Praise for
Jon Armstrong's *Grey*

"*Grey* is a legendary book waiting to happen. It's a mad, stylish, trippy, endlessly inventive romp through the biohazardous wastes of post-genre literature. Jon Armstrong is a genius, with an umlaut, to the fifth power."
— Michael Chabon, author of *The Amazing Adventures of Kavalier & Clay*

"Jon Armstrong's debut novel puts a fresh suit of stylish clothes on the beloved body of cyberpunk, skewering high fashion, consumerism, and... the public fascination with celebrities..."
— *Locus Magazine*

"If F. Scott Fitzgerald had ever imbibed himself into a science-fictional state of mind, subsequently pouring his talent for vivid images and acid observation into a futuristic dystopian extravaganza, the result might very well read like Jon Armstrong's debut novel. This formidable newcomer has given us, in Michael Rivers, a grey Gatsby who will revisit your reveries long after the last page is turned."
— James Morrow, author of *The Last Witchfinder*

"*Grey* is a truly extraordinary and original work—a deft and raucous mash-up of William Gibson and J. D. Salinger by way of Fellini. It'll change your outlook, your brain chemistry, and your wardrobe."
— Catherynne M. Valente, author of *The Orphan's Tales*

"*Grey* is a fascinating book. It's a fusion of the quasi-apocalyptic corporatism of Alfred Bester's *The Stars My Destination* with *Bladerunner* and a big hunk of *The Umbrellas of Cherbourg*."
— Jay Lake, author of *Trial of Flowers*

"Two thumbs up... I couldn't put it down."
— Cherie Priest, author of *Four and Twenty Blackbirds*

"...a stylish, weird, funny, an
— Tim Pratt, author of *The Strang*

YARN

YARN

JON ARMSTRONG

Night Shade Books
San Francisco

Cover art by Anthony Palumbo
Cover design by Ian Morin
Interior layout and design by Ross E. Lockhart
Author photo by Pitchaya Sudbanthad

First Edition

ISBN: 978-1-59780-210-9

Printed in Canada

Night Shade Books
http://www.nightshadebooks.com

To Elba and Caroline

Yarn

I woke early, suffocated by a sweaty and prickling sense of apprehension—exactly the feeling of wool against the skin on a warm day. Yet there, in the dark of my bedroom, the sun seemed impossibly far away. What had set this fear in my veins? None of my current design projects were so difficult or important. I was using a new half-micron twill for a suit, but I had tested the fabric extensively and knew its properties. And though the motor-driven ball gown we were creating was complicated, my assistant and I had spent a whole day installing the mechanics and testing it again and again. No, those projects were essentially complete, and I felt good about their look, materials, and function.

It was no use. Neither sleep nor an answer was forthcoming. I rose, wrapped in swirling unease, and prepared for the day. It was still dark as I drove through the obsidian and gold towers of Ros Begas to the studio. And as I walked the two-hundred-meter metal-and-wood meditation-and-exhibition entry hallway that spiraled in from the building entrance to my showroom front door, I went over the fashion consultations I had scheduled for the day, the calls I needed to make to suppliers, the fabric tests I needed to run, and the gathering swarm of details for an upcoming show. In the hallway, I powered-on the fashion exhibits that I had on display: including two fabric bursting automatons and a pilling analysis machine, and stooped to collect a few dust fibers on the dark wood floor.

At the end of the spiral, I paused at a display that held the yarn

I had gotten from my father. It rested on black velvet and was lit with a single heterojunction crystal which bathed the thread with a warm, otherworldly glow, recalling the dawn when I'd pulled this strand from my father's pocket so many years ago. But my memories could not linger because someone or something was lurking beyond the next curve, near the showroom doors.

Peeking around the last swell of the wall, I saw a figure draped head-to-toe with dark fabric—the weave was a deep dark charcoal green, with the slight sheen like L-flax—a fiber I never used. While it wasn't completely unusual for someone to come unannounced, the hour and the dress were suspect. Tentatively, I stepped forward, waiting for the visitor to move or speak. At ten feet away, I stopped and as the milliseconds ticked by in silence, began to fear that this was some sort of an attack, that this laundry pile covered an assassin. But even as I catalogued the properties of my jacket, titled Water Hold #11, *with both fluid dynamics and charged particle closures, and thought how I might use it to defend myself, my fear seemed misplaced and wrong. I wet my lips. "The showroom is by appointment only."*

The head turned slightly. The voice that emerged was tatty and frail. "I lived a fool's life and will come to a fool's end, but I've come to ask a favor."

The skin on my neck and back puckered with goosebumps. "Vada!" The heels of my Celine-Audis clapped percussive notes on the polished wood. "I never thought I'd see you again. Where have you been? What happened? What are you wearing?"

The outline of an arm came away from the torso and touched the door. A moment later after a small, moist click of what I imagined were her gaunt lips, she said, "I'm sorry. I am dying."

My throat tightened. "No." As though simple denial changed anything. She didn't reply. "Where have you been? What happened?"

"I need help."

"Of course," I said. "What happened? Are you in pain?" Without thinking, I reached my hand to hers.

She shrank back, shaking her head. "I need your help."

Anew, I saw the rumpled, rough material that covered her in contrast to the faultless cut, fine texture, and precise stitching of my garments. Shame flooded me. "I never expected to see you again."

"I had my battles, my deceptions, and my gardens of failure." She spoke like it was her slogan.

I gazed where I imagined were her eyes. "I tried to find you. I even hired a detective, but he found nothing." I wished I could see her face. "Three weeks ago, I was in Kong. You'd never believe it, but there're fifty chrome towers and solar plots there on that old muddy hill. It's completely different."

The cloth shook as she nodded. "You look good, Tane. I'm sorry, but I can't stay. They're closing in."

I wondered what she was running from this time. "You must be hungry… allow me to at least feed you."

Beneath the cloth, she straightened. "I need a Xi coat."

Xi yarn. Old, immoral, and drug-infused yarn. "That's not a cure." I gestured at the materials of the hallway as evidence of my wealth: the rare lumber, the hand-poured high-carbon concrete, and the custom-built fabric test machines. "What do you really need, Vada? Surgery? I can get satellite organs."

Her head leaned forward. Wrinkles of the fabric covered her face. "They're just… No. I can't go on." Her words were so quiet I barely heard. "It's time… I just need pure."

She meant pure Xi, the loving, the universal, the erotic, and the dreaming Xi as opposed to the other kind: dark Xi, skreem Xi, nightmare Xi. It occurred to me that she was wearing the basketweave not so much to hide from the authorities but because she had been disfigured by torture. "Listen," I said, stooping to meet her hidden eyes, "come in and sit. Whoever is after you… I'm sure we have a few moments." I reached for where I thought I would find her wrist or forearm, but bumped into what was probably her hip and pulled back.

The pile of basketweave turned as if to leave. "Vada," I began, "I guess I was looking for you because… I have been thinking about us. The truth is, in some way, there's been no one else."

"I hope you weren't waiting for me!"

"No." I felt small, though the truth was I had not. "I just mean that…" I stopped and chided myself for trying to explain.

"Tane… I'm sorry. I understand." Her voice warmed. "I think of you, too. We had an incredible affair."

She had overstated it. "We had eight months," I corrected her. "Two hundred and forty outfits and costumes in about as many days." I tried to keep my tone light, but felt it strain.

"You know who I am."

I nodded and smiled politely. It was always about who she was.

In the stillness of the hallway, I could hear her swallow. "I've heard about you and your work. I'm proud of you. You've made wonderful things." She seemed to laugh for an instant, but then I heard what I thought was a tiny, clenched grunt. She was still for a long moment, and when she finally inhaled a convex of the fabric formed over her mouth.

I stepped toward her, fearful she might collapse, but she backed away.

"Can you please make me a Xi coat?" She exhaled a ragged breath. "I just want to die without pain."

I had absolutely no idea where or how I would get the Xi yarn. "I'll do it."

"I'll come back tomorrow night."

"Tomorrow?" I laughed. "Wait, Vada. First of all, I don't think the yarn is even still made. I would have to find someone who somehow still has some, get it here, weave it into cloth, and then make a jacket." I waited for a reply, but none came. Whispering, I said, "Tomorrow is impossible."

"You're very talented," she said, and turned away.

"Wait!" Irrationally, I was struck with a terror that I might never see her again, and even as I tried to choke the words in my mouth, I asked, "Did you ever really love me?"

Her body slumped, fabric pooling at her feet.

"I'm sorry, Vada." I felt ashamed. I was unraveling before her. "It's just that I've been thinking about what happened... mulling it over and... I'm sorry, I'm just in shock that you're here."

"Tane," she said very quietly. "I must go. Please, I need the coat tomorrow."

"Vada, tomorrow is impossible. I'll try my best, but it will take days." Even as I spoke, the rounded top of the cloth relaxed like a balloon beneath was losing air. Wrinkles and valleys appeared as the pile descended to the floor. She was collapsing before my eyes. Reaching into the fabric to grasp an arm or a shoulder, I found nothing but more wrinkles of the basketweave. I flung the fabric to the side, afraid I was going to uncover a puddle of flesh.

I found nothing.

Dropping to my knees, I pushed aside the cloth and felt the cool floorboards beneath. I turned my gaze to the showroom doors and down the curve of the hallway. The place was empty. And silent. It was as if I had been visited by a ghost.

Studying the floor where she had been standing, I discovered that one of the heartwood planks had been disturbed, the clear diamond-coat sealer neatly sliced along its lines. Yet as hard as I banged on it, I could not make it move.

"Vada! Where are you?"

Slumping to the floor, I heard the rhythm of my breathing, the air molecules being sucked into and pushed out my bronchi. I heard the rush of blood in my ears and the distant clap of my heart valves. She wasn't the fool; I was—for believing and cherishing the impossible. Picking up the basketweave, I held it to my nose and inhaled. I smelled a mixture of rose, corn, and a hint of smoke.

PART 1
PLY

SEATTLEHAMA: A PECULIAR FASHION BUSINESS

When I am asked about my talents in the yarn arts, I like to say that there is no such thing as talent. When they ask how I came to be one of the world's top designers, I shrug and mutter some cliché like *hard work*, *luck*, or *perspiration*. In an interview a year ago at FiberKon, someone asked when I knew I was a fashion genius. I told him I was not a genius. I believe that. But I do have a few special talents that no one else seems to possess. Maybe I always knew I was different, but it was during my first year in Seattlehama that I saw real evidence.

I showed up for work one morning to find my boss, Withor, standing over my little desk. The drawer was open and on the top sat my secret yarn collection that I had gathered over several weeks. It was significant to me, but wasn't even enough to knit the toe of a sock. "Did you steal this from me?"

"No!" Withor was a cloth jobber who had an office filled with samples. "I found them."

He grabbed a magnitron loop from his desk, held it between his eyebrow and nose like a monocle, and peered at the stuff. "These are all torn bits of junk!" Frowning, he asked, "Where'd you find them?"

"Just around," I lied.

"You're a thief! You stole them from somewhere. I should send you right back to the dirt!"

He meant the slubs, the vast corn-filled world that surrounded the city for thousands of miles in all directions. It was where I was born and had lived until I was nineteen. It was a world dominated by corn and sadness. I never wanted to return.

"I did," I confessed. "I'm sorry."

"From where?"

"T'ups." I hadn't meant to use the slubber word for city men, but he didn't seem to notice. Shrugging, I added, "I just grab them."

"You *grab* yarn from cloth?" He snorted. "Impossible!"

"It's true. I can show you."

In the hallway outside of his office, he pointed one of his long fingers. "The woman in the orange crinoline halo dress. That's a half-denier yarn. I defy you to pluck one of those from her fat behind."

I approached the t'up who stood before a showcase window of pewter, blackroot, and satellite ivory buttons and notions. The fabric's yarn was incredibly thin, but I could see that the grid of the weave was at a forty-five-degree angle, and noticed a small twisted loop near the center seam that stuck out just a thirty-second of an inch. That was enough for me to grasp between my fingernails. With a snap of the wrist, I yanked out a bit, turned, and headed back to Withor and handed him the thing before she knew what had happened.

He studied it with his magnitron. "Unthinkable for the denier…" He tossed the thing to the floor. "Impossible! I demand you repeat it with someone else." He scouted the crowd. "There! The gentleman in the green plaid, strolling suit." He made me take a dozen more yarns before he believed that I wasn't tricking him.

"Fine," he said, and tossed the samples at me. "I've seen enough. You stole the yarn. All this *capacity* of yours amounts to debris only useful to a sparrow building a nest. It's a disgusting frayed mess. They're torn little bits of thing. Don't do it again or I'll toss you out!"

Withor's dismissal stung, but over the next several days, as I looked at my collection, I decided he had a point. The ragged ends were ugly. Using several odd bits of metal, broken scissors, and wire that I had found in his office trash, I made two tiny sharp hooks. At first I tried to hold the tiny knives, but found it was better if I glued them just under my fingernails. Once I had practiced with them, I showed Withor, thinking he would be impressed.

He popped his magnitron on his eye and inspected my hand. "What's the purpose of this? I told you to stop that disgusting yarn snatching!"

"They aren't frayed anymore!"

He glared at me. "I really should have you sent back down to the slubs and get a slave who isn't a criminal nuisance." Then he eyed my fingers again. "You mean you actually cut a single yarn with those?"

"Yes."

In the hallway, he pointed to a t'up in a butterfly hat, vermillion clack shoes, and a long white crepe floor jacket.

I ripped a high-twist yarn and handed it over.

"Ha!" he said, as he examined it with his magnitron. "I should have guessed. Cheap irradiated cellulose!" He let the magnitron drop from his eye socket and caught it in his right palm. "And indeed… it is perfectly cut." Narrowing his eyes, he fiddled with the pin and bolt near his tie knot. "This is nothing! I could do it easily myself." He stared forward for a beat. "Quite easily. Cutting a single yarn from cloth and extracting it. It's nothing at all…"

Three days later, Withor directed me to sit in the guest chair across from his desk for the first time. "I mentioned that odd talent of yours to an associate," he began in that languid rhythm of his as he fiddled with the bondage of his necktie. "Well, *talent* is not the right word. What you have is a perversion of sensibilities."

From his desk he picked up a square of black cloth and kissed it to his lips. "I would have ignored him, but he is offering a substantial reward." He set the cloth down and glared at me. "I fully expect that you will fail. You might even be maimed or killed." He laughed dryly. "Such a tragedy that would be!" He leaned far back on his chair and spoke toward the ceiling. "Oh, I had such hopes for my life… for artistry and grandeur, but it has become overgrown with *deals*. And now another contemptible scheme has found me." Sitting up again, he finished, "But I would be a fool not to investigate the possible lucrative side of your repugnant little *ability*. In any case, this associate happens to have a wet spot for the repulsive and saccharine Tinyko 200. Namely he wants a bit of yarn from her little puff skirt."

It would have been impossible to escape Tinyko 200. As the Celebrity Executive Officer of Bias-Anderson- Commonwealth-Burlington-D her image, sounds, and brands saturated the city in the form of engineered alloy, fan engines, pumps, diagnostics, extruders, fabricators, and a popular line of dresses, gloves, eyeglasses, and radio underwear. Tinyko herself was a tiny, young woman with wide blue eyes and a pert mouth. She was famous among the young Cute Bubble Active style girls, but since her recent birthday, had started venturing into the mature market, or as it was called, Wetting the Show.

So that I would blend in as an IMG collector, Withor bought me my first suit and tie. I remember staring into an audience of mirrors and marveling at how I looked. I was no longer a boy, a slubber, an indent worker, but a city man. To finish my costume, Withor also bought me a knit mask. "IMGs wear these silly cloaks, so you have to too."

The thing was like a super-fine stocking made to fit over the head and obscure and soften the features. With it on, I looked like a mannequin. With the necessary pass in hand, I headed to the banquet hall at the top of the city, and slowly worked my way toward the stage.

The others all held their photo-cams, sight-cannons, airtricity gauges, infra- and ultra-meters, waiting for a glimpse, a peek, for the chance to cut an image of Tinyko's tongue momentarily caught between the raspberry of her lips and her milk-glass teeth, her soft fuzzed cleavage as she leaned forward to laugh, her delicate and slender fingers frozen in an inappropriate pose seemingly about to caress the tiny spike of her left nipple through a silken skullcup of a bra.

Beside me in the crowd, another masked man said, "Last show, I got a shot of her crotch so tight you can smell the salt scrod of her cut." He smacked the black, dimpled barrel of his cam and laughed. I nodded as if in appreciation but soon slipped away. His passion seemed desperate and alien.

Moments later, atom lights flashed. Torrents of blue smoke shot from around the crystal stage and the thundering beat of Tinyko's newest song began to vibrate my gut. A phalanx of dancers and strippers ran out and genuflected as from the center came a roar of a fan-jet and there, in an elongated bubble of orange light, was Tinyko. She waved at the crowd, flashed her fluorides, and then opened her mouth wide and screeched her first note with an ultrasonic intensity. One of her slender fingers riffled through the chiffon at the front of her skirt and for a split second revealed the glistening ultra-white of her radio panties. Like piranha, the crowd pressed forward and spattered her face, chest, and crotch with ricocheting white, green, and pink flashes.

Going sideways, right shoulder first, I jockeyed through the men, pushing an elbow here, nudging against a moist twill there, and made my way toward the right side of the stage where the stairs were guarded by a dozen men who wielded smoking-hot scimitars. Between the men sat black guard dogs with long hypodermic teeth. According to the program, after her flash song, she would come down the stairs, let several fans feel her breasts, and auction off a thimble of her virgin love-juice. It was then that I had my best chance to get close enough to rip a yarn from the puff around her nineteen-inch waist.

As I got closer, it actually became easier to swim through the bodies because most of the others were pushing themselves under the lip of the clear stage and pointing their lenses up. And just as I reached the edge of the long glass stairwell, close enough to smell the rubber and asbestos of the guard's safety jackets and the red-hot of their curved blades, she started down.

Her steps were shaky and clumsy. And up close, I could see the depth and opaqueness of her theatrical make-up, her horsehair-thick lashes, and the way her lipstick was drawn beyond her natural lips. In person, she seemed small, artificial, and awkward.

As she came to the bottom of the steps, I squatted, and when she neared, reached between the legs of one of the guards toward her skirt. The infinity chiffon was the softest thing I had ever felt. It was like fresh corn silk and distant whispers and I touched it a split second longer than I might have just to experience its excruciatingly tender hand. I couldn't see my fingers in the haze of the fabric, but found one of the micro-denier yarns, cut it and yanked it. Next, I dropped to the floor and twisted away just as the thick arms of one of the guards twitched. He smashed his scimitar blade a foot deep into the carbon-cement floor right next to my ear.

Standing, I turned and pushed my way through the worshipping throng, my heart pounding.

SEATTLEHAMA: THE VOLCANO-POWERED SEX AND SHOPPING CAPITAL OF THE WORLD

I looked up at the city of Seattlehama every day of my nineteen years in the slubs. The mile-tall circle of buildings—constructed atop Mount Rainier—was often just barely visible in the ginger haze of the morning sunlight. During the days, as I worked in the corn, the towers split the yellowed sky and tore long holes in cloudbanks. And at night, I would often sneak out and stand in the dark of the fields and the dilapidated and unlit houses where slubbers slept dozens per room and watch as the sky faded to charcoal and purple and the curves and spikes of the towers gleamed like the frozen flames of an enormous rocket ship heading straight into the heavens.

Years later I would learn that the ring of skyscrapers of Seattlehama were not like the tall buildings of other cities. Instead of glass-covered boxes, these were built of woven ceramic. Up close they were covered with fabriclike patterns. Not only was each strong and flexible in ways that older buildings weren't, but the city was built around a mile-wide atrium with the circle of buildings all linked in such a way that supported and was supported by all the others. I've heard it said that half the city's towers could be removed in an instant and the rest would barely sway.

For my first six months inside Seattlehama working for Withor, I lived near the bottom, just a few floors above the simmering pools of the lava that was drawn from Mt. Rainier to power the city's massive turbines. The place was known as the slubber slum, where several hundred brandclanners lived in a dozen dim sleeping and eating cafés. Most of the men worked below with the toxic biofilms that held back the lava, replaced valves on the steam turbines, or fixed the pipes and made repairs on the dark undercarriage of the city. My cleaning and errand-running job with a textile jobber was unusual, and I never mentioned it to the men who returned from the day filthy and bleeding.

In many ways the ghetto was worse than the slubs. There was no view, no sky, no sweet scent of the ripening corn tassels in the fall. It was filthy and uncomfortable. The food was awful. And worst of all, the slubber transplants grew angry, fidgety, unsettled, and unpredictable.

"Watch it, soy boy!" someone would shout.

"You're a corn smut!" another would reply.

Each night it was always the corn-eaters versus the soybeans versus the potatoes, all crops of the major brandclans. Soon someone would throw a punch or a kick and a melee would rage until men in purple satin came in and beat everyone with their long electric sticks. And every few days someone died at their job, or was bashed over the head by the satins, or just didn't wake up. The next day a new man from below was brought up to fill his place.

But the instant I had handed over the pale, almost weightless and invisible yarn from the chiffon puff from Tinyko's skirt, everything changed for me.

"Excellent condition," said Withor as he examined it under his magnitron. He cackled brittlely. "I have three more orders for yarn plucked from the sad asses of our city's blessed corporate celebrities." He glared at me. "You will snatch them as quickly as possible."

While I thrilled at the idea of taking more yarn, I knew I was being used. "What do I get?"

"You're a slubber! You should be happy just to be in our glorious shopping city, away from the retched squalor of that corn all around."

I stared at him unhappily.

"What you do is trivial. Trivial and trifling. I could certainly do it all myself—and much better—if I so chose." His right hand fiddled with the pins on his black-and-white-striped tie. He flit his hand in the air. "Keep that suit and tie."

While I loved my first suit, I shook my head. "The yarns I take are worth more."

"You're a corn slubber! You're a fly! You're a lint caught in the ass crack of another lint! And you don't tell me what something is worth. You don't negotiate with me! You don't even beg. You take my orders and you carry them out and you are glad."

I worried that I had gone too far. In the beginning I had been impressed with Withor as I had with everything in the city. And while I now secretly hated him, what he said was true. Below my suit, minus my yarn ripping, I was a slubber. I was lucky to be away from the drudgery, the labor, and the politics of life in the corn.

"Fine!" he sighed. "I'll give you point one percent of net." From a drawer he pulled out a small rubbery purple card and tossed it at me. "And with that you can purchase all the trinkets and trash you can... well... you can *afford*. All of Seattlehama takes MasterCut."

At the end of the day, I was heading down the familiar stairs that led to the slubber ghetto when I stopped, and fished the card from my pocket. The purple surface was tacky and shiny, and if I tilted it back and forth, I could see a t'up inside it wearing a strange stringy shirt that cut lines across the neck, shoulders, and swollen chest. Below, I heard someone shout, "Soy boy, play with your tiny toy!"

Someone else yelled, "You're corn rot!"

Tucking the card into a pocket, I adjusted my lapels, tightened the knot in my tie, and turned to the city proper. I wasn't a slubber anymore. I had a fashion job collecting valuable yarn. And most of all I had a purple MasterCut!

The first thing I did was head to a store called The Highly Profitable Epicurean Frosting Franchise not far from Withor's office and order a Chocoa 99.71%. I had seen dozens of t'ups walking around gleefully stuffing themselves with the stuff. The sticky brown paste came piled high in a double-D bra cup and was served with a long ivory spoon. It was a dozen times sweeter than M-Bunny cola and like nothing I had eaten before. After just one spoonful, the sugar and butterfat coated my mouth. After three, a buzzing nervousness trembled my fingers and my stomach was filled with lead. I dumped the rest in a noisy and blinking entertrash basket.

Still, the joy of holding up my MasterCut—as I had seen Withor do when purchasing notions for the office—and having the t'up behind the crystal counter nod and then hand over the frosting confirmed everything I wanted that day.

Down another hallway I found the cloth stores. Inside it seemed a rainbow of everything I had ever wanted to see, touch, feel. I found black cloth so black it didn't seem to exist. I saw colors so bright they hurt my eyes. I saw wools, polys, cottons, rayotts, pricons, flaxes, silks, bamboos, and metals. I smelled cashmere, flax, ramie, abaca, basalt, and camel. I marveled at the crispness of the satellite silks; the springiness of the spandicotts, the softness of the French puff-flannels. I inhaled the starch in the taffeta. I rubbed crepe on crepe and enjoyed the sandy grit.

From there, I found a thread and yarn store and laughed out loud at the thousands of colors, sizes, twists, weights, sheens, lusters, plies. This was more than I had dreamed of. This was more than I had ever imagined. I read a sign that said: 46,231 more shades of red available by special order.

In another store I found fashion machines: acoustic jacquards, card punches, loom beams, air-jets, deweavers, flash seamers, water-knitters, flux steamers. Standing before a Control R&H projectile loom, I traced my eyes as yarn might travel along spool holders, through weft tensioners, across conveyor wedges, up and over shedding boxes, through eyeholes, down to spindles, the tooth blocks, guide scissors, and out of the heddles through the wormwheels.

I ran a hand over the smooth brushed finish, the marbled gray paint, and solid brass fittings of an A-Max insta-seamer. Turning, I found a clearing and five feet from me, a t'up stood on a knitting machine that resembled a ski trainer with two long hand poles and foot levers. The t'up pushed one pole to the right and spun the other. A set of floating hooks knit blue yarn into a pair of shorts in midair. I wasn't sure how it worked exactly, but decided that the left pole steered the knitting hooks and the other controlled the number of loops.

Three others stood watching. One wore a white suit and held a thick, jewel-encrusted cane. The second wore all black, but here and there on his jacket were small live, wiggling white worms that had been woven into the fabric. The third, in a camel hair suit, had what I later learned was a giraffe mask over his head.

The knitting t'up pulled the right handle to the side. Now a thicker band was formed around the top of the shorts. A moment later, the t'up pulled the right stick far back, pushed on the right footpad, and the machine stopped.

"Artistic zeal!" said the man in white. "Flamboyance and bravery!"

"Best britches for bitches!" enthused the giraffe. "May I?"

Using a pair of connected needles, the t'up took the shorts from the machine, seemed to knot it, and handed the shorts to Giraffe.

Curious, I stepped forward. "What is this?" The four of them turned and looked at me with varied amounts of confusion and disdain.

"This," intoned the man in white, "is the Stanton-Bell Tex-knitter 222. It's the top-of-the-line artesian, topsumer, craft-gasmic, model with the skivvé form." He blinked several times. "Welcome to my fashion motor boutique. Call me Archibald. Are you… um… are you a knitter?"

My confidence faded. "No. But I think I saw how it works."

"You have fine taste, good consumer, sir, but I wouldn't suggest starting on a stand-up Tex-knitter. We have desktop models for socks, collars, and wrist bands for crafters in all sorts of pleasant and complimentary colors."

Meanwhile, Giraffe was tugging the shorts on over his pants. Only they weren't just shorts, but the front had three pouches: one long and two smaller ones for a root and two nodes—that's what slubbers called genitals. And his root was eleven inches long.

"I am the corporate executive slut of my dreams!" said Giraffe, shaking his hips back and forth. "Watch my fantasy grow!" They all laughed.

Meanwhile, I was studying the t'up who had been on the knitter: the shape of the eyes, the smoothness of the neck, and the contours of the body. She was definitely not a man.

When she wiggled her hips, the long root tube on her identical shorts flopped back and forth. She said something about scratchy yarn and while they laughed again, I stepped backward. If someone had inspected the tag at the back of my neck that instant, it would have read: 50% confusion 30% fright 20% arousal.

In the slubber ghetto the main topic of conversation, besides which crop was best, was about the existence, features, meaning, and anatomy of Seattlehama women, or what we called reds.

I was born into the M-Bunny brandclan and we were the planters of corn. Our special crop dominated the hills around Seattlehama. To the south, L. Segu, the soybean clan, was stronger. And while we had our differences, we had several things in common. For one thing the slubs were filled with men and nothing but men. Men planted the crops, tended them, harvested them, processed them, made them into all sorts of things, ate them, and recycled them. Men cleared old roads, tore up old parking lots, razed useless buildings, and planted more corn.

But once a year, a few men who worked the hardest, praised the crop the most, and recycled everything they could were rewarded with the opportunity to have a son. They boarded one of the buses and traveled to headquarters. They wore different B-shirts there and ate something called *krissmascake*. They thought that it was those cakes that made their roots hard. And when that happened, a *red* would come and would lay down with them.

Ordinarily, no one in the slubs had erections. The only exceptions were those who traveled to headquarters, those who were debranded, and those few who, for some reason, had just gone corn rot. If a rep caught you with a hard root, it was said you would be immediately debranded or just recycled, but I never saw it happen.

It wasn't until years later that I understood that those B-shirts and shorts we wore muted our tempers, our anger, and mostly our libido.

I don't know if she sensed the surging of my heart, but the t'up turned and addressed me. "Shopper…" Her eyes darted over my Teardop suit. "From what finger of the glove have you come?"

I didn't understand *finger of the glove*, but feared it had something to do with the slubs. "No," I told her. "I'm… um… I'm just here looking."

"Adrift," she announced to the others. "*Adrift* in the currents of commerce and unfamiliar with the loft and ply of fashion." Her glossy red lips pinched off what seemed like a growing smile. "Shopper, have you never envisioned skivvé?"

The man in the giraffe masked said, "That's Python Duck Weapon's Celebrity Executive Officer, Kira Shibui."

"I am Tane Cedar," I told her. My heart was beating hard and my palms were moist. "You knit *syrup*." I had inadvertently used a slubber word. "I mean… great!"

Her right eyebrow rose with curious skepticism. "A small but curled wood shaving of praise." She eyed the others. Worm Jacket giggled. Giraffe nodded.

They were laughing at me. "I am also interested in yarn and knitting."

"If you desire, Kira," offered the storeowner, "I'll ask him to leave."

She held up a gloved hand. "Allow him to linger." She narrowed her eyes. "Those who harbor hearts that beat not with the liquids of the pedestrian, but with twists of the fiber… we must always show honor." She squared her shoulders and stared at me intently. "I am a saleswarrior for Python Duck… in the glorious skivvé battles amid the grand foundation war." When she inhaled, her breasts were squashed inside her rather stiff-looking outfit. I didn't know how to describe it at the time, but it was like a sailor suit in shiny orange decorated with several large bows. The flared skirt was so short it didn't cover her underwear. The neckline was low, and around her neck rested a wide collar. Her boots and gloves were the same orange. She peered at me. "You must know *the glory*, dear mislaid shopper."

I didn't know what she was asking, but was glad to have her gaze on me.

Her red lips tightened. "Then know this citizen of credit: we of Python Duck are fighting against the keepers of the dark, the wearers of the empty, and the besmirchers of the cloth. We freed ourselves to oppose the awful howl of the gathering void that is *Casper Union!*" She screamed the last two words.

"Casper Union? What's that?"

My question seemed to please her. She turned to the others. "And thus with his genuine confusion, I have freed him from the realm of the counterfeit and the spy."

"Oh, well done, Kira!" said the man in the worm jacket.

"Brilliant!" Giraffe bobbed his head in a nod. "I didn't even think that he might be an enemy spying on us!"

"Now we know," said Kira, raising her voice, "that he is simply from the dim and the dark bones of fashion." She turned and gazed at me with warmth and sympathy. "Someone should mental him in the ways of the lapel, the seam, and the blessed undergarment."

I knew she was making fun of me, but it didn't matter. "I want to learn."

"Then let me unfold one sleeve of the truth: Casper Union is the skivvé maker that cares not for anything but the lack of their own make." She held up a fist. "They are stealing the glory... No! They are *tarnishing* anything that was ever coated with even the thinnest skin of commerce and pride." Pointing a finger at me, she said, "New friend of our sex and shopping city, you must study fashion and its wars. Come to my flagship: Python Duck on level 609 in the Velour Building and behold the fine art and craft of men's fantasy skivvé."

"Best britches for bitches!" said Giraffe.

"We are desperate for fashion passion!" she continued. "And we are desperate for cutting and needling." She turned her face toward the others. "We need the commanding and the strong and the vigorous to help wage the terror upon those with shallow and muddy puddles of soul."

"*Muddy puddles of soul!*" whispered the man in the worm jacket, nudging the giraffe.

Returning her attention to me, she asked, "Do you, shopper Tane Cedar, with a proud and curious interest in knit—do you have the formidable vision? Do you have clarity of duty? And most of all, do you have the valor to test the capricious needles of destiny?"

Worm Jacket and Giraffe and even the storeowner turned to me. My eyes leapt from Kira to the others and back again. I swallowed and said, "Yes?" hoping that was the right answer.

"Kira Shibui, Celebrity Executive Officer of Python Duck Men's Fantasy Skivvé!" boomed the storeowner. "Visionary knitter, designer, and warTalker extraordinaire. She truly warms the new Stanton-Bell Tex-knitter 222!" He ran a hand along the top of the machine. "I will have this sent to your flagship tonight!"

Worm Jacket and Giraffe began talking excitedly as the storeowner rambled on with numbers and jargon. Meanwhile, Kira's eyes lingered on mine.

"Kira Shibui," I whispered, happy to have remembered her name.

She didn't exactly smile, but something deep in her eyes seemed to warm. Turning, I headed out of the fashion motor boutique. My hands were vibrating, my heart was racing, and I felt like I wasn't getting enough air. In the hallway, I stood for a moment and caught my breath. I didn't know what was happening, but my root had stiffened for the first time.

DESIGN STUDIO

"P*heff!*" I shouted.

"*Yes?*" *came his reply from the storeroom.*

I was in the design room, downing the last of my coffee as I laid out my things on one of the worktables. "*You rescheduled Mr. Nezzo?*"

Pheff returned with a box. "*Yes, Tailor.*"

"*What about the Pings?*"

"*They're coming next week.*" *He set down the box.*

"*Did the button extruder get fixed?*"

"*The guy's supposed to come after two.*"

I thought it was supposed to have happened the day before. "*Okay, but wasn't the Transmission Mills salesman supposed to be here already?*"

"*I jotted him. Told him tomorrow.*"

"*Tomorrow's no good.*"

"*I'll jot him again.*"

"*Did you charge my travel water-shears? The ones with the etched golden tank?*" *On the table was a screen sketch, various travel kits, some clothes, needles, sewers, and several hand tools.* "*Oh,*" *I said remembering,* "*make sure to order more D45 for the WeavePlus.*"

"*I will.*"

I knew what I was doing: I was delaying. I was making excuses. There was a part of me that didn't want to go, didn't want to leave my supplies, my projects, and my space. I had found equilibrium;

I had found happiness. And I worried that traveling through my past would disturb the toxic dust I would find there. There were things I had laid to rest that should probably stay that way.

I picked up the basketweave and sniffed it again. When Vada had appeared before the doors, it had been surprising and overwhelming. A part of me wished I hadn't agreed to make her a Xi jacket so quickly. Besides the fact that it was likely impossible, I owed her nothing. Years ago, I had become the tailor I was today and yet, here I was packing up for a trip for a woman I hadn't seen in a lifetime. And I knew I didn't still love her; I didn't still harbor those same feelings of worship and infatuation. At least that was what I wanted to believe.

There was the detective that I'd told her about, but I had also hired a researcher and bribed two officials from an identity firm. The officials placed her in Bang as a girl. They said she was operated on at some saleswarrior clinic, but disappeared into the slubs of Europa11 before city satins could apprehend her. They figured she was long dead. The identity firm said she was wanted for the murder of a half-dozen CEOs. The detective implicated her in some stolen DNA plot five years ago, but then the trail died.

I took another bite of my eel scone. I had known Vada in Seattlehama. I had watched from afar for almost a year before we met, and it was during that time that I lusted after her as one might a goddess. Later, when I lived with her—and maybe fell in love—I also came to understand (or maybe that understanding was much later) that she could never really love me back. Then again, my attraction to her had always been powered by her unattainable, mythic, and forbidden nature. It had been Zeno's paradox of the heart, I'm sure.

Could some remnant of that desire still be alive inside of me? Or did I feel guilty for having left her? Or did I just now feel sorry for her, for whatever ragged shell she had become of the terrorist and entertainer I had known?

"These?" Pheff returned from the storeroom.

"Yes." For an instant I almost told Pheff to put the shears away

and considered the idea of not helping her, of not trying to find the impossible and illegal Xi and of doing nothing. I didn't need some foolish and dangerous journey. I didn't need any more associations with the outlaws of the world.

The problem was, as I started to form some sentence like, I'm sorry, Pheff… I'm not going after all, let's put this all away… *or a simple and mysterious* Never mind, *I hesitated. Why not spend a day searching for Xi? If I found some, I would make her a death coat; if not, it would only be twenty-four hours of my life.* "Get the carbonate case for those shears," *I told my assistant.*

"I brought the leather one."

"Carbonate," *I insisted. The shears could, with the gritty cycling supply of water, easily cut through a thousand yarns of fabric or steel plate. While the leather one was fine around the office, I was going to have them in my jacket and didn't want to accidentally cut off an arm. As he headed to the storeroom, I called after him.* "Bring a Mini-Air-Juki and a selection of yarn pulls!"

Pheff stopped, turned, and looked at me quizzically. "Yarn pulls? What do you need those for?"

"They often come in handy. And I might as well take a titanium crochet hook, a pair of snips, and a few needles."

He returned with the carbonate case, a silvery hook, a tiny pair of scissors, a card of sewing needles, and a dozen yarn pulls in a jar. Tapping my mouth with my right index, I considered what I had so far and what else I might need. "You know what?" *I asked, as I imagined myself in some polluted and reeking corner of the slubs.* "Add a swatch of 4M biofilter strata inside the right sleeve of my jacket."

Pheff raised an eyebrow. "Where exactly are you going?"

Ignoring his question, I asked, "Do any of our fabric suppliers have a connection to the blackmarket?"

Pheff laughed. "I hope not!" *He watched me sort through the things on the table.* "Really, Tailor, where are you going?"

"It's an excursion," *I told him again.* "Do me another favor. My first job in Seattlehama was with a man named Withor. He was a* *yarn jobber who got into thread thievery and some other nefarious things. There was a jobber named Pilla who ran a boutique. See if you can find either one of them."*

Pheff took a screen from his pocket. He asked me for a spelling and a company name. "No," he said as he thumbed the thing. "No listings in Seattlehama for either. None here in Ros Begas."

"Try any of the cities."

After a beat he shook his head. "Neg. There's something about Withor getting into trouble for importing illegal yarn, but it's from a couple of years back. I don't see anything about the woman."

"What about a listing for the slubs?"

Pheff glared at me. He was right: listings there were as porous as cutwork lace. I wasn't surprised I couldn't locate either of them. I assumed he—and maybe hoped he—was dead. As for her, I felt guilty for having left the way I did, but never had any desire to see her.

I picked up the Mini-Air-Juki, a handheld sewing machine about the size of a thick MasterCut card. Picking up a swatch of muslin, I gave it a quick test. The Mini-Air-Juki's stitch looked tight from the top, but when I turned it over, I saw that it had left large clumps of the sewing thread below. It badly needed adjustment, but before I did that, I opened the container of yarn pulls.

I hadn't used them in decades. They were small flesh-colored metal things the shape of fingernail clippings with a tiny cutter and jaw in the center. With a little glue, they fit under the nail and turned a finger into a yarn collection tool.

I found several sharp ones and added them to my gear.

"I thought I'd visit our fabric suppliers," I told Pheff. "It's been too long."

Pheff stared as if he didn't believe.

"Have we ever bought from Ryder?"

"No!"

I had met Ryder at a fashion convention years ago. I hadn't liked him, and had gotten a slimy feeling from him. "Where is he?"

"He's a ham fighter," said Pheff.

I didn't know his slang. "Wasn't he the one who had that undersea-themed booth?"

"Yeah and it stunk like seaweed!"

Ryder, I thought. That's where I would start. "Oh, and speaking of odor, I need the glue for the pulls."

After fishing it from a pocket, he set the applicator bottle in my palm.

I applied a drop of the clear vinegar-smelling stuff to the pull, pushed the little device under the nail of my left middle finger, held it for several seconds, and did the other.

"You coming back in the afternoon?"

"I doubt it."

"Wait!" he blurted, panicked. "I'm not going alone to the delivery!"

"You will probably have to."

"Cut it off!" he cursed, throwing a forearm over his face in denial. Then flinging his arm out of the way, he continued. "Tailor! You know I'm not good at that stuff! He doesn't want me. He wants you. I can't show up with his suit."

"I'm sure you'll be excellent," I said and then pointed to the mannequin where he had hung my jacket, a single-breasted, five-and-a-half-button front with full climate, a blade-stop liner, and the latest communiqué. "The biolayer in the sleeve," I reminded him.

"Please, Tailor," he pleaded, as he quickly stitched the material inside my sleeve. Once done, he took the jacket from the mannequin, brought it to me. "Please try and be back in time for the fitting. I don't want to go by myself. The needle is, that guy creeps me out."

"Never disparage a client! They pay the bills."

"Sorry, Tailor. It's just that he's so... you know!"

He helped me into the jacket, and as he adjusted the collar around my neck, I said, "It will be an educational experience for you."

I heard him grumble to himself as he dusted the collar and shoulders, but he didn't look at me. Focusing my eyes straight ahead, I concentrated on the weight and temperature of the jacket. When he had finished dusting and had fiddled with the collar, he stepped back, still with his head down.

"Don't judge from the terrain of your life until you have tread upon the rocks and weeds of another's."

"I'm not judging anyone," he muttered. "I'm just saying I'm not you."

I put the travel shears in the inside breast pocket, the Mini-Juki in the other, and adjusted my tie. "The people that fill the clothes, the people that animate the sleeves of our shirts and pant legs of our slacks… they are the ones who bring it to life."

He stared at me, his eyebrows sinking over his eyes. "What?"

"I'm giving you advice." Maybe I was really speaking to myself when I added, "Cherish wrinkles, stains, and small tears. They mean the cloth has lived."

As I walked out into the spiral that led to the building entrance, one of the workmen repairing the floor addressed me.

"No worry, Mr. Cedar." He wiped his wet mouth with the back of his greasy hand. "Besides that it's real tight, there's an open power junction below this board. Any rat trying to get in or out would be roasted."

With a nod, I turned and strode around the spiral. From there I took the stairs down to the parking garage. The attendants saw me coming at a jog and rushed out to remove the cones from around my gleaming charcoal Chang-P.

It wasn't until I was in the driver's seat, with several motors idling coolly, the numbers on the instrument panel glowing a soft peach, the hush of Love Emitting Diode's Eternal Skyline playing on the sound system, that I stopped for a moment. My lips and jaw began to shiver, I struggled to take in air… and I began to cry.

Garage attendants stood waiting for me to exit. I punched the passenger seat and tried to get control of myself. I thought I was *crying for Vada, for whatever gaunt, broken shape she had become such that she wanted to die amid the drugged vision dream of a Xi coat. Maybe I was crying for a lot of reasons.*

SEATTLEHAMA: THE THREAD THIEVERY BANG

During the year that I stole yarn I probably collected enough to make a large, fluffy, and very ugly afghan. I didn't just do celebs, but suicidal salarymen, gastrolace-wearing saleswarriors, C average virgins, blind CFOs, accountants with a missing finger, plump housewives with overbites, and whatever new and quirky category one could image as my customer base began to shift from individual fanatics desperate for a piece of their favorite celeb to costume and fashion designers eager to add meaning, exclusivity, and trend to their lines.

As for me, the yarn collector, bodice ripper, strand snatcher, thread thief, lint lifter, filament filcher, I improved my tools, my technique, my income, and my status. I took the best entervators to the higher floors; I ate at select restaurants where I was the only former slubber, sampling pickled bald eagle eggs and watching scantily clad dancers curse each other, I shopped for clothes in the glittering Full-Fashion Hallway, along the Violet Building's Consumer Revolution Promenade, and in Zé Brag Atrium, where saleswarriors spun bizarre, gruesome, and erotic stories of style and design to lure in the trippers, the holidays, and the world's consumers.

And yet for all my newfound confidence, I made no friends. Seattlehama wasn't the city for lasting relationships. Most of the people there were tourists or shoppers on binges for clothes or sex or both. The people who lived in the city and plied the sales and service arts draped together. As for yarn rippers, for a while there was only me.

Several months after the Tinyko rip, there were so many new orders that Withor hired two men to help. One was named Flak, and the other, Vit. I assumed that the three of us would become friends, but soon learned that I had nothing in common with them. Flak powdered his face and wore filmy white suits that made him look like a ghost. His black hair was teased and starched into a tall point. When I asked if it was supposed to be a volcano, he glared at me with disgust. As for Vit, he carried a large electric pump harp he never played and spent most of his time grooming himself and his endless collection of *de Nimes* pants.

It was my job to teach them how to swipe yarn, but during my demonstrations all they would do was scoff and giggle.

"A former corn prisoner cannot teach us anything," is what Vit finally said. So I left them to figure it out on their own. Sometimes I saw the marks of their efforts: ratty nibbles marring expensive jackets and skirts.

After almost a year of thread thievery, it no longer satisfied me. "I want to make things," I told Withor. "I can't keep handing over the yarn."

"Make things?" he laughed at me. "You can't mean *design*?"

"Yes, I want to design!"

"A corn slubber designing fashion!" He tilted his head to the side and smirked. "How charming! You *do* have a sense of humor!" His smile slowly flattened into a grim line as his right hand crawled—tarantula-like—down the pins that tacked down his tie. "Listen to me: as a former slubber, you are forbidden from quitting, you should be forbidden from even thinking such ridiculous cut." He puckered his lips for a moment, thoughtfully. "But I tell you what: I'll make you a deal. I will release you from your job to pursue whatever ridiculous fantasies you have, but only after one last rip."

It was all I wanted and was about to agree, when he held up a hand and looked up at the ceiling.

"Hello there! Yes, I've been anxious to hear from you. Yes, I know the risks!" He leaned far back in his chair. "Listen to me... there is too much that must be protected! I know!... Yes, she *knows* how to do it.... Well, believe me, I detest her, but she is talented! Listen to me: I just had a luminous idea. It's a perfect back-up plan!... It will all be taken care of. *Trust Withor!* Goodbye!"

He stayed far back in his chair and muttered, "One final rip! Withor, you have done it again!" He sat up, and with quick strokes, began drawing on the screen on his desk. "Let me show you the objective."

"I can stay in the city?" I asked. "I don't want to go back to the slubs."

Withor looked up at me. Strangely, his sour expression soon turned warm, and with a broad smile, he said, "Of course! It's quite possible you may never leave!"

CHARCOAL CHANG-P

The twenty-three lanes of northbound traffic on i6002 was clogged as usual. Far to my left the elevated, neon pink Snuggly Train passed swiftly above, blaring the trademark Snuggly-tune from the speaker towers mounted on each car. I turned down the outside audio.

With my left thumb, I caressed the slight dimples of the forward horn buttons. Directly ahead was one of those odd, low-slung, seven-wheel Haier-Sapporos painted in an awful purple-and-beige check, warning lights flashing. Perched atop the wide back bumper was one of those bumper buddies, as they were called—in this case a beetle-green automaton goose. The bird paced back and forth, flying up and landing back on one leg, speaking, singing, and trying to get the attention of other motorists. Pointing at me with a wing, it hopped around, bobbing its head back and forth. It seemed to be chanting something. I twisted the outside audio knob to the right, only to hear it repeating, "Chang Pee Pee! Chang Pee Pee!" ad infinitum.

With a roll of my eyes, I spun the knob back to near zero, and settled myself in the seat. It would take at least thirty minutes to reach the Loop. I turned my mind to the events of the morning, and the strange fabric Vada had been wearing.

The L-flax fiber and the slight corn aroma meant it must have come from slub mills. While that wasn't necessarily indicative of anything—a lot of yarn and fabric was milled in the flatlands (although I never used it)—I had a hunch that Vada had *something to do with its manufacture and use. Well, Vada or her people, or her clan, or her group, or her associates—I was never comfortable with the word Toue, nor had I ever come upon a definition that accurately portrays who they are. Again, I may have been too close.*

I knew the basketweave wasn't made to wear over one's head. I could think of a half-dozen cloaking materials that would have served that purpose —the light-bending bombazine by Dunlop & Misrahi Mills, the super reflective double-weave from Lux Lux, even that refracting gauze from one of the satellite mills. That was the problem with designers. They used the wrong fabric for the wrong reason. They would turn denim inside out; they would cut super-satin the wrong way, and mix incompatible fabrics like a child mixing gouache and house paint. But the real question was: Where did the basketweave come from, and did it signify anything? And what was that touch of smoke I had detected?

Another cute Snuggly Train shot past us at high speed as if in mockery. When a space opened in the left lane, I swerved in and was finally rid of the checked Haier-Sapporo and its obnoxious robogoose, which had just finished pretending to urinate on my hood complete with (thankfully silent) ribald commentary.

Unfortunately, as soon as I merged, the new lane came to a stop, and I had to sit there while the others passed by. The robogoose was airborne, and as it flew by it imitated an obscene gesture with a wing tip and laughed.

Pushing the interior volume as far as it would go, I was surrounded in an insulating hush like wind coursing through massive stone turrets, vast subterranean ocean flows, or a spiral galaxy blasting through the perfect and silent vacuum of space.

I rubbed my eyes for a second and wondered what was beneath Vada's cloth. Was she as badly injured and disfigured as I had imagined, or was the fabric just to cloak her identity and escape? That Vada had somehow sneaked through the catacombs of the building between walls and floors, through ductwork and forgotten spaces, and then retreated through a floorboard, did not surprise or intrigue me as much as her choice of material.

Traffic was still crawling. I dialed Pheff. "Put that basketweave under the magnitron and tell me if the yarn's labeled—"

"Tailor," he cried, "you're back!"

"I'm not even on the ramp to the Loop yet."

"Cut it off! You're joking!"

"City traffic is its usual dreadful." Since I figured he'd already forgotten my request I repeated it. "See if the basketweave is labeled."

"Listen," he said, "I just got a call. The delivery vessel will be late."

When he didn't elaborate, I asked, "When is late?"

"It won't be here for another hour! That mean's it's not going to get there on time. That means someone is going to have to apologize. That I can't do!"

"The first week my original shop was open," I said, as I nudged the car forward, "I didn't sleep for a week. And when I delivered my first suit, my hands shook. I kept expecting the sleeves to fall off or the buttons to explode. And you know what actually happened?" He didn't respond, but I knew he was listening. "I had used an incompatible interfacing in the collar. The stuff began to combust and when the man put it on, it scorched his neck and shoulders. Had he not attacked me and broken my collar bone, he would have probably won his lawsuit, and I would not be here."

"Cut it!" he said with a nervous laugh. "What'd you use?"

"Fuse-i-Lok D6... industrial base." He laughed harder. "You'll be fine," I concluded. "What about the basketweave?"

"Um... nothing. No label."

Almost all yarn had identifying manufacturing marks. That limited this fabric's origins. "Thank you," I said. "I'll call when I'm on the Loop."

Lost in the hypnotic crawl of the traffic, I thought back to my first days, weeks, months in Seattlehama. Back then the city was growing rapidly. New buildings were being erected every few weeks. They built them on the ground and raised them floor-by-floor.

The whole plan for the city had been the brainchild of a textile engineer who figured out how to spin microscopic metal strands into a kind of yarn that was amazingly strong. Enormous buildings could be woven into the sky at high speed, much like a length-wise or warp-knit tricot loom.

My lane moved forward, and I came up on robogoose again. He spied my Chang, turned and offered the single black dot of his hind end. I thought about stepping on the accelerator, bumping the Haier-Sapporo hard enough to knock the birdbot onto the pavement, but my lane was still moving, and that was what mattered.

I passed him and had a thought: flying and landing. A chill ran down my neck, but I couldn't make the connection.

We continued about a hundred yards ahead before coming to another stop. Foot against the brake pedal, I closed my eyes and an image came to me:

I was looking down at the road and the tops of the cars from a hundred feet in the air, peering through the white gaze of a chiffon window. Above me, stitched to the top edge of the cloth wall, was a large, hydrogen-filled batiste balloon. I couldn't see it, except for a slight curve of its blue-gray flank, but more sensed its shape and buoyancy. Below my feet was a dark and textured fabric floor. Stooping, I touched it, and knew instantly what it was.

I heard a voice behind me. It wasn't words or speech, but a long vocalization—a cry of pain. When I turned from the chiffon window and the view of the road and the cars below, the interior of the airship was too dark to see, but I stepped forward, my hands outstretched, and thought I felt something, but whether it was a cloth wall, a pile of fabric, or just my imagination, I couldn't tell. Beneath my bare feet, I stroked the gridlike pattern of the basketweave.

I woke back in my car. A wagon pulled in front of me and then a long, white limo did the same. Other vehicles streamed around me. The purple-and-beige-check Haier-Sapporo was long gone and so was the robogoose. The sound I had thought was Vada's voice was actually the distant wail of several horns behind me.

I pushed the accelerator and the vision slipped behind me.

SEATTLEHAMA: THE PURPLE AND GOLD ROCOCO ENTERVATOR

The last yarn rip Withor wanted me to do wasn't from the split trundle skirt of some giant Seattlehama celeb, or even a sample from some obscure black and white kalamkari for a designer's mega-creation. Instead it was from an unnamed woman who was going to be in a certain obscure hallway at a certain moment. The only feature I had to identify her was the cloth of her suit: drap-de-Berry, a heavy woolen twill. The details were something of a letdown, but I was just thrilled that it was to be my last, and spent most of the day dreaming about what I might do next.

And as the hour approached, I ate a light meal, bought myself a new navy serge suit and trimmings in the Full-Fashion Hallway 403. The saleswarrior dressed in nothing but gemstones and a belt skirt. "Before my vocal cords are severed tonight," she whispered, "I want you to hear my last words, my last whispers, and smell the smoke of my moans."

I was more surprised that she had finally spoken to me than what she had said. By then I had heard lines like these—warTalk, it was called—from other saleswarriors.

"The fumes of our destiny are salt, acid, and semen." Her eyes, like those of most other warriors, were large, beautiful, but empty.

"I'm busy," I said, shaking my head. "Sorry."

The Full-Fashion Hallway was just five floors above Withor's office in the color building. The rip was to take place on floor 881 in the Parfum Spaceship. All the buildings had wide sets of showstairs, filled with performers, singers, organ jugglers, fortune advisors, and massagers. They also had internal elevators, but the way to get around, the real way to get from floor to floor and building to building, was one of Seattlehama's most famous attractions: the entervator.

Between the buildings hundreds of cables, leads, wires, lines, and supports connected the city. Shuttling travelers along this cacophony of greased links were tiny theaters featuring dial bands, howlers, peek shows, voice wrestlers, tongue cappers, cat-walkers, cheeps, and push shows.

When I first traveled on these odd ships to yarn-rip assignments on the high floors, I found them alien and tedious. In one a band of five men wearing chartreuse crinoline screamed in unison. In another females stabbed each other with satin pins and sewing needles. In another a woman punched herself as she sang about being a cat. But on the way to my last yarn rip, I happened to take the Europa Showhouse. The interior was decorated in purple with gold ornate accents, and the air smelled of smoke and pollen. Once the ship started up, a man in a large red suit and red top hat came on the stage.

"I now present to you, graceful shoppers and consumers, the star of the Europa Showhouse—the only fully invented Baroque-style entervator serving the south and west side—the lovely, the talented, the erotic, the mysterious, the genetically patented *Vada*!"

The crowd cheered and hollered. The woman on my left removed the chrome gag from her mouth and screamed. "I love you, you treasonous whore!" From the point on the chrome plug came a viscous stream of saliva that dripped like spider's silk onto the purple carpet.

Although I had never seen a doll before, in retrospect that's what Vada looked like. Two large circles of rouge dotted her cheeks. Atop her head, her luminous auburn hair was wound into a pile and ornamented with tiny birds, baubles, and golden rickrack. Her burgundy dress was part corset, part gown, and part giant insect shell. She wore the most fantastic and elaborate pair of deep-red boots I had seen, glazed with glowing beads of various shapes and luminosity. The pointed toes curled up and around. And the heels were made of what looked like little machines, with spinning gears, pistons, and exhaust pipes that puffed tiny, pearly beads of smoke.

And unlike most of the faultless saleswarriors and their beautiful and plasticott faces, Vada was obviously in her middle years with a few wrinkles on her neck and an appealing laxity in her face and body. She seemed real and alive.

As I watched her sing a ballad, read someone's fortune, and strip down to her red pellicule underwear, I was mesmerized.

SEATTLEHAMA: DEATH IN THE PARFUM SPACESHIP

From the 888 entervator port in the Parfum Spaceship, I soon found the quiet hallway of my assignment for my last yarn rip. I was early, so I headed to an empty enterjohn beside the Fat White Ninja Chocolate Finger Dipper Bistro, closed and bolted the door, and undid my slacks.

As I shucked myself to climax into the bowl, the blue knitter-kritter frog that hopped around inside the enterjohn glared at me.

"Hey, sh-hopper!" it said. "This porcelain pooper is for select evacuations. Here in Seattlehama, if you want *that* kind of fun, go to Teensy Town Tea and Pillow Room on 621 or Mr. Matto's Hanky Parlor on 622. Be sure to mention me, EnterJohn Frog the Seattlehama Sh-Hopper, for a ten percent discount on your first visit!" His speech doubled in speed. "This offer may not be combined with any other and is time limited for twenty-three hours and forty-three minutes starting now. It is not redeemable for credit, and the terms and conditions of this offer may change at any time. SO 94-B."

After splashing myself with water, I hurried out guiltily. For the next quarter hour I paced the hallway anxiously, trying to convince myself that there wasn't anything wrong with me, that my root wasn't rotting, and that the frog wasn't going to report me to the authorities.

The stores here were filled with electro-logo t-shirts with celebs' faces, the towers, and all manner of logos. There were plush dolls of characters and critters. I saw miniatures of the city made out of every conceivable material: wood, metal, meat, light, and ice. In one store was a selection of carved mini-entervators with suspension wire kits. I stopped for a moment. The most famous entervators were all there: The Ring Bell, SkyPod, The Infinite Puddle, but I didn't see the Europa Showhouse. I thought of Vada and my root started to stiffen again. I thought about finding another enterjohn—one without an annoying knitter-kritter, but by now it was almost time for the rip.

The place Withor had described was an intersection of plain hallways where the lights were dim and clumps of dust littered the floor. The cloth was supposed to head toward the main shopway, so I waited around the corner. Soon hard-soled footsteps approached. A man in a bright yellow suit came around the corner. He was watching a screen in his hand and didn't even see me as he passed. I relaxed, but a moment later I heard several small grunts, a muffled scream, and the *pas de deux* of footwork.

A woman in a mahogany drap-de-Berry suit stumbled from the doorway on the right. She slammed into the opposite wall, fell to the floor, and let out a raw cry. An instant later she was silent, but her body twitched like a dead spider.

I started toward her to help, but a hazy shimmer appeared in the air between us. I heard hard breathing. The shape bent over the drap-de-Berry woman and pulled a rough heather scarf from around the woman's neck. I guessed that the scarf was being tucked into an invisible pocket, but it looked like the material was pushed into another dimension.

I moved to back away, and the hazy figure came at me. I was shoved backward and might have been knocked to the floor, but I grabbed onto the shimmer with my yarn pulls and stayed afoot.

I waited, ready to defend myself, but saw and heard nothing. Seconds passed and then I heard footsteps quickly disappear down the hallway. It was gone.

Drap-de-Berry had come to rest with her face toward the wall, but when I stepped over her, I was surprised to find her eyes and mouth wide open. She looked like she was frozen in screaming pain, and even as I touched her neck to feel for a pulse, I knew something terrible had just happened.

Turning, I ran before it happened to me.

A LOOP NEAR-DISASTER

Once I had turned off Route 6002 into the verification port and my Chang-P had been sniffed, I steered it toward the Loop access ramp, engaged all of the forward motors, and primed the accelimeter, and put the steering on lock, requesting a lane course to Nug Yar on the East Coast, where Ark Textiles and the jobber Ryder was located.

A route came back instantly and as the car accelerated to 4.3, pushing me far into the upholstery of my seat, I finally felt my frustration lift. I would be in Nug in twenty-one minutes and eight seconds, and while it would probably take me twice as long to get to the address and find suitable parking, at least I was moving.

Although I had said I would call Pheff, I did not. He would be busy with the preparations by now and the frenzy of last minute hemming, pinning, steaming, ironing, and folding would be adequate distraction from his anxiety. If he needed anything, he would be sure to check my status, see the blip of my existence reassuringly simmering along the red line of the Loop.

Once the car had reached final speed and the g-forces had released me, I selected a sample book of Probiotic Plurex Maxi-Gabardines from the shelf on my door. I idly fingered the squares as a blind man might read a magazine.

For the past ten years, my work had consumed me. Tailoring clothes for the richest and most famous men in the world had become my life, my calling, and my identity. But it was a lonely existence. My friends—mostly associates—were limited to those in the business, clients, and my assistant Pheff. Vada's visit reminded me of all those before, the phalanx of people I had met on my journey, those I had known, those I had loved, those who died beside me, those who had tried to kill me, the few I killed.

Tossing the fabric samples aside, I turned on the driver's mirror and looked at myself. A wrinkle, which dipped slightly above my nose, scored my forehead. My eyebrows had recently begun to wane. The left, especially, seemed to have thinned from the depth of its youth. On my chin, I touched the single black hair that grew there, tugged at it, and pulled a tiny spike of skin taut. If I tugged another quarter of an inch, I would yank it out and a bead of blood would grow in its place.

Did I feel like a fake? I was indeed a successful and desired tailor. I had taught myself everything from yarn composition, fiber texturizing, backing, weaving and de-weaving, stitching, tailoring, pressing, and all the hundreds of skills I employed with unconscious dexterity. But somewhere else in me, beyond the polished palladium suit racks, the black nano-velvet shirt boxes, the walrus ivory collar stays, the rhino-leather soled shoes, I had never left the cornfields of my youth—still struggling to help the crop, honor M-Bunny, and be loyal to my reps.

The clan I once belonged to had grown stronger and larger. The slubs of my childhood had stretched from Wiskon to Seattlehama, but now reached even farther, pressing north and south. M-Bunny men even worked the land in Antarctica. And while M-Bunny once existed as parts of a larger patchwork with the soy, potato, and truck clans, now it had become a near monoculture up and down the continent.

The hormones previously sprayed onto our B-shirts and shorts were an abandoned practice and so, too, was the gentleness with which we treated one another. Gone was the reverence for corn above all. And instead of the strange loyalty-based mating system, women were allowed in special reproductive zones. The life I knew had vanished.

Despite the hardships—and there were many—my early years

had been filled with blissful delusion. I believed that M-Bunny was going to save the world, that our subservience to the crop, our worshipping and genuflection before the ears, was making a difference—and that those greedy and selfish creatures who lived in the towers were ruining everything.

And then, when I was seventeen, I had an insight that changed everything. I realized just how awful M-Bunny's shirts were. Back then they were made of a stiff and scratchy non-woven corn fiber. They went "on sale" twice a year after the spring and fall harvests. It was one per man, which meant we wore the things for six months. We didn't care. We didn't know better. Besides, we were making a sacrifice; we were saving the planet.

I, like many, developed a rash from the front of the neck hole. Our armpits grew sore where the stiff fabric bunched up, and for those who had put on weight, the things didn't stretch gracefully over the belly, but tore in long frayed lines.

One night, I took off my B-shirt and laid it flat on the floor. The neck hole was cut at the top and the sleeves stuck out at ninety degrees, but as I studied my body and the structure of others, I understood that it didn't match. Our necks didn't come straight up out of the top of our shoulders, but angled forward. And, of course, our arms didn't stick straight out but hung at our sides.

In the beginning I was confused. I asked my rep why M-Bunny's shirts didn't fit.

"We don't ask questions," I was told.

I came to understand that M-Bunny's shirts weren't made for us. They were stamped out of the material without regard to our bodies and our movements. It was wrong. Worse, it seemed easy to fix. And when I told my rep, he forbade me from talking about B-shirts again.

"Another word, and you'll be recycled!"

I felt betrayed! And worse, it meant that if M-Bunny wasn't right about B-shirts, she might not be right about anything.

For weeks I tried not to think about it. I didn't speak to my rep or tell any of the men. I told myself it was my own problem, that I didn't understand something larger. And then, one evening when I had tugged the front of my shirt from the sore spot on my Adam's apple for the millionth time, I headed out into the dim of the cornfield outside the house. Using a bit of wire and some corn silk, I tacked down the front of the neck hole so that it fit. The difference was so wonderful and freeing, I spent the next several days giggling.

Soon other men in the house asked me about it and they wanted me to do the same for them. After I had done half the house, our rep noticed and called me aside.

"It's done with corn silk," I told him. "It's not against M-Bunny."

He told me to stop, but then two days later came back and had me fix his shirt. When he slipped it over his head, he felt the same instant relief.

Soon I was fixing the B-shirts of other reps. And even as I was noticed and being praised for helping M-Bunny, for adding to her splendor, assisting her men, down deep, I was the worst kind of disbeliever.

I woke from my daydream seconds before the Nug Yar exit. If I missed it, I wouldn't be able to turn around until the Greenland exchange, another fifteen minutes away. "Cut me!" I whacked down the emergency lever, slapped the off button that electrified the fast fibers, grasped the steering rods, and nosed the Chang-P down the ramp to the speed reduction Loop—the dreaded thing for which the highway had been named.

Only ten of these Loops still functioned. Improvements in road control and car navigation had made them nearly obsolete. It was only foolish drivers like myself, who actually controlled their cars, who ever needed to decelerate in the Ferris-wheel-shaped things. Basically, it was an enormous loop-the-loop of specialized elastometric and polarized road, which could slow a car to ramp speeds in less than a half-mile of space—that is, if the tremendous centrifugal forces didn't crush the vehicle or kill the driver.

As soon as I entered the Loop and pressed the brake, the road rose straight up into the sky. At first the momentum pulled me toward the windshield, but as the car began to climb, I was slammed back. Weights seemed stacked on me ten deep. I couldn't keep my eyes open. Blood pooled in my feet and ankles.

The dash was awash in warning lights, and every muscle in my body tensed as if to keep my skeleton from flying apart. I couldn't take in air. My lungs were flattened. I couldn't open my mouth.

The Earth spread out below like a celestial dish.

I'm not sure at what point I blacked out. Somewhere near the top, when the Chang was upside down, I imagined I was in a glass gazebo. Blaring light filled the place. Someone else was there, but in the glare I couldn't see. I reached out as if to shake hands, but the figure attacked. I saw my body hit, fall, and lay on the ground.

Next, I was sitting in a plush seat. A distant mechanical tone sounded. Before me was a blurry checkerboard of orange lights. Slowly the dash came into focus. The reset button for the emergency system was flashing desperately. Reaching a hand— with exactly the sense of detachment one might have operating a robotic arm—I weakly pressed it. The car went silent.

I had come to a stop at the end of an emergency ramp. The car was still on the road, but at a thirty-degree angle. I wasn't sure who I was. My sleeves were dark charcoal. I brought the right one closer to my face, and I could see that the weave was a low-twist, dual-satin that formed a satisfying pebbly texture on the surface. Something about it seemed familiar, but the idea was slippery.

Then it came to me: I was Tane Cedar. I was a tailor and fabric designer. I was driving my Chang-P to Nug Yar, to talk to a jobber about getting Xi yarn for Vada. I was on a dangerous expedition and needed to be extremely careful. I knew I had just been warned.

SEATTLEHAMA: WITH EXTREME LOVEEFFORT

I couldn't go back to Withor. I hadn't ripped the drap-de-Berry yarn, and no matter what I told him, I knew he wouldn't believe me. Worse, I worried that he had known the woman was going to be killed. Maybe some designer had wanted a yarn from a murdered woman in drap-de-Berry. Whatever Withor was up to, I wasn't going to play his slubber. But he still had my papers. Once I completed the rip, he'd said he would give them to me so that I could be free.

What was I supposed to do now? I couldn't report what happened to the satins. As a former slubber who didn't have his papers, I knew I wasn't supposed to be stealing yarns. I didn't think I was even supposed to be this high up in the city.

I didn't know where I was heading, only that I needed to get away. At the entervator port, my MasterCut was rejected.

"You'll have to see one of our credit and debit dungeon masters at the window," intoned the woman at the gate. I headed straight out of the port and threw the purple card into the first entertrash can I saw.

When I found showstairs, I started down. Ten flights later, in a large glassy atrium, I stopped dead. Straight ahead was Casper Union. Kira Shibui, the t'up with the beautiful eyes and impassioned speech, had mentioned it. Grateful for something even remotely familiar, I headed inside.

The space was large. Masked customers stood around tall

51

plinths decorated with female mannequins in nothing but yellow skivvé. At the back, a band playing water-pipes and odd machines filled the air with an endless train of percussive thuds and raspy squelches. Saleswarriors in short white plasticott dresses were everywhere. Long, yellow, empty root-tubes hung from their crotches.

One sashayed toward me, all blue eyes and corn silk hair. Her mouth was tiny and as red as a wound. Her skin was as smooth as organza. Her tube swayed with each step.

"The properties of unison and union," she said, her expression firm and serious. "Your skin became *her* skin."

"Listen," I whispered, "I met Kira Shibui a couple of weeks ago…"

The woman's eyes—large before—grew huge as her mouth tightened to a knot. "How dare you come to our motherfloor and speak the identity of our enemy!" Turning, she spoke to two other warriors. "A traitor customer just uttered the wrinkled sound of *Python Duck Weapon* and that sad and starchless traitor, Kira Shibui." She then spat on the floor. "Even the shape of her name acidifies my tongue."

I didn't know what I'd done wrong. "I just wanted to ask a question. She told me her address. It was 609 something… I don't remember the building."

"Kira Shibui will soon be stuck upon the cold metal of my needles. And that will be her final residence!" The saleswarrior pulled out a pair of long, golden, connected knitting needles from a container at her waist.

"I didn't mean anything. Do you know where she is?"

Other saleswarriors gathered around us. One crossed her arms. "Leave now, sorry shopper, or Josephone will knit your intestines."

Josephone jabbed her needles toward my gut with an angry grunt. I had to jump back or she would have stabbed me. Her face was red, her eyes, furious. She was completely rot! Turning, I fled.

I wandered the hallways feeling suffocated by the city and its endless stores, shoppers, and crazy saleswarriors. I passed some shoe boutique and a woman in fluttering red stepped before me. "The destiny of your journey rests in the crotch of my desire."

Reversing my direction, I began to run. My head felt filled with rot. I passed a large group of shoppers all dressed like crying bears. Another group wore black clothes covered with worms.

Frantic to get away, I jogged down a seemingly endless series of staircases and came to a kiosk. The blonde smiled at me. "Hi. I'm your friendly, sultry infofighter, Sheila Top, with tourist, shopping, and fashion fornication information. May I help you in your reality, sir?"

"I'm looking for a woman," I said between breaths. "She's a knitter... Kira Shibui... She said something about 609... I don't remember the building."

"The fashion company you're looking for is Python Duck Weapon Men's Fantasy Skivvé," said the infofighter with a glaring smile. "It's in the lovely and practical Velour Building." She handed me a stack of cards. "Here's a complimentary Enterpass. Here's a complimentary city map... plus a coupon for a free Sweet and Unpleasant Throat Gusher from Melancholy Mouse Burger." She tilted her head to the side. "Seattlehama is the finest reality fantasy destination on the Rim. Have you gotten off in our city yet, sir?"

I said yes, thanked her, and turned.

From a nearby port, I headed back up a hundred floors in The Flying Drop, exited in the Velour, and soon found Python Duck Weapon. The store wasn't a tenth of the size of Casper Union and sat empty except for a single t'up woman who occasionally jangled the strings of a water-guitar. In the center sat a black table with three headless and armless mannequins in blue skivvé with long, narrow root tubes. Since no one was around and the musician didn't seem to be paying attention, I touched one. The fabric felt incredibly smooth and light.

I felt a presence and stood straight. Kira Shibui was three feet away, dressed in the same orange sailor suit. Around her waist, hanging from a belt with a bow, was a long, open pouch. In her right hand she held a pair of knitting needles at me.

I put up my hands. "We met before."

She peered at me for a long beat. "Ah, yes! I smell it now… the smoke of recollection." She tucked her needles into the pouch and then closed it. "You are the lost consumer from the shopping evening I acquired the Stanton-Bell." Her mouth quirked into a small smile. A scatter of freckles across her nose made me think of the beautiful dotted surface of a fried TakoDrop.

I pointed at the display skivvé. "You knit these?"

"On the legendary Stanton-Bell Tex-knitter 222," she intoned, turning toward the displayed skivvé. "The Stanton is an arrogant and glorious sister in the long war of our lives. A sweet sister, but one later tainted by the echo of spilled love." Whipping around, she glanced toward the front door. A second later, she turned toward the musician. "No percussion! In this crisis, I must hear every loathsome footfall!" She looked me up and down. "Come. We will talk in the safety of the design room."

She led me through a hidden door into a room piled with boxes, cloth, notions, and half a dozen complicated machines. It was silent, and the smell was of cloth and concentration.

She folded her arms. "Fill the air with your reasons."

"I remembered you," I said with a shrug. "I liked your kitting."

Her mouth was twisted to one side sourly. "You are not a scout, nor customer… I say you're not a tourist either."

I was much worse. I was a yarn ripping, paperless slubber who had run after some ghost-killed drap-de-Berry. "You told me to come by to learn about knitting." Her expression didn't change. She had laughed so easily at the knitting machine store.

"I do not recognize the slippery edge of your tongue." She narrowed her eyes. "Where are you from?"

While I tried to think of anything but the truth, I just came out with it. "The slubs."

Her eyes widened in horror. "Cut me," she muttered. "I thought I tasted the slur of a flat man… of a prisoner from the thirsty wormholes of the impoverished."

"I'm not a prisoner!" I told her. "I'm from the slubs."

"*Slubs,*" she said, with a laugh. "A prosthetic word. *Prisoner* carries the moral and repentant weight of the dead lives lived. And yet, I understand your indignation as you surely can't be blamed for the devastation of that wide and sad monoculture." Pursing her mouth, she folded her arms. "And your presence… Why are you before me?"

"I'll do anything for food and a place to stay."

She scowled. "Python Duck Weapon requires no warriors of design, credit, or transaction."

My heart sank. She showed me to the front door. I muttered awkward thanks as I stepped out into the shopway. For a while I just stood thinking. I couldn't return to the slubber ghetto. I couldn't go to Withor. Casper Union was out. Could I live on cuisine court samples and sleep in some hallway? Pressing my thumb gently against the sharp of the yarn pull glued to my middle finger, I wondered if I could rip yarn and sell them to the t'ups in the hallways. A woman in a see-through gown and furry black mask strolled by. *Would you like me to steal a yarn for you?* I imagined myself saying. I knew that was foolish.

I started down the hallway looking for a cuisine court where I might get some samples. The only other thing that came to mind was to try to find my way back to the infofighter to get more coupons. I figured I could last for several days like this, but after that, I didn't know. Nearby, I found another information booth, but just stood near and watched the screens for anything about drap-de-Berry. All I saw were commercials for clothes, cosmetics, and costumes.

"Man of dirt!" Kira Shibui stopped and looked me over.

Had she heard about drap-de-Berry? Was she about to turn me in? I thought about running, but she didn't seem like she was about to accuse me of anything. She pushed my shoulder as if testing my weight and then poked at my bicep with an index finger.

"Python Duck Corporate requires a Friday Officer. It's not a prestigious title, but one of muscle and bone."

I was so happy, I laughed. "Thank you! I had a good feeling about you. And I was really impressed how you knit." Her expression was serious. I nodded like I might have to an M-Bunny rep and said, "I'm happy to help."

Now her expression turned dark. "*Help?*" She shook her head slowly. "We are in fashion battles for our lives and we will only survive with true and extreme *LoveEffort!* Nothing will be required but *everything*." She glanced up and down the hallway anxiously. Then she glared at my TearDrop suit with disgust. "We must shop immediately."

AN UNEATEN
TWO-POUND
FLUFFY BURGER
AND
AN UN-DRUNK
KITTY PINK KOLA

How close had I just come to dying on the Loop? Once I blacked out near the top, the Chang-P's safety intervention logic had kept the car on the road. But if I had lost consciousness a few moments before and maybe twisted the wheel to one side as the g-forces began to pull, I might have flown off the up ramp, launched myself a mile up, and gotten my baked remains on all the major one hundred thousand feeds.

"You should pull over and rest," advised one of the Loop officials. "Get your neck and spine checked."

While it was probably a good idea to have a full work-up, I had a deadline and had no intention of stopping before I got to Ryder's office. But as I drove away my hands were vibrating slightly and my throat was dry. Worse, the movies of what might have happened were so bright and loud I found it impossible to concentrate. Just a few junctions later, I pulled into a rest stop. Beyond the station were two family restaurants. I had my choice of the saccharine pink and yellow Melancholy Mouse Burger or the saccharine yellow and pink

Fluffy Fun Bunny. I chose the later because it was closer. Before I went in, I stuffed my ears with grey cotton yarn to cut down on the clatter of bomb-blast happy melodies and shrill sing-alongs.

The place was enormous. A moving walkway whisked me half a mile away to the tables, where a jittery teen girl dressed in what looked like the offspring of a dandelion and a chimp stepped beside me and rattled off the specials.

"Just a regular burger," I told her, "and a normal drink."

She pouted at me. "Well, golly poo! Our superevil desert warlord, Mister Krunchy Smack Tart, will be so glad you're not treating yourself to one of his yummy chocolate and karabola face pies!"

"Good."

I found an empty table and chair and sat. Seconds later the girl returned.

"One mouth-tingling two-pound, Fluffy Bunny meat burger," said the same dandelion chimp girl. "And a frosty, frigid super-bladder Kitty Pink Kola." She plopped a pink plasticott box before me. Blindingly bright cartoon critters, slogans, and logos covered every inch. She leaned in and whispered. "I added six hand-carved Europa1 golden-toasted beef-flavored snap-fries for you to try for free! If you like them, let me know—I can get you half off a Fat Daddy Porker order." She giggled ferociously and was gone.

I used to feel it was critical that I get out of the studio more often, see and smell the world, taste its food, listen to its voice, music, and dreams, but in the last several years, whenever I ventured out, I usually ended up despairing the sheer ugliness of it all—the ever more intensive glare of the colors and the painful jangling of life's soundtrack. Most often I would retreat to my studio and head to my magazine humidifier for a copy of Pure H to cool my retina on the silky black-and-white photos and text.

It was times like that I was most reminded of my client, Michael Rivers. Of course he had been born in the epicenter of the world's noise and chromatic violence, and I had come from the opposite direction. For him the rejection of color was rebellion; for me it was more complicated. It was rejection of the brutality of city color, but it was also, in a way, an embrace of an abstracted version of the corn, of those days at the height of the pollen drop at the end of the summer, when the sun baked away color and left only light and shadow.

For years, I had been pure grey. I assiduously removed all colors from my work, even at the microscopic level. My yarns were finished in such a way never to refract a tiny rainbow. My weaves and knits were created so that moiré patterns would not create interference colors. To white fabrics I added oxygenated films to instantly ameliorate possible stains. To blacks, I endlessly checked that there were not hidden tints introduced in the twists of the yarns and the mathematical dance of twills.

After a decade of religious colorlessness, it was time for a change. Not just for myself but my clients. Fashion must change and even our anti-fashion had worn its jacket too long. After a week of sleepless nights, I chose another color: green—dark green—hunter and phthalocyanine green. And the achromatic dance I had been dancing came to an end. I was afraid of what my customers would think of that first dark green suit I crafted, and, indeed, when the fashion automaton came out into the studio wearing it that nervous day, my biggest buyer sat up, made a face and seemed about to protest. But a moment later, something changed in him, or more likely—I guessed—he understood that he too had evolved, and that his outside would now imitate, mirror, and amplify that.

My client had at last found the vector of his life and stepped into the role he had been raised for. While it might be argued that green was the wrong shade—it wasn't the color of his family company, it held no special history—maybe because it came to him without meaning, he was able to give it his own.

For me, of course, green had significance. But I hadn't chosen the greens of the fields and leaves I remembered—this green was dim, overcast. And as much as I liked the nebulous emeralds in my latest clothes, I wasn't quite sure if this new shade meant future or past, forward or withdrawal.

Focusing on the plasticott food box before me, I snapped open the top and removed the jewel-case-enclosed burger, the sculpted bear blaster drink cup pricked with five straws, and the gratis tray of fries, each individually wrapped and resting beside drops of several gourmet sauces. This was exactly the sort of chaff that Pheff lived on. Every other day I would find the disassembled boxes, cups, trays, and the scraps of peculiar, fashionable food in the office trash.

For a moment, I felt sorry for him. Although he was both talented and competent, I feared he lacked the sand and gravel needed for a life in fashion. His life, from what little I knew, was exactly like this meal: hyper-processed, sweet and smooth, but ultimately safe.

By now, my hands were no longer trembling and my heartbeat felt like it had finally slowed. But I just sat there staring forward the golden-orange of the drink cup seemed the color of the sun setting in the slubs.

I had been coming out of the corn syrup processing factory into the burnt orange of afternoon. Six feet ahead—in silhouette— stood a man. I didn't recognize him—I didn't even pay him any attention—but started toward the bus stop that would take me back to the house where I lived.

The man said, "Tane."

His voice wasn't the same—it had shrunk in depth and tenor— but it stopped me instantly. Gradually, as my eyes adjusted to the light, I saw his face. A dark bruise covered his right cheek. The left side of his mouth was covered with a bloody scab. Worse, his arms and what I could see of his neck through the tear of his B-shirt were covered with pinkish sores. I hadn't seen him for more than nine years. "Dad!"

"I found you." He sounded exhausted, and I got the feeling he had been searching for a long time.

"What happened?"

He shook his head slowly as if counting the abuses and tragedies.

"Were you in a fight?" I figured he had clashed with a group of L. Segu men, but what really worried me was his rash. M-Bunny reps were always on the lookout. While some diseases could be cured with doses from the M-Bunny COM, if it were bad or unknown, the man would have to be recycled.

He looked me over and eked out a smile. "You're good."

"How'd you find me?" Before he answered—not that he seemed about to—I continued. "I never heard anything since you left that night. I was only at that house for another year before they moved me. I asked the reps and the man at the COM all the time, but no one heard anything."

He pulled himself straighter and looked me in the eyes. "I don't have much time." He scrunched his wrinkled mouth to one side as if in thought. "I'm dying."

My mouth was so dry, I couldn't swallow. I shook my head.

"I've got a day... I don't know... maybe two."

I forced a smile. "You're just hurt and... and... tired and probably hungry." As I tried to think of something more positive, my eyes lit on the sores that peeked out the neck of his shirt. It looked like his chest was covered.

"Go south to the slubs around Ros Begas."

"Ros where?" I was still trying to keep my tone light, but the intensity of his glare made me fearful. "Why? What's going on?"

"There's a Europa brandclan there called Bestke. Switch to them."

"Switch?" I knew of the concept, but had never met anyone who had actually changed. The rumor was that most L. Segu men wanted to switch to Bunny, but maybe that was just propaganda. And all I knew of Bestke was that it had something to do with potatoes. "Dad," I said quietly as several M-Bunny men walked past eyeing us suspiciously, "let's just get you a dose or something."

"Do as I say!"

"I will," I said. "But, please, let's get you something at the COM."

"Bestke," he repeated. "I've told them about you."

"Shh!" The idea that he had talked to another brandclan terrified me. I had no intentions of switching and didn't want my reps suspicious. "I'm sure there's some M-Bunny dose that will help you. I know a guy at the COM. He's good. It's near the house."

"You have to go. Promise me you will."

I knew what happened. Dad was debranded! He had destroyed corn somewhere, he had not recycled, or maybe he had killed a rep! When a man did something against the corn or M-Bunny, he would not just be recycled, but his father and his sons would be taken away. That's why he wanted me to go. "Dad," I said quietly, "what'd you do? What happened? Did you do something to the crop?"

He sighed and stared down at his feet.

Disappointment and shame began to harden in my body like another skeleton. In that moment that dad had been debranded it felt worse than his death. "Let's get the bus. The COM's near my house. We can see what they say."

"Promise me."

I was sure I could see disgrace in his eyes. And then I noticed that the sores weren't on his face, neck, or hands. "How'd you get that... those... that stuff on your arms and chest?"

"Promise me!"

My frustration shattered like a pane of glass. "Nine years ago you just walked away! You turned down the path. And I don't know if you know it, but I followed you. As far as I could, anyway." I don't know if I wanted to surprise him or demonstrate my sorry longing. His mouth pinched. "Dad, I figured you were recycled."

He twisted his lower jaw to the right, and I thought he was going to yell. He bared his teeth and clenched his eyes. A small grunt came from him and that was all. Then I heard his teeth slip against each other as he bit down.

"Dad?" My exasperation turned to panic. "Smut! What's the matter?"

His legs buckled and he fell to his knees. I grasped his shoulder to keep him from falling on his face.

I woke from my reverie and glanced around me, hoping the other customers hadn't noticed. A mother and child silently worked on a *mound of fries. Two teenage girls lip-synced to the blaring music. Behind them sat a saleswarrior from some nearby store in her tiny spandicott dress and neon make-up. She ate sullenly as if fully absorbed in daydream or rehearsing her warTalk.*

I opened the jewel case and unwrapped the lurid pink foil. The bun was colored the livid yellow of the sun, the meat dyed a pastiche of reds, blues, and purples. It looked awful. I set it down.

I thought about how I had changed after my father left. Maybe to compensate or lure him back, I tried to be the most loyal and virtuous M-Bunny man ever. I had worked long and hard in the corn. I recycled everything. I praised M-Bunny's food, her clothes, and the corn oil that powered her buses.

But when Dad showed up that day in the slubs, beaten, and sick, my attitude changed forever. I understood that he wasn't the man I thought he was. If that memory was a lie, then maybe I had understood nothing.

I began stuffing my food back into the plasticott box. I couldn't even look at it anymore. When I got up and started toward the trash, the dandelion chimp girl chased after me.

"Sir, would you like me to wrap your treats?" She clenched her small hands together nervously as she peered at me. "Or is something the matter?"

"Something's the matter." When her mouth tightened into a frown and her eyes got watery, I hastened to add, "But not with the food or you. With me."

She offered to have the on-duty nurse come and check me and do a full and complimentary gastrointestinal check, but I told her it wasn't like that. "It's memories," I told her. "Memories."

SEATTLEHAMA: PASTEL RUFFLES

The Black Blossom Shopping Amphitheater and Custom Fashion Art House was a cacophony of competing rhythms, clothing racks, undulating displays, and hundreds of saleswarriors. I found it hard to see anything for the flashing lights, the made-up faces, and the jangle of sounds and conversation.

We passed a nine-foot-tall chunk of clear ice. Frozen inside was a frilly violet jacket. Kira stopped, eyed me, and then the jacket. I got the feeling she had just copied my head and was now affixing it atop the thing.

A saleswarrior in tiny white shorts and a dripping wet shirt came toward us. Her orange eyelids accented her huge blue eyes. "*My theme is cloud.*"

Gazing at the encased purple jacket, Kira replied, "*More than cloud: atmosphere and the passion of the storm.*"

"*Take me,*" swooned the saleswarrior, "*take me to the eye and see me where none have stitched before!*"

The two of them laughed. They had been quoting something. A second later both squinted at me, not undressing but re-dressing.

The saleswarrior said, "He's the visage of Warrior Remon of Loin!"

"With some slight adjustments," Kira agreed.

In the next moment, I found myself being fitted for that violet jacket. The rich material was stronger and more supple than anything I had ever felt, and once the saleswarrior swirled her fingers over a silvery remote, the sleeves changed length and the shoulders fit perfectly. Kira stepped before me and primped the thick flow of ruffles that spilled down the front. She combed the fringe on the sleeves, buttoned the seven buttons down the front, and then stepped back to take me in. Her pupils seemed large, her lips, thicker. She was breathing fast, her breasts swelling above the neckline of her dress with each inhale.

Stepping toward me close enough that I could see the powdery luminescence of the browns and gold around her eyes, the colorless fuzz that salted the corners of her mouth, a few tiny red threads in the white of her eyes, she whispered, "High-fashion fornication."

I didn't know the last word, but the way she snarled it, I guessed. I hadn't seen anyone ever kiss, but had a notion to press my mouth to hers. I leaned close enough to feel the warm atmosphere around her.

"Warrior Remon!" She pushed me back. "You're not fully dressed!"

From there we shopped for a shirt, tie, scarf, kerchief, chemise, hose, shoes, slacks, and a man's non-fantasy skivvé.

At the last booth, Kira told me to sit in a large chair.

"What for?"

"We're going to style your face and hair."

A team of technicians, clinicians, and gender counselors worked me over. My hair was primped; my forehead reshaped, my hands smoothed, and my Adam's apple enlarged with some sort of injection.

"I don't like this," I complained between pricks and twists.

"You're done," announced a woman who wore a crown of lights.

The man in the worm-covered jacket that had been with Kira when we first met stepped before me. Behind him I recognized the man in the giraffe mask. Worm Jacket was gazing at me. "He *is* Warrior Remon of Loin from *Sensitive Dead Penisless Boys.*"

Kira held a mirror for me to see. My hair had been lengthened, fluffed, and highlighted with reds. My forehead was taller, which made me look serious, even severe. Somehow my eyes looked twice as wide. My eyelashes were dark and felt heavy when I blinked. My lips had been puffed and felt tender. I looked like a t'up man, like a friend of Vit and Flak.

Giraffe rocked his mask forward and back. "Beautiful!"

Worm Jacket raised a fist. "To the buttonhole machine!"

"First," said Kira with a naughty grin, "I need a fashion fornication coat."

Both Worm Jacket and Giraffe let out excited whoops.

As the three of us headed through the crowded shopping floor, other t'ups began to follow, and by the time we reached a display of huge jackets, forty more were tagging along.

"The woven lining provides body, hand, and contact." The saleswarrior wore a thick, fuzzy coat. The front was unbuttoned and she was nude underneath. Hers were the first breasts and vulva I had ever seen. I couldn't stop staring. I knew Kira didn't have a root in her skivvé, but now I wondered how she peed. "Electrical and mechanical stimulation is built into the lining," continued the warrior. "Our sensations are industry-leading."

"Get the hunter green!" suggested Worm Jacket.

Kira thought that funny.

"We love you in black emerald," agreed Giraffe. "It brings out the mystery and cruelty in your eyes."

Kira relented and selected a dark green coat. The gathered crowd cheered.

Behind the fashion runway, Kira and I dressed separately. Worm Jacket came to help me. "Remon! Slow down. Take your pants off. This goes on first!" He held a strange silky blue pair of shorts with a round clump of fabric in front.

"What is that?"

"Don't you know what a Mr. Troy is? It's only *the best* men's panty. It's got the Spandik Cup front and Absorb-it technology.

You know, it's like they used to say… *it shapes and cups and helps you go nuts.*" As he sang, his enthusiasm dimmed. *"The skin on your fashion pin…"* He narrowed his eyes. "Kira won't tell us anything about you. Where are you even from?"

I looked him in the eye and said, "I was a prisoner."

He froze. "Cut me," he muttered.

For that instant I was in control. It wasn't a feeling I had often.

"You really are like Warrior Remon."

I was back on my heels again. "Who is Remon?"

"Only the biggest character from the biggest epic. He's *the* dream man. And the thing is, he lived part of his life in the corn. That's the secret unmentionable thing about him. He meets and falls in love with Bunné, who is Neutering Queen JackRabbita. They have a secret affair and he loses his… well… you know."

"This is made-up," I confirmed.

"No. Like all Bunné's epics, it's based on a true story. That's where the power comes from." He struck a pose, stared intently into the distance, and then laughed. "I look a little like Remon, but he's so convinced and strong… I can't pull it off." He shrugged and then gently touched one of the live worms woven into his jacket. "I dress like Commander Sheppard in the Mulberry Jacket. He's Remon's best man." He gazed at me for a dejected moment then picked up the Mr. Troy. "So, anyway… um, when you get *solid*, this fabric stretches and surrounds you with sensitive silk. It's called sensi-silk. And the Absorb-it drains away those unsavory liquids." He peered at me. "Have you fashioned before?"

I tensed. "No."

He nodded slowly. "Well… okay. Here's what you should really know—and I'm not saying this to be a cut—Kira is an amazing knitter and a completely beautiful warTalker. She's my favorite celeb knitter… I mean, she's not a big one or anything… and her fashion company is really beleaguered now. But she's special. She's a real rebel, and she's risking everything and that's stunning. What she's doing with you is such a gift. You have to cherish this." He stared forward for a long beat, and I got the feeling he wanted to be with her. "I guess she knows what she's doing." I heard him swallow again. "Anyway, let's get you dressed. First put on the Troy and then your stockings… and then you've got a nice cream chemise here… and a ruffled lavender shirt…"

When I was dressed, Worm Jacket and I headed to a room just behind the stage. Several t'ups in ornate and lavish costume waited to go on next. Thumping music and the occasional squawk of a voice echoed beyond the curtain.

Kira came toward me in a thick, fuzzy jacket. Her large eyes were filled with warmth and unfamiliar vulnerability. She smiled and whispered, "Hello, Warrior Remon of Loin." She teased the ruffles and frills of my jacket and shirtfront with her lace-gloved hands. "You are truly majesty and honor… you are the smoke before fire… the silence before the crash."

A warm tingling filled me as I stared into her eyes.

"Kira," said Worm Jacket, "I'm not trying to be a cut or anything, but you know that he hasn't fashioned before, right?" He smiled nervously as his eyes darted between us.

"Deep instincts of the forgotten men," she said, eyeing me knowingly, "are never forever lost. Just as cloth remembers the body and the creases of time, so too the warrior lays deep within the breast of the male."

Worm Jacket smiled sourly. He swallowed, nodded slowly, and then stepped away. For an instant I felt bad for him.

"The interlocked closeness," continued Kira, her voice tender and hungry. "Knits rubbing against wovens. The tightness of the stitch. The slight pilling across the friction of our longing. The stretched and then torn yarns of desire."

The black emerald of her coat made her eyes glow with promise. I reached to touch her cheek, but she moved so that my fingers met the thick collar of her jacket. The material was warm and soft and as I caressed it, she closed her eyes and let out a long teardrop-shaped moan.

A second later she pushed me back in a playful faux anger. "Save Troy for the show!"

"Shoppers, customers, consumers, and buyers…" A man in an enormous orange suit spoke at the far side of the stage. "On this auspicious day of late winter afternoon shopping, The Black Blossom Fashion Shopping Amphitheater fashion show continues!"

Kira and I were peeking between the heavy white curtains. Through the glare of the lights I could see hundreds of t'ups around the runway clapping and cheering. As others strutted out before us, Kira showed me the mechanics of the walk, the sort of dower, unhappy face one made, and what we were going to do at the end of the runway.

"Let's have a passionate welcome for our favorite independent men's fantasy skivvé knitter Celebrity Executive Officer, Kira Shibui!"

Kira fiddled with the ruffles of my jacket and sleeves one last time and then turned, and headed through the curtains to the runway. The crowd screamed.

"There she is! Today's shopper! Today's luxury consumer! And just behind her, new shopper to our boutiques… welcome Tane Cedar as Warrior Remon of Loin!"

I held closed my eyes for an instant and then stepped through. A crash of applause hit me in the chest as I started after her.

"Kira is in a Bietnamese tower wool blend with a silk-a-pussi core and dovetail lady lining," said the announcer. "Her warrior is wearing a wounded sky robust purple jacket in pleated zero denier high-twist Halyn with fall curl and spilled ruffle gut details by Rebel Sheep. His blouse is a quad-collared taffeta with splatter-curls by Exceptional Red Self-Injury Santa. His shoes are fine goat scrotum leather cement-skippers from Aurora Boring Alice."

The man went on, but with the screams of the crowd and beat of the music, I couldn't hear and didn't care. Ahead of me, Kira reached the end of the runway, stopped, glanced one way with a haughty turn of her head, and then turned to gaze at me. In the glare of the lights, the blast of the sounds, and the frenzied motion of the crowd, she seemed like the center of the store and the apex of the earth.

Stopping before her, I first glanced away as if I wasn't interested or hadn't even noticed. Then I put a hand on a hip and turned toward her slowly. I could see annoyed amusement in her eyes. Stepping closer, I caressed the thick lapel of her coat and then, as I had seen on some screen ad somewhere in the hallways, I gripped the fabric, pulled it close, and kissed it. She was saying something, but I just buried my face in the soft collar and started nibbling at the edges. Her fingertips traced the seams of my shoulders, to my armpits, and down my sleeves. The sensation was tickly exciting. I bit the collar of her jacket, and she arched her spine.

She pushed me back. Her face was flush, her nostrils flared. She reached down, touched the single, large round button on the front of her jacket and pulled it open. Underneath she wore a white suit as thin and transparent as mist.

I undid the front of my slacks. My hard root was covered with a layer as thin as paint—the blue flowered patterned sensi-silk of my Mr. Troy. Grasping her coat, I moved myself toward her buttonhole.

SEATTLEHAMA: SKIVVÉ BATTLES IN THE FOUNDATION WAR

Each morning I would head to the cuisine court down the hallway for cups of double-concentration java and ice curry doughnuts for breakfast. At noon I picked up whitened fish rolls, hairy pork sticks, and juice pizzas. The rest of my days were filled with cleaning the lint trays, carrying boxes, and unpacking crates of liqui-yarn. I asked Kira about tools, about yarn, about her skivvé. Her answers were in warTalk so I didn't learn much, but for a while I was glad to be safe.

Worm Jacket and Giraffe came by daily to chat and see what she was up to. Once after Kira left them to attend to a customer, I stepped beside the two men.

"How do you find out if someone died?" I whispered.

Worm Jacket peered at me oddly. "Who?"

"Someone I met a while ago."

"Good luck getting real news in Seattlehama!" scoffed Giraffe.

"If it's not on a coupon," quipped Worm Jacket. "I could check for you. Who died?"

I recalled drap-de-Berry's frozen scream. "I was just asking."

"Was it another saleswarrior?" asked Giraffe.

"It was just something I saw in a hallway a while ago."

"They don't tolerate offenders." Giraffe leaned in. "I'm sure it was fixed."

Worm Jacket asked. "What happened?"

Shrugging as if it were nothing, I told him, "I thought someone was hurt."

In the mornings, Kira did most of her knitting. Once she was done, she would warTalk with customers, and then head out to lunch with clients or meetings with investortroopers. During those times, when the front door was locked, I began to sneak into the design room to first look at, then touch, and finally test the heat crimpers, the water-shears, the button extruder, the ribbon maker, the seam braider, the elasti-matic. And then after several weeks, when Kira headed to Melancholy Mouse Burger with a creditwarrior for what I figured would be a long lunch, I stepped before the Stanton-Bell.

Basically I was not to touch *anything*, but at least a dozen times she had expressly and explicitly forbidden the Stanton-Bell in particular. "Refrain from even depositing the dead follicle, the dead platelet of skin even *near* this glorious sister." But it was too tempting. I had watched Kira knit a hundred times and was sure I knew exactly how it worked. I wanted nothing but to try.

The thing looked like the offspring of some upper-body aerobic exercise machine with steps for one's feet and two long handles for controlling the floating knitting heads. After taking a deep breath, I stepped on and gripped the handles. For a minute, I just stood there and imagined. My heart was racing. My palms were wet. I told myself to get off, get out of the design, and get back to my duties.

I didn't. Instead, I reached forward to the round green button and switched it on. It emitted a slow hum, a faint, but powerful vibration, and the magnetic knit heads quivered like the mouthparts of some chrome insect.

My heart beat in my fingertips as I pressed the right handle forward. It moved. The knit heads spun in air and created a thin row of knit. I was doing it! I wanted to laugh out loud. I pushed the handle again and it made another row. Slowly circling the left handle, I began to form a wide loop.

An inch. Two inches. Five inches. This is what I had been born to do. I spun the handle again and again and again.

I had enough for the sides of a skivvé and was approaching the crotch. I didn't really like nor even understand their men's fantasy skivvé, so instead of making one of Kira's, I made a simple pair of shorts that I might want to wear. In less than five minutes I was done. I turned off the power and stepped off the foot pedals. I had made something! I had created a garment. I began to giggle like my mind was rotted. But just as I was about to take it from the knitting heads, the door design opened.

Kira dropped a plasticott bag and rushed at me. "Traitor to the heart of yarn! Retreat your soul. The smoke of disgrace. The undying knots of agony!" Her warTalk came so fast and angry, I couldn't keep up.

"No!" I said, holding up my hands. "I just tried. I didn't break it."

She whipped out her knitting needles and jabbed them at my throat. "The scars of injury have spoken," she said. "Corporate Operations Officer is your title and duty. The Stanton-Bell is jewelry. Do not rest even the heat and soil of your fingers upon it! I will have to have it cleaned and reset!"

Her needles stabbed me. I touched my neck and found blood.

Spinning around, she yanked the shorts I had knit from the hooks. "This... this... sorry rag of loops! Where did it come from?"

Ashamed and embarrassed now, I didn't answer.

She bellowed. "Travel to me now, musician Ginn! Travel with the quick!"

Ginn, the water-guitarist, pushed the door open and peered in with a look of annoyance. "What?"

Kira held up my skivvé. "What is this aberration of crotch? You will not grime and foul the equipment. There is an earth and wind between the vibrating rings on your blunt club and the harmony of the men's fantasy skivvé."

"Cut me!" Ginn scoffed. "I didn't touch your dick tube machine." She let the door slam. A moment later an angry grinding of water-guitar filled the salesfloor.

Slowly Kira turned toward me. Her eyes were disbelieving. "Make harmonies of reason and elucidation. Do it now! From where did this come?"

When I swallowed, the scratch on my neck stung. "I just turned it on... I was just trying it... I'm sorry... I just wanted to make something."

Her eyes were wide and incredulous. "You are a spot! You are a spyglass and an undercover! You are not the prisoner you claim! What house are you from? What mysteries have you stolen? What covert ideas have you slipped?"

I shook my head. "I'm from the slubs."

"Then how?" she screamed. "Prisoner explain: How did you tangle the yarn with such grace and insight?" Her lips were trembling.

I was confused. Did she like what I'd made? "I just got on and did it."

"Training on a craft knitter such as the lofty Stanton-Bell is three long years. And with that stretch comes no assurance of artistry, refinement, or clarity. I have knit for seven years. I am worthy, but no master." She came within an inch of my face. The muscles at her temples tensed, as she seemed to chew unhappily while she looked me over as one might a machine for defects or a sample of knit for pulls. In a flash she held her pins at my face again. "You now will convey the warm luxuries of truth." She enunciated each word as if releasing an emerald or ruby. "Or I will knit your larynx closed."

"I don't know... I saw you do it... You just turn one handle to make it go and pull the other to change the... number of hooks... and..." Her eyes narrowed a fraction of an inch. "I don't understand why it's hard."

Her nostrils flared and her cheeks flushed. "It is a skill and a dexterity, and the number of knotted skivvé I have sung on the Stanton only to abandon as rag would fill the hallway before the flagship." In a flash she had jammed her knitting needles in my nostrils. She hadn't stabbed me, but I could smell the sharp metal. "You were never a prisoner! What be you? Speak before I bobble your brain!"

"I am from the slubs! I was born in Stelikom." Beads of sweat bloomed in my hair and down my back. She was going to kill me. She was just as rot as every other saleswarrior! "I started fixing B-shirts. I sewed the neck holes because they weren't cut right. And I... used to dream about grids and lines. I didn't know what they were... I mean I didn't know it was cloth until I came to Seattlehama. That's why I collected yarn."

"Then what proof have you, purported slubber prisoner!"

Withor still had my papers! Without them I was nothing. "That's the truth," I told her. The points of her knitting needles felt like they were stabbing my sinuses.

"Show me something!"

"I don't have anything."

"Nothing?" She yanked the needles from my nose. "You have nothing?"

I rubbed my nose. I was bleeding, but not badly. "I guess not."

She laughed at me. "Then you are nothing. You do not exist. I don't know if I should stitch you closed or toss you from these towers from the ends of my needles." When she waved the things in an angry figure eight, they swished like swords through the air.

I thought of the one thing I did have. It didn't prove anything, and I didn't want her to take it, but I said, "I have yarn."

She glared at me. "What yarn?"

"I got it from my dad in the slubs. I don't even know where he got it. But it's all I have."

"The dust and smoke of lies! Everything from you is sweaty

fiction! You are no prisoner. You are no spyglass. You are a nothing. I should bind you off."

I held up my hands. "I have it with me."

"Show it now."

I started to undo the closure on the front of my slacks.

"Move with sloth!"

The yarn I pulled from its hiding place inside the seam was thick and dark, and frayed at both ends. Holding it in my palm, I showed her.

Kira stared at me for several moments. I thought she was angry, that she considered it a joke of some sort and might even take it and snip it into a hundred little pieces before she did the same to my throat. But with her mouth puckered into a knot, she snatched the thing from me, turned, and dropped it onto the observation tray of a large magnitron. A second later she was studying the thing as I had done several times at Withor's office when he was out.

She muttered something that sounded like *Bunny*.

RYDER'S BUILDING

I had given the parking and maintenance attendants instructions to replace the Chang-P's tires, recharge the motors, put in new parachutes, and wash and detail it inside and out. Once the work was settled upon, I jogged two blocks down to Empire Square as a few raindrops, from what seemed like just one malicious cloud, dotted the intricate white and black tiles. Circling around a row of shrubs, iron tables, and benches, a crowd clasping their coffee bags and conversation hats were beginning to scurry for cover. I ducked my head and entered the lobby of the Iron Building.

The Iron was one of the smaller auxiliary buildings at Fashion Plaza and housed lesser mill companies, a few artisanal notions manufacturers, jobbers, and a dozen designers on the decline. Although I hadn't been inside it before, the black sand and sapwood lobby was similar to the others in the complex, if somewhat more shabby. To the left was a store that sold samples. On the right a line of hawkers, dressed in various costumes and representational fabrics, kick-started their smiles when I appeared and began their pitches, trying to press upon me their logoed trinkets and absurd promises of luxury, resiliency, economy, forecasted trends, and even minor acts of fashion sex. Ignoring them, I headed straight for the stairs.

The hallway was dim, the dark floor tiles covered with a thick archeology of yellowed wax and hopelessness. Here and there on the wall hung faded posters of weaving machines and yarn texturizers, each machine accompanied with women in big vests, revealing oiled skin in elf bikinis, and those night hats from a dozen years ago. Most of the doors were covered with ad-heads who smiled and began to describe the services or goods within. I passed them all and came, at last, to the far end of the hallway. In wiggling red letters that spelled out Ryder—Textile Jobber, a female ad-head with livid green hair smiled forcefully. As soon as she saw me, her black eyes met mine and she began speaking with the speed of a jet engine.

"This is the day the ocean speaks to you… that the dreams from sixty-thousand leagues beneath the surface, where memory is still memory and love is what it is supposed to be…"

To my right, I saw a men's room. While the ad-head blathered on, I ducked inside. The ancient walls were fake-citron wood, the floor black mesh. Two emerald commodes sat stiffly within. The heavily perfumed air gave me an instant headache. Above the single crystal sink, where six faucets dripped a slow polyphony, the mirror was warped and, depending on where I stood, alternately made my eyes and ears grow closer or farther apart.

I splashed my face with handfuls of overheated water and then raised my head to my soggy reflection. The mirror's distortion reflected some of my restlessness seeded in my harrowing experience on the Loop, but below that I could see the muddied turmoil of my thoughts about Dad, Vada, and myself.

Vada's appearance at my studio—now just hours ago—had, like a tornado, torn apart the intricate balances, arrangement, and denials of my life.

We had only spent part of a year together, but in my youthful fervor her assurance, her abilities, her contradictions, her mysteries, her love of costume had fascinated and consumed me. I was still so unformed and lacked confidence then. Perhaps that was why I had thrown myself into her request with such fever. I wanted to show her that I had changed. I didn't just have an elaborate showroom, design studio, and a successful business, but had matured in probably exactly the way she had wished for me years ago.

Staring into that fun house mirror, I told myself that the more logical and practical reason why I was doing this was to repay her. She had saved my life. She had rescued and put me back together. This was my chance to save her, if only for a quiet death. That idea—one I hadn't yet fully mulled—pleased me in a way I rarely allowed.

The truth was, of course, that as a tailor I was a maker of men. They came to me, frayed, unsure, and crooked, and it was my work that not just mended, protected, and reshaped their body, but also restructured who they were from the outside in. I could give them confidence, even if they didn't think they had any. I could give them authority, even when they deserved none. My suits could speak for them, if only they kept their mouths closed. And as such I saw myself as a mentor, teacher, friend, and sometimes a father to my clients. I enjoyed the restorative and formational power of the fabric arts, working without the bloody hacks of a surgeon, the elastic vagaries of a philosopher, or the sweaty labors of a coach.

I grabbed a silken towel to dry my hands and dabbed my face. This job was exactly the thing I had been preparing for my whole professional life. What greater goal could there be for clothes than to ease one into the next phase? From what I knew of her life, Vada had rebirthed herself with her costumes— how fitting that another costume would end it.

Throwing the towel into the receptacle, I stared at my face again. The momentary triumph I had just felt in ordering, defining, and congratulating myself on my journey, my payback, my grand quest, faded. There was something else going on. I didn't know what it was, but I was starting to feel its weight, its temperature, and hand.

Returning to the hall, I started toward Ryder's door. When I got within ten feet, the green-haired ad-woman came to life.

"Destiny of design," she said, batting her green-encrusted eyelids, "is the buried treasure of your dreams and Ryder Textile Jobber is the submarine, powered with the relentless velocity of love that is ready to take you to new depths of creativity and material

freedom. Won't you come with me, take a dive into the wetness that is pure and clean?"

Turning the knob, I stepped inside.

SLUBS: CORNFIELD

"**D**ad," I whispered, "Dad… I'm sorry to wake you."

In the moonlight, I could just see his eyelids and the wrinkles around his eyes twitch a few times.

"It's me, Tane," I said, afraid he might not even remember me. "I have go to the corn mill. The bus will be here soon."

Finally he opened his eyes. He didn't turn to me, but stared straight up into the black sky.

"That music you hear… that's the early fry." Two hundred yards away on the paved road I could see the lights of a food truck. Several times a day, they circled the fields, delivering fried BurritoPops, EcoDogs, and KobNockers announced by the tinny chimes of the M-Bunny jingle.

"You'll be okay," I told him. We had slept in the field. I had covered him with my blanket. "Just stay here. I told my friend Rik to look after you. You can trust him. He's very loyal. Just don't go in the house. The rep doesn't want you there… yet." Although his eyes were open, I worried that he wasn't really awake, and that he wouldn't remember.

Jamming a hand in my shorts pocket, I continued. "I'm leaving you with two M-pennies so you can get something later if you want. You should drink some Golden. It's good for you."

"Right." His flat voice lay somewhere between acceptance and sarcasm. Then I heard him swallow, and his eyes finally met mine. In that instant, I saw the man I once knew. The strong, capable man I had always looked up to.

"Dad, I missed you." I barely got the words out before my throat constricted. Before I started to cry or he replied, I quickly said, "Anyway, here are some coins." I held out the thin silvery things, hoping he would take them. Instead, his eyelids began to droop. "Dad?"

He was falling back asleep. Instead of waking him, I inched forward, gingerly felt for the pocket at the side of his shorts, and tried to slide the coins in. I got them just inside the flap of the stiff non-woven, but worried that they would easily slide out into the dust. Trying not to make a sound, I attempted to push the coins farther in. And that's when I saw—or I thought I saw—a tiny white light, no larger than a grain of sand inside his pocket.

Sitting back, I told myself I had to go. I hadn't seen anything. It was just some blip in my vision, like the way my eyes seemed to make patterns and meshes in the dark. But then I saw it again.

The only lights in the slubs were corn oil lamps or the pale blue florescent bulbs powered by the truck and bus engines. I couldn't imagine what he might have. Worse, he wasn't supposed to have anything like that. If one found a rusted cluster of gears, a hard green wafer traced with lines of gold, or coils of colored wires, it was all to be immediately turned over to M-Bunny for proper recycling. Besides, it was said a lot of that stuff could kill you.

In the darkness of his pocket, the light flashed again. Dad had something that wasn't M-Bunny. He had something illegal, *unloyal,* and dangerous. I panicked and rose, making my way toward the fry truck.

I stopped after twenty feet. I couldn't leave that thing with the lights—whatever it was—with my barely conscious father. If the rep discovered it, Dad was doomed. I returned to his side. Gingerly poking into his pocket, I grasped the thing between two fingertips and pulled.

It was a thread seven inches long. It blinked and sparkled like it was encrusted with a dozen microscopic stars. And even when I shielded it from the moonlight, the specks didn't disappear. They actually grew brighter and blinked on and off.

In the distance, there was a brief pause as the fry melody reached the end of its loop and began again, and in that blip of silence, where the space around me expanded to include the vast hush of corn and wind, I floated far from the world I knew. The sparkling thread in my hand was like nothing I had ever seen or dreamed of.

Maybe I should have tucked it back into Dad's pocket, or dug a hole and buried it, or grasped his shoulders, shaken him, and demanded to know what it was and where it had come from. Instead I tucked it into my own pocket and started toward the fry truck.

I didn't get a chance to really examine the yarn until I was at the back of the M-Bunny bus heading to the corn mill. I only had a bit of scratched glass as a magnifier and wasn't sure what I was looking at, but that yarn told me things. It told me that there was a place of reason and artistry. It told me that there was a place where I might fit in.

"Bunny?" I asked Kira, confused that she thought it was from the slubs. "You mean M-Bunny."

She pointed at the screen. "This signature is Bunné."

I stepped closer. It would be a while before I had the vocabulary, but I later learned my hidden thread was what's called a "novelty" or "compound" yarn—one made of several components—five in this case. Two were thicker matrix-fibril, one was angora wool with a loose z-twist that looped and spun around the two main mono-fibers like an extended spring— thick and fuzzy here, narrow and smooth there. A micro-mono wrapped around the wool connected it to the others. And threaded loosely among all of these was another very high-twist yarn that resembled a miniature string of lights—in this case light-emitting polymers.

I asked, "What's Bunné?"

"The beating heart of my enemy… and the tap root of my inspiration." Kira faced me. "I was part of Bunné at one time. I dreamed with her and was a proud saleswarrior at her fantasy knitting subsidiary, Casper Union." Her expression darkened. "But I saw what they were doing to the brand. They were replacing craft with rage, silver with tin, and heart with spleen." For several moments she seemed lost in thought. "If you were a Bunné spy, that would explain your handsome knitting, but not your presence before me. And hearing your past… about this yarn from your father… I am moved. Both moved and baffled by what you are."

I was glad that she wasn't threatening me anymore, but she hadn't answered my question so I asked it again.

"Bunné!" she cried. "Miss Bunné is the ruling celeb of this sex and shopping country of Seattlehama. Around her rumors of terror swirl, but she is the tower and she is the light. Truly she is grand, and I haven't stopped loving her even as my heart is filled with the tar of hate." Kira paused as if to gather her warTalk. "I worshiped her and her dreams. But I could not stay with Casper Union. I can't fathom how she has been duped by those who pervert her vision and her love. To my death I will battle back to her feet and clear a wide and bloody swatch of truth!"

She spun back to the magnified yarn. "So, I believe you, Tane Cedar. I believe and hold dear as I have not before that you truly are a former man of the prison crop… but how did your father acquire it?"

"I don't know."

"You did not inquire?"

I shook my head. "He died the next day."

She bowed her head slowly as if offering her condolences. "Remon, you are a cloudy mystery. Someday we will knit that haze into meaning, but for today, your past binds and unites us… it powers our fight together!" She took it from the magnitron and held it in her palm as one might a jewel. "It is quite a yarn."

Tucking it into my pocket, I found myself deeply relieved to have it back. No less a relief was to have gained Kira's trust, even if it took a bloody nose and a scratched neck.

"I sense a deep furrow of talent in you." She stepped beside the Stanton-Bell Tex-knitter. "Demonstrate the rhythm of your knitting for me. Audition for possibilities."

Without a hesitation, I stepped up and grasped the handles.

SEATTLEHAMA: INFINITE LAYERS

Kira had me knit twenty skivvé in a row. She reloaded the cartridges three times, urging me on. "Knot and start again! Yes… Brilliant!… It's sheer intensity. Spectacular! Excellent!"

I worked faster and faster. Skivvé piled up around us. Another cartridge went dry, I stopped moving the handles and we locked eyes. Hers glowed with intensity. I thought she was going to get more yarn, but she grabbed her thick coat, but did not button it. Stepping from the Stanton, I undid the front of my slacks, and we fashioned each other on the pile of my knit skivvé.

"I have found my Remon," she whispered as we lay there cooling off. "Truly a Remon of worth and terror."

"The man in the worm jacket told me that Remon was from the slubs."

It seemed to take a moment for her to figure out whom I was talking about. "That's a Mulberry Jacket! He is dressed as brave Commander Sheppard. But as for Warrior Remon, he is not *from*. He fights wars. He slays ferocious beasts, and he is championed by the city. But then… in a mysterious moment… he is injured. Some songs describe a battle in which a gang of corn prisoners slashed him. Another ballad describes a threat from Bunné who curses his manhood. What ever is the cause, Remon is cut across his groin. While his exact injury is never known, he never again wears a fashion panty. And yet, ravaged by war and the heat of love, he and Bunné find that their love for one another blooms like a glamorous cancer."

She was so adamant I couldn't laugh. "Is this real or not?"

She gazed into my eyes. "What is truth is that Warrior Remon was a man of fashion and talent and so are you." She shook her head and smiled. "If you walked into the knitting conservatory where I schooled and danced with a Stanton-Bell as you have today you would be crowned dark emperor of the loops!" Her face was aglow and excitement flowed from her. "You have all the belongings of knowledge, the twisted fibers, and the precision knotting, but you need lessons of design."

"In the corn all we had were B-shirts and shorts and they weren't even real cloth. I want to learn everything."

"First," said Kira as she flexed her hand before me. "The study is skin. We learn its stretch and wear. We learn its ease and comfort. That is the heart of fashion. All the layers we stack on top must not sacrifice its pleasure and beauty. Our customer is skin. And as the foundation, skivvé are the rhythm of dress."

For a minute we sat there staring at our hands as we flexed our fingers and watched the skin wrinkle and stretch. My eyes wandered to her skivvé, the tube of which rested on her thigh. "Why you wear *men's* skivvé? You don't have a root."

She laughed at me. "They are men's *fantasy* skivvé. Several years ago, in Bunné's *Sweet Way Surgery Duo*, she wore the first pair. From then on it is fashion. The market has doubled every year. The fantasy skivvé has become the badge of honor of the true knit saleswarrior." She pushed herself up, took down a yarn cartridge, and inserted it into the slot on the back of the Stanton. "We will first knit the woman's *reality* skivvé," she announced. I wasn't sure what she wanted, but began knitting and when the knit heads came to the crotch, and I was about to add something, she held my right hand still. We produced a simple, smooth skivvé.

"The female sculpture," she announced as she pulled it from mannequin hips. "The stage is empty, the actor, hidden. There can be no drama. It delights some, but not the saleswarrior of purls. For us, we find dignity, power, and ferocity in *the ghost*." She pulled her dress above her belly. "The man is positive... an appendage of expression... a wand of will... a needle of knitting!"

I still didn't really understand, but felt I could pretend I did. Kira stared at me intently. I didn't know what to expect.

"I promote you, Warrior Remon."

I remembered how Withor had hated me, dismissed my yarn snatching, and used me. "I'm so glad I found you." I hoped her promotion meant I could continue to knit.

She paced back and forth. After a minute, she stopped and spoke softly. "You shall know the inner mechanisms of the corporation and the dire clock mechanism in which we run." Her expression was almost sad as she gazed at me. "Today... the creditwarrior I lunched with had charts covered in the blood of loss. The balance is that Python Duck is in its last minutes. We must profit. We must chart now!"

"I had no idea." Even as I spoke, I recalled my first impression of the empty Python shop compared to the crowded and shiny Casper Union. "What can I do?"

"Exactly! You... Warrior Remon... you will be our sensation! You will be our scandal. No man knits fantasy skivvé and no former prisoner ever did!"

She didn't mean *I* was going to knit Python Duck's skivvé, did she?

"Yes," she replied as if reading my mind. "And it is a smoky and desperate map. But without sensation... without spectacle and risk, the creditwarriors will take our Stanton, our yarn, our needles, and our hope." She took my hands and cradled them in hers. "These are the artistry and honor I have searched for. These hands are the labor and the might. You Remon of Loin..." Her eyes focused on mine. "You are the craft that I do not possess. From now on you are Python Duck's Chief Executive Knitter!"

"Kira," I asked, "are you sure?"

"Time is desperation and we have arrived at the endgame. Tell me now: Can you grace the loops?"

"Yes!" I squeezed her hands in mine. "I will knit for you."

"I will honor and assist you, Remon. We have a day to design your line, and relaunch our glory! We must now loveeffort!"

The next day the flagship was darkened. Workers redid the floor with plush black fabric. The walls were covered with green poles and the ceiling was dotted with thousands of blue lights. Pyramids of dirt were piled six feet tall.

"What is this?" I asked.

"The fantasy skivvé of pure male savagery."

I thought of my life amid the corn and how so much of it was spent working corn plants, pushing the kernels into the dry land, watering them, tending them, and harvesting the ears. It was hardly pure male savagery.

"The real slubs weren't like this. They were much more dull. There were brutal moments, but that was all about recycling. Mostly we farmed and worked in mills." Although she listened, she didn't hear. And maybe it didn't matter. I was happy just to spend that night and most of the next day on the Stanton-Bell. I didn't love making these fantasy skivvé, but I couldn't get enough knitting. I made variation after variation and Kira would come in every hour or so, look them over, and make comments.

"They're robust and vigorous," she said. "They're male and distinct! Try one with a slightly more narrow tube. I'll return in forty minutes."

Near shopping dawn, as designers, constructors, and caterers finished, Kira selected three of my skivvé and dressed them on new full-sized, articulated wooden mannequins. Two were naked except for the skivvé; the third also wore a Rebel Sheep jacket and a violet shirt with layers of ruffles. She introduced me to the two newly hired saleswarriors, who like Kira were dressed in their short orange sailor suits with my blue skivvé below. I also shook hands with a clock drummer who was going to play along with Ginn. For a half-hour Kira gave a rousing, if mostly indecipherable, warTalk. Then the windows were opened, and doors were thrown wide.

To my surprise, hundreds of costumed t'ups were lined up in the hallway, and in an instant the place was full. While some headed straight to the craft and catering tables, most surrounded my skivvé. In my design, the tube was just a couple of inches shorter and open at the end. Below was a single large pouch. As the t'ups stared, pointed, and some even reached forward and squeezed the tubes, I felt exposed and vulnerable. Each frown, each furrowed brow, each small guffaw were jabs to my solar plexus.

"They're the most amazing skivvé in the history of fantasy garments." To my right stood Worm Jacket. On my left was Giraffe. "Truly an achievement far beyond the mere knitting and design. You are a credit to all the prisoners. I think Kira has found both an executive designer and a *cause célèbre.*"

Giraffe spoke, but I couldn't quite make out his words through his mask.

Worm Jacket leaned in. "He wants to see you buttonhole Kira again. He's *dé bazed.*" He laughed and while the lower half of his face was a smile, his eyes conveyed hurt.

Kira greeted both men, took me by the arm and paraded me around for more questions and what seemed like ten thousand photos.

"Are you really a slubber, Remon?"

"How did you learn to knit?"

"Did you really eat nothing but corn?"

"How many flats did you kill?"

"Do they kill the prisoners to feed the crop?"

"What's your inspiration?"

I tried to answer the questions as best I could. Kira usually took over with her warTalk. "He represents the crown of hardship... the transformation of potential into love... the hate of the criminal blossomed into the elemental cruelty of the finest men's fantasy skivvé ever knit!"

For me the party soon became a whirlpool of sounds, faces, and a knot of feelings. One moment I would feel proud and powerful, but a moment later I would overhear some t'up say, "He's a filthy corn needle! She's just using him to save her beleaguered company. Meanwhile she's ruining men's fantasy skivvé!"

And just when I didn't think any more customers could fit into the space, and Ginn and her drummer had cranked up the volume of their hammering melodies, and people were sloshing back milky glasses of something they called corn wine, eating roasted cougar vagina, laughing and gossiping and a few were even fashioning each other, four more entered our flagship—four Casper Union saleswarriors. I recognized Josephone from before.

Once our customers saw who they were, they began to push back. The music came to a ragged end. The crowd hushed.

"This," cried Josephone, pointing her knitting needles at the skivvé on the dressed mannequin, "is infamy. No man shall knit our crotches and certainly not a prisoner! It will not stand. You have finished your fantasy, Kira Shibui. We are simply here to cut the plaited cord and purl you and your knitter." With that she snapped her needles together.

Kira stepped into the clearing before me. Her two new saleswarriors flanked her on each side. She seemed calm and cool. And when she spoke her voice was like curling vapor from pure ice. "The uninvited learn from the heart and the skill of our needles, and now that you have seen majesty, you will retreat and live in the lint below your automated knitting contraptions."

Josephone's nostrils flared. Her mouth shrunk to a dot. Swinging her needles she whacked the mannequin in the face. The thing teetered back and forth several times and then clunked over backward and smashed on the floor. Josephone laughed like she had never seen anything so hilarious. When she turned to her minions, they imitated her exactly.

I was near the back of the flagship, squashed in the crowd of frightened fans, customers, and shoppers. Behind me I heard someone mutter, "Kira's dead and so is that prisoner knitter of hers."

ARK TEXTILE TRADING

In the foyer of the office of Ark Textile Jobber was a twenty-foot-wide model of a sunken ship complete with twisting vines of seaweed, a giant squid with glowing red eyes, several cavorting mermaids, their tails covered with radiant teal scales, and a giant crab with pinching claws. Above this papier-mâché menagerie hung a large lit sign: The offices and consult of Dr. Galvon T. Horse, Textile Prospector and Deep-Sea Fabricator.

I paused for a moment, considered the garish colors, the grating typography and texture of the signage, and felt confident that this man and his company—one I had never dealt with before and would make sure not to deal with again—was the right choice for the illicit yarn I now needed.

A mermaid came toward me. Her skin had been dyed blue and the cobalt glitter on her eyelids was so thick and apparently heavy she had to lean her head back to peer at me. "Babe," she began with a perfunctory smile as fresh as the Paleozoic, "do you have an appointment to see the beloved Doctor of Fibers?"

I tried not to roll my eyes. "I'm Tane Cedar."

"Oh." Frowning, she looked me up and down, she said, "You look thinner than I thought, babe."

"It's the suit."

Her frown, which was maybe the natural inclination of her mouth, tightened for a beat. "He's with some others, but just go on in, babe."

I was tempted to suffix my reply but just said, "Thank you."

Through a door made of old planks, the main room was a large warehouse that smelled of starch, sizing, dust, and a mingling of unconfident colognes and perfumes. Tables were stacked with jagged mountain ranges of fabric in all manner of plaid, check, tweed, print, flock, and solid. Among the tables, here and there, stood dozens of customers pawing the stuff, pulling lengths of ribbon and lace from spools, comparing color samples to the bolts, and bargaining with the seafaring staff. And despite the plentiful sound absorbing material, the volume of talk was like a raucous party.

"Welcome," said a man dressed in a silky white sailor's outfit. "Mr. Tane Cedar, right?"

"Indeed," I said, forming a smile. "I need to speak with Ryder." The man's chalky green eyes slowly passed over my suit jacket and slacks, as if he were adding the thread count, dividing by the tailoring, and finding the square root of the lining. "Now," I added, gently waking him. "It's urgent."

"I can help you, sir." He blinked several times as he held his sand-white smile. "I love your suit!"

"Thank you, but I need to speak to Ryder."

The man's mouth soured in a way that made me think that he had already spent his imagined commission. He fluttered a hand toward the back of the space. "For the boss you'll have to wait."

I started past the sailor salesman.

"I could help you. He's really busy. It's not about the commission!"

In the back surrounded by a crowd of fifty or so, I found Ryder sitting behind a large transparent aquarium desk filled with some glowing blue-green protoplasm. He wore a triple-breasted silver and navy coat. The long pointed collar of his spider-silk macramé shirt hung halfway to his waist.

I had only seen Ryder once before at a fabric convention two years ago and he struck me as someone auditioning to play himself. The one thing I remembered was that each time he spoke, he would first touch the end of his tiny and preternaturally pale tongue to his thin top lip. *The shapes and colors reminded me of the action of some small, nocturnal, insect-eating mammal—a lemur maybe.*

The others were all arguing with him.

"That's not the contract!" he said to one of them. "The yarn count was to be between one fifty and one seventy-five.... No, I can't refund your money.... It is pure chemocott, and I guarantee it. Check the chemical composition!"

"Ryder," I said, nudging my way forward, "I need to speak with you."

As his eyes focused on mine for an instant, they grew large with surprise. "Gloria said a Mr. Cedar was here, but I didn't believe it was you." He raised his voice and said, "Everyone, I want to introduce you to my newest customer and my very dear friend: the revered Mr. Cedar."

Several of the others said hello and I heard someone ask how much hand stitching I did. Ignoring them, I asked, "Can we talk? Privately."

"What about my order?" asked a man in a floor-length ivory jacket.

"About that," replied Ryder, "I can't tell you how very, truly, and wonderfully sorry I am." The wet and white tip of his tongue darted out for an instant. "However, the details of our contract stipulated that all of the said goods would be grey. How this even became a misunderstanding, I cannot comprehend." Ryder glanced at me as if to commiserate.

To my right, a man in black puckered his cracked lips. "I've got to have more of that red double-poplin, Ryder!" Ryder paid no attention to him, but began arguing with someone else.

"Very sorry," said Ryder to me. "You see how wanted and needed I am."

"You told me it would be a high-gloss finish," complained someone else.

"I said it could. Could. With a C! Read the contract. I know it's there, because I wrote it. It's an experimental finish. I understand it didn't work. But you knew that when you bought it." Ryder's *tongue dotted his sentence.*

"I haven't gotten the backing I ordered!" said someone farther back. Turning, I saw a familiar face, another men's tailor from Ros Begas. He had made a splash several years ago with an absurd five-vented jacket and since then had kept slicing his suits into smaller and smaller pieces. Our eyes met, and while I could see that he was surprised to see me here, he bent his head in greeting. I returned the nod. "I need the stuff, Ryder," he continued. "It was supposed to be at the factory yesterday."

"An honor to see you so early," scoffed Ryder. "You told me your delivery service would come and take it!"

"No, I didn't!"

"It's still at the mill waiting for your people." He turned to the mermaid holding his monocle. "That's what you recall, right, my watery paramour?"

She did not turn toward him, but stared forward, her lips seemingly sounding out dialogue to some imagined scene or lyrics to a song.

The tailor said, "I'm going to tear out your ribs and use them as collar stays, Ryder."

"If I could do without my ribs, or any other body part," quipped Ryder, "I would have happily sold them long ago." He glanced at me and sucked in his cheeks. When I frowned, he fluttered an angry hand at his mermaid. "My naughty, algae-covered Mildred! Please scream something unpleasant to the mill yield supervisor, and tell them to rush the backing to his studio." When she did not respond, he leaned closer to her green hair. "Immediately, my naval navel!"

"What about me?" asked someone else.

"All in good time, good sir! I will finish with everyone in order."

"Ryder..." I leaned far over his plasticott-covered aquarium desk, "I am pressed for time."

"Mr. Cedar," he whispered, "but you didn't call ahead. I'm an important jobber as you see!" His tongue flicked his rigid smile.

"On the banquet table over there you will find some sea urchin tarts from late yesterday. Please have one and drink a coffee. I would very much like to discuss your needs, and I will be with you as soon as I can." He then smiled at the crowd and said, "Would someone help Mr. Cedar with a calm coffee?"

Sitting backwards on his aquarium desk, I lifted my legs and spun to face him. Leaning in to bring my nose close to his, I said, "I'm quite pressed."

Ryder sat back in his chair. His face paled and his eyes grew watery. "Scissors!" he chirped. "Are you mad? Get off my desk and get away from me!"

The voices around his desk had hushed.

"Listen to me," I whispered, "I need pure Xi yarn."

"What?" he asked as if I hadn't spoken a language he recognized.

Near his ear, I shout-whispered, "Xi yarn!"

He leaned far back. His tongue dotted his lip nervously, his eyes darted toward the others as though to elicit their help. "B–But that's illegal," he stammered with a pasty smile. "That's been prohibited for years. You should know better. No one has that. No one! It's quite immoral. It's nasty stuff." Out of the corner of his mouth, as if I might not hear, he muttered, "Mildred, call security."

"I just got the mill manager!" she complained.

I spoke to his clients. "Please excuse us. It will just be a moment. Thank you." The other Ros Begas tailor stepped back. A woman rolled her eyes angrily. "I apologize for being rude," I said to Ryder, "but I need it now."

"It's not made!" he snorted. "It's amoral. It's terrible! Now please, get off my desk and leave. I'll report you to the authorities and have you dragged out."

"Can you get it?"

His tongue held against his lip. He seemed about to answer, but then glanced away. "Mildred," he said, "security! Call them now! Right now!"

I eyed her and shook my head once. She frowned, not so much

as if unhappy with me, but everything, and folded her blue hands in her blue scale-covered lap.

I returned my attention to Ryder. "Can you get it?"

He dabbed his forehead with the lace of one of his cuffs and laughed tightly. "Maybe five days... maybe... possibly. Just go away now!"

I shook my head. "I need it now."

"That's impossible! I will have to check with my sources. That will take some time, but I'll let you know. I'll call you. I will. I'll call you as soon as I hear something."

I grasped the long right collar of his shirt. Bending the fabric around, I touched the sharp point to his soft neck. I did it gently, but knew he could feel it. "Then I need your sources."

His Adam's apple rose and fell, and I thought of the time Kira had scratched my throat with her needles. Was I turning into a tailorwarrior?

Dots of sweat shone across his forehead like sequins. "I admire your work, sir. It's tremendous. You're talented. Very talented! But I'm sorry... I don't have what you need. Just don't hurt me!"

"Your source," I repeated, getting tired. "You said you had a source."

"That's the thing. I don't know if he has any. I would have to check." One clear bead of sweat rolled down his right temple, stopped a moment as it neared his chin and then was lost in the folds and deltas of his neck.

The room was so silent it felt as if all the electrons had stopped their frenzied orbits. "Tell me your source!"

"This is not how I am accustomed to doing business, sir."

"Nor I," I agreed. The soft flesh around the collar point was white.

His eyes met mine and were steadier than they had been since I came in. "I can't even be sure he's got any."

"Who?"

"Fine," he muttered, as another drop of sweat ran down his forehead and was absorbed in his left eyebrow. "It's CeeCee Textiles.

The man's name is Zoom Langsin."

I released his collar, which impotently flopped back down across his shirt. Spinning around, I was off his aquarium desk, heading through the bolts of fabric, and past his employees and waiting customers. I saw several eyes follow me as I passed, but no one spoke. As I crossed the threshold, however, I heard Ryder shouting. "God damn slubber! They should slaughter all those disgusting prisoners once and for all! Did you see how he attacked me!"

SEATTLEHAMA: BLOOD AMONG FIBERS

Josephone stepped before another mannequin and pulled back her knitting needles as if to bash it. Kira leapt forward with needles outstretched, and tore the sleeve of Josephone's dress, drawing blood. With a war cry, Josephone swung back. Kira ducked, but one of Josephone's minions jabbed her shoulder. Kira hit the floor, but jumped up instantly. Josephone tried to spear her. They locked needles.

Meanwhile, the terrified customers began shoving their way out. Several were knocked to the floor and trampled.

A Casper Union warrior, eyes watery and teeth clenched, rushed at me with needles aimed at my throat. Just a few feet before she reached me, one of the new Python saleswarriors leapt forward and plunged her needles into the base of the woman's throat. A spray of black blood shot from the wound and she crashed to the floor like a cut corn stalk.

I felt sick.

Kira and Josephone shoved each other back and forth. Kira swiped her needles and cut Josephone's left hip and leg. Josephone spun around and slashed Kira across the side of her head. A clump of bloody scalp and hair fell to the floor before my feet.

"Stop!" I yelled. "Stop fighting!" No one listened. Kira circled Josephone warily, waving her needles and warTalking. From the top of my right sleeve, I ripped out a yarn two feet long. Stepping forward, I whipped it at Josephone and caught her in the eye.

Screaming, she instinctively reached for her face… and jabbed one of her needles into her right pupil. She fell to her knees, her face glossed with her own blood. Before she collapsed, the remaining Casper Union saleswarriors grabbed her. Kira went in for the kill, but the two fought her back, pulled Josephone out the door, and ran.

Two bodies now lay on the floor: the Casper Union woman who had attacked me; one of the new Python saleswarriors, face down in a large pool of blood that soaked the plush fabric.

After the Casper Union saleswarriors retreated, the last few trapped customers ran. Kira threw the injured Python saleswarrior over her shoulder, and with Worm Jacket and Giraffe following, carried her down the hallway past the cuisine court to the nurse station. Promising to return, she exhorted Ginn and me: "Guard the flagship with your life!"

Ginn dashed into the design studio and reemerged with shears for both of us. We stood on the bloody floor, surrounded in broken cups, abandoned hors d'oeuvres, torn fabric. The air smelled of salt, rust, and solid recycle. At one point, I began to gag, and stepped away from the fallen enemy saleswarrior. Outside the window, shoppers stood with their hands cupped around their eyes, staring at the destruction. I stood strong, even as my stomach threatened to heave and my knees shook.

"Have you forgotten purity of line and the hand of love?" complained Kira as she tossed my newest skivvé into the trash.

I stepped off the Stanton-Bell, where I had been working for hours. I was exhausted and hadn't slept well for days. The nervousness I had felt about being without my papers and witness to drap-de-Berry's death was replaced with the dread of the Casper Union saleswarriors showing up again.

The store had been cleaned up and reopened, but I hated to

go out of the design room. "They're going to come back and attack us!" I told Kira. "We shouldn't be open."

"The frayed yarn of your heart! You disgust the Python Duck."

"Aren't you afraid?"

"Of art? Glory? Celebrity?" She scoffed. "Your prisoner courage is a tangle." She pointed at the Stanton. "I command you to peel the sticky fear from your skin. Now stand on the controls and knit as you did!"

"I don't want to be killed."

Her eyes grew wide. "You doubt me! You question the point on my needles and the edge of my shears!"

"No," I told her. "But those Casper Union saleswarriors will be coming back. And there are lots of them."

She curled her lip. "How can you shrink like this? Why is your being so cotton?"

"Kira," I said, exhausted, "do you want to die for skivvé?"

"That would be the jewel of honor!" She laughed. "What would you die of, Warrior Remon? Would you prefer to perish from the sniffles? Perhaps you wish to be killed by tripping down an escalator!"

Reluctantly, I stepped back onto the Stanton and started another skivvé. When I was done, Kira took it from the hooks with her needles.

"Neither the exact promise of dawn nor the witchcraft of dusk," she muttered. She started toward the salesfloor with it, stopped, and twirled a finger at me. "More."

Although the next weeks passed without incident, I still jumped at loud sounds and barely slept. My legs and back ached from working the knitting machine, and I had lost weight despite a diet of snacks from the cuisine court.

"I must butter and scone with creditwarriors!" chimed Kira early one morning. Despite her misgivings about the quality of my knitting, sales were booming, and she had big plans for Python Duck. "Warrior Remon," she told me, "guard the flagship!" With that she was gone.

I cracked the design room door and saw that she had left the store open. Kira hadn't showed me how to take credit and lock the front door. The musician, Ginn, wouldn't be in for another hour. I was alone.

I thought about running. I could be across the new blue sales floor in seconds and out of this building in a few minutes. But then what? And what if I ran into the Casper Union saleswarriors?

A woman entered the store. I thought about closing the door and hiding in the design studio, but she was not with Casper Union. Instead of their sharp black and yellow, she wore a green dress with white boots and a little hat. I didn't see any indication of a skivvé.

Stepping out, I drew a shaky breath. "We're not open yet."

She peered at me as if unsure of something. "Tane Cedar?"

"I'm Warrior Remon," I told her, afraid she was some sort of an official who had come to take me away. "Chief Executive Knitter for Python Duck Weapon Men's Fantasy Skivvé."

She glanced around the store as if at the products. On her right hip hung a long pair of silvery shears. Her hair was orange; her skin, spotted, and grayish around her eyes. If I used just one word to describe her it would have been *tired*.

"If you want a fantasy skivvé," I told her, "you'll have to come back later."

Her expression was pained. "Sixty percent of the participants in the foundation war died last year. Mostly were in little houses like this." She frowned. "The foundation war is the bloodiest of all. They're littering the hallways with fallen bodies, you know."

I worried that she was talking about drap-de-Berry. I swallowed, but stood firm. "I just work here."

With a sad laugh, she said, "You can see yarn or something, right?"

This warrior wasn't from one of the stores along our hallway,

I didn't think she was one of Kira's fans, nor did she seem like an official, but something about her seemed familiar. "You'd better talk to the CEO, Kira Shibui."

She stepped around one of the tall plinths, peered up at the skivvé, and then looked me up and down.

I asked her, "Are you a knitter?"

"No."

"Fashion?"

"Cut and sew," she replied. "Mostly cut."

"What's *cut and sew*?"

She smiled for an instant and continued to admire the skivvé. When she turned, I saw that her dress didn't cover her bottom. "What matters to you is that those of us in weaving are just not as murderous as these *loopers*." She stepped behind the far plinth.

"What do you make?" She did not reply. In fact, she had not reappeared from behind the skivvé display. Stepping around, I said, "Hello?" She was gone. The store was empty. I dashed toward the design room, afraid she had somehow gotten by me and was stealing supplies. She wasn't.

A moment later, Kira came in the front with two creditwarriors in short, navy pinstriped dresses.

"Warrior Remon!" she announced as she stepped beside me. "The breathing pride... the escaped menace... *the* sculptor of *the* skivvé."

From the glow in Kira's face I could tell things were going to change. And what was her great idea? As I soon learned, she wanted to expand the flagship and move it closer to Casper Union!

"Our needles will *pierce* not simply poke!" she declared when explained her plans to Ginn, the other saleswarriors, and me. "We float helpless in the foundation war, but today we craft our continent of final victory."

The saleswarriors clapped and pumped their fists. Ginn gave a battle cry. I could only muster a tense smile as I pictured our blood spilled across some immense gleaming salesfloor.

Over the next days, as I knit long into the night to try to stockpile skivvé for the new space, Kira and the other saleswarriors were constantly heading out to check on new locations and attend countless meetings. Usually one saleswarrior stayed to guard the place, but twice I ended up watching the flagship alone. The second time, as two other consumers browsed the store, the woman in green returned.

"Where did you go last time?" I asked her quietly.

She just shrugged. "Do you want to work in wovens?"

I didn't reply.

One of the consumers brought over a pair of blue skivvé with an extra long tube. "I'm such a fan," she enthused. "You're so brave and beautiful. I feel so bad for the prisoners, but so many of them deserve it, you know."

"Sure," I agreed. By then Kira had taught me credit. I quickly wrapped and bagged it, handed it over, and thanked her.

Once the consumer was gone, Green spoke softly. "You're better than these fantasy skivvé." She twisted her mouth to the side. "And there's plans for Python Duck to move across from Casper Union. It's the big rumor around here."

I tensed at the thought of Kira's suicidal plans. "What would I do for you?"

Her melancholy brown eyes held on mine. "Do you trust me?"

"I don't know."

My answer seemed to please her. "We'd better go before the loopers return." She stared toward the door.

I didn't move. "What would I do? And where are we going."

She stopped. "A different building… a different level… a different world!" Behind the sorrow in her eyes shone a tiny hope. "We'd better go. I'll explain everything later."

Kira stepped in.

SEATTLEHAMA: FULL-SPEED TAILORING

With a disgusted expression, Kira looked Green up and down. "Shopper, are you interested in fantasy skivvé?" To me she said, "Remon, retreat to the design room."

I stood firm. "Kira, moving closer to Casper Union doesn't seem like a good idea."

Her eyes widened first in surprise and then in outrage. "Return to the safety of the design room, Chief Executive Knitter Remon!"

The green saleswarrior spoke calmly. "He doesn't want this anymore. He doesn't want to die for your loops."

Kira grimaced at the warrior's clothes. "A woven dress of pure shame!" She stepped closer. "Are you lost? Are you without credit and starch? What say you, *consumer?*"

Green bristled, but did not reply.

In a flash Kira pulled out her needles and screamed. "Go or I will release the blind snakes of your gut!"

I cursed myself; I had just started another fight. "I learned so much from you, Kira, I'm grateful for your belief in me, I really am, but when I started I didn't know you actually *killed* each other. And your new flagship seemed like self-destruction. There are a dozens of them!"

When Kira glanced at me angrily as if to curse me, the green saleswarrior drew her silver shears. "Get back or I'll cut your cut," she said.

Kira laughed at her. "Is that your warTalk? Is it from a beginner's textbook or the back of a cuisine court coupon?"

Green jerked her shears at Kira's face, but she didn't flinch. Instead, she snapped her needles at the woman's mouth and said, "Let me knit your tongue into a true beast of language."

"Kira, please… I'm just saying that this move is too dangerous. We're going to be killed."

Without taking her eyes from the other saleswarrior, she replied, "Words of disgust! Would you rather die of time and boredom?"

Green said, "Let him go."

"Get your own talented Remon." Curling a lip, Kira moved closer. "Who are you, salescut?"

The green saleswarrior bristled. "A jobber."

"A jobber!" Kira snickered. "A jobber of what? Cloth? Felt? *Backing?*" She shook her head. "Maybe you're a jobber of torn buttonholes."

Green's mouth tightened. "He doesn't want to knit your boy panties for you anymore."

I said, "Casper Union is going to come back. They're going to kill us."

Kira turned and glared at me. "Without the threat of death there is no life! Those fallen heroes of skivvé have given everything for us." She shook her head slowly. "In our post-capitalism and dragons… in our glorious fashion… in our loveeffort… I will knit and I will kill until the very last fiber of my blood."

While she glared at me, the green saleswarrior smashed her scissors against Kira's needles. Kira was knocked off balance, and Green bashed her shoulder into Kira's chest. The maneuver seemed crude compared to the deadly ballet of the knitters.

And yet Kira was knocked flat onto the hallway floor. Her needles clattered against the store window. She looked small and defenseless. The squashed tube of her blue skivvé rested across her thigh. "Wrinkled fighter!" she cried at Green. "Iron your ways! No warTalk! No grace!"

"You sick, knitting cut!" The green saleswarrior pulled back her shears.

"Stop!" I shouted.

Green froze. Her eyes met mine.

I pushed her away from Kira and began running down the hallway as fast as I could. A second later, I heard Green following.

As we flew down one set of showstairs after another, I kept checking behind us but Kira hadn't followed. Finally we came to an entervator port. While I still was catching my breath, we boarded.

Part of me felt guilty that I had left Kira, another part was elated to be away from her, her needles, and her lust for blood.

"Thank you for stopping me." Green eyed me. She wasn't as young as Kira, nor was she as old as Vada. But her eyes were confident. "You still want to leave skivvé knitting?"

I nodded and said, "What do you think will happen to Kira?"

"I don't know."

"Do you think she'll come looking for me?" I hated to add her to my list of enemies like Casper Union, the ghost who killed drap-de-Berry, and Withor.

Green shook her head. "Even if she did, it's a huge city."

I slumped forward and held my head in my hands.

We exited at the lowest level, *the Keep* as it was called, and Green led us past the tourist places to a dim little cuisine court. We sat at a small round table. We ordered from a bored waitressrebel in beetle green super-shorts and were soon snacking on cabbage, octopus pancakes, and mercury waters.

I asked Green, "So, who are you?"

She smiled as if she had been waiting for my question. "Pilla."

"And how do you know me?"

"I've heard a lot." She smiled as if at a private joke.

"From where?"

Pilla opened her mouth and then turned her head to a look at the scraggly man approaching our table. He plunked down in the seat next to me.

"Why meet in this lonely selvage hole?"

Pilla nodded at the man while introducing me. "Kastle owns a famous costume store. I think it'd be a good place to work for a while."

"YeOld#1CostumeShoppee," he said proudly, "is the second largest in Seattlehama. Our salessoldiers are completely dedicated to our grand mission of economically and fashionably dressing the tourists in their epic dreams."

I wished he would just go away so I could talk to Pilla. "Salessoldiers?" I asked her. "I thought you said this was safer."

"It is," she insisted.

"You can work your way *up* to salessoldier," said Kastle, "but you'll start in our alterations army. We all work from shopping dawn to dusk. It's hard but rewarding." He smiled dimly, but I didn't know what to say.

"He's interested," Pilla said. "He can do it."

The man narrowed his eyes as he glanced from me to her and back again. "You start tomorrow." He opened a case and handed me a shiny screen. "That's got all our costumes. Look them over. You'll have to get your own hand-Juki, so I've put a small advance on a MasterCut." He slid a rubbery purple card toward me, stood, and said, "Welcome. *Remon.*" With that, he shrugged at Pilla and headed off.

"I don't want this," I told her. "*Alterations army?*"

"Relax." She laughed and then peered at me. "This is just a place to start. You'll be sewing plushes and wovens. Believe me it's better than that loopy world of knitting."

"Who are you, really?"

Pilla seemed taken aback. "I'm here to help. Come on." She stood. "Let's get your equipment. I think you're going to like this."

"I want a straight answer. How do you know my name?"

She sat back down, wiped her face with a crumpled silk napkin, and sighed. "I know you through Withor."

SEATTLEHAMA: RASH

YeOld#1CostumeShoppee, or *Number Two* as the employees called it, was part of the Golden Triple Quadruple Best Mall on the lowest level. It was *the* most touristy mini-mall in a giant touristy maxi-mall of a city. The space was famous for the Electri-Coco ceiling, which pulsed a constellation of perfumed beauty faces, perpetuity lace, and scenes from the most famous epics. Here the hundreds of salessoldiers wore costumes from komiks, dream, and nightmare. Bang, rage, and throb beats ricocheted in the air. And everywhere were thousands of masks, jackets, puffs, acid-dukes, hump-wigs, podium shoes, and plasticott swords for rent. When the trains from other cities disgorged their customers, they rushed straight at us.

I worked in the alteration rooms, where t'ups of all sizes and ages crowded in with their newly rented and ill-fitting costumes. Stepping up on the platforms before the mirrors, they stripped down to their foundation and waited impatiently as we fitted, tacked, and hemmed up the Choky Bears, Reginald Ball Faeries, and Blackwitch Breaths.

"If you make it through the first week," said Dill, who worked next to me, "get some good support hose and mud-soled shoes. And be glad you're not down in renovation. When these costumes come back, they have to use scrapers to get off all the dried bodily fluids."

The job wasn't easy. Many of the t'ups were anxious and rude. They complained about the materials, the length of the dwindle skirts, the lack of fringe on the jackcoats, the cheapness of the plasticott worms woven into the Commander Sheppard blazers. They wanted us to hurry and to make them look "just so" when that meant tall instead of short, slim instead of lumpy, gorgeous instead of unsightly.

But it was all worth it for the chance to use the Juki Magni-Needle 66-11 Handseamer with the liqui-thread attachment. A flexible cord stretched down my right arm from the power and supply pack on my back to the detailer wand that I held in my hand like a small pistol. It operated as an extension of myself, and it was a thing of beauty.

I simply pointed the laser tip of the wand and smoothly hemmed or stitched. I could do stretch, decorative, seaming, safety, double or pick stitches by selecting the shift. And while the other fixers hurried to adjust the length of sleeves, pants and attached bow, gloves and capes in the same amount of time, I could reach the Juki up pant legs, down jacket backs, and inside the panels of plush bellies like a plastic surgeon, and tuck and smooth the cloth exactly.

In the last throng of customers on my first day, a young man stepped up onto my platform. When he pulled off his hobble pants and his leather reverse shirt, he stood nude. But that wasn't what shocked me. His entire torso was covered in sores just like my father's: pink and yellow and centered with a crusty white.

"Yeah… I know," he said with a proud smirk. "I burn too bright."

As I worked gingerly to fix his sleeve length, stitch on his ties and hem his pants, my hands were shaking. Should I tell him that he was dying? Didn't he know?

When he was done and stood primping the fluff down the front of his shirt, I worked up my courage and pointed to his chest. "What are those?"

He didn't take his eyes from his own reflection, just smiled. "Honorary cancers of glamour and dream."

It sounded like warTalk, and I didn't know what it meant.

I sought Dill out after my shift. "That customer in the hobble pants. Did you see him? He was covered in sores."

"Oh him," Dill laughed. "He's awfully fashionable. He's a serious Xi burner." Dill tucked his long white hair behind an ear and leaned in. "Some of us from the shop are going to a Xi boutique later. You should come and test it out."

"What's Xi?"

"It's a special yarn. It's kind of against the law, but it's big. Supposedly virgins spin it, and when they're done, they die. It's very cosmic and dimensional. It makes you dream in pure fashion. You definitely need to test it!"

Ten of us sat at an archipelago of little tables at the nearby cuisine court. While they ate and complained sociably about customers, costumes, bosses, friends, and lovers, I picked anxiously at my food, worried about what I was going to find.

We headed near the bottom of the city to a dark hallway where the storefronts were covered in thick drapes. The saleswarriors here were all young men with enormous frosted hairdos, paintslacks, and choke coats. I heard one say, "Desire burns the night burns the desire burns a hole in your *night desire*."

We crowded into one of the places seemingly at random, entering a room dressed in tarnished silver and moss green. From behind a lichen-covered plinth, Pilla stepped forward, greeting and air kissing my companions. She stopped when she saw me. She suppressed a smile. "Hello again."

In the shocked silence of the cuisine court the day before, I had asked her how she knew Withor.

"We work together sometimes."

"You're a yarn and cloth jobber like him?"

"I deal with specialty yarns."

I tensed. "I'm never going back to Withor. He was a smuthead."

She laughed, pleased. "I don't want that either. You're with me now." She shook her head. "You should have heard him rant about you."

"He made a fortune from my yarn rips and paid me almost nothing. And he insulted me every other sentence. What was he complaining about?"

"He's a bigoted old bag." She frowned. "He hates that you have some gift, though he'd never admit it. Honestly, he loathes anyone with talent. He pretends that he's the platinum sewing needle."

I studied her face, her overworked hair, the crackle pattern of her lips, the warmth in her chocolate eyes. I had that feeling again that I had met her before. "On my last yarn rip, I didn't get the yarn and didn't go back."

"I heard something about that."

"Is he looking for me? Is he angry?"

She eyed me mischievously. "We're just not going to tell him."

I debated whether I should mention it, but did. "He has my papers."

She nodded thoughtfully. "They're not going to be easy. You just have to stay out of trouble until we can get them."

After all of Kira's warTalk, Pilla's plain talk was an air I hadn't known I missed. "So, why are you helping me?"

"Your talents are valuable. But whatever we can make, I'll share it fairly."

I picked up the MasterCut. "What percentage are you taking?"

She had scoffed at that. "YeOld#1 doesn't pay enough to worry about. But it's a safe place to practice sewing. Later we'll figure how to *make*."

"I don't know if I should thank you or not."

Pilla eyed me. "You'll thank me."

Now she escorted all of us Number Two employees into a dim room with several couches and small beds. Swirling sounds—I couldn't call it music—filled the space. On the way, Pilla had opened a large black closet and pulled out a sad-looking off-white cardigan, which she now held up. She asked, "Who's going to lead?" I noticed that she was wearing rubber gloves. The group clamored for her to go first, but she kept begging off. "I've got to work the closet," she said several times.

Clearly this cardigan was special, but why, I didn't know. The texture, sheen, and thickness of the yarn reminded me of the scarf I had seen pulled from drap-de-Berry's neck after she had been killed.

One of the salessoldiers from the front of Number Two stripped off his Steam jacket and shirt. He had a half-dozen of the same sores on his shoulders and the back of his neck. "Hand me that cutting sweater. I'm freezing in here!" The other employees laughed as if he had told a joke.

I eyed the sweater and his sores and wondered if my dad had worn Xi.

"Wait," said Dill. "Tane just joined Number Two today. He's never burned Xi before. I think he should have the honors."

"A Xi virgin?" cooed several of the women.

"Burn! Burn!" chanted others.

Pilla held the sweater toward me, but I didn't move.

"Strip," Dill ordered with a smile.

"Put it on!" complained the half-naked salessoldier.

"It makes your mind brocade," said another.

I stepped back. "Keep that away from me! My dad died from that."

SLUBS: SMUTS, ROTS, AND RUSTS

The M-Bunny COM on the old highway was one of the few buildings left from what was said to have once been a thousand. It was a windowless cinderblock structure, but inside tables and shelves displaying all of M-Bunny's many goods were laid out below a translucent ceiling. In the front stood racks of B-shirts and shorts. Farther back were oils, powders, beads, and solutions. In another area sat spare parts for the buses, corn oil generators, and night lanterns. I headed straight to the pharm, and bought a salve, a cornbox of something called M-Bunny Skin Fat, and several packages of tarlike black corn pest gum, paying with the last of my M-Bunny coins. When I got back to the house, Dad wasn't where I had left him.

"Dad? Dad!"

Rik came down the row, expression grave. Thumbing over his shoulder, he whispered, "He's over there."

"Why?"

"Rep wanted him farther from the house. He's down next to that drain thing where the corn doesn't grow." Rik followed me. "He looks the same."

Dad was asleep on the ground. His eyes were closed, his mouth, open. His breathing seemed irregular.

I stooped next to him. "I'm back."

He opened his eyes and peered up. "Where'd you go?"

"I had to work but look, I got some stuff for you at the COM."

His breath came out in short huffs. "Where's your rep?"

I held up my purchases one after the other. "I've got corn salve… skin fat—I've heard that's good. And I got pest gum. That should help the rash."

"No," he grunted. "Get your rep. Recycle me. Take the bonus." Straining, he pushed himself up. "Take the money and get to Bestke. You understand?"

I was horrified that my father had mentioned another brandclan with Rik standing just three feet away. I tried to smile reassuringly at Rik. "Dad's just a… um… he's a little rot."

"Try the pest gum," said Rik. "Looks like he's got smut. Want me to help?"

"Thanks. I'm okay. Just tell the rep I'm going to sleep out here."

Rik's calm eyes held on mine for a long beat. I could see my father's death in them. I looked away first. "Sure," he said, and disappeared into the corn.

I turned back to my father. "Stop talking about other brandclans! You could get us debranded!" I stuffed my mouth with five of the black gum sticks.

"Get your rep," he repeated.

"Stop saying that!" I worked my jaw, softening the gum. The corn tenders used pest gum when they found anything bad on a stalk or an ear. You spit the black juice onto the rust or the blight. It tasted like rot, but it worked. "Take off your shirt," I said, as my mouth began to fill with the sour juice.

"Stop," he told me.

I wanted to scream. "Dad, please, lay back. This will help!"

He rubbed his face, coughed wetly. Giving up, he flopped back down on the dirt as if exhausted. He muttered something when I pulled up his shirt, but didn't open his eyes. Strangely the sores that covered his chest ended abruptly an inch above his shorts. I chewed a few more times and then began to spit the pesticide on his rash.

Pilla shook her head. "Pure Xi can't kill."

"He had sores all over," I told her.

"Sounds like he was a very heavy burner." She pursed her mouth sadly. "Who told you he died of Xi?"

When the fry truck melody woke me before dawn I checked my father. He was resting quietly, but in the dark I couldn't tell if the pesticide gum had done anything.

"I have to go," I whispered to him. "I'm going to try and get more gum tonight. Just stay here. Rik will check by later. You'll get better."

When I returned that evening, my father was gone. All that was left was the flattened ground where we had slept. I found Rik in the front field.

"The rep's in the house," he said quietly. His face was long, his eyes cheerless. "You should talk to him."

Our rep was a heavy man with thick features and a long, heavy beard. He had a way of looking off into the distance and twisting his mustache when he spoke.

He was talking with several other men inside the foyer, but when he saw me he dismissed them. "Good news! The regional rep came by before, and he looked at your dad!" He gazed out at the mountains on the horizon and smiled. "M-Bunny is very interested in rashes." Twirling a clump of hair below his chin, he reached into the pocket of his shorts with his free hand, and pulled out a small bag. "His recycle bonus was big. Even after my rep's take, and mine, you have quite a lot of metal."

Recycle bonuses were coveted and honorable. Large ones were rare and were only given to the most loyal men or for special circumstances. I stared at my rep. I couldn't understand. Goosebumps covered me, and it seemed the world was shrinking away. "Where is he?"

My rep smiled and shook the little bag. I had seen my dad a total of twenty days. Now all I would have of him was a handful of M-Bunny's stamped tin coins.

"He was sick," I told Pilla. "I figured it was the sores."

She gazed at me sorrowfully. "Was he in bad pain?"

"He was hurt. He didn't complain."

"No." She spoke softly. "Pure Xi doesn't work like that. Neither does dark."

"Are we going to burn?" the salessoldier with sores interrupted. "I'm ready!"

Pilla reached into one of the sleeves of the cardigan, yanked out a square of Xi cloth and tossed it at him. He began rubbing it over his neck and chest as the others cheered him on.

Dill stood beside Pilla and me. "You think it was dark Xi?" he asked.

"He said his dad had many sores. That just means he burned Xi often. Dark Xi is completely different. It will leave a sore, but it kills long before you could get more than one."

"Do you know dark Xi?" Dill's voice was edged with awe and fear. "Have you touched it? What's it like?"

"I've dealt with it." Pilla shrugged. "It's spun hell." She touched my shoulder gently. "I'm sorry about your dad. But pure Xi isn't what hurt him. Pure is an extraordinary painkiller. It's a dreamer. If you don't want to try it, that's calm, but you know what I think? I think you should just touch it and know what it is. It seems like you don't know much about him."

"Almost nothing. He disappeared for nine years and then just showed up one day with that rash all over his arms and chest."

"Xi shirts... Xi sweaters... Xi jackets. They're most popular." She pursed her mouth. "He must have been burning to take away some pain." She undid a button at the front of her green saleswarrior outfit. She had a sore across her left clavicle. "If you do it a lot... it causes lesions, but they don't hurt, and if you stop they heal quickly." She whispered, "I burn a lot... so watch me." She then closed her eyes and wrapped the cardigan around her neck. The others crowded in.

After several moments, red patches, like continents of emotion, appeared across Pilla's neck and face. A sheen of perspiration glazed her forehead. She parted her lips and moaned softly. Her expression reminded me of Kira's face when I sewed her buttonholes. Pilla let her head roll back and let out a loud wounded cry. I felt like I shouldn't watch, but I couldn't stop staring. And when she finally opened her eyes, she smiled at me. Tugging the sweater from around her neck, she held it out for me.

It was a simple rib knit in low-twist wool. Up close, I could see that it was a mix of white, gray, and jade. I took it from her. Most in the room were watching me. I put it around my neck like Pilla had done, ready to fling it off the moment something went wrong.

Some in the room started chanting, but Pilla shushed them. "Burn a little flame," she whispered.

I stared at her, waiting. The thing felt warm and a little itchy. That couldn't be all there was to it, but I didn't feel anything else. It was just like a woolen scarf.

"Is he getting warm?" someone asked.

"Maybe," answered someone else.

Was it me? Was it because I was a slubber? I pressed the sweater to my skin and closed my eyes, but still nothing happened. I was just about to give up, take it off, and open my eyes when suddenly an expanding warmth started around my neck. The warmth soon turned hot, and just as I began to panic, ready to fling the thing off me, the heat turned liquid and sunk into my flesh, into my blood. It seemed to circulate though my head and body and felt sleepy and comforting. Was this what my father had felt? This was okay. It was soothing and relaxing.

And then it seemed like the yarn began to melt, as if fusing with my skin. It wasn't bad; it didn't hurt, but I knew something else was coming. I don't think I opened my eyes, but I could see the room again. The others seemed far back, but Pilla's face was as large as the harvest moon. She smiled. Her lips moved but instead of sounds, colored fabric filled the air. Chestnut organdie. Burnt yellow needlecord. Orange tulle.

She reached out a hand and touched my face. Instead of skin—instead of the slight roughness of the swirls on the ends of her fingers—I felt crepe.

I tried to tell her what was happening, that the world was turning into fabric, but when I spoke, folds of dark merino came from my mouth. It was shocking but also funny. I laughed in white chenille.

She came closer. She smelled of cotton and starch. I put my arms around her, and understood that she wasn't flesh and blood anymore, but layers of intricate woodblock printed chintz, red velvet, white horsehair, and black swanskin. I squeezed her close to me, as I had never held anyone before. I loved who she was and what she had become.

The others in the room were smiling. Some congratulated me as the sweater was passed around. I touched them and they too were stitched together from layers of fabric, lace, and bone.

If this is what my father had experienced, if this is what he saw and felt... then I understood why he had returned to me covered with sores.

SEATTLEHAMA: SEAMS RIPPED OPEN

I woke in the largest bed I had ever seen. The sheets and pillows were Hunter green satin that felt slick and cool. Sitting up I faced floor to ceiling windows that looked out on the city atrium. It was night and the costumed shoppers were in full force. When I called out, "Hello?" my voice sounded small and weak.

Pilla came through the doorway, a pink plasticott cuisine court mug in her hand. "You're up!"

"Where am I?"

She smiled. "My bedroom."

"What happened?"

"You burned Xi. Don't you remember?"

For a panicked moment, I checked my neck and shoulders for sores, but didn't see or feel any.

She shook her head. "You'd have to burn more than that to get a sore."

I remembered when I had hugged her to me. "Everything was made of fabric. You were chintz, velvet, and swanskin."

Pilla smiled. "You were hard dreaming."

"But it was like the dreams I used to have as a boy back in the slubs. I would dream of stuff like that... about how the world was made of patterns. Last night was just deeper and more real."

"That's calm." She sat on the side of the bed and smiled at me. She looked fresher than usual and her hair was neatly arranged.

"That's very calm."

"You don't see cloth?"

"For me it's more of a feeling. It's like I'm connected to the universe. If I see anything it's vast purple clouds and fields of stars." She sipped her coffee. "You talked about your dad, but you weren't making too much sense."

"What did I say?"

"You kept saying you understood. It was as if you were seeing the meaning of the cosmos. That's not unusual. There's something vast about Xi. It's supposed to connect the non-verbal part of the brain." She eyed me. "So, it was good to try Xi, wasn't it?"

"Yeah." I exhaled. "But why was my dad doing it? You said Xi is a painkiller. Do you think he was in pain?"

Pilla shrugged. "Financial, emotional, psychological, physical... there are millions of reasons to burn. Was he successful?"

"I don't know. When I was a boy, he was an M-Bunny rep. He seemed so strong. But when he left, I figured he must have done something terrible. I thought he had ruined the crop somehow, but I don't know if I'll ever learn much else."

Pilla was silent for a beat. "Sometimes it's better not to know."

I recalled that bag of M-Bunny coins. I never spent one. I threw a handful into the corn, some kind of angry offering. The rest I gave away. "I didn't have a choice."

"It's possible he was protecting you. Maybe there was someone who wanted to do you harm and he wanted to keep you from that. That would be a good thing."

Like I had many times before, I felt guilty that I had not switched brands as my father wished. Bestke was a strong Europa brandclan, but it didn't control land near Seattlehama. One night I even snuck away from my corn-tending duties and started walking south. Somewhere in the middle of the night, cold, tired, and hungry, I turned back. From what I'd heard, I would need to somehow walk for five days straight to make it to a small Bestke enclave. The journey itself seemed impossible.

Pilla interrupted my thoughts. "You hungry?"

I dressed, and we headed out. My arms were tired, my legs, sore. And maybe it was the lingering effect of the Xi, but the colors and sounds of the city seemed magnified. As we passed shoppers, I couldn't help but thread count their pants and jackets. Every conversation and spill of music from distant doorways bloomed in front of me.

After we ate at a dingy little place, I headed to YeOld#1 and took my place beside Dill. We didn't have time to speak, as the hordes and their costumes descended on us, but he winked at me.

"I just can't decide," said a pouting t'up girl with the caped AngerFrog costume draped over her arm. "Last time, I was Charcoal NirvanaBitch, but that got repetitious. I went for this because it's cutting, but not too hook. But is this material all ventilated? I don't want to get all sweaty when I bustle!"

"It's good," I told her.

Before she even slipped on the suit, I had hemmed the legs. And prior to zipping it up, I reached in with my Juki Magni-Needle 66-11 Handseamer and made two quick darts over her kidneys.

"Oh," she admired in the mirror, "that's splattered! I look hot-hot!"

Next, a young man held an Envoy Duvet and a BallerinaHead Girl. "I credited both, and they said I can combine them!" he screamed. "It has to be done instantly. I'm already late!"

I'd been told not to mix the costumes, but this t'up seemed like he was about to rage. "Of course," I told him. Ballerina and Envoy had similar constructions, so I knew I could do it quickly. Besides I could try the seam-ripping mode on the Juki. Dill had showed me how it worked when a t'up came in with a defective Choky Bear.

Engaging the ripper, I opened the seams on the arms and legs as easily as slicing white bread. Switching the Juki back to sew, I married the gold-embossed sleeves of the Envoy with the torso of Ballerina. Envoy's hat, I tacked cockeyed on the man's head, and on his legs, I used her stockings and the envoy's floppy white boots.

"Not too bad," he muttered, before he dashed off.

Seven hours later when the shift was over, I was exhausted. When we headed into the barracks to wash up, the owner, Kastle, stood waiting for us.

"Someone down here mixed a costume!" he growled. "We charge extra for refinements, adaptations, and any character redesign! That's custom work! That's not your jobs down here! Now who was it?"

At first, no one moved. Finally, I raised my hand. "He seemed like he was in a hurry."

Kastle stepped before me. "We have rules, soldier. You broke them."

I feared he was going to ask for my papers. But in a flash, he yanked the Juki from my hand, tearing it from the power cord. "Return all your YeOld#1 articles to the company exchange. You're court-martialed!" With that he turned and left.

I couldn't believe how crazy he'd acted. Glancing at the frayed wires in my hand, I asked Dill, "What was that?"

His face was white. "You're fired."

I looked where Kastle had gone and wanted to shout, *No!*

"When I saw that BallerinaHead and Envoy mix walk out, I had a bad feeling. I wish I saw you and could have stopped you, but I was deluged with a bunch of fat Fairies."

"They credited him both costumes. He said it was okay."

Dill shook his head. "You can't trust our customers."

"I was just trying to help." I stared at the floor and worried what Pilla was going to think.

"Don't fret." Dill patted my arm. "You'll find other costume tailoring work. You're really good. I thought your mod was real calm!"

Dill invited me to dinner and Xi burning. Thanking him, I said I would catch up later, but figured I had better deliver the bad news and headed to the Xi boutique.

Pilla looked at me as if she couldn't fathom what I'd told her. "Wait. What'd you do?"

"I mixed two costumes. I know they told me not to, but this customer was shouting, and I just thought it would be better just to help him." I waited for her to go rot like Kastle.

Instead, her nonchalance surprised me. "We'll find you something better. That was a waste of time anyway."

"I loved using the Juki."

Shaking her head thoughtfully, she said, "You're not labor. You're design."

I thought about catching up with the others from YeOld#1, but decided against it. I didn't want to wallow in my firing with Dill, nor was I in the mood to hear their usual complaints.

Idly winding my way down several sets of showstairs, I passed singers and snake dancers and then slowed and stopped. Vada's face flashed in my head, so I headed to an entervator port to look for the Europa Showhouse.

The port was crowded with trippers and consumers, and as I made my way to the info desk, I came to a group all dressed in Blackwitch Breath costumes.

"Ye Old Number One," I said, knowingly.

"Anger's my super shake. Suck thee down!" sneered one with an affected accent.

They laughed and headed off to a waiting entervator. For a moment I hated them and their warTalk curses, but then I noticed the crooked hems, ill-fitting shoulders, and sagging bodices of the cheap rented costumes and I felt two small satisfactions: my alterations would have been better, and most t'ups wouldn't know the difference.

The Europa Showhouse came, but I saw that it was heading up to the 800th floor in Parfum Spaceship where the drap-de-Berry rip occurred, so I waited for it to come back down before boarding, raced on, and got a seat in the front. When we started down, the stage lights came on and Vada appeared in a red bobbin lace dress and brass-colored boots.

Shielding her eyes from the spots, she peered out at us. "I need the brave assistance of one of the fair shoppers in the audience. I will read the humors and veins of your mind and assist you in divining your heart and your steed. I see hands… thank you. Among you, do we have someone from out of town? Good! And maybe not just out of town, but someone who doesn't truly belong, but someone who wants to…" She ran a gloved hand seductively over her crotch. "…*fit in*." The crowd laughed.

A man came forward and stood beside her. Closing her eyes, she touched his neck and around his ears as the man squirmed. As she guessed his name, where he came from, and his age, I imagined how the caustic dimity of her gloved hands would feel against my skin.

While she sang a quiet song accompanied by water-harp music, she stood in front of me for several moments. Unlike Tinyko, who had been disappointing, up-close, Vada was more beautiful, powerful, vulnerable.

SEATTLEHAMA: TORN AND MENDED

"We're going up to meet a designer," said Pilla the next evening as we walked to the entervator port. "I'd like you to apprentice with him. We'll see what could happen from there." She smiled wistfully. "It's a long shot, but I would so love to see Withor's face if it happened."

I didn't like the idea of taunting him. Didn't he already hate me?

An entervator soon came. We ascended to the 700s in the Shangtung and then walked along a balcony that overlooked the immense near mile drop to the atrium. I slowed for a moment as I tried to locate the Velour Building, where Kira had been, and the Parfum Spaceship, where I had ripped yarn from Tinyko.

I caught up to Pilla as she headed into a dinnershow. The dark room was studded with tables made of black lava and the waitresswarriors wore nothing but black pearl lamé masks. Pilla ordered drinks for both of us.

"Are we meeting the designer here?" I asked.

She peered toward the entrance. "He should be here in a few minutes. Listen, he used to be huge in Europa. He's fallen, but he's very bright... if a little eccentric. Maybe that's typical of a top designer... or a *former* top designer. Have you ever heard of Zanella?"

"No."

As she stood and smiled at an approaching man, she

whispered, "Pretend you have."

The man had black hair and a stubbly beard. He wore a long coat. A pair of enormous yellow-tinted shades covered half of his face. "Pilla has told me all about you," he said as he sat. His accent was hard and heavy on the saliva.

"It's an honor to meet you," I said.

He narrowed his eyes as if he doubted me. When the waitresswarrior came with our mercury floats, he ordered a hemlocktwist.

"You were *involved* with that yarn-ripping boom." His tone was disapproving.

"Kind of."

"He's from the slubs," Pilla added, as if that explained anything.

His face was a study of wrinkles. "And you want to learn fashion from me? With an out-of-line designer who goes around wearing fornication coats in Seattlehama?"

"I do."

"He was knitting skivvé," enthused Pilla. "You know, those fantasy sex panties that are big here. Tane made them without any training. Usually those knitters study for a couple of years."

The waitresswarrior returned with his drink. He downed it in one long gulp and handed back the glass. "Another." Frowning at Pilla, he said, "Knit skivvé are not *real* fashion. They are just an accessory and a trifling one at that." He looked at me. "Was this underpants your own design?"

I shook my head. "Not really."

"Those awful things popped up in Miran six months ago," he told Pilla. He then went on about some boutique, jobbers, and a group of weavers involved in some Xi scandal in Europa2, but I couldn't follow.

Zanella's second drink arrived with the food. Pilla and I had walrus stakes. He devoured his albatross sushi so quickly I wondered if he'd eaten in a week.

"Can you show him something?" asked Pilla at the end of our meal.

"He seems unlikely." Zanella smiled sourly. "But for what you mentioned earlier, Pilla, I will endeavor to introduce him to something of the world of true fashion."

She reached across the table and they shook. It was like I was a slubber again and these two reps had just bought and sold me.

"Pay attention to him," she whispered before we left. "He's a legend. You have no idea how lucky you are that he's in need. You'll study with him during the day and stay with me at night. I'll see you later. And listen to everything he says." She headed to the Xi boutique; Zanella and I boarded the Shangtung entervator and traveled across the city to The Marcella. His place was in the six hundreds, and although The Marcella was opposite The Velour, Kira and her sharpened knitting needles were not far.

Our ride was silent, and Zanella spoke to me only once to say, "I came to Seattlehama to think about existence, contemplate the flow of time, and to learn how to play the steam koto." I got the feeling he expected me to laugh, but I didn't know if it was funny. Zanella rolled his eyes and sighed deeply. As I sat staring down at my feet, I imagined slinking back to YeOld#1 and begging for my Juki.

The sleep boutique Zanella was staying at was quite select, which made the mess revealed when he unlocked the door all that much more shocking. Magazines, clothes, dishes, papers, screens, clocks, towels, masks, even bits of braided hair covered the floor.

"Oh," said the designer, as if he had forgotten. "Meet the mess." He cleared off a chair for me and had me sit. "You don't know shit about me, do you?"

"I don't know designers."

"Glorious!" Zanella rolled his eyes. "Well, a deal's a deal. I get high-quality Xi from Pilla and you'll get some... I don't know... *advice* sounds too unstructured... some *fashion lessons* from a former star." He pointed behind me. "Let's see if you've got some fashion bobbins. Over there in that... *stuff* is a suit safe. Bring it over here."

In the corner was a pile of junk taller than me. Most of it seemed to be dirty, wadded, and torn clothes. Buried in the chaos I found a gleaming, four-foot-tall, chrome safe with a large black dial in the middle. Even though it was on wheels, it seemed to weigh two tons and was difficult to maneuver. Zanella did nothing while I struggled with the shiny beast. As I pushed it toward him I let the wheels crease the magazines, boxes, and papers on the floor out of spite.

When I finally had it positioned before him, he inhaled deeply, and muttered, "What's the number..." He peered at me. "Any ideas?"

I shook my head. He puckered and unpuckered his mouth, obviously hoping to conjure the combination; I watched him for signs of obvious psychosis. A second later, he turned the clicking dial this way and that. The door popped open with a solid click.

Inside the lit interior hung a simple navy suit jacket. "Its one of mine. It's not that wonderful. It was a hit about twelve years ago... wait... no... god, it's been twenty-two years now. Anyway, your first task is to take it apart and then put it back together." He pushed himself up and headed to the bathroom. A minute later he emerged in a transparent suit. Through it I could see his droopy arms and the loose flesh between his legs. He scowled at me. "I'll be back tomorrow night to see how you're doing."

As he opened the door to head out, I asked, "You're going to burn?"

"It is none of your shit business." He seemed to go, but then stared forward as some momentary sadness seemed to fill his eyes. "Yes. I am."

"I tried Xi yesterday. Everything was made out of cloth."

"Cloth? Curious."

"My dad was a heavy burner." As I spoke, I wondered why I

was telling him.

"Most burners in this city are young and fashionable. And they burn to free themselves from their suspicions and inhibitions." He stopped. Wrinkles scored his face. "This old man burns to ease his soul into the tight suits of senility and death."

For several moments after the designer had gone, I saw my dad sleeping in the corn, his chest covered with Xi sores. I wondered why he had burned so much and hoped whatever it was the yarn had been a comfort.

Waking from my thoughts, I cleared some space on the floor by pushing all of the junk into a corner, and spent the night taking that jacket apart. It was what I had wanted to do since I had gotten to the city, but hadn't been brave enough. I had snatched yarns because I had been afraid to take more. I had knit and tailored because it was a job, but this felt like the sex I had always wanted.

As for the navy jacket, it was unlike any I had seen in Seattlehama. The shell material was the best part. The heavy high-twist wool felt like what I imagined Vada's cheek felt like. The front of the jacket was dotted with double buttons, the left side slashed by an angled glove pocket. The bottom hem would have fallen a foot below the hip on most men, and the shoulders were heavily padded, which gave it a top-heavy look. The collar was wide with asymmetrical notches, and inside, the bright red lining seemed deliberately worn, even a little frayed in the left armpit. Dozens of tiny pockets covered the inside, as if to house a magician's colony of performing sparrows. On the inside back I counted nine labels, each with intricate logos and text: A production of Ottoman & Poplin, In Cooperation with Wadmal Council, With Assistance from Silesia Partners, Development and Coordination by A & U Industries, with thanks to Arch Velani. At the top a black label read: Executive Production by L. F. W. M. Nathan Zanella ACE.

While cleaning the floor, I had found a sewing needle and used that to pull the seams. I started below a fold of lining on the inside of the left sleeve. Each piece of lining, cloth, backing and pad, each pile of scribbly thread, all the buttons, stays, and labels, I laid it all out like an exploded view.

Along the way, I found dozens of odd and interesting curiosities. The outside pockets were all triple stitched with a curiously strong, red thread. One pocket was lined with a silvery lamé, which I guessed had something to do with either electronics or heat. As I got further into the matting and horsehair layers over the shoulders, a layer of white felt nearly disintegrated as I removed it. Other places, the deconstruction was like a puzzle, and I had to figure out in what order the parts had been assembled so as to pull them apart without damage.

Once it was all laid out, I stood, stretched my hands and neck, and got to work putting it back together. That went surprisingly quickly. As I held the pieces together, I found I could actually insert the needle in the original hole and pull it so that the stitches matched exactly.

Sometime late the next day, the door opened. L. F. W. M. Nathan Zanella ACE stepped in. He was now wearing a long, dark fornication coat. His eyes were red, his cheeks hollow, and his hair splayed in all directions. He glared at me unhappily, but then noticed the jacket hanging in the open vault. Bending, he peered at it. He checked the sleeves and then the tags in the back. He pulled it from the hook.

"So, you didn't even try? What did you do, just sit here the whole time? Oh, this is shit sad indeed!"

I pointed my chin at the top of the vault where I had put a single horsehair. It had occurred to me that I would need some proof that I had disassembled the jacket. That fiber had come from deep inside the layers of the right shoulder.

Zanella picked up the hair and felt it between his fingertips. He seemed about to laugh at me, but then something changed. It was like he recognized the fiber and its specific crinkle. For several frantic moments, he turned the jacket inside out, checked the numerous pockets, felt around the back of the collar, and inspected the armholes. When he finally hung the jacket back in the box, and closed the door on it, his expression was confused and maybe annoyed.

Picking up the horsehair again, he stood silent for a long moment. "Shit," he finally muttered, "you did it."

PART 2
Z-TWIST

PART 2
WINTER

SEATTLEHAMA: SINGLED OUT ON THE ROCOCO ENTERVATOR

"If you don't know history," said Zanella, "you can't repeat it. Fashion is about cycles. It's about sensing what's about to happen. It's about seeing into the future. No... it's more than that... it's about *making* the future. If you guess right, you will have created next year. There are few who work so intimately with the future... cherish that."

He would often deliver these lectures standing before the windows, looking far down at the circle of buildings while he applied his make-up and sprayed his hair with an army of products. For the first several days he talked and talked.

"To be successful, you must know not just cloth, body, and ease, but time," he said another day as rain poured down outside. "Our job is to make love to the zeitgeist, listen to its moans, and interpret their meaning."

After a week he led me to another room in the sleep boutique. There he stored his collection of historical garments, fashion magazines, cloth and seam samples, yarn recipes, and fiber formulas. Unlike his living space, it was immaculate. It was a museum, a library, a laboratory, a design room, and for me—the world's most wonderful playground. We spent weeks unboxing and unwrapping one treasure after another.

I had to memorize his entire fabric samples collection and he would quiz me by showing me the three-inch squares.

"Damask… gambroon… pellicule… dornick… chiffon…" I stopped when he showed me the next.

"Hello? What's the matter?"

I woke from a daydream. "Sorry… drap-de-Berry…" His sample was darker than the woman's suit, but it was like seeing her paralyzed scream again.

Zanella told me where things had came from, who made what, who stole what idea from whom, how it was marketed, how the mills ruined the order, how the product deviated from the contract, and a hundred other stories. He quizzed me constantly, and soon I had answers about fabric, construction, patterning and draping. Identifying and discussing other designers' work took longer.

"You must see this," Zanella said one day, opening a sealed black box. Inside was a highly constructed pale yellow suit with clear buttons, no pockets, and low drop shoulders. Zanella laughed as he picked it up and handed it to me. "Poor Marrion! He's gone now. Rest his soul. Lister Erik Marrion Chat was his name. Marrion was his mark. He loved these pale and destitute yellows. He wore them all the time. His house was covered with them. And he adored those thick glass buttons. He made them himself with some mad high-fire technique. But he was a genius at tailoring. There are few more exquisite suits than his, but…" Zanella let out a long exhale. "He just kept doing the same silhouette in the same palette. I told him to experiment, but he clung to his ideas. He thought those ideas were his being. For years he was loved. He made dresses and gowns; he made popular *de nimes* in yellow, of all colors. He sold and sold… but then… overnight… he was hated." He met my eyes. "Fashion changes and fashion is the universal constant."

Those were my days. As much as I could, I traveled up and down in the Europa Showhouse admiring Vada and her endless costumes. Once she wore a stunning dress layered with tapestry and bone, next a sheer caustic dimity clung to her curvy figure, another time her face was barely visible behind feathers and Chantilly.

I decided that I wasn't just attracted to her appearance, or her magnificent and often risqué clothes, but to her maturity, her being, and the way she stood. When she was on stage, she was balanced, solid, and rooted to the floor in a way that reminded me of corn stalks at the height of the harvest. She belonged in a way that I could only wish.

When the Europa Showhouse docked the last stop, and Vada thanked, waved, and blew air kisses, I would slink off, my hands stuffed in my pockets hiding my excitement.

Thus would begin my nights. But instead of a few frantic moments in enterjohns listening to the admonishments and coupon offers from knitter-kritters, they were filled with fashion of a different sort when Pilla introduced me to something called Pearl River Love Tights.

"I'm not into the whole epic character stuff," she explained. "With these it's just a body and a minimum of fabric."

The bright yellow, pink, and teal bodysuits came in sealed packages, covered with cartoon frogs and pigs and promises of fulfillment, improved function, and ecstasy. The knit fabric within heightened touch and warmth like a giant magnifying glass. The first time, it was just the two of us sliding against each other in her green bedroom. The next night we headed to her Xi boutique and in one of the back rooms found a pile of others all dressed in Pearl Rivers.

I liked the tights better than Xi and soon got to know all the styles and weaves, from the slightly rough Tricolene, to the sheer Visiweave. Tights parties brought an intense and anonymous fashioning, where I often imagined I was with Vada. Some nights I only got an hour or two of sleep before finally collapsing in some corner of the boutique.

One morning, I woke in a pile of sleeping bodies. After peeling off the knit, and starting to re-dress in my usual clothes, I stopped. Staring at myself in the mirror, I hated what I saw.

I was dressing in a clumsy approximation of Warrior Remon of Loin, with violets, dark purples, fringe and frills. Worse, my face was as it had been shaped that day with Kira at the Black Blossom Shopping Amphitheater and Custom Fashion Art House. The man I was looking at wasn't me. Over coffee, I told Pilla.

"Finally!" She handed me her MasterCut. "Yes! Get a makeover."

A gender consultant reshaped my face and hair. I found a men's store nearby that sold a designer that Zanella had introduced me to—Cloque, a reclusive and little-known designer rumored to be nearly one hundred years old, had been designing since he was six. His clothes were not about trend, drift, or boom; instead they were about the integrity of cloth, simple tailoring, and cool colors.

When I walked into Zanella's that afternoon, I expected him to be stunned by my new look, but I was the one to be surprised. Zanella's room was immaculate. A stack of suitcases stood by the door.

"You're leaving."

"Back where I belong!" Behind the yellow lenses of his glasses, tears streaked his face. "I have stayed in Seattlehama long enough… I have contemplated long enough… I have fornicated enough coats… and I only took one steam-koto lesson. I actually burned my fingers!" He pulled off his glasses, wiped his face on a sleeve, and eyed me up. "I have something for you." He pointed to the old cloth-covered book on the coffee table.

Historical Highlights of Extraordinary Tailoring, Draping, and Costume Design. Editor Betran Feldspar.

I picked it up and began to page through the yellowed volume.

"Two articles are mine," he said. "'The Lost Drape Technique,' and 'The Secrets of Gravitational Deformation Tables for Woven Cloth.'"

"You can't go," I said.

"It's time."

"There more things in your collection! I haven't seen everything."

"Only a few trifles."

I stared at the book. "I'm not ready."

"Please have a seat, Tane, I want to tell you something." Zanella clapped his hands happily. "And would you like a juice? When I cleaned up, I found a service-fridge in the corner." He laughed. "I had completely forgotten about it. I hate what a slob I am."

I sat, declining the juice.

"I must tell you something, Tane. When we first met, I did not think you were worthy. I didn't want to teach you anything, but I needed the money and the Xi that your... paramour... sugar... whatever you call that peculiar saleswarrior of yours... provided." He tilted his head back and propped the large frames back onto his now dry nose. With a white cloth, he dabbed an errant drop of juice that had splashed on his shirt. "But I've been surprised by you. You have vision that I do not possess. You have an innate command of fabric." He clasped his hands together. "So, I have two things to tell you. First, you still have much to learn. You are only now ready to *begin* in fashion, but you must first design women's clothes. I know that you have an interest in menswear, but study the female form. You will learn everything and more from her. The male and what he wears is a single planet to her solar system of silhouette and couture."

I didn't like the idea, but said, "Okay... I'll design for women."

"And second, don't let anyone ever tell you that fashion is superficial. It's the only thing that distinguishes humans from the critters. We have our fashion and our fashion is our culture. Leave people naked and not only will they freeze or fry, but their society and language will collapse to the hunter-gatherer of fifty thousand years ago." He leaned forward and spoke in a hushed tone. "Listen to me, Tane, as a designer... you are the shaper of men. You are the builder of order. It is through the tailor... that kings are fashioned."

I wandered toward the entervator port clasping Zanella's book to my chest. I didn't want him to go. I didn't want anything to change. I didn't even want to head back down, so I plunked myself in a chair.

After idly paging through the book and finding his article about gravity's effects on cloth, I glanced up at the t'ups, the holidays, and the costumed customers around me. I did not yet belong among them—as I had wished for so long—but I was beginning to sense who I was and what I could do.

More and more my thoughts were dominated with the shapes I could make, the seams I might sew, the folds I might make, and the bodies I might hide and reveal. Of the pants, vests, shirts, jackets, skirts, and gowns around me, the colors were wrong, the silhouettes, unseemly, the fabrics, squandered. I was here to shape them as I could.

I wanted to laugh. None of these t'ups knew it yet, but I was the one. Maybe not today or tomorrow, but as I sat there, holding Zanella's book, I felt all-powerful. All I needed was sharp shears, a tape, and some needles, and I could heal all that was broken.

Before I had seen just the yarn, or just the fabric, or just the darts and fasteners. My nights of fashioning bodies in what amounted to sensual foundation and my days of designers, lines, and ideas fused. It wasn't just about cloth. It wasn't just about skivvé, or jackets, or skirts. It was about the bodies inside.

As for Zanella, I knew I would never see him again. I had hugged him, thanked him a dozen times, and wished him well. I knew I was taking a small piece of him forward.

The Europa Showhouse arrived to take me down. I took a seat in the front on the far right, and after the door closed and the lights dimmed, Vada appeared in a red gown covered with beads as small and shiny as fish roe. Her hair spiraled around her head and something about her eyes seemed especially attentive and bright.

Shading her hand from the lights, she peered toward the back. "I am looking for a brave shopper who wonders about the price of happiness and the depth of credit. I need someone who is not afraid of the shine on the cosmos tonight. Someone from out of town, preferably!"

Since she always picked someone from the back, I was shocked when she pointed her red-gloved hand at me, and said, "You!"

My body froze. All I could do was quiver my head in an approximation of *no*.

"Cram your cut!" said the t'up woman beside me.

"Go on up!" shouted someone farther back.

My face must have been as red as her gloves when I finally stood. Someone next to me pushed me forward and I stumbled up onto the little stage. My hands were shaking. My mouth was dry.

"Are you a fan of mine or is your taste in vertical transportation simply purple and rococo?"

I shrugged, and once I had unstuck my tongue from the roof of my mouth, I said, "I like you." The words slipped out, but as I tried to explain them away, I was drowned in the crowd's screamed approval.

"Well," said Vada to the audience, "more white for my goblet… more muscle for my plate… another needle for my cut." While several in the front rows stood and whooped, she grasped my elbow and pulled me closer. Leaning in, she sniffed my face the way one might a freshly baked pie. "My olfactory intuition tells me that my very good new friend is just twenty-one years old…" She lifted my right hand and inspected my fingers. "My ocular intuition tells me that he has flair for certain *materials*."

Those in the crowd who seemed to think everything she said was innuendo screamed, but I wondered if she actually meant cloth.

"But what we must know," she said to the crowd. "What we must know is what is *inside his suit*. What secrets are inside the lining?" Turning toward me, she grasped the lapels of my navy jacket as if she were threatening me, yanked it toward her, and somehow removed my jacket without tearing the back. She was now holding it up for the audience's approval.

And it was that moment that I saw someone I knew sitting toward the back of the ship. He alone wasn't cheering. He alone wasn't smiling and clapping. Vit, one of the two city boys Withor had hired to rip yarns, recognized me. From his odd, conniving expression, I got the feeling he was just waiting to run to Withor and tell. What that meant, I wasn't exactly sure, but knew it wasn't good.

"The cloth touches the skin," continued Vada, "the skin touches the blood… the blood touches the heart." She held the jacket open and then, with a dramatic sweep of her arm and a loud tearing sound, ripped it in half—as she did, a spatter of red liquid burst from the lining. Several t'ups in the front leaped out of the way. Red dots freckled one woman's cheeks and nose.

"Inside the heart," Vada continued, her voice filling the ship, "is the talent and the quiver… and inside the quiver is the mind and the trust." As she spoke, she wadded up the torn jacket and reared back. "And in the trust, there is nothing but the smoke of love." She threw the jacket. It burst into flame.

Someone screamed. Most applauded. Many waved their arms as if in apoplexy. I saw a woman pat her hair as if it might have been singed. I stared at the dissipating puff of smoke and felt like I had been punched.

"And in the natural realm of the vaulted if extinct imagination of our lives, just as the snake molts to grow, you too—my new friend—you have grown before us. You have expanded your air and your mind." Stepping behind me, Vada said quietly, "Hold still." She wiggled her hands under my arm, which tickled. Several in the crowd whooped salaciously.

"After the last shopping hour tonight," she whispered in my

ear, "come to the entervator Keep below the city atrium and *join*."

Before I could answer, she grasped the placket of my shirt and tore the starched material. Below the shirt was my navy serge jacket and my shirt and tie just as before.

"Check the veracity and impunity," said Vada, as she stepped to my side. "We will have no dread of the truth. Speak the reality!"

Hurriedly I undid the jacket button to check the lining.

"Tell us! Is it yours? Is it yours exactly?"

"Yes," I said to the crowd. "This is my jacket!"

Vada bowed and the audience roared with approval.

SEATTLEHAMA: FREEDOM FIGHTER, SABOTEUR... TERRORIST

I stood outside of Pilla's door for several minutes, not sure I should go in. I liked Pilla, I loved Pearl Rivering with her, but Vada wanted to see me. She wanted me to *join*. I hoped that meant *join* her, as in fashioning, but maybe all she wanted was to offer me some job carrying boxes, or vacuuming the purple carpet and drapes. But whatever it meant, I had to go to her and find out.

Pilla and I hadn't talked about our relationship—we just put on Pearl River Love Tights and jumped into the piles of bodies at her store—but there was something unscrupulous about her. As much as I liked her and trusted her, I knew that all she really wanted from me was to make piles of money and show up Withor somehow. For all she had done for me I did owe her, but somehow, tonight, for the first time, I had to get away.

It didn't help my nerves that Vit had approached me in the Showhouse. As we exited, he had stepped before me. "You're in big trouble."

I rolled my eyes at him. "I am not."

"You're supposed to be dead."

"No, I'm not!"

"Yeah, you were supposed to die on that last rip!"

Did he mean drap-de-Berry? Had the invisible person meant

146

to kill me?

"You are a corn. You're a prisoner. You're an *illegal slubber*!" He shouted as if to shame me in front of the other exiting passengers. "I'm telling Withor I saw you. He's going to get you, corn boy."

I flitted a hand at him. "Go away, Vit!"

He smirked at me, turned on a heel, and sauntered off. I didn't know the laws, but I wasn't supposed to be in the city unless I had the papers that Withor possessed. I hated to imagine being transported back to the corn, and shoved out off the back of a truck into the dirt. I couldn't live down there again. How could I eat another TakoDrop or, worse, ever put on a B-shirt?

If I ever saw Vit or Flak again I would have to run. I cursed my most recent makeover because I had reversed all that Kira had done and I looked like I had when I worked for Withor. If I had been dressed—and looked like—Warrior Remon of Loin, I doubted Vit would have recognized me.

Before I went in to Pilla's, I wondered if I could say I was sick and later sneak out? Or should I tell her the truth? Unsure, I pressed my hand to the door.

Pilla sat in one of the blue chrome study chairs that overlooked the atrium windows. In one hand she held a tall glass of Unhappy Rhino. Around her shoulders she had draped a Xi scarf. Her gaze was distant. "You say goodbye?"

For a second, I thought she was talking about maybe Vada or Vit. "You knew Zanella was going?"

Pilla laughed at me. "He told me he was impressed with you." She took off the Xi scarf and set in on the arm of her chair. On the right side of her neck she had developed another sore. She had six by my last count.

"There's a haberdashery in the Coin Building in the three hundreds. Not the greatest place, but a hundred light years from YeOld#1." After sipping her Unhappy Rhino, she laughed maliciously. "The owner of the place has been burning hard every night, and he's deeply indebted. Tonight I'll introduce you and propose that you start there tomorrow."

I resented her presumptuousness. "Actually... tonight," I said, as I gazed out at the flow of shoppers in the atrium, "I was thinking that I'd go out alone and window-shop."

"What?" Her thin eyebrows knotted over her nose. "Why?"

"I want to think about what Zanella said today."

"What did he say about me?"

"Not you." I laughed at her paranoia. "He said I should design for women and that I have more to learn. I just want to think about that." I wanted to get away from her. I thumbed at the door. "I'll be back later... maybe late."

"Wait!" She pushed herself out of the chair and stood there swaying back and forth the way Xi made one move like a cornstalk in a breeze. "You must be careful."

"I'll be fine."

"I've pulled a lot of threads for you. Tomorrow you will be working that haberdashery." She frowned. "Do you understand?"

She was just like Withor. "Yeah."

"Listen," Pilla shook her head, "I'm not bad. I'm really not." She stepped toward me. "We are everything, Tane. Together we are the make. And I've risked everything on you." The expression on her face reminded me of Kira and her visions of Remon of Loin.

"I'm just going window shopping for a little while," I told her, as I pointed toward the door. "I'll be back. I promise."

I feared she would follow, but maybe she was too burnt. I checked a few times, but didn't see her. I hated that she saw me as a slubber who was supposed to do exactly what she wanted. I didn't want to work for some Xi burner at a haberdashery in the Coin Building in the three hundreds. A part of me didn't even want to see Pilla again. At the same time, though, I knew that was selfish, that at any point along the way, I had felt grateful and guilty for all she was doing for me.

As I crossed the atrium, I kept my face turned from her

window, but imagined that she was watching me the whole way. Mindful of her gaze, I zigzagged my way from cuisine court to fashion shop, to club entrance, to souvenir shop. After a few minutes of wandering, I headed into the lower floors of the Harmony Building, where I lost myself among the shoppers, tourists, and saleswarriors.

At a cuisine court I ate and wondered if my fascination with Vada, my secret rendezvous, was just a way to separate myself from Pilla. And maybe I'd overreacted. If Pilla really had risked all her credit on me, like she seemed to have said, maybe she was just worried that I was going to run off. She had introduced me to Zanella and for that I owed her. I would work at haberdashery, I told myself. I was acting like I was already a designer, but I wasn't. Zanella would have been the first to tell me.

When the stores finally began to close their doors and gates, however, I started down into the darkness of the entervator Keep… and Vada.

As I descended, the air began to taste of dampness and grease. Uncluttered by traffic, the thick cables of the entervators revealed themselves streaking into the heights of the city.

At the end of the line, the dimming schedule board was clustered by a choir of jangling vending machines. Only a few of the entervators were still in service. Vada's entervator, The Europa Showhouse, had come ten minutes before.

The birds of the city, most entervators were brightly colored with small wings, fins, and tails. One was painted like a tuna. The one beside it, pink and shaped like a phallus. I came to the purple-skinned Europa.

The door was closed. When I knocked, the sound seemed hollow. I waited, breathless, but heard nothing. I chided myself that I had misunderstood. *Join* was some t'up word or warTalk that meant something completely different. She had probably said that she was glad I had *joined* her fans. I knocked again. I was a fool! They weren't even here.

I jumped back when the door opened and the man in the red

suit and top hat glared at me.

"Hi. I was on the ship earlier this evening…" Not a muscle had moved in his face. "Vada did a trick with my suit jacket. She took it off me, made it explode, but then it was okay." I wondered if he were deaf. "Well, she said I should come by after shopping midnight… I think she said *join*."

He stepped back. "Come in."

It was an invitation, but hardly inviting. Now I wasn't sure this was a good idea. I didn't really know anything about them. They might be planning to rob me or beat me to death just for fun. I stepped inside, my heart hammering in my ears. The house lights were dimmed; the stage was black. Most of the upholstered chairs were stacked to the side. The air smelled of smoke and claustrophobia with a swirl of perfume.

"Sit." Red Hat pointed at one of two chairs near the stage.

As I did so, he closed and bolted the door behind me. He was an inch taller than me and looked muscular. The only weapon I had to defend myself was a tiny pointed pair of scissors in my sewing kit. I wondered if he was Vada's husband, if he was possessive. "Is Vada here?" ·

Leaning against the control board, he took a crumpled purple box from inside his jacket, opened the top, and pointed it toward me. Confused, I shook my head. He shrugged and from the thing extracted what looked like a black bead twice the size of a corn kernel and set it on his tongue. I could hear the hard thing click against his teeth. "So, he hid you?"

Even as I asked, "Who?" I knew he was talking about my father.

Red Hat tossed another black bead into his mouth. "He was a good man."

"The *exploding jacket* went beautifully, didn't it?" Vada stepped before me, in a long red dress and red gloves. The rouge dots on her cheeks and the thick lipstick were gone. She looked both younger and older. "You have to pick someone who has the right sort of jacket. Then it's a matter of cloaking the clothes without the mark noticing." She turned to Red Hat. "We haven't done that in a long time. What has it been? A couple of months?" He just shrugged.

How could she be so casual? "You wanted to see me?"

"Yes, I did." Turning the second chair to face me, she sat. She smelled like some exotic dessert flavored with honey and pepper. Her dark eyes darted toward my hands. "We know you can steal yarn."

"No," I said. "I mean... I don't do that anymore." With a nod toward Red Hat, I asked, "He said something about someone hiding me?"

She glared at Red Hat indignantly. "What are you telling him?"

"Nothing."

She rolled her eyes and then focused on me. "What did your father tell you?"

I glanced from her to him and back again. "What about my dad?"

She smiled. "We knew him. Mark was a special man. A very graceful, intelligent, and prideful man. There aren't so many men like him anymore, don't you think?" She glanced at Red Hat as though to confirm. He ate another candy. She smiled at me. "In the end he fought with us, even if we didn't always realize it. He was one of the most talented men at espionage I've ever met. We'll miss him terribly. And we need your help."

I didn't want to believe that these people could have known my father. I wondered what would happen if I stood to go. "Who are you fighting?"

Smiling sadly, Vada turned to Red Hat. "It's uncanny, isn't it?"

"Eerie," he agreed, with a bored shake of his candy.

I didn't like that they were being so flippant. "What do you want with me? And what do you know about my dad?"

Vada sat straight and seemed to glare at me. "He became one of us." She smiled for an instant, but it quickly faded. "He was a corporate saboteur who was on a mission that happened to be intertwined with our strategies. If you want to know who he was, that's not easy. I'd guess if you talked to those who knew him, you'd never hear the same thing twice. I don't know, maybe that's an exaggeration. But there were probably too many of him for us to know. For us he was a showman, an actor, a con man, and in the end a terrorist."

SEATTLEHAMA: FAR ABOVE EVERYTHING

"Engage," Vada told Red Hat. He had tucked his candy away, stepped before the control board, pushed several buttons, and then pulled a lever. I felt the ship's hook catch a cable, and we started up.

"Where we going?" I asked.

Vada stood. "Tonight," she said, her voice loud as if the ship were full of consumers, "without further compunction, doubts, and delay, we will venture to see both the shimmering highs and the sinister depths of our brilliant and festering world. We will head to the peak of the city, to the night star, where exists *the* boutique and *the* epicenter of shopping, where resides the queen of the epics, the de facto sovereign of Seattlehama: the infamous, dangerous, mysterious, and glorious Miss Bunné!"

That first yarn, the sparkling strand I'd taken from my father's pocket—Kira had said it was from Bunné. I tried to keep the tremor from my voice. "She's one of the big celebs."

"Correction: she's *the* celeb. *The* apex celeb. Seattlehama's mega-celeb."

I played back what she'd said a moment before because I'd never heard her called *Miss Bunné* before. "Are Miss Bunné and M-Bunny related?"

Vada pointed at me as if I had won a prize. "Yes, good customer in the front and back row! Excellent deduction and gastro-molecular computation." Her eyes glowed. "They are, in fact, the very same."

"What does a t'up celeb have to do with the slubs?"

"Ah, the workings, the mechanisms, and the logic. The key and the rhythm of the history and the chronicle!" Vada put her wrist at her forehead and assumed a woeful pose. "How can it all be revealed and explained?"

"Tone it down," complained Red Hat. "You're scaring him."

Vada let her arms drop. "Shut up. We're just having fun."

I glanced between them and despaired. They were definitely a couple.

"*Anyway,*" she said, narrowing her eyes at him. "Yes… it's odd. It's strange, but Bunné runs M-Bunny. She has consolidated her authority and her reach. It's high art and low power. It's a vast and vertically integrated business, and it's her psychosexual playground. The city and the slubs are in fact connected at one deadly fulcrum."

Red Hat peered at his screen and then hurriedly yanked a lever. "I got the master cable!" he crowed. The ship lurched hard. Vada crashed on top of me. I almost tumbled off my chair but managed to stay on and held her up.

"Thanks." Stepping back, she brushed herself off. "Sorry about that." The theater was gone from her voice. She picked up her fallen chair and sat.

Out the windows, I could see that we were moving up at three times the normal speed. I whispered to Vada. "You don't weigh anything."

"My bones are light like a bird's."

"So you *are* genetically patented?"

She smiled as if glad I had remembered the line from her introduction. "I suppose you could say that all the last Toue were."

"Toes?"

"Toue!" she said with ire and amusement. "We're an ancient line from the lost tribe of weavers." Her expression darkened. "Now, we are a dying few."

I figured this was more of her version of warTalk.

"One hundred stories," said Red Hat.

"The Toue were as talented and strong as the fabrics we wove, but we were persecuted for our art and our insular ways. We were thrown from our homeland, and for years lived in the depths of Europa10. Despite the conditions, we produced beautiful fabric, but, sadly, we became more militant, more paranoid, and we lost our way." She glanced at Red Hat, who was concentrating on the controls. "Before the treaty that protected us ran out, the elders tried to create a new breed who would carry on the tradition. We are a part of that sorry lot." She paused for a long, thoughtful beat. "At least that's the official storybook version."

I nodded, but I had gotten lost. "So, you knew my dad?"

Vada spoke in a serious and thoughtful tone. "Mark Tar Octopus was your dad's *nom de fashion.*"

The name sounded ludicrous. "*Mark Tar Octopus?*"

Vada laughed as if she agreed. Red Hat said, "Two hundred."

"Textiles, texturizing, and non-wovens were his original focus. That was before we knew him. Later, he became CEO of a fabric company and changed his name again. I never liked that name or persona." Her mouth shrunk thoughtfully. "He traveled all over the world for his business, and I think it was through the travel that he saw how things truly worked and the desperate imbalances. I'm not sure when it was, but he decided to fight and that's about the time we met him."

Traveled the world? I felt a clenching inside my chest. "I knew him as an M-Bunny rep." Beyond the windows the lights and textures of the buildings sped by.

"Three hundred stories," said Red Hat.

Vada glared at me skeptically. "He could do just about anything he wanted."

This explained why I almost never saw him, but then I remembered when he showed up in the slubs bruised, battered, and covered with Xi rash. "What happened to him?"

Vada seemed reluctant to speak. "For now, let's just say that he tried to assassinate someone and failed. If you'll be patient, the goal of our journey is to help you understand. So a better question is: How many men are recycled in the slubs?"

I couldn't think. I stared out a window as the city raced by and wondered why my father hadn't told me anything? He wasn't just an important M-Bunny rep who traveled to different regions. He was a city man who did all sorts of things. The idea—while impossible—didn't actually surprise me. There had always been something different about him.

"Four hundred stories," announced Red Hat.

In the end, I hadn't known him at all. Maybe my father hadn't liked me, hadn't loved me. Maybe he hadn't thought me worthy. He had left me out in the corn like an unwanted child, an orphan. "He wanted to be recycled for the bonus. He had a Xi rash—I didn't know that—and he wanted me to switch clans. I didn't know about anything else."

"Your dad came to think of recycling as a terrible crime."

"A crime," I repeated. "He wanted it. I wanted to try and cure him, but he fought the whole time. I bought stuff from the COM, but he didn't even want it!"

Vada pursed her mouth sadly.

"I was there when he died... or almost there. He *wanted* to be recycled." I stopped and began to choke. "All he wanted was to help the corn."

"Maybe yes... maybe no." Vada gestured beyond the ship. "In the slubs, corn is put ahead of human life." She bit her bottom lip. "And maybe that is the way to save the world. Or part of the world... or some concept of the world. *Or...* maybe it's just a marketing ploy and a way to rationalize cheap labor." She paused for a moment and looked me over as if unsure she should go on. When she did, her voice was softer. "What I'm saying is that your dad didn't believe that was the way to save the world, that a world like that was worth saving. In fact, he thought it was better to fight against it."

I remembered one of the few days we'd been together, walking through the early summer fields. The corn had been as tall as me. I had looked up and it was as if his eyes had gone gold with the joy of it. He'd seemed more at peace than I had ever seen him. When I spoke, I couldn't stop my voice from vibrating. "He didn't say anything to me."

Vada swallowed. "I know. I am sorry."

"Coming up on seven hundred."

"Shit!" Vada jumped up, and slapped a red-gloved hand on my shoulder. "Give me a boost!" She lifted her chin to the ceiling and I saw a round doorway I hadn't seen before.

"What for?"

"Hurry! You'll see."

I didn't feel like doing anything. I wanted to find some empty corner of the city and unravel. Knitting my fingers together, I bent my legs, and when Vada put one of her red-booted feet in my hands and stepped up, she was like a bird in my arms. Balancing with a hand on top of my head, she stepped up onto my shoulders. For a moment I was inside the hush of her long red dress. The smell was of honey and musk. Her stockinged legs were patterned with the lacy octagons of the city's towers.

Her hips twisted to the left and she grunted as she worked them. I peeked up at her crotch. There, held in with two small straps, was a gleaming pair of silver scissors with three-inch blades. I felt afraid of and for her.

She lifted herself through the opening onto the roof and turned to peer at me as the wind tussled her hair and dress. "Stand on a chair. I'll help you up."

I was still caught in the weave of desire and fear I'd found in the curtain of her dress. Was she going to cut me up there? Was I really safe? I stepped onto my chair. Vada reached down, I, up. Grasping my wrist, she pulled me up onto the roof of the ship with one arm as if I were the one who weighed nothing.

Outside the plush interior of the entervator, I suddenly felt every inner chill made real on my skin. It was like being thrust from the womb. The ship wasn't moving up anymore, but was gently rocking back and forth.

"Hold on!" The wind quickly whisked away her words.

Circling the roof portal and the cable mechanism was a thin metal guardrail. I grabbed at the icy metal, unmoored. From here we could see the rooftops, the points, the spires, and the antennas of the other buildings. Leaning forward, I peered over the edge of the Europa. It was like looking down the lit barrel of a gigantic cannon. All lines focused on the wide atrium a mile below. Beyond the buildings the rest of the word was black. I shivered and imagined myself falling—spinning back down to earth for hours.

Above us loomed only one tower—Bunné's, which was called The Zea. I could see the edge of the enormous open-air amphitheater atop the high rise.

I turned to Vada. "It's amazing!"

She grinned. "Scary, right?"

"Yes."

Vada glanced to her right. The air fluttered her hair. "The wind tonight makes this a little more dangerous to navigate, but I think we'll be fine."

I glanced up at the Zea. I thought I heard sounds coming from the top of the building—the cheering of a crowd and the hammer of a party beat. It suddenly seemed a horrible distortion—the music of my suicide. I wanted desperately to return to Pilla, to the simple chains of her expectations.

A strange smile passed Vada's face, and she shouted, "We're ready!" down the porthole.

The lights inside the entervator shut off one by one. It felt like the two of us were floating in space.

"Go ahead!" came Red Hat's reply. "Release."

My heart stopped, but I knew he could not mean *release* the ship. "What are we doing?" As if to answer, Vada pressed her cheek to mine. Her skin was soft and warm. As I pulled her toward me I realized she had extended her right arm behind my head. Turning I saw that her gloved hand gripping a thick brass lever connected to the cable hook.

"Ready?" Without waiting for an answer, she cranked the lever to the right.

With a ratcheting sound, the hook opened. The cable seemed to shoot up into the darkness as the ship began to plummet. Vada's dress blew up into our faces, a fluttering tulip. Every corpuscle in my body screamed *No!*

IN THE SHADOW

As I sped forward, across the elevated highway of the plains, far above the simmering fields of corn and soy, over the heads of the millions of dirt-covered men tending those hybridized stalks, the tops of the towers came into view hundreds of miles before I had to start braking. "You're sure?"

"It's just outside of the old Seattlehama perimeter," said Pheff. "Its called Royal NuSity Estates. He's in Tower 23, forty-first floor. Apartment E." After a beat, he added, "The place looks awful. Knit aluminum towers, doublewide moon balconies, watervators, and every other semi-modern cliché of super-luxury 'rises. Who is this guy?"

I had not been back to Seattlehama since my days of thread thievery and skivvé knitting. "I'm just following a lead."

"I thought you were going to see Ryder?"

"I did. Now I'm checking here."

"Way out in Seattlehama?"

"Seattlehama has a burgeoning local textiles industry."

"Not really. Have you ever been there?"

"Years ago."

"That's so knotted! Did you get all dressed and… you know?"

"I did, but I'll tell you about it another time."

The city was ten times larger than it had been. Originally the project had been the brainchild of a particle theorist and singer named Zika Emerald. She spent her fortune on building an enormous four-mile-wide foundation around Mt. Rainier and *fourteen buildings that made the original core. But she had died a week before the final tower was topped, and by that point, she and the project were bankrupt. A few years later several rim cities joined together to rescue the project and transformed it into a sex and fashion tourism destination. As a slubber boy, gazing up at the structures, I had no idea of the politics, money, and lust that went on in there, not that I would have understood.*

As the Chang sped closer, I saw how Seattlehama had changed in my absence. The city had been towering and thin, an awe-inspiring monolith. Now the original towers were lost in a garden of thistle, monocot, and dandelion buildings.

As the exit ramp curved hard to the right, I caught a glimpse beyond the guard walls of the slubs surrounding the new city limits. I couldn't help but wonder if some boy were out there, in the cornfields, looking up at the colossal mass of this new Seattlehama, and maybe even at the red and blue lights of my car and wondering who and what was up there.

The road straightened, as I set a course for the secluded Royal NuSity Estates. I wished I hadn't come back.

As I passed the city center, glancing through the star roof of the Chang at the cloud-shrouded towers, I could feel the crystalline memories of my youth shattering like glass.

SEATTLEHAMA: FALLING FOREVER

The muscles in my hands and arms felt so rigid, I was less afraid that I might let go of the rail than they would snap like plasticott under the strain. Below I could hear Red Hat shouting, but his words whipped away in the wind.

"We're dead!" I screamed.

"We're on a voyage," was Vada's reply, her lips against my ear.

We plummeted straight down. The buildings became elongated blurs as the air whistled past. In one instant, I saw our eventual impact—the sprained metal and shattered wood, the crushed bones and soupy aftermath of my organs. Then I remembered all the wires and cables woven between the buildings. We would be sliced into hundreds of pieces.

The ship's motion changed, tilting and gliding forward, rather than down. The weightless terror of freefall receded and the metal hull once again sat solidly beneath my feet.

I felt the cream of Vada's lipstick on my ear as much as I heard her words. "And now, ladies and gentlemen, I'd like to introduce you to the majesty of illegal flight craft!"

We crossed the empty middle of the city, heading straight for the tops of the buildings on the other side. And just as I thought we were going to crash, the ship turned and darted between the Velour and Foulé. As we rushed past the two intricate spires, I swore I saw the distorted silhouettes of writhing consumers inside. And then, with a whoosh of turbulence, we sailed past the city's edge. Turning, I saw the glowing architecture of the city receding behind us, as I struggled to swallow my fear.

"We should get inside!" said Vada. "We're going to be landing soon."

I didn't want to let go of the rail, but she grasped my arm and led me to the portal. A dim glow illuminated the interior. I lowered myself down, trying to land on the chair I had used to climb up, but my left foot missed, and I fell in a heap onto the purple carpet. I was shaken, cold, and furious.

"What are we doing?" I asked as Vada landed beside me. "Where the rot are we going? I don't want to leave the city!"

"Close the hatch now!" called Red Hat.

Vada looked at me. "Another boost."

I didn't move.

"We'll be going back to the city tomorrow."

I knotted my fingers together and she stepped up. Again I was inside the red atmosphere of her dress, her stocking-covered legs framing my face. Above I heard a clank of metal and I glanced up. Of course all I saw was the crotch of her stockings and that small pair of silver shears.

Vada jumped back down, smoothed her dress, and smiled at me.

"Why do you have scissors down there?"

She frowned playfully and whapped my shoulder. "I can't believe you looked!"

She smiled so invitingly, I knew I hadn't imagined her interest. I stepped toward her, and placed a hand on her waist as I had done on the roof. She raised an eyebrow, amused. I started to move closer.

"Slow down!" She pushed me back and glanced at Red Hat hunched over the lit screen. "Not here!"

As if on cue, he said, "Landing in two minutes."

The touchdown was closer to a crash. The ship hit and then pitched so far forward I tumbled into the wall, and half the chairs came crashing down on me.

"Muddy shit," muttered our pilot as a curse or an excuse.

When the main door opened, Vada and I stepped out into squishing mire. Dawn was beginning to temper the eastern sky. The smell of corn, dirt, and a hint of solid recycle felt like a time capsule of memories.

I shivered. "I don't want to be here."

"No one does." Vada glanced around, taking the measure of her surroundings.

Intricate cloth wings were slowly folding into the sides of the ship. "So that's how it flies."

"Wings are as illegal as all untethered transportation. But we specialize in illegal." She barked in laughter and waved a gloved hand. "Come."

"Why are we here?"

She faced me. "You want to understand a little more about what we're fighting against? I know you were born in the slubs, but that doesn't mean you really know what they're about. We're going to see one of the things your father hated." She pulled up her dress a foot and started walking. Her boots sank into the sucking mud. I followed, not sure I wanted to. Eventually, the mud gave way to firmer ground, and soon we were in rows of corn three feet high.

A quarter of a mile later, we came up over a hill, and upon a large complex of low buildings, the largest of which was three stories tall and dotted with red and white blinking lights. At a wire fence, which surrounded the place, Vada reached under her dress and used those scissors to cut through the metal like it was cold fat.

"Stay close to me."

"What is this?"

"M-Bunny headquarters."

I glanced at the structures. This is where men went to have sons and this is where everyone went to be recycled. I backed up a step. "I'm not going."

"I'm coming with you. We'll be safe; we have a sympathizer here."

"I know what's here."

"You haven't been inside, have you?"

No slubbers I knew worked at headquarters. Some men drove buses to and fro, but they weren't allowed inside. That's just how it had been. We didn't question it. Frankly, unless one was chosen to have a son, most slubbers didn't want anything to do with the place.

I stared at the facility. I had imagined it consisted of recycled building. All the houses I had lived in were two-hundred-year-old structures stripped of their appliances, plumbing, wiring, and most of their interior. So too, all the factories were housed in former schools, fast-food places, and shopping centers. This building was made of corrugated metal walls and had electric lights. From the top a few slanted puffs of steam or smoke drifted into the morning air. "Is this new?"

Vada's face crinkled in confusion. "No. It's been here for about fifteen… almost twenty years."

I didn't want to say it. The muscles in my throat fought me, but I got it out. "They took him here."

Vada frowned. "I know."

The roughness in her voice made me feel worse. "I already hate M-Bunny."

A sad smile flitted across her face. "Good," she whispered.

When I reached toward her, she gently clasped her fingers around mine.

SLUBS: M-BUNNY HEADQUARTERS

A man opened the door. His face and hands were caked with dirt and what I soon realized were blood and bits of flesh. The front of his B-shirt was so encrusted that the slogan had long been obliterated. The material across his belly, under his arms, was cracking like dried mud. The hollow emptiness of his eyes didn't seem to connect to anything human. They were two fleshy cameras processing lights and darks, identifying corn, food, cola, and things to recycle.

"You gotta change," was the first thing he said. I heard the sloppy, guttural accent that I had lost by then. As he showed us to a corner where B-shirts and shorts hung from pegs, Vada and I glanced at each other. She smiled and raised her eyebrows in a casual if fretful *well, here we are* kind of way.

The place smelled mostly like solid recycle, but there were notes of rust and salt. And swirling in the air were what seemed like a dozen different sounds: the harmonic and enharmonic whine of several motors, soft thuds, wet splashes, and occasionally what sounded like distant gun shots.

I took off my jacket, hung it, unbuttoned my shirt, released the cuff locks, and unbarred it from my foundation. Next I released the tension hook on my pants and slid them down my legs. Finally, I stood in my chemise, socks, and briefs, reluctant to continue. Pinching the B-shirt that hung before me between my thumb and index, I held it up, and grimaced at Vada.

"I know." She was pulling on a pair of near-black shorts over her tan stockings.

It hadn't occurred to me that I could leave on my foundation, but I decided to do the same. Sniffing the shirt, its pungent sweat and sewage odor, made me sick. When I was a slubber, my B-shirts had been dirty, but I didn't think they were this bad. I pulled up the shorts up over my briefs and then stood there, afraid to move. Vada and I looked at each and grimaced.

"This way," said our guide.

As we followed, I whispered to Vada. "Who is he?"

"A recruit for the opposition."

We walked past large metal vats darkened by years of splatters and drips. Here and there the uneven floor was covered with puddles. Some smelled like chemicals; others, salty meat.

Following the guide up a set of stairs, we got a view of the whole place. It was easily two hundred yards long and half as wide. From translucent squares in the ceiling, parallel blocks of light dappled the machinery and men in a checkerboard.

"They come in here," began our guide, raising his voice over the din as a large garage door began to open at the far end. Through it, I could see blacktop and a triangle of nearby corn. "They come on the buses." As he spoke, several slubbers began to wander into the door where a couple of workers greeted them.

"We give them a special M-Bunny cola. It stuns them. We call it Blue, because it's sort of bluish." He shrugged. "I mean the syrup is." Frowning, he finished, "Let's go down."

From the platform, he led us through a maze of machines, conveyers, and holding pens. Two dozen men now stood just inside the garage door. Some were looking around, but most stared down at their feet with what seemed like a sad resolve. A worker passed out plastic cups. "Proud day," he told each of the men. "Proud day for M-Bunny."

"It stuns them," whispered our guide. "I've tried it. It's good. Real syrup."

The slubbers were then instructed to take off their clothes. "Final recycle. Final recycle!" was the call.

In the middle of the group, I saw a man with sorrowful eyes and a long nose. I shouted, "Rik!"

He gazed at me for a beat. His brown eyes seemed distant and faded.

"It's me, Tane."

Rik had been my best friend. I hadn't seen him for two years, but he seemed to have aged ten. As he came toward the link fence that separated us, I saw that his right hand was crusted with blood and dripping puss. The smell made me gag.

He studied my face and my hair. "Where have you been?"

I didn't know how to answer. I just shrugged and glanced at his hand. "You injured?"

He nodded slowly. "I cut it digging up asphalt. That black tar isn't good for the crop, and it isn't good for the earth." He looked at his rotting fingers. "I tried the pest gum and the corn salve, nothing worked." His voice was calm and his eyes were filled with acceptance.

"That's not so bad, Rik. That can be healed."

He smiled at me and began to recite one of the M-Bunny's songs. "*Our earth… we cherish you. And today as the day before, we have tried to help you.*"

"Rik, listen to me!"

"*We hope you can feel the souls of our feet, the way we walk with modesty upon you and the way we use only that of you we need. And corn… the eyes… the life… and the ears of our earth, we tend to you. We nurture you… we feed and water you with ourselves… we honor you and we ask that you grow strong and recycle our love.*"

When we were young we tended the corn together. I had admired how gentle and nurturing he was with the crop. "You don't have to recycle yourself for that. They can cure your hand."

"*They?*" He looked me up and down. "You live in the city?"

"It's good there. It's different, but it's a million times better."

He scowled at me. "Are you a t'up now?"

I didn't know if I really was or not. "Rik… they can fix your hand." I looked at Vada to confirm, but she had turned the other way, as if to give me privacy.

Rik shook his head. "It's time to recycle."

"Remember the rash my dad had? It wasn't anything. Remember I spit the gum juice on him? It wasn't a rot or smut." I could see that Rik didn't understand or believe. "Really, they can fix your hand! It's not worth recycling."

"I missed you." He smiled. "I was sorry they traded you away." Now he frowned. "I tried to be your friend, but maybe you weren't meant for the corn. I remember you fixing shirts like they weren't good enough." With a shrug, he finished: "We're all just kernels of corn. One isn't better than the other."

One of the workers shouted for Rik, "Over here!"

"He's coming with us," I told Vada.

Vada smiled stiffly.

"He was my best friend," I told her. "He really knows the corn." As I spoke, I could see what I imagined was a tinge of confusion and even disdain in her eyes. Like all city people, she could not really understand the beauty of corn, dirt, and wide skies. "But they can fix him, can't they? It's just his hand."

"Not allowed," said our guide.

Ahead of Rik, several nude men had lined up. A worker nearby held a pneumatic gun attached to a machine. The gunner had a long face with drooping eyes. If I had seen him in another context, I might have described his expression as serene. "You won't feel nothing," he said.

"You are all helping the corn and M-Bunny," shouted the other worker, now collecting the cups. "Good work!" he said to one of the naked men, who gulped down the last of his Blue cola.

The gunner raised the blackened device toward the first man's head. For an instant, the man peered up at the end with confusion and maybe awe. With slow, deliberate motions the gunner then pressed it to the man's forehead, and held it there as if to let him get used to its temperature.

Run, I thought. Turn and run!

Nothing moved for a beat. Sound ebbed away until a staccato but muffled pop came from the pneumatic gun. The man jerked, his legs, spine, and neck going soft. Before he collapsed, the gunner set a hook through the bottom of his jaw attached to a chain that carried the body up and into the workings of the factory.

"The bolt kills them without pain," said our guide. "The conveyer takes them up to the de-boners. Bones are used for one thing... flesh for another." He shrugged. "Different levels of toxins from the pollution. It's all sorted."

"You won't feel nothing," repeated the gunner as the next man stepped up.

Rik started to turn.

"Wait!" I said grabbing the chain link between us. "There's a whole world beyond the corn. It's not like they told us, Rik. It's unlike anything you can imagine."

"The corn had such hopes for you." He eyed Vada for a confused moment—she was surely the first woman he had ever seen. "The crop is good." Rik nodded at me as if he were the one who understood. "Goodbye, Tane."

"Rik! Stop." I turned to our guide. "How much?" I dug out my MasterCut from a pocket on my foundation.

He laughed and shook his head. "I'd like to take your money."

"Rik, stop! Hold on!" To the guide I asked, "How much? I'll pay!"

Rik tugged his B-shirt up and over his chest and head. "I don't want that, Tane. I love the corn." His belly was distended. The skin was smooth, almost as if it had been burnished to a shine. I didn't know was wrong, but figured a simple dose of something from the city would cure it, too.

"Rik, hold on! Listen to me! It's not what you think. It's killing!

M-Bunny is just killing you like they killed my dad!"

"They are recycled," refuted the guide. "Everything is reused."

"Rik!" I screamed. "I know the corn. I know what it is. I love it, but it's not everything! There are other things... there are other worlds." Now he wouldn't even turn around and look at me. I smashed my fists into the fence. It rattled and wobbled. "Rik listen to me!"

"Don't knock that!"

I turned to the guide, my hand raised. Vada stepped before me.

"Tane," she said coolly and softly. "I'm sorry."

What are the chemical and mechanical processes that cause one's throat to tighten, eyes to water, and chest to harden like cement?

The pneumatic gun fired again. Now there were only two ahead of Rik. He stood with his back straight and his chin high as if to prove his righteousness.

Something came halfway up my throat before I could choke it back down. "Let's get out of here," I told Vada.

She stroked my shoulder, and said to the guide, "His dad was recycled."

"No," I told her. "He had a rash. M-Bunny took him."

"For smuts and rots... that's called a cultivation," said the guide, as the gun discharged.

"It was a Xi rash," I screamed at him. "No one in the slubs knew what the hell it was! It was nothing. He died for nothing."

The man frowned and pointed past me. "Cultivation is on the other side of the building." The gun fired again. "I can show you."

I had to get away. I turned and started walking. We passed large dirty machines that chugged and rattled so loudly I couldn't hear Vada or the guide. The hot air smelled terrible and I thought I was going to vomit.

We stopped in a clearing of machinery. "Those are the

incubators." The guide was pointing to a row of what looked like portable enterjohns. One was being washed out by a man wearing a soiled non-woven mask over his mouth and nose.

And then, above the noise, I heard the gun clearly. Rik. I stopped. Water swelled in my eyes and my throat seemed to shut. Years ago, when we were only half as tall as the mature corn, we had pretended to be men together. We had pulled clumps of silk from the ears and stuck it on our faces to make mustaches, laughing when it fell off.

Vada stepped beside me. "I'm sorry. I had no idea we would see someone you knew."

Wiping my eyes, I wanted to turn and run, but I couldn't even speak, my windpipe was so taut.

The guide was going on about how long the sick men were kept in the boxes, what they were fed, and how the germs were harvested if they got worse.

Before I knew it, the tour was done and Vada and I stood outside again in the dry swirling heat. The sky was impossibly bright and the corn leaves reflected the sun like mirrors. Closing my eyes for a few moments, I exhaled all the way, trying to empty my lungs of the bitter factory air. I could hear Vada beside me still fastening her clothes.

"I hate this place." I squinted at the undulating leaves. "It should be destroyed. This shouldn't exist. I mean all of this... the corn... the men... the reps! And this damn building! It's all a huge lie, and I used to believe it. I used to think that the cities were the problem and that we were saving the world. I loved the corn and thought it was better than people."

Vada closed the last button at her neck and nodded. "This is a nightmare created by Bunné. There are fifty other buildings like this. She has to be stopped."

I could have ended up exactly like Rik. If my father hadn't found me, and if I hadn't taken that yarn from him, I would have eventually walked into the recycling center beside Rick, proud and ready. I had eaten Miss Bunné's EcoDogs, her KobNockers, her TakoDrops, and drunk her colas. I had worn her awful B-shirts and shorts. And most of all, I had believed the promise of M-Bunny's vision: of her sweet corn, of her reclaimed land, of her quiet and gentle men, of the stinging, beautiful smell of her pollen drop.

Vada looked up. "We need to get back to the Europa."

SEATTLEHAMA: FIRST GLIMPSE OF THE INCOMPARABLE SUPREME CELEB: MISS BUNNÉ AND A BLUE MINI-T

Once I knew what to look for in Seattlehama, I began to see Miss Bunné's influence everywhere. She hadn't just influenced Kira, her warTalk, and her skivvé. While Miss Bunné's face wasn't as ubiquitous as Tinyko 200, Elodi, or Strawberry Five, I learned that all songs, dance, and stories were *cloth woven with Bunné yarn*. If it didn't reference her, it didn't exist. She was language; the rest, merely words.

I watched clips of her epics from popular surveillance. The sapphire of Seattlehama was a tall, beautiful woman with sharp cheekbones, green eyes, and a wide, pouting mouth. Some said she was just eighteen, others speculated that she was closer to one hundred and eighteen. To me, she looked like she might be in her early forties with hints of age around her eyes and mouth. Sometimes her hair glittered chrome, others a rich neon black, others a glowing isotope red. And as malleable was her hair, so were her mannerisms, and from what I could tell, her personality. Sometimes she was demure and shy; her head tilted slightly to the side and her eyelids fluttering like moth wings. Other times her eyes glowed with fury, bright beams in the night.

Her epics, *Wicked Lover Coma Dancer, Sweet Way Surgery Duo*—and her biggest—*Sensitive Dead Penisless Boys* were violent, heroic happening/dramas that always began with her in distress only to be saved by her real-life love interest. They included impossible feats of group fighting, syrupy songs, speeches, elaborate dance numbers with thousands of participants, grotesque sex scenes, and long talks about her philosophy, opinions, and shopping experiences.

During my times in Seattlehama I rarely heard anything but admiration for her, so it wasn't until years later that I heard rumors about her shadowy underworld origins, immorally auctioned egg-splits, her influence on the Xi yarn factories, the reports of killing squads, and the massive corruption of her corporation.

After returning to the city, still shaken and angry, I headed back to Pilla's bedroom thinking she would be concerned. Instead she was furious.

"Where were you?" she demanded. "You didn't even show up at the haberdashery! I looked all over!"

"I was shopping."

She stepped closer. "After your work, come straight here. No more shopping for you. Understand?"

"Zanella told me to study women's clothes."

"The only women's clothes you will study will be my Pearl Rivers."

I laughed at her. "You don't own me."

Pilla scowled at me. "You shouldn't be walking around the city like you are! Trust me, get a makeover. Dress like some epic character."

I snorted. "Like who? Rose Farmer Soundless Assassin?" I had tailored a Rose Farmer at YeOld#1, and recalled the elaborate and absurd petal-covered mask.

"No assassins! Get something good. Do you understand? I thought you were dead! I had no idea what happened. You must be careful!"

Guilty, imagining her running down hallways shouting my name, I wondered if she was afraid of Withor or his yarn rippers finding me. I didn't dare tell her that I'd run into Vit.

"I'll tell the haberdashery you're going to be another couple of hours." Before she headed to the Xi boutique, she dropped me off at a salon near her place and, for the next hour, I sat in an enterchair while my hair was bleached and lengthened and my eyes darkened. I was then dressed as epic character Fleece Swansdown from *Super Cut Powder Boys* in a layered blonde suit and a floor-length gulix jacket.

When I arrived at the haberdashery the saleswarrior in charge just shrugged and pointed me toward the design room. Inside, I found a jumble of weaving machinery, design equipment, shirts, stays, handkerchiefs, belts, ties, and cufflinks across the floor.

"You the new one?" asked an old warrior, sitting at a sewing machine. "Start straightening up."

"What happened?"

"Attempted hostile takeover."

For hours I silently picked, sorted, and stacked up the stuff from the floor while the old warrior scowled. I hated the job, but didn't care as all I could think about was heading up to the top of the city to see Bunné's Boutique.

When the store closed, the warrior grunted, "Be on time tomorrow."

I nodded on my way out. From the store, I raced out to the nearest entervator port, boarded the Ring Bell, and headed up to floor 999 of The Zea Building.

While the entertainers in the Ring Bell, dressed as decapitated cats, danced and fought with long, sharp claws, I wondered what I would find, but assumed it would be like the usual Seattlehama store with lots of empty space, loud, live music, soulless saleswarriors, and dresses, parasols, fleck shoes.

It still seemed impossible that the M-Bunny I knew, the one of suffering, and corn, could be the same powerful celebrity whose boutique capped the city I had gazed up at from the crop so many times.

It took thirty-five minutes to reach floor 999. The pure white port was nearly empty and the platinum-floored shopways weren't crowded with the usual hordes. Only a few shoppers strutted here and there and they wore real and elaborate costumes—not the rented junk from places like YeOld#1CostumeShoppee.

A saleswarrior loosely wrapped in black ribbon stood before a shop with a pearl and smoke entrance. She looked me up and down with disdain and then opened her mouth wide. Instead of teeth and a tongue, hers was filled with whirring gears and spindles. What that was, what it meant, I didn't know. Clearly, the top of the Zea was different.

At the end of a cul-de-sac, I came to the entrance to Boutique Bunné. From the outside, it looked like an average store decorated in midnight blues with an array of light jets weaving patterns, but once I stepped past the muttering saleswarriors, the place expanded. Inside, the boutique was hundreds of tinted-glass-floors high, spider webbed by a network of miniature entervators fluttering up and down. Directly above, on the roof, I could see an enormous open-air atrium filled with consumers.

A saleswarrior in a sky-blue jacket, with short black hair and pyrite eyes, stepped before me. "The tides of darkness, shopper Fleece Swansdown. I am your heart and credit. You will surrender with me before the ornaments of happiness and liberty." Shiny leather boots rose to her hirsute crotch. The heels were as sharp as pins. "One hour…" she said, as red numbers flashed inside the black beads of her choker. "If I have not assisted your material freedom and truth, the necklace will cut my air."

"I'm just looking."

She closed her eyes and when she reopened them the beads on her necklace flickered to 59:99:99, and began counting down. "Our shopping has begun. My death has a moment and time." She eyed me and smiled. "My life remaining is all to help you."

I glanced at the other customers and the other saleswarriors and wondered if I could get away from her. "I'm not here to buy anything."

"My breath is but interest on tomorrow." Two more saleswarriors came toward us. Necklace introduced both, but I didn't get their complicated names and titles. One held an IMG wand; the other had on an antenna jacket and was writing in the air. "They will document our journey, our trials, and our success."

"I'm just looking," I repeated with a sigh. "I'm just curious about Bunné."

She shook her head slowly. "Souvenir is memory."

The warrior with the wand flashed us with light. Covering my face, I said, "No, I just came to look!"

"Come," said Necklace with a bow. "I will show you the true universe of Bunné."

Reluctantly, I squeezed into one of the small entervators with them. Necklace whisked us to another floor, and the doors opened on a circular showroom where dresses, slacks, and blouses hung suspended in the air. The space was silent, the air sweet and cool, and as I stepped out, I could see that the garments were incredible. Each yarn, each stitch, each pleat, each button was in proportion and rhythm. I stopped before a simple blue skirt.

The yarn was some incredibly high-twist satellite wool, deeply saturated, and while it was nothing more than simple twill it was gorgeous and fine. When I touched it, I found it as warm and supple as the side of a woman's neck. The drape was absolutely true. The two darts, the waistband, the single small button on the side closure were all refined and perfectly in balance with the whole. And the topstitching around the waist was pure music, for somehow Bunné had sewn on the beat of the cloth, that is, each stitch fell the same exact number of yarns from the last.

I found more garments with ingenious refinements, luxurious fabrics, and stitches metered in perfect harmony. And as much as I had admired the workmanship of the skivvé saleswarriors, Kira included, and the geometry and details of Zanella's jackets, Bunné's creations stirred me in a way I could not describe.

From there, Necklace took us to another showroom, where I considered the hems on Bunné's jackets, the finishes on her foundation garments, and the weave of her six-million-count broadcloth. I was in awe. Her ideas were incredible, her technique, faultless, and the execution, complete.

"This is astonishing," I told Necklace. "I've been studying fashion, but her things… are perfection. They're ideals, like pure forms somehow transformed into real yarn. It's like I'm seeing truth for the first time." I gazed into the saleswarrior's blank eyes and saw my own reflection and my own dreams. I was meant to find this. "The way she cuts and sews is exactly right." Images of wrinkled landscapes, grids, and rhythms of my youth came to me. "This is what I dreamed."

Necklace's sharp eyebrows dipped suspiciously as the other two furiously documented what I had said. "You see beyond the bag and beyond the credit," she whispered. With a bow, she added, "It's an honor to shop with you."

On another floor she showed me Bunné's miniatures: tiny hats suitable for a thumb, shirts that could lay flat on a palm, and slacks that fit two fingers. "We sell a thousand times our hot couture in minis."

And in fact this floor was filled with customers mixing and matching little shoes with dresses and handbags, but I wasn't impressed. These had none of the artistry of her real clothes. The materials seemed stiff and cheap; the sewing was haphazard, and while they were cute, they weren't at all the same objects of art.

I asked the saleswarrior to take me back to the couture floors, but at the end of the hallway, before we came to another mini-entervator bank, I saw a simple blue T-shirt in a large gilt frame. On the front in precise embroidery it read: *Whisper in My Ear.* I stopped and gazed at the shirt for a long time. In the slubs, our shirts had slogans sloppily printed with some rubbery-smelling off-white paste that attracted dirt and were usually unreadable in two weeks: *Rows of Love, I Heart Fructose, Drop the Pollen, I P Golden, Future Fertilizer.* Most slubbers didn't even know what they meant.

Staring at this perfect shirt, its micro-ribbed collar, triple-core shoulder seam, full-fashion sleeves, and hand-rolled picked hem, I couldn't believe that the thing existed. It was an affront. It mocked the non-woven ones I, and millions of others, had to wear.

"What is this?"

"A micro-denier satellite water-cotton slogan T."

"No! Why is it here?"

"It's just on display."

"I had to wear the opposite, recycle version of that for nineteen years. Why couldn't she even make a good neck hole? She knows everything about clothes. She could have done it perfectly!"

The three of them stared at me.

"Why does she hate me?"

"She hates no one," Necklace replied with a shake of her head.

"Where is she?" I looked around. "Where is Bunné? I can't understand why she made those B-shirts so terrible."

"Bunné is above." She pointed toward the barely visible amphitheatre above our heads. "Tonight is an egg-split coronation."

Somewhere I'd heard *egg-splits.* "What is that?"

"Only royal coronal customers can obtain the chance to offspring with a split of one of Bunné's queenly eggs."

The idea seemed repulsive. "Who wants that?"

Necklace stared at me blankly. "*Her* heart, *her* mind, *her* flesh is the ultimate product."

"She's up there? I want to see her!"

The numbers in the saleswarrior's necklace began emitting a tiny chirp. "Less than four minutes left," she said.

"I told you, I'm not buying anything! Just take me to Bunné."

She smiled a wan smile. "You *want* what Miss Bunné has made for you."

"She has never made anything for me!" I looked up at the shirt. I wanted to break the glass, tear that thing down, and rip it to shreds.

"Once you buy *it*," said Necklace, "you *will* know. You *will* understand."

I laughed at her. "You can't understand. Have you ever seen her non-woven shirts? The ones she sells in the slubs? They're horrible. I tried to fix them, but they're the worst things ever made."

"She made something for you. For you alone." Necklace spoke the way one would to a child, and then she headed toward another entervator bank.

"What did she make me?"

"Your shopping destiny awaits."

She wasn't going to take me to Bunné or anything else real. I'd seen her stuff, and it was time to leave. Necklace held the door to the small entervator for me as the numbers in her necklace ticked down. At first her gaze was the empty stare of the Seattlehama saleswarrior, but then her lips tightened, her complexion paled, and the liquid in her eyes trembled. She said, "Please," with feeling and urgency.

This was a mistake, I thought, as IMG and the writer followed me into the mini-entervator. Necklace touched a lit button and we were whisked upward. The beads on her necklace read 0:55. She yanked a lever and the doors slid open to a small, empty room. Straight ahead was a counter. On a square of black velvet sat a beautifully crafted, blue mini-T, barely three inches tall, with the words *Bunné Hurts* perfectly embroidered in silver thread.

"This?" I wanted to laugh. "This is what I'm supposed to buy? *She* hurts? This is smut! It's complete rot!"

The numbers on the saleswarrior's necklace blinked 0:00. She tried to grip the strand, pull it away as the thing was tightened, but she couldn't get her fingers under it. She was choking. Tears streamed from her eyes.

"The moment!" said the IMG saleswarrior as she splashed us with light.

I tried to break the necklace, but it was too strong. I looked for a latch, but it didn't have one. The beads were sinking into her flesh. Her face was white.

"Do something!" I screamed at IMG. She just flickered her light at me as the other drew frantic descriptions in the air.

Necklace collapsed in my arms. Her body felt heavy and limp, but her lips moved. I pressed my ear to her mouth and heard, "Buy... the... T."

I glanced up at the counter. "Okay!" I shouted. "I'll take it!"

The necklace expanded instantly. The saleswarrior gasped for breath.

YARN JOBBER

O n the large sign at the complex entrance of NuSity, I saw that someone had graffitied it into NuShitty. From the lurid colors, the painful smiles of the model family lounging in a living room with over-stuffed purple furniture and the requisite explicit acrylics on the walls, I could tell that the anonymous speller no doubt had it right. Beyond the sign, I passed an out-of-order security hut, and as I followed lights to the parking, a woman came jogging toward me. While I wondered if she were some guard, with her lilac and black thong-back gown and roller sleeves, she looked more like the half-naked muchacha-ko warriors that Pheff might have wished for.

I scrolled the window.

She leaned against the Chang, attempted a smile, and asked, "You want to touch some bias-cut charmeuse?" While she looked like she might be only twenty-two, her voice was as rough as the back of that fabric would be.

"No thanks." The oldest and second oldest professions: prostitution and weaving—a potent duo.

The crumbling parking pavilion housed an assortment of dented and elderly Karmans, Pips, and even a few of those cheap one-wheeled Bolbos that I doubted were street legal. I parked and started toward the towers.

The air was warmer here and, despite the blocks of bright sunshine between the close-set rocket-shaped towers, smelled of mildew and mold. In the building's shabby lobby, a sign announced *that the watervator was out of service. Inside the open doors of the people mover, a fat man in ratty overalls lay snoring. Back outside, I squinted up into the glare. No entervators connected the buildings, so the only way up was the external stairs that circled the moon decks.*

After twenty floors, I stopped to catch my breath and wipe my brow with an oxygenated cloth. What stuck me about this development, besides the decay—the long streaks of white oxidation on the metal-skinned towers and the aesthetic sabotage of the bright and haphazard piles of junk on the decks—was the lack of occupants. On several floors I heard the thump of music and the drama of amplified voices, but I hadn't yet seen anyone going up or down.

Then I saw a woman in tight stretch step out to the deck of the next building three stories above. She flopped a neon yellow rug over the rail, and raised a large wooden fork. Then she noticed me. Although she was haloed in glare, I could see her face clicking through several emotions, like a gun barrel rouletting past empty chambers, before ending up with a wide smile—accompanied by a preening tug of her top and twirl of the fork.

When I shrugged, she beat her rug, sending a cloud of dust and debris toward the ground. I continued my climb.

My legs ached when I got to the forty-first floor. There I found apartment E surrounded by piles of boxes. On the door, crucified with wide swatches of tape, was a yellowed business card reading CeeCee Textiles, Zoom Langsin.

It seemed to me that behind this door stood a terrifying absolute edge and end of the fashion world. My knock produced a hollow pot-metal sound. After a beat of silence, I knocked again, more forcefully. "Hello? I'm looking for Mr. Zoom Langsin." Cocking my right ear toward the door, the way a robin might listen for a worm, I heard what sounded like shuffling and desperate whispers.

I tensed and imagined several men with weapons. Ryder had called ahead to warn them! I backed up a step, waited, but nothing happened.

"Zoom? It's Tane Cedar, men's precision tailor." I heard nothing. "I just want to speak." After a beat I upped my offer. "I want to buy some yarn!"

"Go away!" It was a woman's voice. Was Zoom a woman?

"This could be lucrative."

"I'm not open!" Now a man spoke. "Come back tomorrow!"

"Zoom, can we talk for a few moments?"

"I'm not open!"

"Please. Just a few minutes." I heard no reply. I knocked again. "Ryder sent me. He said you're the best." I could picture the two of them in there, standing still, their eyes locked as they listened. "Zoom! I need a specialty yarn! I'm willing to over-pay."

No answer. What was wrong with him? He lived in this rotting tower and yet seemed happy to ignore a begging customer.

"Zoom! What is going on? I need the yarn! Speak to me at least." Met by more silence, I beat on his door angrily. "If you don't open this, I will!"

This was more than just the Xi. This was basic civility. He couldn't even crack the door and tell me to go sew myself? From inside my jacket, I pulled out the stitched black-polyoxide case for the water-shears and opened it. The golden device looked much like a pair of non-powered shears, except that above the top jaw was a pressurized water-tank the size of an egg.

When water-shears were used to cut layers of cloth, the wider bottom jaw acted as the take-up and recycled the high-pressure stream of grit-filled water. But, of course, I wasn't going to cut fabric, so I unlatched the bottom, returned it to the case, and deposited it in my outside jacket pocket. I put my ear to the door and thought I heard him swearing. "Can you hear me? This is business! Talk to me."

I pointed the shears toward the lock, momentarily considering what laws of city, state, and decorum I was about to violate. "Stand back!"

Squinting, I aimed the top jaw at the lock. I imagined that I might need to spin it around to cut a circle around the lock, but with just a short burst, the screeching jet, like the blunt foot of a karate dancer, punched a wide hole in the aluminum, removing the lock itself, a good chunk of door, and five inches of the frame.

Pushing on the now useless door, which fell inward, clattering noisily to the floor, I stepped into the black room. "I'm very sorry about this. This is an emergency and I have to speak to you. I will have your door repaired."

"What the hell?" screamed Zoom. "You're crazy!"

My eyes began to register the surfaces and outlines of the small room. In the middle was a wide bed with pastel floral sheets. Stretched out across it was a wiry nude man. His wrists and ankles were tied. A woman in a scream shirt and a hole skirt seemed to be trying to undo a large knot of black yarn wrapped around his crotch. "Oh... shit," I said, turning away. "I didn't... I mean... I'm sorry."

"I said I'm busy! You couldn't wait a minute? What's wrong with you?"

"I had no idea. I need to speak to you about some specialty yarn."

"No!" he cried. "You get out! And give me two thousand for that door." He gestured at the closet. The woman pulled a black-and-white-striped jacket from the closet, tossing it over him as one might a towel on a spill, turned, headed into the toilet, and slammed the door.

I pointed to the yarn ball that had fallen on the floor. "That's not Xi, is it?"

He laughed as if I'd told a bad joke. "You are crazy! What's the matter with you? You broke my door! I said I was busy."

I smiled an embarrassed smile. "I need Xi yarn."

"I don't have that shit! And you know what? That was a brand new door! It's worth three thousand. You better have cash!"

"I'll pay for the door, but Ryder said you have connections."

"He's selvage! Give me the money and get out before I call the satins!"

"I'll give you what you want for the door." I stepped closer. "I

need Xi yarn."

"Stitch yourself."

"Zoom, I'm sorry about your door. I'm sorry about barging in here and interrupting your leisure. I wouldn't be here except that I need Xi for a project."

He laughed at me. "Leisure? I only can afford one fabriwhore a month." He pointed toward the toilet. "You just ruined that!"

The bathroom door was flung open. "I'm a seamstress! Don't you dare call me a fabriwhore. You say that again and I'll never come back!" With that, she marched past us and out the doorway, even as Zoom begged her to stay. When she was gone, he flopped back his head and let out a moan.

I dug out my wallet, pulled out a Calvin, and placed it on the bed. "Where can I get Xi?" He stared up indignantly. I added another Calvin. "Zoom, where can I get some?"

He snorted. "Last factory is closed."

I added another Calvin.

Zoom blew out an angry sigh. I added another.

The color of his face changed. He peeked at the bills for an instant before returning his gaze to the ceiling. "It's not made in the hemispheres anymore."

"So... where is it made?" I took another bill from my wallet, pretended I was going to drop it on the others, but then scooped them all up, turned, and started out the door.

"Fuck!" he cried as if I had yanked the yarn around his bobbins. "Wait! Come back here! All I know—there's supposed to be one mill left in Antarctica."

I stopped. My Celine-Audis gleamed in the sunlight that cut across my shins. Turning back to the darkness inside, I asked, "Where in Antarctica?"

"Gimme the Calvins! Ten of them."

I counted them out and set them beside his bare feet. He laughed at me. "So, the tailor of the super celebs is a Xi burner!"

"Hardly. It's for a design project."

"Sure it is." He looked me up and down. "You're probably covered

with Xi sores."

I imagined punching him in the face, but of course he didn't know about my father. "What's the address?"

"I'll tell you what I know, but I want twenty percent."

"Take the Calvins," I told him. "The project is gratis."

He snorted in disbelief. His expression darkened, and then he stared up at the ceiling for a beat. I could just imagine his sad life, his failed schemes, his punishing quasi-legal yarn jobbing, and his monthly mistress visits. "All I heard is that the last factory is somewhere near Birudu." His voice was flat and sullen. "That's all I know."

I added another Calvin to the pile at his feet. "Get yourself a skein of that new Pfizer-core bouclé."

SEATTLEHAMA: A KISS

held the mini-T in the palm of my hand and stared at it. When I had first seen it, I assumed *Bunné Hurts* meant that she was in pain. That for all she had done in the slubs, for all the misery and death she caused us, she was the one grieving. But staring at it in the dim interior of the Time Integral entervator on my way back down, I decided it probably meant that she knew she *caused* pain, that she maybe even reveled in it. And the reason she had made those awful non-woven, ill-fitting B-shirts was because she wanted to torture us. For the first time in my life, I understood that the injustice and cruelty of the slubs was by design.

When the entervator stopped at 200, I didn't get off to return to Pilla's, but instead traveled all the way down to the Keep.

I now knew why Vada had taken me to M-Bunny headquarters. It wasn't about my father, or Rik, or even me—it was about the whole system, and the person who had designed it. Stuffing the mini-T into a pocket, I told myself that I had fully awakened, and was ready to fight. Only where my father had failed, I would succeed.

The entervator Keep was packed. I had to push past legions of costumed WaterButties, Tomoki Jones, Val the Impliers, and some guide droning on about the inventor of the entervator to reach the schedule board. The Showhouse was due in ten minutes. I headed to their parking place and waited.

189

The craft landed right on time. A beat later the door opened and about forty passengers exited. When the last stepped down, Vada came toward the doorway. I could tell that something was wrong the instant I saw her face. When she saw me, she just grasped my arm, and jerked me inside. She almost dislocated my rotator cuff she pulled so hard.

"Ouch!" I said rubbing my shoulder. "What's going on?"

"Shh!" She bolted the door. "The satins are looking for you!"

"Me? What for?"

"They think you killed Izadora." Her eyes were angry. "She was murdered half a year ago."

"I didn't kill anyone! Who is Izadora?" I looked from her to Red Hat and back. "Really. I don't know what you're talking about." An instant later, cold dread filled me. "This woman who was killed... what was she wearing?"

Vada waggled a hand in the air. "I don't know... clothes! But you're the one they're looking for. You have to tell me the truth!"

"What kind of clothes?"

"I heard she was wearing a suit by Chester Brilliantine." Red Hat was leaning against the controls and fishing candy from a pink box. "Made of mahogany drap-de-Berry."

I felt as if I'd been slugged in the gut. "I know her! I mean I don't *know* her. But I was just supposed to rip a yarn from her! Someone else was there. Some man in an invisible suit bashed her against a wall. He tried to get me, but he missed and ran. I didn't know what happened."

"Shit!" Vada covered her face with her hands. "Shit on everything!"

"But I swear I didn't do it! You have to believe me. I was just supposed to rip a yarn. I didn't even do that."

Vada let her hands flop to her sides and gazed at me. "No. I believe you. But—and this is the terrible part—you've been pinned for the crime."

"Me? How? And that was months ago!"

Vada frowned at Red Hat and released a long sigh. "At first the authorities said her death was an accident, but the opposition wouldn't let it go. They demanded more investigation. And then just a week ago, a Bunné opponent stole the body and did tests that showed Izadora was killed with dark Xi."

"Her expression was a terrible scream."

"It's a horrible way to die. Since Bunné controls the quasi-legal Xi trade, there was a call for a new investigation, but yesterday, Bunné's people said they had new evidence that pinned you: they had a yarn you ripped from her."

"I didn't rip a yarn! I saw some ghost thing strangle her."

"Yes. It's not truth they're after," added Vada with a sigh. "They want a convenient solution."

"An illegal slubber is the perfect crease," said Red Hat.

Vada nodded slowly. "We were about to ask you to help us."

"I want to help!"

Vada smiled forlornly. "We wanted you to do one of those yarn rips for us."

"Bunné," added Red Hat.

Vada rubbed her eyes. "Two years of work down the sewers!"

"But I could do that!" I laughed giddily. "I can rip a yarn from Bunné. No problem. Just tell me when and were."

Vada looked at Red Hat. "What's he going to do now?"

He pulled a small glowing candy from the box and tossed it into his mouth. Looking me up and down, he said, "Hide."

"Just tell me where Bunné will be and what you want," I said to Vada.

She shook her head slowly. "It's much too risky. The satins are looking for you. You're the current top anti-shopper. They'll find you."

She didn't understand how good a yarn ripper I was. "Vada, listen. I can rip any yarn anywhere from anyone. Just tell me what you need!"

She shook her head. "It's impossible now."

"Let me try. I can do it."

"When the time is right." She glanced at Red Hat. "The story is that because she trusts no one, she wears all her company information in the clothes on her body. If we could get a yarn off it, we'll have enough to destroy her… or at least cause terrible problems."

"That's easy!" I said with a laugh.

"Nope," said Red Hat.

"You have to understand that Miss Bunné is a top weave scientist besides being a talented businesswoman, a singer, and an epic master. We're dealing with someone on a very high level."

"He needs to go, and so do we." Red Hat crunched down on a candy in punctuation.

Vada ignored him. "She invented the self-spinning cluster, the Konkordia knit language, Bosweave, and expanded dark-knot theory. We believe it will be difficult."

I patted a pocket. "I've got my pulls with me. I just need to glue them in, and I'm ready."

"Time," said Red Hat.

Vada glared at him. "Xavier," she said, "could you give us a moment?"

Xavier, I told myself. That was her husband's name.

He exhaled. "There's no time."

"One minute."

He shook his head. "Twenty-nine seconds."

Vada rolled her eyes. "By the way, Tane, this is my brother, Xavier."

"Oh." A grin spread across my face. "Nice to meet you!" I held out my hand.

He shrugged noncommittally, then ambled past me to a little door at the back of the ship and slammed it closed behind him.

"He's just…" she stopped. The idea of explaining seemed to

instantly exhaust her. "Tane... I... I appreciate your willingness to help. You don't know what that means to me, but..."

I stepped before her, sensing an equality between us. Touching her right forearm, I leaned in. I had never kissed someone without a mouth stocking or any fabric between us, and the idea seemed a little disgusting and maybe dangerous—yet I put my mouth on hers.

After just a few seconds, she pulled back. "Wait... you're complicating this right now. I like you, but we have to wait. And Xavier and I must go. If you've been followed we'll be linked and we will be killed. We had an agreement that we could stay in Seattlehama only if we keep absolutely clean and uninvolved." She frowned at me. "Do you understand?"

"I'll go with you."

She glanced toward the door, fumbling for her next word. "If you're with us and we're caught, you're dead for sure. You're safer on your own."

"I want you," I told her. I kissed her again.

"Shit!" Xavier burst from the back and sprinted to the controls. "They're coming! Get him out. We're going up!"

Vada's lipstick was smeared. She turned away.

"Where are you going?" I asked her. "It doesn't matter. I'll come with you!"

When Vada turned back to me, her mouth was wiped clear. "Tane, for your sake, you must go! If we're involved, they will want us more than dead. You can escape. Just stay away from the entervators. Hide somewhere. And try and get out of Seattlehama. You'll be fine."

"Get him out!" cried Xavier. "We're starting up!" He turned a lever and I could feel the entervator latch onto a cable.

"I'm sorry, but you're really better off alone!" said Vada, hurriedly unlocking the door. "We're Toue. We're wanted in all cities. I'm very sorry, but you must go."

The ground was slowly falling away. I had to jump before it was too late. I landed hard on the cushioned pad where the ship had rested, and rolled to look up at the Showhouse.

I stood, straightening my Fleece Swansdown jacket and brushing off the dust. I didn't like how she first kissed me back only to then shove me out. What was the rush? I was the one in trouble. And if she really needed help, I knew I could rip a yarn from Bunné. I could do it without looking. I thought about going right now and doing just that to show them. She had to be somewhere in her boutique. Maybe Necklace knew where.

And then I heard it. "That's him, officers! That's the killer." I knew the voice.

CUT AND SEWN

Barreling down the showstairs, shoving the Handy Breeders, and Wayward Bug Ladies to the side, came seven men dressed in navy satin, brandishing long silvery sticks. Withor and Vit followed behind.

"He's the murderer!" cried my former boss. "I have the drap-de-Berry yarn rip he took to prove it!"

"He's making it up," I protested, sprinting around one of the entervators. Jumping over a box of tools, I slid to a stop as one of the satins was coming at me. Turning, I reversed direction.

The only way out of here was the showstairs or the cables. Two satins guarded the stairs while the others played cat and mouse with me between the parked ships.

Behind a pink entervator, two men worked on an open panel of tubes.

"Can you take me up?"

They didn't meet my eyes. One shook his head.

"Please!" I had to rush away as one of the satins closed in.

"I sent him on an authorized and completely ordinary yarn acquisition errand," continued Withor louder as men with photo-cams and sight-cannons crowded around the stairs. "He killed the poor woman—who happened to be a member of the Fashion Board—for no reason at all. I tried to rehabilitate him. I have great sympathy for the prison class, but they're a nasty, ungrateful people!"

The satins moved in as I raced back and forth, desperate for a way out. Between a long silver entervator and the back wall, four of them cornered me.

Vit sneered. "He's a corn boy slubber."

"Indeed," Withor agreed. "This is unfortunately another example of that race's tendencies to irrational violence."

"I didn't do it!"

None of the satins spoke. Their grim expressions made me fear they weren't going to send me back. They were just going to kill me.

"There was someone else there! It looked like a ghost. I don't know who it was, but that's the killer."

One of the satins lunged. I jumped back, but slipped on the oily floor. Before I could get on my feet another rushed forward and punched me. His heavy, gloved fist felt like it cracked my ribs. I fell face down as if I had been run over. Another satin put his knee in my back. I couldn't move.

Withor stood far behind the satins, as if I were some dangerous beast.

"Okay," said one of the satins. "Bag him up."

"I didn't do it," I said with the tiny amount of air I left in my lungs. "He sent me. He knew! And there was someone else! Someone in an invisible suit." If the satins heard me, which I doubted, none paid attention.

An explosive roar came from overhead. I had to twist my head as far as it would go to see. Two hundred feet up, where Vada and Xavier had been headed, was a smear of black smoke hovering between the buildings.

"Two more Toue dead," muttered one of the satins.

Someone—maybe another entervator entertainer—gasped and said, "They shot down the Europa Showhouse."

PART 3
NOVELTY

KONG: MUD-SOAKED THERMOSET CHIFFON

The first sensation to return to me was sound. And not a particular sound, but an ambience: the harmony of a space, the pulse of air, the hum of the cosmos. The second was temperature. The air above was hot and moist, but whatever I was resting on was cold and felt like it was slowly sucking the warmth from me. And the third, smell, was the one that actually woke me, as a stinging combination of rotting garbage and sulfur filled my nose.

Pushing myself up, I blinked several times to clear my vision, but all that I could make out was a blue-tinged haze—like hundreds of layers of voile. Beneath me was a soggy towel. I was naked except for a few splatters of mud here and there. My ribs were visible below my skin, and my stomach curved inward toward my spine. Below, my slack genitals hung in the heat. I wanted to stand up, but the muscles in my arms were already trembling from the strain of lifting my shoulders. I sank back down. The sound of my own harried breathing filled my ears.

I didn't know where I was, but I guessed days, maybe even weeks had passed. After I had rested a moment, I strained to sit on my haunches. The small change in elevation made me dizzy, and for a moment I feared I was going to be sick, but then the sensation in my throat settled. Beyond the borders of my towel was nothing but dark mud dotted here and there with a few sad tufts of vegetation, the odd rock or lump, and a few bits of trash: a sloppy scrap of paper, a shard of once-white plastic, a fluttering ribbon of black metallic tape.

I tried to speak, to call for someone, but could only produce a whisper before I began to choke. Coughing flooded my skull with pain, and when I put my hand to my forehead, my fingers found a rough line of scar tissue now stretched from my hairline to my neck, slicing my face in half.

If I had the strength, I would have run from myself. Instead, my fingertips crawled along the slick and knotted skin like ants on sugar as I tried desperately to conjure what had happened.

I remembered Kira's beautiful eyes. I recalled standing on the Stanton-Bell knitting a skivvé. I saw Vada performing in the Europa. I remembered Pearl Rivering with Pilla.

My stomach clenched. I vomited a dribble of clear goo. The scar down my face felt like it was going to pop open. Holding my head, I moaned, and slumped forward. This pain wasn't just the scar, something else was wrong. For an instant I knew I was dead, and that this was some empty stage for the soul or memory. I was stuck here forever in this stinking hot air and cold mud.

And then, as if a set of complicated gears engaged, somewhere in the reawaking mysteries of my brain, I remembered being in the entervator Keep and Withor pointing at me. After the Europa Showhouse had exploded, the satins had stuffed me into a large cloth sack. I had been beaten unconscious.

I felt my face, but couldn't understand why I had one big scar down the middle. When had I been cut?

Steadying myself, I rose onto one knee, clenched my teeth, and then pushed myself up. I was standing, but I had to negotiate my own violent dizziness like a surfer pitching his weight from right to left and from the balls of his feet to the heels and back. Stepping off the cloth, my feet sank into the recycle-smelling mud. I saw tire tracks and figured someone had dropped me here. I wobbled twenty feet before I had to stop. Resting on my haunches, I huffed down the noxious air.

And while I knew this was the slubs from the smell, where was the corn, where were the houses, and where were the M-Bunny men? All around was nothing but mud and fog.

"Hello?" I held my head with both hands as the pain felt like it was going to split me in two. I shouted, "Is anyone here?" I heard nothing. "Hello? Anyone!" Pain blinded me for an instant.

I had been struggling inside the bag. I remembered trying to push my way out. It had been so black I had seen nothing but spirals and checkerboards. Then I remembered lying on a table in some noisy echoing space. From high above, I had seen harsh parallelograms of sunshine. And it was there—wherever that was—that my head had been torn and the flesh on my face had been sliced off with sharp metal gears.

And then I knew! I had been taken to M-Bunny headquarters. I remembered the factory skylights, the hum of machines, and the grinders that deboned the recycled. But unlike my dad, and Rik, and millions of others, I had somehow escaped. Feeling my head, I tried to find the hole where the bolt had gone in, but of course there wasn't one.

They hadn't given me Blue to stun me, nor had they mercifully killed me before they recycled me. I had been thrown straight in. But then something happened.

I heard a wet suck of mud. A second before I had been screaming in hopes of finding someone else, now a cold fear covered my skin. Turning around, I peered into the fog. I heard more squishing sounds. They were coming for me! I searched the ground, and grabbed at what I thought was a metal scrap but it turned out to be paper. Ahead I saw something shiny, and grabbed for a small shard of glass. Feeling the edges, I found the sharpest point and held it up.

I saw movement in the fog. A flutter of what looked like cloth. Glancing about, I wondered if I could try to run, but even as I stumbled backwards, the shape solidified. A man in a long coat—Withor!

My heart was hammering. My scar throbbed. Wobbling, I

bent my knees like Kira in battle. First I would cut his throat with the glass. I'd slash it back and forth. Then I would bash his head. And bash it again. I would keep on slamming my fists into him until he stopped moving.

ANTARCTICA

It might have been prudent to slow on the tiled surface of the *Antarctica Extension, as one moment tremors seemed to come from the nose of the car, and next the back would hum an odd harmonic, but I kept up my speed, afraid that I was falling behind.*

Five hundred miles from my destination, an emergency call came in. "Mr. Cedar," said the cool voice of a Mz Foss of the Security Board, "I need to ask you a few questions."

I cursed myself for not turning off all communication. "Yes please... go ahead." I tried to make my tone as light and cheery as possible.

"You had a visitor."

"I did?"

"We believe a woman visited your design studio yesterday."

"A client did."

"We suspect this client *may be a freeboot."*

I shook my head even though she couldn't see. "I doubt that."

"This matter is of extreme concern." She had stretched the second syllable of extreme *like spandex. "To be blunt, the woman in question is wanted for crimes against humanity."*

"I didn't know. I don't quiz clients about their personal lives."

"Mr. Cedar," said Mz Foss, her voice shifting into a lower, more powerful, gear, "the Security Board is fully aware of your history, actions, and associations." She paused as if waiting for me to confirm.

"I am aware of your awareness," I replied.

"Am I to assume from your insouciant tone that you spoke with this wanted criminal and are possibly engaged in criminal acts yourself?"

"I'm just stating the facts as I know them, Boardmember." Grasping the steering, I mashed the accelerator to the floor for a moment in anger. Letting up, I finished, "Please accept my apology, Boardmember."

I heard nothing for several seconds. I hoped that the connection had been cut, but just as I had positioned my index finger above the off button, she spoke again. "You are hereby charged with aiding the enemy of the families. You must immediately report to the Security Board headquarters and plead your case."

"Yes, Boardmember," I replied, pulling down the skin beneath my eye to give her a Red Hole! "I'm on my way now." I switched off the communications and pointed the Chang toward the exit ramp activating the mercury brakes.

From the off ramp, I found the highway heading toward Birudu and sped along. The drivers here, mostly in ancient Wangs, Arlies, and Maxis, were an aggressive bunch, but not enough of a distraction from the call and its implications. A storm was building on the horizon, and I worried that Vada would be caught before I ever made it back. I hated to imagine what the satins would do to her.

I gazed out to my left, where the land slowly descended to reveal a tangle of crowded roads lined with shops and coffee houses and their twittering and blinking signs. The windowless, hulking warehouses, the drab slabs of factories, and above it all—the product of a hundred smoke stacks darkening the sky—a writhing mass of black smoke lit by the flashing licks of flame from the oilrigs below. A travel poster for hell.

KONG:
THE PACIFICA
SHOWHOUSE

Color began to saturate the coat. It seemed to change from near black to maroon. The collar and sleeves were trimmed in black, but the shirt and pants shone bright in the gloom. As I stood waiting, nearly hyperventilating, I noticed the man's gait. Rather than Withor's artificial tiptoeing bounce, this man's stride was solid, firm, and calm. He didn't carefully set his feet, but plopped them onto the ground with relaxed authority.

As the figure came closer, the maroon of his coat was revealed to be a vibrant red, and I could see that the trim was made of a fuzzy feather-like substance that shimmered and shook in the breeze. And when my mysterious visitor's features became clear—I knew for certain that it wasn't Withor. The eyes were dark with shadow. The bee-stung lips were burgundy; the eyebrows arched and curious. Each cheek was dotted with a large circle of rouge.

"Y—You!" I stammered. "You're dead!"

She stopped six feet away. Her initial smile turned to puzzlement. She glanced around. "Where the shit are they?"

"Who?"

"Those idiots! They weren't supposed to even bring you yet. And they weren't supposed to just leave you." Vada focused on me, and her eyes lingered on my nude body for a beat before

I dropped the glass and covered myself. She laughed at my modesty. "How do you feel? Are you all right?"

"Not really."

She frowned sympathetically, gathered up the sides of her skirt to her hips, and began working down her full panties—a red and white pair with embroidered white dots and ruffles all over the bottom. Stepping forward, she held them out. "I don't know why you didn't even get a gown. I guess you have to be explicit with that shit hospital."

I didn't move. I wasn't sure this was a good idea.

"Oh, go on. They're clean and comfortable." Wincing, she glanced down. "You need something!"

In what felt like an emulsion of embarrassment and gratitude, I took them. Her warmth still lingered in the soft material. She turned to give me privacy and after I tried to scrape off some of the mud from the bottoms of my feet and ankles, I carefully inserted my legs and pulled the panties up.

"You look good!" she said with a smile. "Sort of. Are you really okay?"

I nodded. "I saw the Europa explode. They shot you down."

"Yes." Scowling, Vada let out a long exhale. "She *almost* got me."

She meant Bunné. "How'd you survive?"

"We got out of the ship a couple of seconds before." She pursed her mouth. "The United Sisterhood of Entervator Entertainers and Pilots."

I should have known that someone who could blow up a jacket only to make it reappear would have other tricks. "This is the slubs, right?"

"Outside of Kong." She squinted up at the sky, then down at the mud. "And what a cut of a rendezvous spot! This is shit. I'm sorry."

"What happened?"

She frowned. "Mostly awful things." Her shoulders sank and she peered at me doubtfully. "I'm very sorry. We thought you had much more time to get out of the Keep."

"Satins came for me. Withor was there. He said I killed the drap-de-Berry woman."

"I believe their original plan was to leave you next to that drap-de-Berry woman, as you call her. Your dead body was supposed to take the fall. Someone knotted it." She squinted at me. "Why didn't you tell us about Izadora?"

"I didn't know."

"From now on, please tell me everything that *might* be important. Actually just tell me everything." Vada looked skyward for a moment. "We got out of the ship before the rocket hit it, but on our way out of the city, Xavier was captured. They tortured him." She frowned at me.

"I'm sorry." I brought a hand to my face. "What happened to me?"

She pursed her mouth tenderly. "You were almost recycled. We checked outgoing from the city and found a prisoner who was returned." She shook her head slowly. "It was kind of lucky actually that the orders were to toss you into the deboner alive. They do that sometimes for special cases. When our sympathizer realized who it was, he shut down the line just as the blades started on your head."

"I kind of remembered that! It was terrible."

"I caught up by then. It was completely awful. I didn't know if you were going to make it. We pumped you full of nem-d. We headed across the Pacifica and… well… I'm very sorry."

I touched the stitches on my face. "Did you sew me up?"

"Oh no!" She snorted a little laugh. "Don't even think it. I couldn't. No, I know a tissue sculptor here in Kong. That's why we're here." She shrugged. "And it's a good place to start over." She gazed at me sympathetically. "You had very little flesh left. I want to warn you that you look a little different and you'll have some scars." Her eyebrows rose as if anticipating my surprise. "I had him do a flat-fell down your nose." She suppressed a smile. "That's my favorite."

A flat fell seam is formed by interlocking the seam allowances with two parallel rows of topstitching. I couldn't tell if she was joking or not.

She pointed her small nose aloft and snorted. "And of course *he's* late."

Who could she mean? I peered above wondering if some other Showhouse entervator was about to glide to a crash landing nearby.

Vada was still studying the sky. "How well can you sew?"

"I can sew. Thank you! Thank you for saving my life."

She made a face. "It was really close. I don't know how you really survived that grinder. Just getting you out of that thing was a huge mess, and then transporting you to Kong was a disaster. You almost died. We ran out of nem-d and had to stop in Fiji for more... anyway... everything completely unraveled."

"Why go to all that trouble for me?"

Vada stifled a smile like a gardener pinching an unwanted flower bud from a stem. "You have talents."

I was about to ask what they were, but crouched and caught myself before I fell into the mud. The earth seemed to have shaken.

She stooped before me. "You all right?"

"I just got dizzy."

"You need some rest and some food." Vada glanced up again. "Damn it, where are you?"

"What's coming?"

"The Pacifica."

"What's that?"

I heard a rush of air and looked up.

"There it is!" Vada raised a shiny black-gloved finger. And like a flower unfolding from the rumples of cloud and fog, a sky-grey dirigible silently emerged and floated down to the dark earth to where we were.

THE HIGH EUROPAS AND PACIFICUM: TWO HUNDRED AND FORTY COSTUMES IN TWO HUNDRED AND FORTY DAYS

Once we were inside what they called the low port or the mudroom, Vada buttoned the hatch. I touched the cloth walls and stared out one of the chiffon windows at the twists and curls of fog as we began to ascend.

"Welcome honored consumer to the adjunct airship of the magical traveling show... we call her *The Pacifica Showhouse*." Vada's eyebrows rose with the promise of a marketer. "It is made of nothing but silk and longing."

"I love it," I whispered as the ship breached the fog and the orange light of a sunset illuminated the cloth, the world, and us. To the right, I saw an impossibly huge city. I was used to Seattlehama, which was all height. This one wasn't as tall, but was easily a thousand times wider. Buildings, bubbles, towers, Turkishes, scrapers, and beepers created a dazzle of lights, grids, and patterns. It was a crazy tapestry—a jacquard loom gone mad.

"That's Kong," said Vada.

Far to the left the sun melted into a glowing coal as it sank to the horizon.

"Listen," she said, quietly, "Xavier escaped, but was badly hurt. Don't ask him about it, don't look at him, or mention it. He hates that."

"Sure. I'm sorry. How'd he escape?"

Vada just grimaced. After a beat, she glanced at the sunset. "Kong is a glorious city."

I turned to the window. "That's where we're going?"

She shook her head. "South."

I had no idea where Kong was and thus no concept of *south*, but I was satisfied. Vada unbuttoned a door, and we stepped into the central hallway. The basketweave floor stretched and warped underfoot and I could sense that my weight slightly twisted and bent the whole craft. I tried to step lightly, and worried that even in my emaciated state, I was too heavy.

"There are two floors," she whispered. "Your room is here." She unbuttoned a door that led to a small cabin. "Tomorrow, when it's light, and you've had some rest, I'll show you around."

Beside a narrow mattress on the floor sat a low table, holding a nano-denier crochet bowl filled with what looked like steaming water.

"There's linens and clothes for you in the closet. We don't have running water and when we're traveling—especially near cities—it's lights out. It might take you some getting used to the airborne movements, the feel of the ship, the turbulence. And there's not much heat, but we can talk about that later." She eyed me. "You should clean up before that gets cold. I've left some food here. Sleep well. I'll see you in the galley for breakfast." She then stood and her expression seemed to vacillate between anticipation and hesitation. She then said, "Welcome," leaned in, kissed me on the mouth, and was gone.

I stood for a long moment savoring the lingering warmth and moisture of her lips. She had saved my life. I wanted to laugh, but just then the floor shuddered, and the bowl with the water would have spilled had I not leapt at it. After I had washed and changed into a simple pair of red pants, a button-down shirt, I ate, felt incredibly sleepy, and crawled into bed.

When I woke, it took me a moment to remember where I was. I heard distant laughter. Unbuttoning my door, I stepped into the hallway and followed the sounds.

Up a spiral oilcloth stairs, I found the ship's galley where five sat around a table. Their conversation and laughter stopped as soon as I entered, and when I swallowed, I was sure they could all hear. As Vada smiled and stood, I was overcome by the childish disappointment that I wouldn't have her all to myself.

"Good morning. You look rested."

"Thanks, I feel better."

She introduced the others. At the far end sat Xavier. Gregg, his first mate, sat to his right. Haas, who I almost never saw after that first meal, was the cook. He sat next to Gregg. Vada was on the other side of the table. Marti, the captain's boy—a young woman—was nearest the door.

Gregg glared at me with what seemed like preemptive loathing. Marti didn't look up from her bowl, but sat with her spoon hovering before her mouth like she was waiting for someone else to speak. Haas stood and rushed past. Xavier looked at me blankly. His right arm and his right eye were missing, and the flesh of his face was lumpy as muffin dough. Beneath his bare pate, his mouth now twisted to the side in a permanent snarl. I quickly glanced away.

"They just left him there in the mud!" said Vada. Gregg harrumphed displeasure. "Come in… Come in!" She waved me toward her. As I wedged myself into the chair beside her, she patted my shoulder once.

"He shouldn't be here," Gregg muttered.

"He *is*," replied Vada, staring him down.

"Could have got you both killed," added Marti, finally downing that spoonful of stew.

"He has as much right to be aboard as either of you two half-breeds!" Vada closed her eyes for a beat, gathering herself. "And it was not his fault. Caam was talking too much, and Ffem, bless her bones, was also linked and slaughtered. Our cell broke too many rules and procedures."

Gregg cocked his head to the side. "But he's the enemy!"

"Shush!" said Vada, who glanced at Xavier for an instant. "I will have no more of that! He's with us! Treat him with the respect you do all crew members."

I held my head up and tried to smile, but I wondered if I should be here, if I even wanted to be here—if I would last.

"He can help." Xavier's voice, which had been as full and deep as an oak, now sounded like a twig scratching a windowpane. Frowning—or snarling less—which seemed the best he could do—he held up his remaining hand and the two gnarled finger stumps. "I can no longer sew."

I glanced at Vada and the long red-and-white-striped jamdani robe she wore. Was Xavier saying that he had made it and the rest of her costumes?

Marti stood and left the room. As the rest of us sat in silence, I had just enough time to wonder how I had offended her before she surprised me by returning with a bowl of dark soup and a spoon, which she set before me. I thanked her, receiving just a grunt in response, but I sensed the beginnings of a grudging acceptance.

"You have to understand how protective they are," Vada said quietly when we were alone in her room that evening. After I ate, I napped the whole day. Now it was dark, but light from the three-quarter moon filtered through the layers of fabric of the dirigible above us to hazily illuminate the curves of her face and the open pages of her writing book.

"Were they with you in Seattlehama?"

"This ship was folded and put away." She eyed me. "They were working with another cell, but they got news every few minutes."

I lowered my voice to a whisper since I had found that the

oilcloth walls of the ship didn't absorb much. "What happened to Xavier?"

"Yes… that…" Her voice cracked. She shook her head and started again. "We're just thankful he's alive. They hurt him badly. He's got all sorts of internal problems too. They used dark Xi."

"I've heard of that, but what is it?"

"There's pure and dark Xi. They're almost identical yarns, but are treated differently. The—" she stopped again. "I'm sorry I just, I can't talk about it."

We were lying across her wide bed, our heads propped up on the pillows, our legs loosely intertwined. Vada untangled herself and stood.

"I didn't mean to upset you."

"Everything is upsetting!" she said loudly. "Everything is going wrong. And don't think that you're the only one to blame!" She tossed an arm at the door. "They want to lay it at your feet, but that's not right. It's all of us and all of our incompetence and our pettiness and our lousy tactics!"

I had lots of questions, but didn't dare ask.

Vada sat with her back to me. "Everything unraveled."

"How long was I… out?"

"You were in a suspension coma for two months."

"Two months?" I had figured it had been only a few weeks.

"Miss Bunné pinned the Izadora murder on Xavier and me. And because we're deadly, horrible Toue, in the ensuing panic, she disbanded the city's Fashion Board so that there's no opposition. Bunné is in complete control. And like the peons they are, the rest of those horse-hairless CEOs are all going along. The Toue have been flushed out and the tourists are coming and spending."

"I knew that drap-de-Berry thing was bad, but when nothing happened, I just hoped it would all go away."

"When the satins followed you to the entervator Keep when you came to see us, they made it into a grand Toue conspiracy."

The ship rocked gently, and then began to move in a slow wide turn.

"Why are you illegal?"

"Basically my very talented and proud ancestors couldn't get along with anyone. We've been labeled and hated."

Vit's words came to mind when he and Withor were accusing me of Izadora's murder: *Corn boy slubber.* The words felt like they burned my skin. I wanted to bash him. While the satins chased me down, he and Withor had watched like it was a sport. "Bunné makes the satin's clothes," I said with a sad laugh. I had seen the perfect stitching on the cuffs and pockets. "Their suits were beautifully tailored."

Vada snorted angrily. "Her personal army of cut men." The way she spoke, it almost sounded like a slogan. "A lot of them are recruited from the slubs. And she's got colonies all the way down to Antarctica now." Vada stopped and looked up. Through the ceiling and the ballonets, we could see a white moon.

"What do you mean, *cut men*?"

"Bunné's a castrator." She gazed at me sadly. "Even of herself. She's got a love-hate relationship with the male organ." Vada twisted her mouth left and then right. "Mostly hate, I suppose."

"Like that epic of hers with Warrior Remon called *Sensitive Dead Penisless Boys.*"

Vada rolled her eyes. "Right! And the real shame about Bunné is that she's brilliant and fascinating and wonderful—if morbid, crazy, and deadly. In many ways she… well, she *was* a wonderful person." She stared ahead, lost in thought. "She's one of those rare geniuses in history. When she was five she was weaving jacquard, building electronics, and composing music." Her voice lost its edge and volume. "I haven't seen her in years. But, from what I've heard, she's not the same person."

"How do you know her?"

"Know thy enemy." She didn't continue.

"Why did you want me to rip a yarn from her?"

"Xavier came up with the idea. She's turned herself and her clothes into her own data-processing repository. Somehow if you could have gotten close and had taken a yarn, we might have gotten something very useful."

I feared Vada wouldn't be happy about what I was about to say, but I wanted to tell her everything this time. "I went to her store."

Her eyes darted toward me. "Whose?"

"Miss Bunné."

"What happened? Was she there? Did you see her? Did she see you?"

"No. It wasn't anything." I shrugged. "A saleswarrior just took me around."

Vada grit her teeth. "Just a saleswarrior?"

"And two others."

Vada closed her eyes—had I ruined everything, again? "Documenters?" she asked. "One had a light-gathering wand?"

"Yeah, but all I did was buy a shirt." I remembered the beads pressing into the flesh of the saleswarrior's throat, her face going white. "I just bought a mini-T that said *Bunné Hurts.*" The ice of panic filled my chest. "I had the mini-T in my pocket when the satins got me!" In that instant I finally awoke. "And the yarn from my father! I forgot about it! It was in my pocket too!" It felt as if my spleen had been torn from my gut.

"We recovered them."

I could hardly breathe for the relief. Her words were salve. "Where are they? Do you have them?" When she didn't immediately answer, I said, "I'm sorry about going to her boutique."

"No." Vada frowned thoughtfully. "It doesn't sound too bad. As long as she didn't see you." She motioned toward the hallway. "The things are in your room. I thought you'd found them already."

I stood and stepped to her door. "I just need to see my father's yarn."

"Look for a twill bag in the bottom of your closet."

I started to unbutton the door.

"Tane," she said, "you're *absolutely* sure you didn't meet Bunné? And there wasn't anything unusual about shopping, was there?"

I told myself that a saleswarrior almost choking to death wasn't rare. "No." I stopped unbuttoning. "Why?"

Vada pursed her lips. "If she recognized you… if she saw you again… she would almost certainly strike." She gazed at me apprehensively. As I opened her door, she said, "And I need a costume designer."

"What?"

"It's my weakness," she pouted playfully. "My one real weakness. I love clothes. And no offense, but I don't want any of those creepy skivvé with dicks and balls! I want beautiful, gorgeous, luxurious, and wonderful things."

Her unabashed greediness made me laugh. As absurd as it was, mingled with my horrifying memories, such frivolity seemed a release. I found myself answering, "I can do that." The last thing Zanella had told me was: design for women next. A wash of gratitude filled me. "I'd love to… I'd be honored to."

"I need a new costume for each show." She held up her hands as though I had protested or was about to. "I know! The vanity… the narcissism… Well, there's that, but I've found that it keeps the show fresh. And the costumes are not really so new. We recycle old ones and use every scrap, so you'll have to be inventive and resourceful."

"Shows?"

She blinked at me with theatrical surprise. "Good gracious, lovely shopping consumer, of course we're still doing our shows! And over the years, I've done many more shows in the slubs than in the cities. These are the people who really deserve some…" She paused as she thought of a word. "*Entertainment.*"

PERFORMANCES IN RAM-POOR, MANIRA, SHI-ON, ZAK3, K'KOM

We flew mostly at night and stopped in clearings, muddy fields, or the crazed macadam of former parking lots early in the morning. While turbulent near-crashes seemed to be Xavier's specialty, all that we suffered were small abrasions, popped seams, spilled soups, and bruised elbows. Once landed, we would spend most of the day assembling the stage and getting ready. At dusk we would put on a show. In the darkness we would pack up and sail off.

Since Xavier's voice wasn't strong, Gregg did the barking. He also sang and accompanied himself on a crank electro-static harmonium. Marti wore flash pants, juggled glass spheres and knives, and sometimes told funny bawdy stories. But of course, the star of the show was Vada. She told fortunes, sang ballads, danced, stripped, told jokes, and ate fire.

I never tired of watching her, and now that I was living and sleeping with her, I saw and understood her performances differently. She gave of herself on stage in a way that she didn't—and probably couldn't—in the rest of her life. It was like a switch turned and the only emotions that came through were pleasure, happiness, and power. It wasn't that she was unhappy the rest of the time, but when onstage, the enthusiasm that radiated from her was like heat from glowing coils. Often the best moment of the day was when she would come to me at the side of the stage after a show, exhausted, but smelling of lilac and sweat.

"The audiences are so quiet," I complained after one of her first shows in a dusty, forlorn place called Ram-Poor. "It's like they're dead."

"It's the slubs," she said. "Multiply their response by ten." She exhaled deeply and laughed. "I'm telling you, they absolutely loved it."

"Well," I said, kissing her, "I did."

She pushed me away and whispered, "Not in front of the others!"

Each evening, once we were airborne, Vada and I would retire to her room for a fitting. She would strip to her foundation, and I would carefully drape and pin the various parts and pieces I was working on. As I made my adjustments, she, unstitched from the day, put her hair up in spools, and massaged in her face creams.

While I never grumbled about the tools aboard the Pacifica, they had a terrible assemblage of dirty, sticky, bent, and corroded satin pins, needles, thimbles, shears, rippers, and rulers. Worse was the irritable, balsa wood, pedal-powered Singa sewing machine that never really worked. The fabric and notions came from the storeroom, which was filled with shreds and pieces of old costumes. I recognized a few things from her shows on the Europa.

But while the materials were difficult and the tools sad, it was during those eight months—those tiring, endless days and nights—as I first repaired and patched mag-gowns, ribbed corsets, and Jupiter dresses, and then, as I got to know the curves of Vada's body and became familiar and confident with the conventions of woven fabric: the darts, the seams, the finishes, I began to create my own dresses, skirts, corsets, and gowns, that I became not a ticker, a knitter, a stitcher, an apprentice, or student of fashion, but a real tailor.

"It's a little tight here," said Vada as she stood before me in a low-bust bodice and cantilevered symbol skirt.

I quickly re-pinned the edge and allowed for more ease at her waist.

"Yes," she said, smoothing the skirt over her hips. "It's beautiful. I love how it flows. It's like… high clouds… or water in slow motion."

Once our fitting was over, she would put on her robe and settle into her desk to write in her notebook. I never asked but assumed it was a diary.

While she wrote, I sewed by the moonlight that seeped through the oil organza ballonets, or by oil lamp. Some nights, when we passed Bankok, Lumpur, or Malay, and we were dark, I sewed by feel in the pitch-black. Once she finished, I would lay down my needles, and, as Xavier steered the Pacifica over mountains, meandering rivers, and dark valleys of the world's slubs, we explored the landscape of each other's bodies.

One night, a month after I had boarded the Pacifica, Vada and I lay across her bed, the sweat of love cooling my forehead and back, I confessed, "I love being here with you. I love watching you in the things I make for you."

She unfurled a long, low, satisfied growl, exactly the sort of sound one would expect from a panther. "Your creations are celestial."

"I want to do this forever." I sat up and faced her. "You know what I mean?" In the dim of that evening I could just make out her face, but not her expression.

"I do." Her tone was disappointingly cool. I had hoped she might say that all she wanted was to tour the slubs, with me designing her costumes.

Glancing up at the silhouette of the moon just visible through the ballonets, I asked, "Where are we going?"

She laughed softly, sadly. "Eventually… back to the city."

She meant Seattlehama. "Why? You're not going to get another entervator, are you?"

"No."

"This is good. We're happy. I see how the shows make you feel. We can keep doing this. You don't have go back."

She exhaled slowly. "I'm not."

I felt elated for an instant, but then I understood. I flopped back down and stared up at the faint scratch of high clouds in the night sky. "I'm not going back either."

For a minute there was only silence and the occasional vibration of turbulence. A moment later the ship bounced hard, and I heard two seams pop. By that point I could tell from the timbre of the thread where the split had occurred. It was my duty to find and fix tears.

Vada spoke softly. "Were you happy in the city?"

"I'm happy now."

"What about the slubs?"

"No!" I laughed. "I mean, in a way, yes, I was. I loved the corn. I worked at growing it and tending to it. I had friends. But I was only happy because I was so ignorant. But even so, when I looked up at Seattlehama, I just knew there was something else, that there was something I was meant to discover." I touched her arm and found it cool. "I like this. I like you." I waited for a reply and then heard the slow even rhythm of sleep. I lay there, watching the filmy haze of illuminated clouds through the layers of organza. "I love you," I whispered, and kissed her cheek.

The next day we set up our stage south of a city called K'Kom. That part of the world was dominated by the rice clans: Mitsu, Senter, and Wan. Most of slubbers were docile, emaciated, and sad-looking in their rice-cloth tunics, in their reds, blacks, or blues. As we set up the stage and the tent covering, a crowd began to grow and by the time the show was ready to start, there were a thousand instead of our usual several hundred. And unlike most slubbers, these men were boisterous and angry.

"Cover me up," said Vada as I helped her dress for the show in a red beach peignoir. "There's testosterone in the air." When I laughed at her, she frowned. "The Senter clan is strong here, but the Wans are trying to push in. So what do the brandclans reps do?" I shook my head. "They change the hormones in the clothes so the men get aggressive and angry."

I found a white petticoat and helped her slip it over her ruffled polka-dot panties. "Did M-Bunny ever go to war?"

Vada's expression darkened. "Not around Seattlehama. To the south, it's constant war. There, Bunné is ruthless. Originally, the slubs were her labor and manufacturing base, but now it's her lab to culture new war diseases."

I had been fixing her collar, smoothing the fabric around her neck, when I stopped. I had spit the pesticide gum all over my dad's chest desperate to save him. "Why did my dad burn Xi?"

I heard her swallow. "It was fashionable then. He did a lot of fashionable things." Her voice was small and distant. "Toward the end of his life he was brokenhearted. I never really understood."

"He was in love with someone?"

She nodded.

"He was covered with sores when I saw him in the slubs." I laughed at myself sadly. "I thought it was some corn smut or something. I chewed this pesticide gum and spit it all over him. I had no idea what to do!"

She focused her coffee-brown eyes on me. "I'm sorry. I guess he knew the local reps wouldn't know a Xi sore from a corduroy patch."

"M-Bunny paid me a bonus because they thought it was a new disease."

"Oh, that's what happened!" She shook her head. "They wouldn't pay much just for recycling. I'm very sorry, Tane. I didn't realize he gave himself up for incubation. That's terrible!"

"He wanted me to take the bonus money and use it to run away, but I couldn't. I tried, but as soon I would see Seattlehama sinking over the horizon, it felt like I was leaving home."

"If it's any consolation, M-Bunny didn't get anything from

his Xi sores."

"Why does M-Bunny pay for diseases?"

"From weapons to medicines. A couple of years ago, Bunné realized that the slubs were perfect for incubating new viruses. There's some pox that she just used in the lower Californias. It was reported that seventy million L. Segus died."

I imagined piles of bodies amid dying soybean plants. It seemed impossible. "Bunné and M-Bunny seem so far away." I closed the button on her right sleeve. "Even so, I feel guilty... like I got away, and all those other M-Bunny men never will."

She frowned. "It's not fair."

Gregg started the show early, but the crowd wasn't interested in him, and soon I couldn't hear the twangs of the electro-static harmonium over the shouts and boos. When Marti appeared in her light-green spread suit they howled with approval, but when they realized all she meant to do was juggle, they grew restless again.

Vada stood at the side of the stage with her arms folded over her chest, her frown etching lines around her mouth. She shook her head. "Tell Xavier to start the motors."

"You haven't even gone on."

She let her arms flop to the sides of her long gown. "This looks bad."

As if on cue, a man holding a pointed bamboo pole rushed onto the stage. He pulled up his tunic and flashed his semi-erect root at Marti. She shoved him back as two more came up. One swung at her. She stumbled avoiding the blow and fell.

Vada, Gregg, and I rushed out. I tried to shove one of the slubbers off the stage, but even though he probably lived on a half cup of cyst rice a day, he was surprisingly strong. He twisted around and knocked me backward. Pushing myself up, I saw Vada lean to one side, supporting herself on just the fingertips of her right hand, and leap horizontally to kick one of them with both feet. The man flew off the stage and into a gang who were climbing up behind him. In a cartoon it would have been accompanied with the crash of scattering bowling pins.

More men rushed the stage. One held a pole, but Gregg ripped it from him and used it to hold the others off while Vada kicked two of them back down. The crowd loved it.

While Marti held back the crowd with a rifle, the rest of us knocked down the stage, bundled it up, and threw it into the storage hatch of the ship. Meanwhile, Xavier started the engines and began adding the lift to the ballonets. In just thirty minutes, the Pacifica was off the ground and Gregg, Vada, and I were climbing the rope ladder to the sky.

By then the crowd had thinned, but those remaining began throwing rocks. One hit Gregg in the face and he lost his grip. I grabbed his jacket, but the fabric strained and started to tear. Vada reached down, grabbed the golden sash around his middle, and hauled him up like he was little more than a laundry bag.

It was then that I heard the pop. One of the slubbers had speared the ship with a bamboo pole. The gases soon pushed the pole from the hole, the ballonets began to soften, and the ship began to sink.

From above Vada said, "We have to set down and repair it."

The crowd below was screaming, stones flew through the air.

"No! Keep going. I'll fix it."

Since the dirigible wasn't fully inflated, I was able to grasp the loose organza in my hands and climb out below the hole like someone hanging from jungle gym bars.

The slash was just five inches long, but if it wasn't stitched up we were going to lose all the half-hydrogen. I had a needle and thread in my pocket, but as I hung there, constantly re-gripping the fabric so I didn't plummet into the mob below, I realized I didn't know how to fix it.

"Tane," shouted Vada, hanging from the lower portal. "You'll fall. Come back!"

"Keep going!"

"We have to set down. Climb back!"

"I've got it!" I still didn't know what to do. Just then the powder engines turned on, and the ship lurched forward. Desperate not to fall off, I jammed my hand into the tear and felt the cold half-hydrogen rush down my sleeve and into my shirt. With my hand inside the ballonet, I grasped the seam allowance with my nails and found I could support myself with just one hand. With the other, I retrieved the threaded needle from my pocket, I sewed my sleeve to the ship, securing myself and sealing the hole in one move. The only problem was that now I had to dangle there as rocks whizzed past my head.

Vada called down from her perch on the ladder. "Hang on! We're landing up ahead!"

"I fixed it!"

She gazed at me proudly, and for that absurd, dangerous, yet perfect instant, I knew she loved me exactly as I loved her.

ANTARCTICA: BIRUDU

I slowed the Chang to a crawl. The last sign I had seen said: Entering Birudu / Population 48 Million. *And while I could see fields of house-towers in the distance, even cheaper versions of the vertical aluminum cigars that Zoom Langsin lived in, I was in the industrial side of town, where the buildings were squat, windowless, and covered with the varnish of smoke and greed.*

Thirty feet ahead of the Chang stood the first man I had seen for miles. He was covered head to foot in a yellow suit with a long visor and articulated black gloves. In one hand he held a long pole with which he was poking at the bottom of a jagged overhang of a building with the measured and bored motions of an hourly worker.

When my door swung open, the biting rot of the outside air seeped into my nose even before I had inhaled. The viscous humidity soon sheened my face, and beneath the soles of my Celine-Audis, the ground was spongy and sticky like risen sourdough.

I stepped to the front of the car and cupped a hand beside my mouth. "Any yarn mills around here?"

The poker man startled. "You're not supposed to be here!" I could just make out the dark triangles of his eyes, nose, and mouth, like charcoal smudges of a sketch hidden in the glare of the plastichrome of his visor. "Get on out!" He turned to the building as a door opened.

From the medical green interior, the silhouettes of two men emerged. Shielding my eyes, I saw that the first wore a short sleeve

B-shirt and shorts, while the second was dressed in a HAZMAT suit like Poker. The M-Bunny man's face was covered with a dark crust, like a blackened steak. His eyes were bloodshot and his lips shrank back from mottled black and brown teeth. While his eyes met mine for an instant, I sensed that his will and dreams had withered away to nothing but a sad residue.

I put my right arm to my face and breathed through the filtering material Pheff had hemmed into my sleeve, watching these two men walk to a trailer beyond Poker. Hazmat opened the door and pushed the M-Bunny man inside, shutting it after him. On the door, I could just make out a handwritten sign: Incubation. Below it were five interlocking black triangles.

As he returned to the building, Hazmat saw me, stopped, and raised an accusing finger. "Restricted area!"

Meanwhile Poker was idly prodding here and there. "I already told him."

Hazmat shook his head solemnly. "This is a restricted area!" The level of self-righteousness in his voice identified him as a boss. "There's a biological restriction."

My dad had surely encountered someone just like Hazmat. I thought about running at him and leveling him with a heel to the throat, but I turned to my Chang and, while still pressing my suit sleeve to my nose, got inside, quickly lowered the door, and turned the cabin air control to MAX Purify.

My hands were shaking and my stomach was acid. I had long avoided thinking about what it had been like for my father after he gave himself up. Even when Vada and I visited the M-Bunny headquarters, my anguish for Rik's regular recycle had diverted my imagination. And much later, when I had the means, I had searched for my father's past, for where he had been and what he had done—not how it had ended. But as I released the brakes, and engaged the forward motors, I was flooded with the vision of my father's last hours. He had been stuffed in some small space, allowed to get sicker so that they could scrape his skin to collect whatever viral or bacterial prize they thought he had.

M-Bunny's real product wasn't corn, or the products of its mills and factories, or even more prisoners—it was biological weapons.

KOM: NEARING THE FINAL HEM

From that day in K'Kom, Gregg called me *Darn it* for my emergency darning, and while I can't say I enjoyed the nickname, at least he always said it with a laugh or a smile. As for Vada, her reaction confused me. Even as Xavier and Marti praised me, she didn't say anything, and when I finally asked her what she thought, she only said that I'd been brave—the word she used was *valiant*, stretched out in a way that seemed to dilute its power. I got the feeling she resented what I'd done, as if perhaps *I* wasn't supposed to save *her*. And from that point on, the space between us cooled a few degrees. Of course that only made me long to be closer.

"I want to keep doing this forever," I told Vada late one night. "I see how much you love performing—I saw that back in Seattlehama, but it really gives you joy. It nourishes you. And that I'm making your costumes—that's a dream for me."

"I try to give something to the men in the slubs, but this is not my life. This is just a part of who I am."

Even more than her words, her tone seemed to render what I'd said inconsequential. "This *is* a good life."

"This is just what we do while we need to raise funds, hide, and plan."

"Vada… all I'm saying is that I'm happy and so are you. I can see it when you perform. That's what attracted me to you on the Europa."

She exhaled. "The shows feed my joy, but not my anger."

I wanted to scream. She seemed to think of her own anger as an organ, a poblano-shaped thing that rested beside her spleen. Not only did it exist, but required certain nutrients, demanded to be exercised, and most of all, couldn't be appeased, let alone extracted with forceps, happiness, or love. It wasn't the thing to ask, but I did anyway. "*What* anger?"

"We all have an ache somewhere. You do too."

"I don't," I told her. "Not when I'm with you… not when I'm working on your gowns."

That night was dark, and the ship was lights out, so I couldn't see her, but the way she sighed, I could tell she thought I was the broken one. "I can't let Bunné do what she's doing."

I wanted to laugh. "Bunné's a million miles away."

"Seven thousand twenty-eight."

"You're joking!"

She laughed for a moment. "Well, *approximately*." When her laugh faded she sat up. "Every minute that we're out here, she's killing thousands and consolidating her power, becoming more entrenched. Don't you care?"

Her single-mindedness exhausted me. "I do and I don't."

"You should hate Bunné. You should despise her for what she did to you, let alone that she ground your father into a paste."

Her word *paste* infuriated me. "Bunné didn't do that, the M-Bunny reps did. Besides, my father allowed it. He did it—" Guilt and rage swelled in my throat. "—He did it so I could have the bonus."

Vada thrust herself from the bed, and plunked down on her chair. "I don't expect you to understand the larger context. I *wish* you did, but I don't expect it."

The problem was, I was beginning to understand the *larger context* all too well. And as if to show her, I said, "We're heading to Seattlehama."

"Yes." Her tone was bitter, her delivery, sharp.

"You told me that you want me to rip a yarn from her. What

that means exactly and what will happen to Bunné afterward, I don't know. I can guess, but what I… what I see now is that there are no plans for us after that."

By then, I had made Vada two hundred and forty outfits, dresses, gowns, corsets, jumpers, mornings, evenings, and even a variant on a wedding dress. I had darted, hemmed, milled, cobbled, ironed, finished, tailored, stitched, beaded, shirred, ruffled, darned, frogged, zipped, tied, chained, over-locked, embroidered, top-stitched, zigzagged, padded, and stiffened.

More than that, I had heard about her childhood spent hiding and training in the Ukraine, Africa, the North Pole. I had heard her stories of being shot at, poisoned, savaged, beaten, locked away, and spit upon. I had listened to her recount her experiences fighting, singing, fire eating. I had enjoyed the tales of the people in her life: Qem, Adana Feez, and The Astonishing Zoré (obviously, she was a performer). I had even learned a little of her early life at the Toue camp, although that wasn't a favorite topic of hers as it was mostly overcrowded with tragedy.

She hadn't moved since I had spoken. "Vada, what's going to happen to us?"

"Tane," she began, her voice soft, "what we're doing now is lovely. It's wonderful, and it's not very dangerous. But if you stay with us… you will end up killed. And I absolutely don't want that. You don't want that. It can't… I mean… we can't… we're just too different. Our lives are too different."

I got up from her bed and stepped gingerly through the darkness to her side. Sinking to my knees, I put my arms around her. She in turn put an arm over my shoulder even as I heard her sigh wearily. "Vada," I said, willing our differences to silence, "shhh!"

"Come on, Darn it!" Gregg stood on the sand in nothing but a braided black thong and water goggles. Behind him, submerged to her neck, was the skinny-dipping Marti, who waved merrily at me before somersaulting and paddling off in the greenish murk. "The water only looks bad, but it's not." Gregg shrugged. "Well, maybe you'll just grow another toe."

For the past two weeks we had done just five shows as we flew over more water than land. We were now on the northern coast of Fiji. Vada and Xavier had left for town early in the morning.

"We're meeting someone" is all she had said that morning as she dressed in our double room at the Pair of Dice Algae Ocean Motel and Spa.

"You mean you're not going to tell me."

"And that's for your sake. If you…" She stopped, closing her eyes for an instant before she buttoned the top of her blouse—a veri-peek net with embroidered red polka dots. "Look," she began again, her voice softer, "even the time you've spent with us is something you'll always have to hide. If it's discovered, you'll probably be banned from the cities… and I'm beginning to regret that I—"

"What about what I want?"

"What you want can't change who I am."

"I'm not leaving you. I need you."

"Tane, please. Let's not start."

"Damn it!" I said, not caring who heard through the thin walls, "I want *you*. That's what I want! I wish you wanted me as much."

"I'm not something to *have*."

"I didn't say that. I said I want to *be* with you. I want to sew for you. That's all I want." I had been shouting. When I stopped I was as empty as a husk. This was a waste of my time. It was never going to happen. With my hand to my forehead, I spoke toward the floor, "I wish you wanted that."

"Tane…"

Turning, I opened the screened door and stormed across the cement, past the T-shirt carts, the smoked rat-on-a-stick huts, the plasticott sandals sellers, and the ocean-tar necklace vendors to the water's edge. I stood there staring at the slop of the algae-filled ocean feeling furious, foolish, and hoping like hell she would come after me.

When I finally returned to our room, all I found was the puckered bed of our night and the words *miss you*, scrawled in her narrow loops on the back of a drink coupon for Magoshi's Seaweed Cabaret. I felt abandoned. I angrily jammed my clothes into a white plastic laundry bag, as if I might just toss it over my shoulder and march off into the distant tropical hell. But when I stuffed my second pair of pants into the bag, it split open. I grabbed my things and hurled them at the lurid sunset painting bolted to the wall.

That evening, she returned. "I do *need* you," she said over dinner, the words awkwardly hollow in the post-Tiki, sea-monkey-squalor of Magoshi's.

"You *need* me to rip a yarn, and then you're leaving me."

Her mouth tightened to a hard line. "You're acting like a child."

"You're treating me like I'm your foot soldier. I'm glad you saved me and brought me in to your life. I understand how unprecedented and risky it was. I could tell the way Gregg and Marti first looked at me, but you're trying to use my talents like Withor, Kira, or Pilla."

She tilted her head to the side. "That's not how it is."

"That's exactly how it is! This is actually about us. *You* took me in and *we* were together. But now it's like you don't think I'd have feelings, like this was just a job. But when I sew for you, I feel you… I really feel you. I know where your bones are, I know the folds of your flesh… I love you."

Vada lowered her chin, eyes on the table. "I feel the same way." She smiled sadly. "I'll never forget anything."

I stared at the condensation on my glass and shivered. "You already have."

She clenched her fists. "We can't be the husband and wife like you want." Her hands relaxed and she dropped them to the table. "Not like you want. You know what I am. I have wonderful feelings for you. But I'm… I can't fall in love."

"You mean: you don't want to."

"I didn't say that."

A tray stacked with our BBQ stingrays arrived. Vada was ravenous; I downed the rest of my blue algae cocktail and ordered another.

Later, the two of us strolled down the boardwalk—cementwalk, really—under the strings of colored lights and the spiraling swells of night flies.

"What was that meeting this morning?"

"We met someone who has studied the material."

"Bunné's?"

"Shhh," she admonished, if the boy-girls in grass crowns were all listening in. "From what we heard, it's going to be extremely difficult."

I shrugged unconvinced. "Sure."

"Four days from now, she's going to have a show at the open-air amphitheater at the top of her building. It's called The Suicital."

I stopped and turned to Vada. The red and orange bulbs overhead washed her color away. Her dark eyes looked black, her skin, white. "The closer I push, the farther you retreat."

She closed her eyes slowly. The corners of her mouth darkened and a few faint dimples appeared on chin. "I'm… I guess in some way I'm afraid."

"And you're supposed to be the outlaw." Grasping her hand, I led us on.

We came to a collection of carnival rides: a giant Parris Wheel, a Spin-Tron, a Vorvox, and something called Hell Tunnel. I insisted we get in the last.

"This is silly," she said, but didn't otherwise resist.

We sat in a little car, which trundled along through stale water and various black rooms where worn projections of spiders, scorpions, and blood patterned our bodies. We barely paid attention though, for as soon as we had started, I grabbed her, and since I had made all her clothes, I knew their secrets. I had her exposed in an instant. We fashioned, and at least for those few minutes on that *silly* ride to hell, on that polluted island paradise—in the flesh if not fully in spirit—when I pushed, she pushed back.

ANTARCTICA: A BAR CALLED JUNIP NESTLED BETWEEN FEATURELESS FACTORIES AND WAREHOUSES

I nside it was so dark, I couldn't see anything. The music consisted of a steady grind and what I imagined were the perverted mutterings of a hunchback. The place smelled of body odor, spilled mash, and darkness.

From the low ceiling, crusted with decades of forgotten and unlit lighting options—including two dilapidated chandeliers, missing most of their faceted teardrops, and several cracked low-hanging sconces—the only source of illumination was a strange swirl of red plasticott that looked like some amateur's representation of the beginning of the universe or a massive nosebleed.

Once my eyes began to adjust and the walls and floor came into view, I could see twenty slubbers slumped over a flock of small black tables to the left. All were dressed in ill-fitting t-shirts. Among them I recognized recent versions of uniforms by M-Bunny, L. Segu, Bestke, and even two Wans—with their five useless empty eyelets down the front. The men were mostly all the same, except for the thickness of grime on their faces, the shapes of their frizzy beards, and the degree of misery curving their spines.

On the right, a dozen more sat before a dark bar, decorated with *a backlit rack of bottles of cheap liquor—corn mash, green-o, and what they called white maze.*

If any of them looked up when I had first entered, they had repositioned their heads at precisely the same angle of desolation and misanthrope as before. When I moved toward the bar, I saw only one overtly watch—his eyes glazing my suit and tie with suspicion as his left index wiggled halfway up his right nostril.

I saw two empty plasticott stools at the bar: one just a foot away at the end and the other halfway down. I stepped toward the second and I took my place as the men on either side inched away. After studying the bar surface, I found a relatively clean spot to rest my elbow.

I sat there for at least sixty-four bars of the noisy robotic music until a middle-aged woman in a tiny and too-tight red plastic dress finally emerged from behind a dank curtain and took up her place behind the bar. Her hair was florescent pink; her rubbery mouth liberally smeared with a sparkly green lipstick. From the middle of her red plastic necklace, a simulacra of a scrotum hung between her breasts and above that a long red erect phallus curved toward her mouth like a pacifier or microphone.

Once she had freshened the drinks of several others, she slopped her rag at the bar around my elbow and said, "Yeah?" Her voice was as smooth as crackers on sheets.

"I'm looking for a yarn mill."

"To drink?"

The men on either side of me laughed.

Without acknowledging her joke I just said, "Xi yarn."

She rolled her eyes "I don't make it!" She got another laugh from her audience, probably hoping for comps.

"Of course," I said, abandoning that tack. I gestured at the shelves behind her. "A bottle of your best acid mash."

"That's three thousand!"

But before she had finished her sentence, I had flipped out three fresh bills. Once she had registered the Calvins, I added another. "Three for you and one for the handsome red lad around your neck."

When one of the men laughed at my joke, she swiped his drink away and scooped up my bills in the same motion. A moment later, she smacked a bottle of Sir Admiral Dooganberry's Hot Pink Mash down in front of me. Then, in a clearly practiced move, she sucked the dong far into her mouth only to spit it back out in disgust, before turning on a heel to retreat behind the filthy curtain.

A show barely worth one Calvin. *I unstuck the bottle, slipped off the stool, feeling the plasticott momentarily cling to the high-twist wool of the seat of my pants. Holding up the bottle like a lure, I spoke over the music,* "I'm looking for a Xi yarn mill around here."

For several beats, no one even moved. Then a man with a red-and-gray-peppered beard knocked back his drink, and burped. Glaring at me, he blew out and let a wad of snot hang from his right nostril. A moment later, as if playing yoyo, he sniffed it up.

Undeterred, I caressed the flat bottom of Sir Admiral Dooganberry enticingly, and then turned and headed out into the sulfur-filled air outside. I strolled toward the Chang P, leaned against the side, and waited.

There was something tragicomic about the single-minded machismo ire of the modern slubbers as they oscillated from horny to angry and back again. In the last ten years, freedom and sympathy movements in the cities had put an end to the harsh chemicals and hormones once added to the B-shirts. But given this new alternative, my placid childhood in the corn had been a blessing.

I examined the bottle in my hand. The man on the front—Dooganberry I supposed—was elaborately decorated with medals and ribbons on his white jacket, golden epaulettes, a thick black handlebar moustache, a monocle, and a pink iguana on his shoulder.

After a few minutes, the man who had laughed at my joke exited the bar and started toward me. When he was fifteen feet away, he stopped, and pointed at the Chang-P. "This thing go?"

"*Xi yarn?*" I confirmed.

He nodded. We both got in and zipped off.

"*The bottle.*" He held out a worn and trembling hand.

I tightened my grip on Dooganberry's neck. "*Once we find the mill.*"

After a tremendous sniff, the sort of slubber thing I had forgotten about, he raised his chin toward the road. "*Ten miles straight.*" He reached for the bottle.

"*When we get there.*" I nestled the prize in the storage bin of my door.

"*Don't believe me?*" he grumbled.

"*Yes and no.*"

In my peripheral vision my passenger eyed me suspiciously. "*You from the cities?*"

"*Yes and no,*" I repeated.

"*It's one or the other!*" he argued, confusion lining his voice.

"*It's both.*" Turning to him, I met his stare. "*Right?*" I asked when the road forked ahead.

"*Yeah.*" The man sniffed again. "*The Xi for you?*"

"*Yes.*"

He loosed a typical two-huff slubber laugh. "*Got yourself spun on it?*"

"*Basically.*" This man could have been me, had I stayed. I wanted to ask him about his life, what it was like out here these days, but I didn't want to get too friendly either... too close to my past.

Two more amused huffs. "*No one liked you at the bar.*"

"*No new friends,*" I agreed. "*A shame.*"

We drove a mile in silence. Then suddenly, as if the question had been building up inside him, he blurted out, "*What are you?*"

"*A tailor.*"

"*For clothes?*"

"*Exactly.*"

"*Okay... up here,*" he said, pointing. "*Turn here. Past that tank... turn left. Then it's down there until we get to a gate. It's blue. I forget what it says.*"

We had been driving past warehouses, sheds, non-descript factories, and stacked containers colored with logos of shipping concerns, the ornate flags of ports, and the stylized fury of taggers.

We passed a large beige cinderblock building on the left. Beyond it was a small road under a blue sign. "That it?"

"No. It's bluer. And it's a gate gate." A beat later he asked, "What kind of car is this?"

"A Chang-P," I told him. "You're riding in the 660 with fifteen custom forward engines."

He snorted in disbelief. "How fast?"

"Quite."

"Hard to drive?"

"Somewhat." I felt bad for the man, for how little he knew, for how little he had experienced… and for how far I had come in comparison.

"Okay," he said, pointing, "up there. Past that barrel on the right."

I slowed. A blue gate was open. From one of the sides hung a jangle of chain and several locks. Beside the road a sign read: Warning. Clearance Required—By Order of M-Bunny Corporation a Division of MB-I. *I didn't see a guard—or anyone—for that matter. I nosed the Chang through the gate and continued. The road sloped down and to the right past more forgettable buildings. We passed a fenced courtyard, where a dozen slubbers stood. Several watched us pass.*

"How much farther?"

"Uh… well… not much." His confidence seemed to be fading.

I wondered when my friend was going to make a move, or if he had called ahead to arrange a trap with his buddies. I glanced at him, the wet shine below his nose, the filth in his matted beard, and told myself he didn't have communications; he probably didn't have friends.

The buildings grew more and more sparse. Between them sat fields of junk planted with gloomy, undersized corn.

"Stop here!" the slubber barked, his voice startling me in the silence.

The Chang came to a crunching stop. To our right was a pile of slag and sand; to the left, another windowless two-story structure.

When I glanced back at the man, he held a six-inch serrated knife in his right fist. The tip was slightly bent. "I'm an honest corn," he began, his voice tight, "and I want to help you. It's just that things cost more in Antarctica... especially for a shirt tailor." He punctuated his sentence with a laugh.

Here it was, I thought. "What do you want?"

"You tossed three papers at Pricilla. Five is good for me."

I glanced around at the buildings and nothing outside. "So, you're saying there's no Xi?"

The man laughed again. "There's Xi here. Pay me and I'll tell you where."

I pretended to consider his offer for a moment, then grasping the Admiral by his neck, I flipped open the door, and jumped out before my knife-wielding friend had even moved. I closed the door and glanced about. Straight ahead were three buildings guarded by men holding flash sticks.

I heard the slubber pounding on the windshield from the inside. After rolling my eyes, I said, "Passenger door." The lock clicked open. His breath was swear-strewn as he scrambled out and stumbled around the front of the Chang with his knife extended. "Don't corn me again!"

"If you cut the yak upholstery," I told him, "I will skin you and use your hide it to repair the seat. Now, do you want to earn the pink mash or not?"

The slubber stopped and squinted at me for a long beat. In the orange light, his eyes were hazel, complicated, and beautiful. A bubble of saliva formed at the side of his mouth as his whole face twisted into a disappointed frown. Then his eyes dropped from mine to the dusty bottle I held at my side and, just as quickly, his urgency and power faded. Turning, he gestured with the bad tip *of his knife. "It's the far one."*

I started for the building, but after five paces, turned, and tossed the bottle to him. The bottle somersaulted through the air. Flinging the knife to the side, he caught the bottle in both hands, but then fumbled and juggled it all the way down. The glass clinked against the dry hard ground, but didn't shatter. Relieved, he blew out a sigh, and wrenched off the top for a long desperate drink.

PACIFICUM OCEAN: FORWARD OBSERVATION PORTAL

We flew a hundred feet above the vast floating garbage-covered surface of the Pacificum Ocean. Near the Hawaiian Islands, roped-together junks, floats, rafts, and hulls formed masses that stretched for hundreds of miles. Since we weren't doing shows and I didn't have any costuming duties, I spent most of the time on my stomach in the small forward observation portal sharing the eyescopes with Gregg.

"There's a couple over there!" he said, handing me the scopes. "He's sewing her cut hard."

I took the scopes, but I didn't seek his find, instead scanning the dirty faces of the algae and seaweed brandclan slubbers that gazed up at us. Children often threw things at the Pacifica Showhouse as we passed—until their parents smacked them when the debris inevitably came raining back down. "It's all sad," I said.

With a disappointed snort, Gregg snatched back the scopes. A minute later, the ship having drifted, we were past the couple and he raised his head. "We'll be in Baja in two days." He shrugged. "I haven't been sand chipping in years."

I didn't know what that meant and didn't ask. These slubs seemed far worse than the corn. I couldn't imagine living on floating garbage and subsisting on little but the emerald algae that filled the water.

"Over there," Gregg pointed to the right. "Is that a cut-ko getting undressed?"

I just shook my head. Gregg frowned at me for a moment and turned back to watch. "She's going swimming," he said. "Wait… never mind… it's a man." He took the scopes from his eyes and stared ahead glumly. Turning, he glanced over his shoulder and spoke quietly. "Vada's had *others* along for her show tours."

The news didn't surprise me. "Oh?"

"But she's different around you."

I raised my head.

"She's nice to you." He frowned and scratched his nose. "I can see she really likes you." He laughed and then whispered. "I'm afraid of her, but it's juice that you guys are *fashionable*."

Although I pretended I didn't care one way or another, my chest fluttered with a strange mix of joy, relief, and worry. It confirmed exactly what I wanted to believe and exactly what I was beginning to fear.

"You floaters, looking for tits again?" Marti stood glaring at us. I rarely saw her these days, as she was always on the bridge helping Xavier. She poked her head into the organza bubble.

"Cut off!" said Gregg. "There's not supposed to be more than two in here!"

"Shut up!" To me she smiled and asked, "You doing it?"

"They've been doing it the whole time!" said Gregg, before I could speak. "Don't you hear them?"

"I'm talking about him getting Bunné, floater!"

"*Getting?*" I asked. "I'm just supposed to rip a yarn."

"Rip a yarn?" Gregg scoffed.

"No," said Marti. "I heard you're *cutting* her."

Vada sat at her desk staring at her open notebook. Folding it closed, she spoke toward the wall, exasperation in her voice. "You were talking to the crew."

"Is it true?" I stood just inside her cabin's door.

She turned and faced me. "We need the yarn."

"You told me I'm ripping a yarn. Marti says I'm *cutting* Bunné.*"

She sat up. "You're not *cutting her,* whatever that means. Marti probably means that the information we can get from the yarn—as we understand it—could take her down. You might only be setting off a long chain of events."

I chewed that for a moment. "Okay," I said slowly, "and it's the end of us?"

Her gaze fell away from me. "Each of us—I mean everyone in this cell—will go a separate way. We'll go under the heavy blankets for months… maybe years."

It was then, standing in her cabin with the gentle vibrations of the ship thrumming beneath my feet and the sunlight filtering down through the ballonets, that I finally saw, understood, and began to accept the end—the end of my adventure, the end of my affair with the showhouse entervator entertainer, and maybe the end of everything I had known. I hated it, but didn't know what I could do to stop it.

Vada frowned. "I know you're angry."

"No," I lied. "I'm not."

She pursed her lips. "For us to be together like you want, you would have to give up your life."

"I would."

"You don't know what you would be giving up."

"Isn't that my choice?"

She shook her head slowly. "It's not fair to you. You're supposed to sew, not do what we do." She sighed. "I love how I looked in your work and, believe me, a part of me wants you just for me, but that's not fair to you and your talents."

"That's your excuse," I told her. "I'm the one who decides about me and my shit *talents.*"

Her head slumped forward wearily. "Look… there are other things, too. I'm older than you think, and I've done terrible things. You have to understand who I really am. I'm not just the entervator entertainer you think I am."

"I know that!"

"I'm wanted by all the cities!" she said loudly, angrily. She covered her face with a hand and whispered. "I'm even wanted in Budai. And those people don't give a stitch if you cut out your own mother's lungs and eat them."

"I don't care about any of that."

Vada sighed. "And I wish I didn't either."

Two days later, after hundreds more miles of polluted ocean, I heard the call *Baja ahead!* from the bridge. For the next several days we flew north along the coast, closer here, farther there. We passed huge metropolises of G-Diego, Lax, Esefoh, and mile after mile of slubs everywhere in between.

"M-Bunny is pushing inland against L. Segu," said Vada. She and I lay on our stomachs in the forward observation port. "She's got masses of M-Bunny men as far down as Pelu. There's another corn clan down there called Rima, but they have been decimated with pox skirmishes. No one knows how many dead."

"Are you telling me so I'll be angry at Bunné?"

Vada paused. "I am."

"You don't have to."

"I just want you to understand."

"I do understand."

She frowned at me, but I ignored her, staring at the iridescent blooms of color in the water below.

Vada pushed herself up slowly. "I'm tired."

After she had gone, I lay there alone, a tingling fury racing up and down my body like charged electrons. I had to fight hard not to punch, kick, or scream.

Then the floor shifted. I turned, expecting Vada, but her brother Xavier lay beside me. I had barely even seen him on the ship over the past several months. He was always on the bridge. I glanced at the clump of chewed gum that had once been his ear.

He stared forward at the landscape below. "We're both a little bit doomed."

I didn't want his pity, or worse, to think that she had sent him to deliver the final blow, to tell me how impossible and tragic and different they were.

"We've both been hurt," he added. "In different ways." He stopped and shook his head. "Listen, all I know is that she thinks you're special. If she could… I think she might have run off with you." With that, he stood, and headed up the stairs to the bridge.

I know he had meant to comfort me, but his assurance only made it worse. It was close, he had meant. Just not close enough.

I didn't go to my room that night, but stayed there in the observation portal. Around dawn I fell asleep. When I woke in the afternoon, I used the toilet, ate, and then returned to the portal, where I spent the rest of the day staring blindly ahead as the earth flowed past.

I didn't see Vada.

Finally, we stopped in some slub place that Marti called Union. The tenting, the stage, and much of the gear was unloaded to lighten the ship. The crew was pared down with Gregg and Haas staying behind. At dusk, we turned north, and it wasn't long before I could see the top edge of the glowing towers of Seattlehama in the distance. I had imagined that I would feel some sense of homecoming and relief, but it was the opposite. I felt dread.

Through the eyescopes, I located Bunné's building, the Zea, and could see the lights of the open-air amphitheater on top, above her boutique. They were preparing for the show Vada had mentioned: *The Suicital*. I lowered the goggles. The stitches on that dress in Bunné's Boutique had been exactly seven hundred warp yarns apart. Standing, I hurried down the cloth corridor to the costume storeroom. Most of Vada's costumes and notions had been unloaded in Union, but a few remained, and after scrounging around in the darkness, I found the blouse I was looking for—a simple off-white number with black pick stitching. I checked the material: two-up twill with a high-twist blend warp and a low-twist weft. I guessed it was satellite silk as the hand was soft, supple, and coolly logical. With my thumb, I felt the pick-stitches and started counting the yarns.

A moment later, I tossed the blouse aside and made my way to Vada's room.

"I understand something."

Vada turned slowly from her notebook, her face grave. "Button the door."

I stepped in and closed the cloth behind me. "You're sisters."

ABOVE SEATTLEHAMA

Turbulence rumpled the walls and floors. I touched the twill beside me and waited. Vada closed her book and put it away. I could see her lick her lips and heard the tiny click of saliva. She didn't seem surprised, just resolved to provide the facts that were my reward. "We are sisters. Although, originally *she* was a boy. Her name was Qem." She snorted. "I don't know where that name came from. Maybe that's the reason... I mean... maybe that's when the problems began."

"You said you had a baby brother who died."

"I... well, that was a lie. That was Bunné. And my *brother* did die. She changed back then. And I don't mean her gender operation. One day I saw something in his eyes that scared me. I tried to help him. We snuck away to Umsterdam. I thought that surgery would help. We both thought that would fix her. But it didn't. I remember sitting next to her in recovery and her staring up at me with this awful sadness. It was like both of us knew we were fighting something else." She was silent for a long time. "Something inside her."

"You never told me much about your parents."

"That was another lie. We didn't have parents. The Toue custom is for the group to raise the young."

"But you loved Bunné," I said.

Vada nodded, and for a moment seemed to be lost in thought. "I still do... in a way." Her voice wavered. "I love who she *might* have been. Not who she became and who she is. These days, honestly, I can't be proud of even the good things." She sat up. "I just keep counting my regrets like fibers in a yarn."

"I don't understand what happened."

"No one does. I've gone over our childhoods a million times. Everything seemed normal. We had our looms, our secrets, our time scavenging. She was so happy in the beginning. You know what I've come to think? Some illness came over her. Some personality disease… some narcissism ailment… I don't even know." She slumped forward. "Mostly I blame myself. Maybe I could have done something else… something more."

I sat on her bed. "So you're trying to kill your sister?"

"You have to understand that we are part of a special generation. We're different than most Toue. We were bred to save the world." She laughed as if it were now just a joke. "We're smarter and we're stronger. We're more talented. We smell like shit petunias." She paused and stared at me for a long moment, as if trying to fix me in her memory. With a shrug she began again. "At least that's what we were told. So we set out to change the world. And then we were going to do the same in Seattlehama. Only in the end, once Bunné had assassinated the bastards, she decided *she* was going to run it. She made herself into the celeb… you know that part of it… and over time the city seemed to adopt her as some lost queen." Vada's laugh was laced with bitterness.

"When did she start M-Bunny?"

"M-Bunny." She paused. "That was one of the first things she did. She overhauled the prisons. She was going to *save the men*." Vada shook her head slowly and then focused on me. "You have to understand that before you… I mean years ago… the slubs were terrible in other ways. They were violent wreckages. Bands of gangs roamed around… killing… beating… you heard stories that there were ten million rapes a night out there in the darkness." Vada put her elbows on her knees. "Bunné neutered them all. She gathered them up, clothed them with her shirts. She made them into sexless simpletons. *They're happier*, she said. *We've done a good thing for them.* Maybe they were." Vada gazed at me sadly. "Anyway, it was a huge success. The city wasn't being attacked; the tourists came. That's how it all started. And she was just a kid then. She was nineteen."

"She's the one in the posters." In the COM in M-Bunny buses and on the back of the fry trucks were posters of a smiling young woman, maybe fourteen, with apple cheeks and clear eyes. In most of them she is holding a basket of corncobs. In others, she stands amid rows of corn with sunshine blessing her hair.

"I know!" Vada said, as if I had said it a hundred times before. "Those paintings... I did those."

I thought of all the years I had stared at those posters in awe. "You painted those?"

"I tried to stay close. I tried to steer her as best I could. I painted her how I wanted her to be." She rolled her eyes. "I've never seen any royalties on those, either!"

"I remember staring at those posters at the COM. I didn't even know what she was, but I grew up loving her."

"I know," she said softly. "I know."

"She started with M-Bunny and built her empire from there?"

"She invented those B-shirts with the hormones in them. From there, she just kept going."

"Why are those so awful? That's the one thing I just can't fathom. Why isn't the neck hole even right?"

Vada stared at me for a beat and then laughed. "You are crazy!"

"I hate those shirts!"

"I'm sorry. I shouldn't laugh. I've never worn one very long." Vada shrugged. "What else can I say? She can sing. She can dance. She knows how to tell a story. It doesn't hurt that she's gorgeous. She's a brilliant researcher. I've told you all the things she's invented. As soon as she had her gender, she never looked back. And there were people begging to help her."

Through the front of the ship, I could see the glowing towers straight ahead. They were only a few miles away. "You sound almost jealous."

"No…" she said with an exhale. "It's not jealousy. I'm in awe. Or I was. All that she's done is amazing. It's just that now there's no one to tell her to stop."

"Except her older sister."

Vada snorted bitterly. "She'd cut me if I did."

From behind a dozen layers of oilcloth and organza, I heard Xavier slur from his wounded mouth, "Begin city ascent!" The nose of the ship began to rise, and I could feel the strained harmonies of the powder motors.

Vada's voice sounded a thousand miles away. "Let's get you ready."

As I re-dressed in black super-stain, fingerless gloves, and Jacque 24 chameleon sneaks, and applied my yarn pulls, the Pacifica began its long climb to the top of the city making a slow corkscrew around the buildings. Once I was ready, Vada and I slipped into the forward observation port. The height of the city, the dazzling kaleidoscope of colors, the humming spires, towers, and constellations of color and geometry seemed to so fill our senses that for several minutes we didn't utter a word.

Here, at last, was the communion I had expected to feel upon my return. I was taken back to the wonder of my first dazzling sight of Seattlehama as a boy. And even as I remembered the endless hallways, the miles of souvenirs, and the costumed t'ups in their worm coats, elaborate hoop gowns, chrome chokes, giraffe heads, and ball-shirts, I couldn't help but be awed by the structure of the city itself.

Vada nestled beside me and we kissed. And then in the confines of the observation—little more than a sleeping-bag-sized bubble of the organza—we said goodbye.

"Three hundred," came Xavier's voice just as we were re-dressing.

"We should get down to the mudroom," said Vada. "You've got everything?"

"Yarn pulls," I said, holding up my hands. Patting my pockets, I continued, "Suicital pass... Gecko gloves... and my dad's yarn."

Vada smiled. Just then the ship lurched to the right, and I heard a wall seam pop.

"She going to make it?" I asked as we felt our way down the now-sloped corridor to the bottom of the ship.

All Vada said was, "Hope so."

Marti stood inside the mudroom, her arms crossed. "All finished with your biological farewell?"

"That will be enough," said Vada.

Marti frowned, and pointed toward the floor. "Don't unbutton the hatch until we give the call—we need the aerodynamics." She held out a hand. "Good luck."

I shook it and thanked her.

When she left us, Vada and I huddled in the growing cold. The engines began to choke as the air thinned and the balloon's lift stalled, and I found myself straining as if to raise the craft with sheer resolve.

"Eight hundred stories," he called out. It seemed to take forever as the ship strained for each inch. Winds buffeted the ballonets and sometimes it felt like we were plummeting hundreds of feet at a time. Outside, the city continued to slowly spin around us. When we finally crested the neon green static of Infinity Tower, Xavier announced, "Nine hundred."

Slipstreams of cloud and haze filled the air giving the buildings a crystalline glow. I heard several more seams snap.

Marti whispered through the speaking tube, "Open the hatch!"

Vada crouched down to undo the buttons, letting in the freezing night air. Straight down it was pure black and cold, but when I leaned far to the side, I could see the vista of the buildings stretching a mile down through layers of mist. I grasped the walls and held on. Above us, the ballonets quivered like soap bubbles. They seemed barely able to support us. The ship trembled and when I peered down to check, I could see that we had come to a stop.

"We're not moving."

"Shh!"

More threads snapped. Several sounded like they were far above and I worried that the ballonets had broken. On either side of the gondola the motors were vibrating so violently that I feared they would rip from their moorings.

Vada leaned toward me. "Tane," she murmured, "I do love you."

Her words arrested me. And it was the first time in my life I heard them. My heart swelled, my throat tightened, and for the next minute—maybe more—I could barely breathe, let alone speak. I nodded my head, but knew she could only see the barest outline of watercolor on black from the city lights.

Xavier's voice stretched down the tube. "Is the hatch open?"

"I told them already!" came Marti's voice in the background.

"That's why there's too much drag!"

Ignoring the argument on the bridge, I put my arm around Vada's waist. "I love you."

She kissed me, but in the darkness her mouth missed mine so that her upper lip knocked into my teeth. She pulled back with a yelp. I think she was cut.

"Sorry!"

"Shh!"

Through the open hatch, I saw that we were now fifty feet above Bunné's huge, scalloped, open-air amphitheater at the top of her building. Rows of seats were filled with thousands of costumed t'ups. Through the gusts of air I could hear snatches of applause and the thump of a beat.

"Destination target approaching," said Xavier.

Vada grasped the flax rope and held it for me. "Good luck."

"Twenty feet!" called Xavier.

I took the rope in my gloved hands and stepped to the edge of the hatch. In the cover of darkness, the Pacifica was invisible.

Because of the music and the noise, the motors were inaudible. It was eerie watching the costumed t'ups below so oblivious to our presence.

"Fifteen feet."

Some were eating; others, laughingly throwing back glasses of brightly colored liquor. I saw a row of men, each dressed as Warrior Remon of Loin, dancing back and forth. Farther to the right I saw two Choky Bears fashioning each other.

"Ten feet."

We were nearing the stage and the mosh, filled with women dressed as Maiden Hunk, Pricilla Filth, and several Fine Sensual Rats. Grasping the rope tightly, the muscles of my arms and legs shook from cold and excitement.

"Eight," shout-whispered Xavier as the ship began to shudder. I could hear the motors whine.

"Five!... Four!"

"Vada," I said as I heard several fabric tears.

"Three... two..."

"I'll always want you." The cloth above our heads ripped.

"Zero! Jump! Now! Destination! Target!" Xavier's voice was a pistol discharging into the air.

We were above the far edge of the mosh where it met a glass fence at the edge of the amphitheater. Beyond was only the sheer drop of the tower, an ocean of vapor, and, far below, the hard earth. I tried to find Vada's eyes amid the shadows and darkness to see if she had heard, but except for the shape of her dress, the puff of a sleeve cap, and the wrinkles of her bodice everything was black.

"Now!" shouted Xavier. "Jump now. Jump now!"

Re-grasping the rope, I leapt through the opening and plunged into pure icy cold. Clenching every muscle, I hung on to the rope as it was pulled taut—vibrated a low C—and then yanked me backward. When I let go, I spun head over feet.

ANTARCTICA: MB INDUSTRIES BUILDING #9

The windowless building was made of brick and painted the color of exhausted earth. And as I slowly approached, I saw a guard sitting at the bottom of the dry moat that surrounded the place. He peered up at me from shadow. While his shirt was fresh and smooth, his pants didn't look like they'd seen the affection of an iron in a long time. Worse, the knees had been distended and probably not just from protracted sitting, but weak fibers, low-spun yarn, and the application of some cheap finishing solution for shine and fit. When I stopped ten feet away, he uttered his predictable taradiddle, "Can I help you?"

I stopped at the edge of the moat and pointed at the structure with my chin. "Inside." I trusted the guard to add both subject and predicate.

He squinted up at me unhappily, chewing the inside of his right cheek. After a long moment, he spoke. "You need credentials."

"Name's Tane," I told him.

He stopped chewing, his mouth flattened into a thin line. "What?"

"Tane Cedar," I enunciated. "Men's Precision Tailor."

"You got credentials?"

"Tell the rep I'm here."

"No one goes in without credentials."

If he said that word once more, I thought I might rip his shirt apart and make a gag with it. I pointed at the building behind him. "They know me." I hoped it was true. Glancing up at the sky as if content to watch the filmy clouds swim by, I noted that I didn't hear gravel beneath the soles of his plasticott shoes. I inhaled, and then as loudly and angrily as I could, screamed, "Do it now, smuthead!" I saw my own spittle fly toward the shadows and fall near the scuffed toes of his shoes.

It was the man's belly that reacted first, stretching in pulls and wrinkles across his shirt. Then he swallowed, and I could see the strain around his eyes as he tried to shore up his front of disinterest and disapproval. For a moment, his lips flexed as if he were about to speak, maybe even mention credentials *again, but then he looked away, fumbled his weight left and right, and finally, muttering a string of curses, pushed himself up, and trudged to the left.*

A minute later, I heard "Tane Cedar?" The guard stood, his hand clasped protectively over his belly. "Very sorry, sir." Turning, he pointed to the far end. "Use the green stairs to the office."

I eyed the guard and nodded. The way he stood there, the orange light heating his face, eyes, and plump body, I felt sorry for him and ashamed of my outburst, even if it was the currency of influence.

The green paint on the stairs was bubbling here and there, where rust sores were about to pop. While my reputation and notoriety hadn't done me much good with Ryder and Zoom, maybe they would be more impressed, here at the end of the slubs.

Under the soles of my shoes, the metal clanked hollowly and the whole staircase swayed. At the roof, the green staircase became a walkway with handrails on either side leading to the peak of the roof, where I was surprised to see a greenhouse about thirty feet across.

As I approached, I saw that the door was slightly ajar. Through the glass, I could see what looked like hotel furniture.

"Hello?" I heard no reply and pushed open the door. Inside sat a black desk and chair, a bed, and a night table. Straight in back

was another glass door that probably led down to the mill, and beside that door stood a dressing screen where a figure was visible through the pebbly glass, dyed burgundy hair peeking above the edge. All I could tell through the distortion was that the person was lean and was apparently dressing slowly.

I licked my dry lips. "I'm looking for the rep. I have business."

The figure paused and then with renewed energy finished buttoning something around her neck and stepped from behind the screen. I felt a shock of recognition: Pilla. It was impossible—and yet I knew immediately it was her. Though her skin was a shade lighter, probably bleached from the long darkness of Antarctica's winters, and her hair was no longer a cartoonish orange but a dignified shade of oak, the tiny and heartbreaking sadness that had filled her eyes remained. The real change was the ring embedded in her neck.

A brilliant gold, two inches wide and a quarter of an inch thick, the metal pierced a good pinch of her flesh on the left side of her throat. It took me a second to decide that the ring wasn't some antipodal fashion statement. In that knot of flesh, the ring passed around her jugular. And from there the ring was tethered with a titanium rope to an I-beam above. It was not jewelry but a leash.

Her eyes traveled to my shoes and back up. For a moment a smile played at the corners of her mouth, but quickly soured. "Don't tell me you're here to see me."

"Of course I am. I'm on a supply errand and was directed here by a couple of fabric jobbers." I stepped across the threshold as the door closed behind me. "I love your new hair color! It works so well with your skin tone, it must be your original shade. It's a perfect juxtaposition." I smiled a little harder. "Curiously, I used a shade of brown exactly like it in a necktie just the other day." My eyes darted toward her jugular—she wasn't in charge here; she was another prisoner. "We never said goodbye in Seattlehama. Things changed quite quickly and drastically, and I had to leave. So I never got to really thank you for my time with Nathan Zanella.

His influence was enormous and I doubt I—" I stopped and swallowed. "How are you?"

She laughed at me with bitter delight. "I don't think I ever saw you lie so badly!" I could see the artery encircled by the golden ring pulse.

I peered past her through another glass door that led down a set of stairs. On the floor below, I could see rows of workers sitting on what looked like large plasticott recliners. "This is a Xi mill, isn't it?"

"The last in the world." Pilla stepped toward the desk, touched the screen and fiddled for a moment. She then narrowed her eyes at me. "What the hell are you doing here?"

"I could ask you the same thing!" She did not respond, but gazed impatiently. I had delayed enough. "I need pure Xi. Enough to make a coat."

"You don't still burn, do you?" Her tone was caustic. "It's not the fashion it once was."

"No. I haven't since Seattlehama."

Her fingers moved swiftly over the screen as she tabulated and finished what might have been a factory report. Her fingers stopped. "I never thought I'd see you again."

"Nor I, you!" I tried to smile.

She peered up at me. "You left me in quite a lurch."

"I'm very sorry about that."

"You don't know how bad it was… is." She craned her neck to the side. "How do you like my beautiful golden ring?"

My heart was filled with the itchy wool of shame. "I don't know if you know this, but satins pinned Izadora's murder on me. I was arrested and almost killed."

She shrugged sadly. "But you weren't."

I had run a marathon around the globe only to smash into a brick wall two feet from the finish. "Is the Xi for sale?"

"What's your rush?"

"It's for a client. I have a deadline."

She snorted, "Of course," and idly swiped at the screen.

"Is it for sale?" I reached for my wallet. "I'm willing to overpay."

"Why should I help you?"

"I'm sorry about leaving you like I did. And I know I owe you. Name your price for the Xi."

Gently adjusting the golden ring, she shook her head slowly. "What good would money do me?"

"Can't you bribe your way out of here?"

She glared at me.

"Pilla, how did you get here? Who did this to you?"

"I'm not telling you!"

"I'm sure they could be persuaded to let you go."

She laughed heartily at that.

"I've come too far to leave without the Xi." She didn't even look up, just continued working her screen. "What do you want? Don't you want out of here? Don't you want to get out of that ring?"

Pilla frowned at me. "Maybe I like being tethered in this little office atop this factory in the middle of nowhere!"

I pointed over my shoulder. "I have a pair of water-shears in the car. I'll get them recharged, and I'm sure I could cut that thing off."

She flicked angrily at the screen, which went black. "Do you know how much I risked for you? Do you have any fucking idea?"

SEATTLEHAMA: EDGE OF THE AMPHITHEATER STAGE

I came down hard, bounced, and crashed into the floor. As pain flashed in my bones like dots of a constellation, I took stock of myself. I was hurt, but alive.

"Hey," I heard from behind. A t'up in a heavy fornication jacket glared at me. "That's not dancing!"

"No," I agreed as I pushed myself up, "I call that falling." Glancing up at the sky. I thought I saw the outline of the Pacifica—a swollen grey torpedo—as it headed back down. *Goodbye, Vada. Goodbye.*

Just forty feet ahead was the black stage, where in a cluster of colored spotlights, an old woman rode a large unicycle. Instead of a rubber tire, though, the wheel was made of outward pointing scissors. As she shakily clattered around in a circle, some scissors points seemed to stick into the stage while others slipped. She seemed about to topple at any moment.

A Bunné saleswarrior in a sky-blue minidress and shiny thigh-high boots stepped to my side, eyes bright. She held out a hand. "Presence in the super executive fornication pit necessitates the Super-Core Black Platinum Pass for the Great Suicital Recital Highlights Show. Present your honor, good costumer."

From the inside pocket of my jacket, I took out the printed woven square that Vada had given me. The woman looked it over, her small mouth tightening into a frown. I couldn't believe it. After all that, I was going to be tossed out and never even get the chance to get close to Bunné? The saleswarrior thrust the cloth back at me and produced a tiny smile. "Pain encompasses forgiving." Turning, she strode back to her post. I guessed that was warTalk for *enjoy the show.*

The house voice said, "And now, the apex of the evening... the grand and the magnificent... the craft and the art... the center of our cherished being... the inventor... dancer... singer... model... designer... mathematician... the egg-mother supreme of our sex and shopping city... the slayer of men... the wise of woman... the unity... the harp... the magical... the mysterious... the wet... the impossible... the brilliant show of cause! We bring you the greatest epic creator, the most fashionable leader the world has ever seen... your love... your heart... your mind... your sex! The incomparable and unbelievable pinnacle of humanity and affection: Miss Bunné!"

As the women around me shrieked, flailing their arms, and flung themselves into each other—many fell and were trampled—I pushed back to the glass wall so I wouldn't be knocked flat.

A blast of lights like the exhaust of a rocket enveloped the stage. The glare was so bright I squeezed my eyes shut and covered my face with my forearm. Even so, the light reached me, illuminating an eerie veined world of red behind my eyelids. Once the brightness died down, I was left in a sea of blobby green afterimages. I heard what sounded like massive turbines and then a staccato rhythm began to hammer.

Male dancers in dark jackets, ties, and white tutus entered the stage and flung themselves back and forth frantically. Then two voluptuous, large-eyed women in painted-on nurse uniforms and complicated gas masks wheeled out an empty gurney to the middle of the stage. The crowd seemed to know what this meant and began clapping. And then from above, a woman—Bunné I soon realized—was lowered onto the stage just twenty feet from me.

Her neck, ears, hands, and eyelids were bejeweled with heat sapphires and particle lace. Her short, fluffy, and pure-white hair matched her long, glaring ultra-violet white wedding dress. When she moved, the diaphanous train floated behind like magnetic fog. Even from where I was, I sensed a chilling logic about the garment. It wasn't cut and sewn, but woven whole on some preposterously complicated loom that had been built to make this—and only this—exact dress. For a moment, I was overwhelmed by the geometry of such a thing—this half-woven, half-knit masterpiece of such complexity and ultimate effortlessness.

When her solid silver pumps touched the floor, two boys in black leather shorts rushed out to attach large, pear-shaped earrings that looked like forty-pound anger diamonds. Each boy then labored to support the jewel so it wouldn't tear her lobes.

"In the faint and tarnished vectors of our past," Bunné began, her voice soft and ethereal, "my mother groveled for ears. And when I was hatched among the kernels of despair, my father cut her down for giving him a girl." The dancing men retreated to the shadows as a woman in golden veils came forward, squatted, clenched her face, and then left a large yellow egg on the stage. "As a daughter, I was ravished a thousand chain of moon, I bled from every cut, but I lived on…" Behind Bunné, three of the tutu men came forward. One picked up the egg. For a beat he seemed mesmerized by the thing and then he rubbed it against his crotch. The others laughed, grabbed it away from him, and tried to hump it.

"But I lived on," said Bunné, her volume rising, "because I heard the rhythm in your beast… I lived on because of the kindness in your hands… I lived on because I felt the curds of hope in your mouth…" She was surrounded by a blaze of light. "I lived on…" She raised her right hand high in the air. "I lived on…" Her palm was lit by what seemed like some internal light. She held her pose as her expression wilted from what seemed like hope to fear and anguish. The amphitheater went silent. The characters around me held absolutely still. One of the tutu men, who had been thrusting at the egg, slowed, turned, and stared at her as though waiting for her next line. Then he slipped and dropped the egg. It seemed to take several instants before it fell, but when it hit the stage with a crack that filled the space, the shell split into two large pieces. A puddle of red goo oozed out and there sat a writhing mass of painful tumor and bone.

I stared at that thing in horror even though I knew this wasn't the truth.

Bunné's mouth opened wide, and she screamed in terrible pain. Her knees buckled and she collapsed. The two leather boys frantically detached the earrings. One ran to the side of the stage, dragging the huge jewelry, crying. The other hovered over the crumpled body, whispering, and tentatively tapping her back as if to revive her.

A frantic web of whispers covered the audience. Was this part of the show or had something gone wrong? Soon the murmurs grew in volume. Some called to her, and others shouted for help. I took a step closer, thinking that this might be my chance. Ahead, several women began to try to climb up on the stage perhaps imagining they were going to save her.

In a blink, Bunné's body was gone, as were the tutu men, the cracked egg, and the sorry, broken embryo that had crawled from it. The stage darkened for a moment, then seemed to explode in a tower of sparks. From that violence and pearly smoke a man stepped forward, dressed in a feathery violet jacket embellished with lace, beads, and ruffles. His shirt was a flowerbed of violets and azure. It was Warrior Remon of Loin! He strode to the front of the stage—his muscular legs painted with the sheerest white stocking—and stood there, his shoulders wide, his chest puffed as if he were king, emperor, dictator, and CEO of the world all at once. He began to sing warTalk in a rumbling baritone.

Once he had finished his song, he stood and surveyed the audience, his steely eyes projecting both power and angst. Cold tremors shook me as the crowd cheered. Not only did I see myself in him, but felt he connected me to something else— something I couldn't quite identify. And now I understood Kira's admiration. I wished I had truly been more like this man.

In a flash, he held up a palm as presenting us with something— his innocence, his humanity, his potential. Music began to build. A thousand violins sawed an arpeggiated minor chord. Bass drums beat faster and faster.

A ghostly image of Bunné stood beside him. She clutched at her abdomen as if in pain. When she took her hands away, they were covered with blood. The audience gasped and Bunné's ghostly image faded away. When she disappeared, a single red dot appeared on Remon's tights-covered crotch.

He gazed down in horror as the spot grew larger and gradually drips flowed down his white tights. His eyes rolled up in their sockets, and when he tipped over backward, a hospital bed rose from the floor to catch him.

From off stage, a younger looking Miss Bunné ran to his bedside. Her long, diaphanous, unsewn gown made of unfinished cloth of gold was the opposite of the wedding dress. I wondered if it was somehow symbolic that the wedding dress of hope was impossibly complex; the dress of sadness, uncompleted and never finished.

She clutched Remon's hand and sang softly and sadly. Baffled and horrified as I was by this grotesque play, Bunné's heartfelt song touched me in a way for which I had no defense. I started toward the stage, curious and leery of what I would find.

ANTARCTICA: CRYSTAL OBSERVATION ROOM

I met Pilla's gaze. "I know you sacrificed a lot."

"You don't know shit! Do you know what happened to me when they pinned you as a Toue terrorist?"

"I'm not a terrorist."

"You were in a conspiracy with known Toue terrorists! You met with known terrorists and were planning terrorist crimes against the shopping city!" Her complexion had turned fuchsia. The flesh pierced by the ring was throbbing.

"You know that's not true."

"I was in shit!" she yelled. "I had to beg for my fucking life. It's taken me years just to get to this shithole. I have my own desk. I have a lovely private toilet. And I eat all the algae burger I want!" She shook her head slowly as she touched the pinch of flesh in the ring. "And no, Mr. Tailor, you are not going to fuck with the ring in my fucking neck with a pair of fucking scissors!"

I stood silent, letting her anger ebb. "How did what happened to me matter to you? You were just sponsoring me in fashion and the last thing was: I never went back to that sad haberdashery."

Her shoulders sagged disappointedly. "I worked for Bunné. I was one of her top assassins."

I wanted to laugh, but her sour expression worried me. She couldn't be an assassin! Sure, I'd heard stories about cloaked ninja-kos wielding deadly knots, plam needles, and satin throwing pins, it all sounded like a pinkomic Pheff might read. It was not Pilla.

"You didn't kill people."

"Not people." Swiping her screen from the desk, she turned and hurled it at the wall. It spun through the air, hit the glass, and smashed. Bits littered the floor. The glass wall was unharmed. "I killed Bunné's enemies." Her eyes traveled from my shoes to my hair and back down. "You are one of her enemies."

"I wasn't one of her enemies. And as for what happened, I was just caught in the middle of—" I stopped. In that dusty hallway on floor 888 in the Parfum building where I was to make my last rip for Withor, I had seen a ghost kill Izadora with a Xi scarf. The ghost then pushed me to the floor, hesitated, and ran. "You killed Izadora. You were the one in the Parfum!"

"There's no visual record." She eyed me slyly. "And that dark-knot cloaking suit I wore does not even officially exist."

"You were supposed to kill me."

She nodded and lowered her head, down at the debris across the floor.

"Why didn't you?"

She peered up at my face. "Your eyes."

I didn't doubt her at all now, and maybe the sadness I had always seen in her was some reflection of her horror at her own deeds. I watched as she now fingered the top of her desk. I spoke softly and with as much angst as I could muster. "I'll never forget when you first came to Kira's."

She laughed bitterly. "I haven't thought about that ridiculous skivvé looper for years! She must be dead!"

"Actually, I heard she's still in Seattlehama teaching warTalk."

Pilla rolled her eyes. "Useless cut."

"You were different than those saleswarriors. There was always an incredible depth and power to you, but also a warmth and vulnerability."

"Don't shit me."

"Remember how we fashioned in those Pearl River tights?" I asked, shifting lanes again. "You introduced me to those. And of course Xi. I'll never forget that." I whispered, "We had a lot of good times together, Pilla. That's what I remember. I know things didn't end well, but that wasn't our fault. Now, I'm sure we can work something out about this Xi and what you might need."

Her brown eyes narrowed. "You know what you can do for me?"

I hoped she wasn't going to suggest we don some of those love tights. "I'd love to help."

She held out her right hand, palm up like a magician starting a trick. "You could help fix things for me."

Was she asking for a handout? "Sure! What do you need?" I started to go for my wallet again.

With her other thumb, she pressed firmly on the tendons in her arm. A five-inch-long, white knitting needle—more like a spike—with a point as sharp as a satin pin, stabbed out of the base of her wrist. She smiled a cockeyed smile. "You can die."

"Shit!" I stepped back.

She started around the desk. "I had this installed years ago. I almost used it once." She gazed longingly at my face. "These days, no one gets close enough."

Retreating, I felt for the door handle behind my back, but found it locked. "Pilla, I'm very sorry about leaving you in Seattlehama! It wasn't what I wanted. You know that, right?" I tried wrenching open the door, but it wouldn't budge.

She stepped closer. Blood flowed where the needle had stabbed through her skin. "You're locked in."

"Killing me doesn't get you anything! I'm rich now, Pilla! I must have something you need. Something you want!"

Her mouth tightened to a pucker. "Look at you, talented tailor to the world—a cringing cut!"

If I screamed, I doubted the guard could hear. Even if he did, he was not about to come running. Worse, I was defenseless. The empty water-shears that I might have used as a knife were back in the car. The Mini-Air-Juki sewing machine in my pocket was designed expressly not to puncture skin. The crochet hook and snips hardly seemed worthy opponents to her needle. The only *other tools I had were the two tiny yarn pulls under the nails on my middle fingers. I couldn't think what to do or say! "I don't need the Xi yarn." My voice had lost power. I strained like I was shouting, but barely made a sound. "I'll just go."*

"They say that every needle eventually loses its point." She tested the tip with a finger and drew a red dot. "But this one is still very sharp."

Flattening myself against the glass door, I balled my right hand. "Pilla, please, this is crazy. Just let me go. I never meant to hurt you. I had no idea."

She stepped closer. "What I should have done was killed you in the Parfum building. That's where I went wrong. I had a job, and I didn't do it."

As hard as I could, I smashed my fist against the door. The glass shook but didn't break. My knuckles screamed in agony.

"The glass is very strong." She smiled.

"Pilla, listen to me: Don't you want out of here? Who's keeping you here? I'll get you out! I've got money."

She raised the needle toward my chest. "I don't want your money. I want to mend my ways."

SEATTLEHAMA: RIP

Warrior Remon died while Bunné kissed his jacket, shirt, shoes, and slowly worked her way toward the bloody center of his crotch. Just as her lips touched the bloody material, the amphitheater went dark. After a long moment of complete silence and pure black, the crowd stood, and screamed.

When the lights came back up, Bunné, now surrounded by saleswarriors—armed with long shears—and purple satins, stood with the others from the show and smiled and waved. Her precisely tailored navy jacket—exactly like the design Vada had showed me on the Pacifica—gave off a shimmer like a school of silvery fish.

The audience, me included, stormed the stage. Soon a hundred surrounded Bunné, and when I saw that the saleswarriors were letting her fans greet her one at a time, I knew this was my chance. I pushed through the wools and sheers, grasped the edge of the stage, and hauled myself up.

Slipping between two Black Dead Breeders, I saw that one had on a skivvé and was rubbing the tube furiously. Farther back, a Magnificent Wasp Female with a ten-inch corseted waist let out a wobbly exaltation and fainted, caught by a Warrior Remon in violet frill. While I didn't feel the same lust and love as the others, I had been captivated, even mesmerized, by the show, and standing there, waiting my turn, I studied Bunné closely, hoping to understand how this one woman could be the ruling celeb of the city, the inventor of M-Bunny, Vada's sister, the most talented seamstress I'd ever seen… and the castrator and killer of millions of men.

"Truth is a gingham parasol!" said Bunné, hugging a Sorry-Girl in torn rags. A moss-green WaterButtie stepped before her. "A lumen of hope," she said with a kiss. To the next she said, "A flock of history." A Pricilla Filth, nude below her flowing gown, wept as Bunné whispered, "A single kernel of myth."

She was a heavy warTalker. I don't know why that surprised me. After all, this was where Kira and all the other saleswarriors got it.

"Three seconds," said one of the satins guarding her. "Three-second hugs only."

"Left arm up… right low," said a saleswarrior demonstrating. "No more than five words or ten syllables."

"One air kiss," added another satin. "Off her right cheek!"

"Keep moving," growled another. "Say your line, give respect, and move on."

Bunné spoke with two Blackwitch Breaths. "The heart of the infinite!" she said with a laugh, and then her expression fell. "Crushed by the swooping fall of a lone Chesapeake leaf."

"Once you greet and hug," said a saleswarrior, pointing to stage left, "release and travel."

A Commander Sheppard in a worm jacket stepped before Bunné, but couldn't remember which arm went where.

"Right arm down! Right arm down!" barked a tall satin.

"I'm sorry," sputtered the man, "I'm nervous… I just wanted to say—"

"Time's up! Move on!" One of the satins grasped his arm. "Only five words!" He dragged Commander Sheppard away.

"I'm sorry!" he called to Bunné. "I'm terribly sorry. I love you dearly!" By then, half of the real worms on his jacket had been squished.

"Next," a satin intoned.

Bunné seemed not to hear or notice her guards and handlers. She smiled at a woman dressed as Reginald Ball Fairy and said,

"I am a new humanity." It was as if she had a special phrase for each of them. When Bunné hugged the woman, her luminous blue eyes met mine.

I shouldn't have been looking at her. I should have been gazing down at the stage or the tops of my Jacque 24 chameleon sneaks, trying to remain unseen and invisible. But I couldn't look away from her, even as every nerve in my body screamed to do so.

Bunné released the Reginald Ball Fairy, and peered at me suspiciously. She pointed one of her long fingers. "Advance."

PART 4
TWISTS PER INCH

ANTARCTICA: CRYSTAL OBSERVATION ROOM

Pilla stood three feet away; the tip of the needle was just two. She was staring at me with those russet eyes of hers. All the sadness I had ever seen in them was long gone, replaced with diabolical curiosity.

"Back then," she said, her voice distant, "I didn't know my kills. I just did them. I didn't really care."

I said, "Ah," as if I were interested. In my peripheral vision, I was trying to measure the length of the titanium rope from the I-beam to the ring around her jugular.

"Your eyes are still remarkable. Do people tell you?"

"Sometimes," I said, as I furtively flattened my palms against the glass behind me. "A client wanted a shirt to match them."

Pilla blinked several times, perhaps conjuring the item.

"And actually…" Instead of continuing, I threw myself to the right and slid into the corner. Having caught Pilla off guard, she swung instinctively. The needle scraped nails-against-blackboard across the door. "You shit!"

Meanwhile, I squeezed into the corner as tight as I could and as Pilla came toward me, I watched the tension on the titanium rope, hoping it would keep her from me like a toothy Dobershark's chain.

Pilla followed my eye line up the rope to anchor on the ceiling. "I see!" She sounded delighted. "Clever. But I'm not sure you've guessed right!" She proceeded to move toward me inch-by-inch with her arm outstretched—the needle unicorning her way. When she was two feet away she stopped. "Still quite a bit of slack, Mr. Tailor."

She was right. There was more than enough of the rope for her to jab the needle out the back of my spine. I cursed whoever had designed this prison. "Listen, Pilla, it isn't right what they've done to you! You're chained like an animal!"

"What's happened to me is not right!"

"I'm your best chance to get out! You're going to kill your best chance?"

She touched her jugular tenderly. I could see that the ring passed under both the artery and a thick tendon. Ripping the thing from her neck would be impossible. Her eyes turned cold. "Don't worry about me. Your dead body will get me out. I'm going to send Bunné your head in a box!"

"But then what? Maybe you will be out. But what will you have? I own a mansion in Ros Begas! I have a massive fashion collection—I don't know what it's worth. Take it. Take it all. You've never lived like that. I remember the lousy cuisines where you ate in Seattlehama. Live like a real celeb for once!"

"You don't know me at all, do you?" Pilla scoffed. She stepped closer. The needle's point was a foot from my chest, quavering to the beat of her heart.

"Okay! I'll take you to my place and you can smash all of my things! If you hate me, then destroy my studio! You can tear up all my projects." I stopped. She would never go for this, and I couldn't even imagine her destroying the yarn from my father in the display box before the entrance.

She came closer and paused for just an instant. When her mouth tightened, I grabbed her wrist and pushed back just as she threw herself at me. It was like trying to stop a train, and the needle pierced my shirt and stabbed my skin.

Grunting, she leaned her weight onto the needle while slapping me back and forth with the other hand.

"No!" I screamed, even as the point began to pierce my sternum.

Her teeth gritted, Pilla muttered, "Stab your damn heart." She anchored herself and tried to thrust the needle deeper, but with my elbows wedged against the glass, I kept her back.

"Damn it!" She spit at me. She clawed my ear with her left hand. "Let go!"

Focusing on the needle's point and the radiating pain from the deepening wound, I tried to push it out, but couldn't get leverage. I felt like I couldn't inhale or I might help the needle through the bone. All I could do was strain to hold her back. If I didn't, she would run me through.

"Pilla! Stop!"

"You corn!" She groaned, "Die!" Again she threw all her weight forward.

I felt the spike bore in another millimeter. My arms ached. Sweat poured into my eyes.

"Bastard Toue!" Her hair was jangled, her lipstick, smeared, mascara, running. She let up only for an instant to shove forward again. "Damn fuck!" Her hip bashed into my thigh. I tried to kick her backward, but I was losing purchase.

She shifted her weight back again to finally drive the needle through. She had momentum and my arms were weakening. She gnashed teeth and smiled as a drop of sweat fell from her nose.

When the pressure lessened, just before she leaned forward again, I let go.

My move shocked her. Her eyes opened wide. "Ha!" she screeched, and just as she started forward, I raked my middle fingers across her face. With my yarn pulls, I snagged both of her eyelids and pulled straight down.

The effect was like closing two tiny window shades. I stretched them as far as I dared and then dug the metal hooks into her cheeks, twisted hard, and snapped off the yarn pulls. The right took a chunk of my fingernail, but the left broke cleanly where it had been glued. Her eyelids were tacked down.

She let loose a horrible screech of pain and fright. Instinctively trying to coddle the wounds, she wrenched her hands to her face and plunged the needle through the bridge of her nose.

In an instant, she was a howling, writhing bloody mess on the floor.

Sidestepping her, I adjusted the shoulders of my jacket, hurried to the inside door that led to the factory floor, and yanked it open.

SEATTLEHAMA: CUT

Bunné's beautiful eyes, streaked with white and sapphire, darted from my left to my right and back again. "You cross the divide... the walls of cells..."

I didn't know what she meant, but her voice felt like a hand running over a wide swatch of chrome silk.

Somewhere in the distance I heard a satin snarl, *Hug and move!* I positioned my arms with the left higher and the right lower and stepped before her. She smelled of tea and sweet musk. Bunné held up both hands to stop me from coming closer. "The tides of moon wash away lives, but never the yoke of our dreams... never the essence of the twisted yarn."

I stood a foot from her. Empty instants ticked by. I needed to act, but felt spellbound.

"I know you," I said. "I know who you are."

Her eyes grew wide, but then narrowed warily. Her thin eyebrows tightened. "The vapors of history tell me that you are the cause of the twist... the force of the needle... the bias of the bias..." In a flash, her arms, which had been hovering between us, grasped me, and hugged me close. "You are the stolen prisoner! You are the illegal cut boy." Did she think I was a character from one of her epics? She began squeezing me so tight, I couldn't inhale. I tried to pull away, but her muscles were like steel cords. I couldn't breathe!

"A predominate love!" said someone.

"But what costume is he wearing?" asked an irritated voice.

"Succession into arrest," muttered Bunné. "I sew vengeance."

My lungs burned. It felt like if she squeezed any harder my ribs would collapse, but instead of trying to escape, I wrapped my arms around her, and felt the back of her jacket.

When the Pacifica had stopped outside Union to let off most of the crew and fuel up, a strange scarred and wounded man, like Xavier, had come aboard and soon disappeared into the galley with Vada and Xavier.

"They're talking about you again, Darn it." Gregg laughed.

"I know."

His smile faded. "Listen… if I had the chance, and the genes, and the stud buttons, I'd slice Bunné in half myself."

I studied the resolve in his face. "Why do you hate Bunné?"

Gregg snorted. "She's evil. She skinned my brothers alive. Listen," he continued, "you have *all* the reasons to hate the cut, too."

Once the scarred man had left, Vada invited me into the galley, where she and Xavier sat at the table. He seemed to be glaring at me—although it was hard to tell since he glowered all the time. Vada pushed a drawing toward me. On it was what they called a flat of Bunné's jacket. It had raglan sleeves, a short stance, and three buttons. Dashes around the notched collar probably indicated pick stitching. Fringe hung from the bottom. At the bottom of the sheet, several numbers and words were written, including *core warp.*

I studied Vada. "That's what you want?"

Xavier's voice was barely a grunt. "Rip a yarn."

Without acknowledging Xavier, I asked Vada, "What do you need it for?"

"Rip a yarn," Xavier repeated.

"Well," said Vada, smiling even as the skin at her temples pulsed, "we need a sample."

"Okay." I pushed the paper back. "What happens then?"

"Just rip a yarn," said Xavier for the third time. "And hand it over to us."

Despite all his scars, I wanted to give him another. I focused on Vada, who wearily pressed her eyebrows with her fingertips. "Bunné doesn't trust anyone with much of anything, so *she's* the corporate info depository. She carries everything with her in her jacket. If we can get pass-codes, some operatives, or even what they call p-junctions, we can break into her systems."

"That's in the yarn?"

Vada nodded slowly. "Everything's in the yarn."

Xavier shook his head, fed up. "Just rip it!"

"What happens when I do?"

Vada's eyes fell toward the table. Her lips parted for an instant and then closed before she started again. "We don't know."

"You don't know?"

"We don't know *exactly*. But she… I mean… her clothes may be a part of her. Or maybe she's a part of her clothes." Some energy seemed to leave Vada. Her voice turned quiet. "She has been attacked before. And we've not succeeded, but we've never had someone with your skills. Anyway, there's a possibility that her clothes keep her alive."

"You mean ripping a yarn is like ripping *her*?"

"I doubt that taking just one yarn…" Vada stopped and glanced at Xavier as if for confirmation. "We don't think that will *interrupt* her." She swallowed. "That's what we think."

I shifted my weight to the side. "What else?"

Xavier slapped the table. "Just rip the yarn and give it to us!"

Vada avoided glancing at him. "We have a plan. Please have a seat." I didn't move. "It is risky," she continued, "but it will work. You'll be fine. There's time to practice some maneuvers." She frowned at me. "Please sit and we'll go over everything."

It was at that moment, standing before Vada and Xavier in the Pacifica galley, that I decided that this was Vada's fight. I wasn't going to tell her, but I wasn't going to go through with the yarn rip. Not really and not completely.

The crowd around Bunné and my embrace cheered as if they were witnessing the reunion of two long lost lovers.

"Behold the shine!" shouted someone.

"She was hatched among the kernels of despair!"

Her arms were as strong as hickory cloth, and I swear one of my ribs cracked. Pressed so tightly against her, I couldn't see the back center seam of her jacket, but I felt Core Warp yarns that Vada had described. I couldn't inhale and wasn't sure that my heart was beating, but I managed to position my pulls, cut the ends, grasp one side, and rip the yarn.

I hurried down the steps that led to the mill floor. As I had seen earlier from above, the factory workers sat in large plastic recliners. Many were middle-aged, but some looked no older than fourteen despite their luminous white hair. They were all dressed in blue non-woven dresses. Above each one hung glass bottles filled with an assortment of liquids: some clear, some a milky pinkish, others as dark as coal. From the bottles, long tubes were plugged into a yellowish lump of jelly on the sides of their necks.

Standing amid row after row of sleeping women, I understood the true horror of it. Stepping closer to one of the younger ones, I could see that her eyes weren't just closed, but had been sewn shut long ago. Beneath the wrinkles of skin and the faint comb of her eyelashes, I thought I could see her eyes moving back and forth as if dreaming...

Beneath the loose gown, the girl's body looked emaciated. Her hands resting on the arms of the chair were bony, the straight-cut nails were the color of plucked chicken. Her skin was so translucent it was like looking at a cutaway diagram. The weight of long white hair hung behind her, supported by fine netting. The flowing strands were impossibly thin, barely the width of spider silk. It was so brilliantly bright that I couldn't look upon it for more than a few seconds before tears formed and I was forced to squint and turn away.

Her hair was Xi! I'd heard the rumors. Xi was supposedly harvested from the heads of virgins. Afterward they were slaughtered and their bile was used to bleach the strands. I'd also heard that the women were fed nothing but spiders and silk worms. It was horrifying, preposterous. A story to scare children. And yet, here, these captive women were being fed chemicals like mutant orchids. A knot of anger exploded in my chest.

I wanted to tear the needles from the girl's neck, but as I stood watching as the corners of her mouth tightened and relaxed, and her powdery white eyebrows, like two thin wisps of butterfly dust, narrowed over her nose, I didn't dare touch her for fear of harming her.

It took me several moments to process the sound coming from my right. A female voice said, "You're not authorized to be in here."

At the far end of the row, a worker dressed in a yellow jumpsuit and darkened visor was walking toward me. In one hand she held a screen; in the other, a large golden brush.

"This is how they make Xi?" I demanded.

The worker stopped fifteen feet away. Through the dark shield, I could just make out a frightened face.

"This is barbaric!"

"Kill that intruder!" shouted Pilla from the top of the stairs. She held a wad of bloody fabric to her face, her eyelids now unpinned. The leash at her neck was pulled taut. Pointing at me, she yelled, "Get some shears and cut him down! I order you to kill him."

The woman came closer, but as I held up my hands, ready to fend off a blow from the golden brush, she stopped again.

"Damn it! Do something, you little cut!"

"Where is the Xi spun?" I asked her, determined to get what I needed and leave. "I need pure Xi yarn." She shook her head vaguely. "Where is it?"

"Attack him! I'll kill you if you don't!"

Stepping close, I grasped the worker's mask and yanked it off. Above fearful brown eyes, damp curls of wavy blue-black hair clung to her skin. "I'm sorry about this, but I need pure Xi."

Cowering, she sputtered, "Spools are in the spinning room."

"You're trapped in there, Tane. The guards are outside—you'll never make it. And get away from the girls!"

"Where's the spinning room?" I asked the worker.

She flustered a hand in the direction she had come.

"Come." Gripping the back of her yellow suit, I hurried her beside me as we passed through rows of Xi girls. A few of them moaned softly as if Pilla's shouts had woken them. At the back of the factory, I found a large metal door.

"This is it," the worker confirmed, tears trickling down her cheeks.

When I opened the door, the loud hum of machinery burst through, carried on the cool air. To the right, I saw a cart filled with spools of brilliant white yarn. I had found it! When I released the worker, she turned and ran, knock-kneed and frantically. A few steps later, she tripped and fell flat.

I couldn't find a label on the cones or the racks. Carefully wedging my pinky finger into the top of a spool, I picked it up, but didn't see any marks inside. Holding it toward the light, I studied the yarn itself, but other than the almost luminous glow, I saw nothing.

Steeling myself, I placed my palm directly on the thread. It felt cold and slick, like a water-repellant monofiber. Within a second, a stream of warmth began traveling up my arm, like an injection of honey and compassion. It was pure! A whole rack of pure Xi! I had ten times what I needed.

An instant later, the warmth turned hot and felt like molten metal traveling through my veins. Worse, I smelled an acidic smoke and when I yanked my hand from the yarn, I saw that my palm had been seared. Through charred holes in my skin I could see clumps of yellowish fat, muscles, and tendons. Screaming, I threw the cone to the floor, but the burning raced up my arm and into my chest. Fire raged in my lungs, searing the delicate tissues. It travelled into my throat and a cloud of black smoke curled from my mouth.

Falling to my knees, my whole body convulsed. And then the pain eased. I checked my hand. It tingled and smarted, but the flesh was whole and pink.

In the distance I heard voices and footsteps. Leaving the cone of dark Xi where it had fallen, I stood and checked the next cart. Grasping one, I flattened my palm against it.

The yarn felt cool and slick just like the previous one. And that was all. I waited, but nothing happened. Was this even Xi? And then I laughed out loud. And I kept laughing with the kind of cleansing near-hysteria that can surpass orgasm. An instant later, I saw myself standing before Kira, my rigid member encased in the expanded fabric of my perfect Troy and the tip an inch from the tight buttonhole of her Ten Million Yarn Super Channel-Haier. Then it wasn't Kira, but Vada in the same coat, and we were on the Europa entervator surrounded in purple and gold. She and I stood on the stage and the crowd was cheering us on. Over her face was a delicious Pearl River Love Mask, and I was kissing the infinite tender knit that covered her chin and neck. As I did so, my eyes were wide open, watching the intricate mathematics of the cloth playing over her skin.

And then I was flat on the floor, the room spinning around me. My heart slowly returned to normal and my body, which had seemingly expanded to fill the universe, to contain all the atoms and all the galaxies and all the power and all the energy, gradually shrank to the shape I knew, that of my two legs, two arms, and a head. And even as I was relieved to have my body back, a part of me considered wrapping the rapture Xi around me, cocooning myself in its genius and love.

Someone hammered on the door.

Pulling the crochet hook and my snips from my jacket, I hurriedly unwound a foot of the pure Xi, balled it on the hook like spinning spaghetti on a fork, cut the end, and without touching it with my fingers, nudged the ball into the bloody hole in my chest. The bleeding and pain stopped instantly. Touching the cardboard cones, I stacked five spools one on top of the other, turned, and was about to start for the door, when I stopped, struck by an idea. I scooped up the cone of dark Xi. With all six stacked on top of one another, I was like a child balancing a huge cone of ice cream *scoops. Whoever had been beating on the door had stopped. I pushed through with my back.*

The worker woman held a pair of shears larger than her head.

"Stab him!" Pilla's voice came from above. "Stab his neck or gut!"

On command, the worker thrust forward. Swinging a foot, I knocked her hand and sent the scissors clattering on the floor. The woman let out a squawk and stumbled backward.

"Shit!" screamed Pilla. "You're a useless cut! Tane! Tane, come here! You can have all the Xi you want, just come up here. I have to tell you something."

I ran past the moaning Xi girls, and as I swerved around the stairs that led up to the crystal room, where Pilla's stream of shouts and pleads fell upon me like welding sparks, I passed the first girl I had seen. She opened her mouth and let out a plaintive little groan, a cry, a lament. I slowed for an instant, gazed at her sewn-shut eyes, but then kept going.

At the far end, I could see large doors outlined in glowing light from the sun—but after a dozen more steps, I slowed, stopped and gazed questioningly at the cones of Xi in my arms. I had all I came for, and yet, I couldn't leave. Hurrying, I returned to the Xi girl's side and imagined what it might have felt like to have my eyes sewn shut.

Still balancing the spools with one hand, I tugged the feeding needles from the jelly on her neck. She flinched, but hopefully not in pain.

"It's okay," I told her, not sure she could hear or understand. Then I set the spools of Xi on the floor. I couldn't believe what I was about to say: "I'm taking you away from here."

"Stop!" shouted Pilla. "Don't touch her, damn it! Get away from her."

Once I had unlatched the seatbelt that held the girl down, I raised her in my arms. She couldn't have weighed more than sixty pounds. Draping her over my left shoulder, careful not to touch her hair, I could feel how skeletal and fragile she was.

"She'll die! You take her away and she'll die!"

"You're going to be fine." I told her. Crouching, I picked up the stacked spools of Xi, and like some kind of circus plate-balancing act, made my way to the doors again. A man stood before them.

Bunné's arms wilted and slipped from me like vapor. She staggered backwards. Grasping the yarn rip between my index and thumb, I turned and immediately pushed through the crowd toward the back of the stage.

A second later, Bunné's scream burst in the air—loud, horrible, and animal. Glancing back, I saw her on the black stage, writhing in pain. And though I didn't quite believe her, figuring this as an exaggerated display, another show—a sick knot settled in my stomach.

"Contain!" a satin shouted as he rushed toward her. "Contain the area."

"Secure Bunné."

"Get the medics."

"Emergency red! Emergency red!"

A satin tried to grab me, but the satin material of his gloves on my super-float jacket was like oil on grease. His hand slid off, and I raced past.

Flashing lights made the air into a vibrating storm. I turned again to see a Pink Dollop Boy dash toward Bunné as if to help, only for a saleswarrior to pull out her water-shears and, with a compressed hiss, slice him in half. The torso keeled over. The legs toppled a moment later.

I wedged myself past a group of Choky Bears and crawled the rest of the way to the wall. From here all I had to do was scale the partition and make my escape. But just as I laid my hand against my pounding heart, I realized that I no longer held the yarn I had just ripped.

Frantically, I glanced all around the black floor, but couldn't find it. Then I raised my eyes and saw it. Up above—floating over everyone's heads, caught in an updraft of the crowd's wild frenzy, flew the sliver of yarn.

"You?" I wanted to smack my forehead in surrender, but of course I was carrying both the Xi and the Xi girl.

"I'm terribly afraid so." He lingered on the word terribly, riding the first syllable over a hill and then the second and third down a wide ironic gully. As he spoke, he patted his black-and-white-patterned tie with his hand, checking the links, locks, pins, and bars that held the cravat in its un-fashionable bondage. "And," he continued, arching this word like a suspension bridge as he eyed the girl over my shoulder, "I'm doubly afraid to see you still acting like the talentless slubber, corn worm you always were."

Withor appeared almost exactly as I remembered him except that his hair was a shade darker, his teeth brighter, and his skin taut, not with youth, but stretched like an overripe plum.

I laughed. "You run this hell hole?"

"Put the creature down," he said, flatly.

"She's not a creature."

From far back, I heard Pilla. "I have this under control! He's not getting out with her!"

Nodding behind me, I asked, "What's she doing here?"

"In fact," he frowned bitterly as he tugged at the knot of his tie, "that cut is my wife. We have a devotion-disgust relationship." He smiled toothily. "She is devoted to me. I find her disgusting." Muttering, he added, "I should have tethered up the useless cut years ago."

I had always wondered about their connection. Adjusting the weight of the Xi girl on my shoulder, I said, "You're the brains and she's the muscle."

"In a manner of speaking."

"But what the hell are you two doing here?"

"In Antarctica? I'm here for exactly the same reason I find your miserable countenance before me. The mysteries of Xi." He patted his clipped-down necktie as he spoke. "Fashion has its cycles, and *while we still have a small but lucrative market, we are poised for a new wave of popularity. It's starting to happen, only this time, consumers want to explore the dark side of the yarn."*

"This damn factory is a nightmare!"

"Hardly! Bombyx mori used to be dropped into boiling water to preserve their precious silk! Our yarn-makers live until old age. They're fed. They're wiped clean every couple of days." He pulled a ceramic knit revolver from a pocket. *"Anyway, enough of these dreadfully unpleasant pleasantries. Put the creature down and hand over that Xi."*

I stared at the object in his hand. I knew little about guns, but it looked deadly enough. I stepped toward him. He grimaced as I handed her over, and while he warily adjusted her on his shoulder, keeping her hair away from his skin, I quickly plucked the Mini-Air-Juki sewing machine from my pocket, pinched a thread of the dark Xi between my fingernails, and stabbed it into the uptake hole. I ran the silent Juki up and down the shirt sleeve of his right arm sewing a messy zigzag with the dark Xi.

"The hell?" Withor pulled away.

Dropping the Xi cones on the floor for a distraction, I palmed the Juki and tucked it away. "Shit!" I stooped to gather the yarn.

"Don't get the product dirty, corn!" He waved the gun at my head. *"Hurry up, you incompetent rot!"*

As I worked carefully to stack them up again, I snuck a look at his sleeve. When I had tried the Mini-Air-Juki back in the studio, it had been badly out of adjustment leaving snarled knots of extra thread on the bottom of the piece of test muslin. I hoped it had spewed a similar mess of dark Xi on the inside of his sleeve.

Reaching awkwardly around the girl, he peered at what I had done. "What is this shit?" Just then the girl began to howl. "Shut up!" he barked, giving her a rough shake.

Come on, *I urged the dark Xi.* Start working.

In the background I could hear Pilla. "You got that slubber Toue? I caught him. He counts as a kill!"

"What a cut!" Withor rolled his eyes.

It wasn't enough dark Xi. I had wasted my one chance at escape. What else could I do?

"Corn boy, take those back to the spinning room... and then we'll... we'll have to..." Withor stopped and a strange sickly expression came over his face. Pushing the girl farther up on his shoulder, he inspected the sleeve I had sewn. "Is that... that dark? You slubber shit!" His eyes bulged. He frantically tried to unknot his tie and take off his shirt, but all those clips, bars, and tacks made it impossible. His lips shrunk from his teeth and a ghastly sound boiled up from his gut.

I knocked the gun from his hand, and took the girl as his knees buckled, and he hit the floor.

"You... shit... you... fucking slubber shit!" In a spastic maneuver, Withor tried to grab at me, but flopped face down on top of the cone of dark Xi. He began to shriek and writhe. "No! Help I'm burning! Damn it! Kill! Shit!"

Gathering up the cones, I glanced down at my former boss. His impeccable hair wild, skin flushed, he sputtered and writhed on the ground like an animal trapped in a sick nightmare. Using the heel of my Celine-Audi, I kicked open the doors and started up a set of worn stone stairs into the light and haze of Antarctica.

"Stop!" The fat guard stood silhouetted by the sun. "Put that... that..." his eyes bounced from the yarn to the girl, "those things down."

"Withor's dying!" I snapped with as much panicked authority as I could muster. "The mill's on fire. Get the other girls out!" He stood staring. "The girls! They're inside. There's a fire! Get them out!"

Once he rushed in, I headed across the dust and gravel. The Chang-P was where I left it. I saw Mash man leaning against the driver's side. As I neared him, the girl began to moan and sob. "It's okay," I soothed her. "Everything's okay now. The bad couple is gone."

Mash's head was down. Straightening, he blinked. "There you is!"

"Please, get off the car's finish."

"No... wait... sorry... listen..." he slurred. "I want to say this: I'm sorry about before... you know... with the knife. I'm... listen... the thing is... I really admire you!" Between his blurry gaze at my face, and the upraised bottle, I wasn't sure who was the lucky object of his affection. For a moment he seemed confused at what was over my shoulder. "Syrup!" he cried, his eyes growing wide. "Let's plant her!"

Stepping to his right, I lifted my leg and placed the sole of my shoe against the side of his shorts. Then, as he gazed down at my Celine, curious and confused, I gave him a solid push. With the mash lubricating his joints and sense of balance, he stumbled, and fell in a cloud of dust, snot, and profanity.

Setting the yarn on the roof of the car, I opened the door, and gently placed the girl in the passenger seat. She muttered fearfully.

"You'll be fine," I said, not sure she could even understand.

I heard a shout and saw two other guards running toward us. One held a 'tricity stick in his hand. I tossed the Xi cones into the back. While I was careful to only touch the cardboard, a few fibers must have come in contact with my skin, as once I was in the driver's seat with the door closed, I began to giggle uncontrollably. The guards are coming, I told myself. The idea seemed hysterical. And they've got a 'tricity stick! Those can shoot lightening bolts and fry a man to a carbon crisp!

Slapping my face a few times, I finally got the car in a forward gear, and jammed the accelimeter. First I swerved around Mash, who was scrambling after the slowly emptying bottle, then turned hard, and headed straight for the two guards. I gunned the forwards, scattering them, squealed away at the last second, and headed back to the highway, back to my life.

Two saleswarriors carried in the hospital bed from the show and set it beside Bunné. Through the bodies moving back and forth, I saw her rise, with help, and lie down. She was alive, then.

"All exits are sealed. Remain in your positions!"

"Be calm."

"We will be searching everything and everyone."

I kept my head down, pulse pounding as I wove my way through the panicked swarm of woolen Dead Breeders and sheer Maiden Hunks. Every few seconds, I looked up to spy the yarn floating above us, now caught in some powerful current, twisting and turning, falling and rising like a dandelion puff along the back of the stage, taking my fate with it.

ANTARCTICA EXTENSION—NORTH

"Xi yarn?" *Pheff laughed nervously over the car phone.* "You're fashioning me!"

"No. I'm not."

"That's completely 'boo! We'll be arrested! They'll take us away."

"Pheff, listen to me, you'll be fine. If there are any repercussions, I will take full responsibility. But we must do our best for our clients."

"Who wants Xi? People have died from touching it!"

"Relax. Everything is under control. I'll explain later." *Reaching into the glove compartment for something safe and interesting to occupy the girl's hands, I continued,* "Listen carefully, we'll need to blend it somehow. The stuff is absurdly powerful." *I found a pack of titanium satin pins and quietly deposited them safely in my door pocket.* "Oh, and research compatible dyes." *Back in the glove compartment I found some blue tapestry yarn. Where it had come from, I couldn't remember, but after I sniffed it to make sure it was clean, I handed it to her. She had already spent several minutes feeling my gloves, a stack of non-woven napkins, several bubble chips, and a stack of cloth samples I had left in there from a recent conference in Kong.*

"He went and got Xi yarn!" *Pheff laughed to himself.* "That's what he was doing."

Maybe I should have warned him about my journey earlier.

"Pheff, you with me?" He affirmed that he was. *"Get us a supply of gloves. Are you researching dyes?"*

"Uh… yeah. I got something here. What color do you want?"

Vada hadn't specified anything, though tradition would call for either white or black. *"Red. Get the cover to Love Emitting Diode's Third Symphony Note,"* I said, recalling the graphic—liquid blues that changed to purples and then reds near the edges. *"Match a dye to the bottom right corner, half an inch in from the edge."*

The girl began to cry again. The blue yarn rested in her lap. In the pocket on my door, I found a plastic spoon and handed that to her. Her moan rose from a dark unhappy to a curious murmur.

"Tailor," Pheff asked, his tone incredulous, *"what's that sound?"*

Farther down in the pocket, I found a stack of pop magnets, part of a spongy Nexilla bar wrapper, a small Rux screwdriver, two Juki-Decker bobbins, several small frogs, a small coil of black yarn, and a swatch of double-felted perpetuity cotton. The last was a treasure, I suspected, as it had the softest hand in the world.

"That was nothing," I told my assistant.

"No, I thought I heard… like a cry?"

"Indigestion," I said.

"Wow… okay. So, when are you going to be back and when do we need this job?"

"I'll be back soon. The job is due tonight." I heard nothing. *"Pheff?"*

"Tonight? Cut me! Oh! I forgot to say: the Diplomat police from the Security Board were by again. Okay, I've got something here! For red Xi…" he said as if reading from something, *"tymethikoke 9. But that needs kiln drying."*

"We'll have to re-spin it with some supersaturated fibers."

"Right. Well… I'll figure out something." I heard a muffled sound and imagined he had plopped onto a chair. *"Tailor, are you sure about this?"*

I watched the girl gently caress the double-felted perpetuity cotton like a child might eagerly and adoringly pet a baby rabbit.

I'd done good, *I told myself.* "Yes. One more thing: check the Yarn and Fiber Guide for self-renovation accidents."

He laughed. "*Self-renovation accidents?*"

"I think there was something about a self-destructing magnetic yarn a few years ago." The Xi girl yawned. Her teeth were tiny. I wondered if they were her baby set. "Oh… and a couple more things actually." I was sorry I wasn't there to see the action of his eyebrows. "Pick up some soft foods—gurts and vegi-blends—and a pack of diapers for a small adult. And get a bunch of toys… some blocks… and a ticking clock." For a long beat, I heard nothing.

"*Wait… what'd you say?*"

"Play it back," I said, unwilling to repeat myself. "And one last thing… I need a copy of the *Miss Bunné's* Life and Love Compendium Volume 100 Lover Epic Collector's Super Good Gold Edition Three—I think that's what it's called."

Pheff laughed that little blip of a laugh of his. "*What the cut, Tailor? Xi yarn, diapers, and Bunné's Gold Edition? You're fashioning with me, right!*"

"No. I'm not."

"*Tailor,*" said Pheff, his voice low, "*… are you… are you, like, really okay?*"

"I'm fine," I said, and terminated the call. I glanced at my passenger, ready to give her the double-felted cotton, only to discover that she had fallen asleep. In the quiet, I studied her face as I hadn't been able to before.

There was a pinched and frail quality around her eyes and nose, but her mouth and chin were larger and more rugged. Instead of the angelic beauty I had seen in the mill, I imagined if she had had been raised normally, she might have been something of a tomboy, spending her afternoons at the edge of some pond, looking for mutated tadpoles or racing a remote-controlled hydrofoil she had built herself.

Hopefully she wasn't blind under her sewn lids, or had some irreparable brain damage from the chemicals they had been giving her. Hopefully she could learn to speak and read and function. I *imagined I would have to feed her from a bottle until her system acclimated to solid food.*

Several times, I panicked that she had died, only to see her chest rise a moment later. Once, when I couldn't determine that she was breathing, I pressed my ear to her chest to confirm her heartbeat.

I was going to have to come up with a good story about where she came from. No doubt I was going to have to bribe some agency or official along the way. I'd kidnapped *her from an illegal Xi mill. The word* kidnapped *sounded unthinkable and foreign, but I liked that I had gotten her away from there. In that moment in the factory, maybe I had taken her in spite, or overwhelming sympathy, maybe I saw myself in her. Whatever the reason, I felt determined that this Xi girl was going to blossom.*

I switched on ZZZZ's "Infinite Nothing"—the sound of one ton of sand being dropped grain-by-grain onto a pile of timpani and woodwind instruments. As the quiet sounds filled the Chang, I tried to get a few moments of rest by letting my eyes defocus on the oncoming rush.

SEATTLEHAMA: SPIN

Clasping my hands over the top of the wall at the back of the stage, I discovered that it wasn't one thick pane, but two, and that between them blew a powerful slipstream of air. I guessed the purpose was to keep the atrium warm and shielded, but this was the current holding the yarn aloft!

I hoisted myself up using the sticky soles of my Jacque 24 chameleon sneaks, and stood atop the wall. I didn't want to look over the edge, but that was the first thing I did. It was like balancing on the edge of a mile-tall rifle. The other buildings completed the barrel, and in the chamber, partly hidden in a filmy layer of cloud about halfway down, were the specks of the entervators set against the distant lights of the atrium. Even as I tore my eyes away, it was impossible not to imagine myself plummeting to a final instant of pure white pain.

"There's one on the wall!"

"Get him down!"

Above me, the yarn was spinning in the air jet four feet above my head. Jumping, I tried to snatch it, but missed. My right foot slipped over the edge. For an instant I was falling, but I smacked the glass with one of my Gecko gloves. It snapped on like Velcro, and I managed to haul myself back up.

"Terminate the intruder!"

Spotlights were turned on me. Shouting voices argued and ordered.

"He's the one who hugged Bunné!"

Meanwhile, eddies of air around my body seemed to push the ripped yarn farther away. Arms outstretched like a tightrope walker, I took four steps until I was under it and then jumped. I had it! I had the ripped yarn. I was complete.

A purple satin shoved one of the Choky Bears out of the way and stood below me. In the blazing light, he looked like a mannequin. His skin was a chalky orange, his hair looked hard and plasticott. In his right hand he held a 'tricity stick, trailing smoke from one the end. He raised it toward my leg. "You are prohibited!"

I turned toward the circular city, toward the pointed crystals and the hellishly deep lines of perspective. For an instant, I let my toes dangle over the edge of the glass wall. Then, before the satin could move, I leaned far forward, and jumped.

FASHION STUDIO

Pheff and I had never worked so hard or fast before. I was proud of my assistant, the way he had anticipated problems and ran to the storeroom a dozen times to fetch things I didn't even realize I would need. The Xi was difficult to work with especially in our masks and gloves. Had we more time, I would have sent it out to be re-spun, but we did our best with our equipment and materials. Once the fabric had been woven, Pheff finished it with several acidic washes to try to soften the hand. While we had some success, it was still too stiff for my liking.

While Pheff washed it again, I draped a jacket in muslin on a form that I had adjusted to what I guessed was the current size and shape of Vada's body. From the drape, I quickly made a pattern, and then fed the finished cloth into the Juki-Decker for cutting and sewing. Pheff took it to the buttonhole machine and then stitched on matching covered shanks he had made. I fabricated a belt and attached a buckle. Finally, he dressed it on a female mannequin that stood in the center of the studio and arranged it into a fashion pose.

"Too seductive," I told him. He lowered the right arm and let it hang, while the other perched on the jutting hip.

The jacket we made was red-and-white-striped with light princess darts, a softly rolled collar, capped and tapered sleeves, a waist seam, the belt, and was slightly flared below. And the more I stood before it and studied the line, color, and silhouette, the less I liked it. It was the old Vada, the one I had sewn for, the one

I had fallen for. I feared it wouldn't fit the current one. But there was no time to make changes.

Out the windows, the sky was at its deepest purple. I was exhausted. My shoulders ached and my back hurt, I felt like a huge spool of yarn was tightly wrapped around my insides. While Pheff was in the storage room, I pulled off my long plasticott gloves, undid my shirt, and investigated the wound in the middle of my chest. The Xi had stopped the bleeding and ended the pain, but I worried about infection.

"Wish I could sleep that deeply!" said Pheff, his voice buoyant and giggly. "She's like completely plonked!"

"Don't touch her hair!" I reminded him, quickly buttoning my shirt.

"I didn't!" He tried to suppress a giggle, biting his lips as his face turned fuchsia. "Cut me, but I'm just... No! I mean, I didn't mean to."

I glared at him.

"It was an accident! I just brushed against it." A giggle escaped, and he slapped a hand over his mouth. "Sorry!"

"Pheff," I sighed, "please."

"She'd be great at a rage party!" His enthusiasm soon faded, and then he nodded contritely. "Um..." he began, again, his voice quiet, "want me to stay?"

"No," I replied. "But thank you very much for your work tonight. It was your finest hour."

"Thanks, Tailor." He thumbed over his shoulder. "I forgot to mention, the night chef left fox and shoo-shoo corn soup. It's in the temp."

"No thanks. Take it with you if you want. Good night." Turning to the windows, I gazed out at the city of Ros Begas. Beyond the lights, the flutter of signs, the haze of motion, and the soft brush-stroke of the desert dust in the air, lay the dark slubs. I'd heard that the new crop had just been planted.

Pheff turned back. "You okay?"

"Yes." I faced him. "Thanks. I'm fine."

"*The girl's going to be sync.*" *He shrugged.* "*It's just going to take her a while to get used to… you know… food and everything.*"

I was glad that he, too, seemed to be discovering a fatherly instinct. "*Sure.*"

He nodded toward the door, but didn't move. "*I never imagined you a dad raising a child.*"

Glancing down at the front of my shirt where my wound was, I thought of the Xi sores I had seen on my father. I had never spoken of my father to Pheff. "*At the end of my dad's life… I tried, but I wasn't able to help him. I mean, I couldn't save him, and I've always felt terrible about that. I guess in some way this journey was a way to remedy…*" *I stopped.* "*I don't know what I'm saying. I guess, when I saw the girl, I saw myself, and I couldn't leave without her.*"

He stared at me. "*So where were you and what happened?*"

I inhaled, not to tell the story, but to propose that we talk later, when a woman's voice said, "*Tane?*"

Vada stood beside the mannequin. By her left eye, an angry scar ran from her forehead to her chin. Her skin was slightly shiny, puffy and tender like the dough of a steamed dumpling.

"*Oh!*" *Pheff's gasp filled the workspace.* "*I—I'm sorry…*" *he stammered. With his head down, he said,* "*Excuse me,*" *and sped toward the galley. A beat later the door clicked.*

Vada stood as crookedly as a bent tree. She turned her attention to the coat and looked at it up and down as one might a newly groomed dog. I slowly stepped closer.

Her condition wasn't as bad as I had feared—she certainly wasn't a diseased lump—but my heart ached for her. Clearly she had been attacked and injured a dozen times. I guessed she was in pain.

A small laugh reverberated at the back of her throat. Her eyes met mine. "*The coat is lovely. It's so… you know what? It reminds me of the wonderful costumes you made for me. It's not what I was imagining at all, but now, seeing it I think it's…*" *She stopped as if to gather herself.* "*It's exactly what I should wear.*" *A tear trickled down her cheek. She wiped it away.* "*It takes me back.*"

She returned her gaze to the garment. "This represents who I want to be… and that is exactly who is dying." She looked at me again, and now I could see beyond the scar to the strain and ache in her face. "Like everything you made for me, it's wonderful." She finished with a whisper. "Thank you."

"You're welcome." I stumbled for my next words. "What happened?"

"More torture." *She paused, her gaze going distant.* "My life was filled with it." *She shook her head clear of memories.* "So," *she said brightening,* "they are still making Xi!"

"Antarctica. That's a whole other story." *I considered mentioning the Xi girl, but didn't. My eyes darted from Vada to the coat and back again. She was a couple of inches shorter than before, and her body seemed thinner and bonier. I had made the Xi coat smaller than her old costumes, but I feared it was still too large.*

Vada glanced around at the studio, and I saw her eyes light on the materials spread out across the worktable—the one hundred gold prints from the Miss Bunné's Life and Love Compendium.

"I just got that today. I was looking it over before."

She didn't move.

To change the subject I said, "You'll never guess who's running the Xi mill down there." *She didn't reply.* "Withor and his wife… Pilla. That was an adventure."

Vada didn't seem surprised or especially interested. "I hope it wasn't terribly difficult."

"Actually… it was… somewhat."

"I'm sorry." *Vada nodded once perfunctorily.* "Thank you again." *She started to reach toward the jacket as if to take it.*

"If I could say something…" *Stepping toward the worktable, I picked up one of the golden prints that depicted Bunné in a satellite silk bulimia dress from* Sensitive Dead Penisless Boys. *She stands with one arm raised to the heavens. Her mouth is open and she is about to sing the word* penis. "Years ago, when I ripped that yarn from Bunné… I felt something really strange." *I turned; Vada was gazing at the jacket.* "At the time I didn't know what it was. But I *just felt that I couldn't fight her. That I couldn't cause her death, if that's what would have happened. And today, Pilla said something in Antarctica that got me thinking. She called me a Toue. I didn't really notice at first, or maybe I just took it as a slur, but on the drive back... I began to wonder about that."*

With her injuries, Vada's expression was especially difficult to read, and she still didn't speak.

"So, do you know?" Her eyes met mine. "Am I one of Bunné's egg-splits?" Egg-splits as they were called were the way the celebs bred, trading parts or their whole genome to other celebs, favored clients, and highest bidders.

Her answer came reluctantly, dredged from the depths. "A stolen one."

I was Bunné's son. That was what I had felt or intuited or guessed when she tried to hug me to death. That explained my strange affinity for her clothes, my lifelong aptitude for yarn. "That's why father hid me in the slubs."

Vada nodded once.

"So I'm half Toue." She didn't contradict me. "That's what I was thinking. And what I'm curious about is, I guess, when did you know this?"

"Much later."

I felt a twist in my gut that told me she had known when we were together. "I bring this up because there's a part of me... and I didn't know it until now... but I still have feelings for you. I didn't think I did, but I wanted to get you that Xi to show you something about me and how I feel. And now..." Vada stood staring at the jacket as if she didn't want to hear. "I was thinking about your main argument for why we shouldn't be together. You were worried that I would be dragged into your world." She seemed to be clenching her jaw. "But with Bunné as my egg mother, I'm half Toue. I was already halfway into your world."

She turned to me, angry. "It's not that! You would have been dead long ago! You would have been squashed." She pressed her lips together and continued more calmly. "You want to know what *happened?" She touched her face. "This is just one cut. I have many, many more. I'm not going to show you; listen: Xavier was shot in the head. Gregg was cut in half. Marti was electrocuted. Haas was pushed off Wah Tower."*

I felt like I'd been kicked in the gut. Memories of my time on the Pacifica Showhouse, of Gregg and the others, flashed in my head. I opened my mouth but it took a moment to find my voice. "And that cloak you wore yesterday, the basketweave... that was from the Pacifica Showhouse. It was part of the floor."

"Yes. The ship was shot down and burned." Her voice was saturated with frustration. She blew out a long breath. "The Toue have been killed off." She shook her head. "I tried to do what I could. I just wasn't... I mean... I've failed."

"I'm sorry."

She snorted a laugh, and said, "We're now, really gone. I always knew we were doomed, since that morning..." Her voice faded away for a moment. "But I didn't know that one of us would kill the rest." She stopped again. "I involved you, and I shouldn't have. I am sorry. I have come to regret it, but I am very glad I got you away from it before it destroyed you, too." She stared at me intently. "I'm glad I pushed you away... no matter what you are."

I nodded slowly. Truth burned in my stomach. Glancing at the worktable, I found another print and held it up. "My dad fell in love with Bunné, didn't he?"

She didn't glance at the image of Warrior Remon of Loin, but glared at me. "It's what killed him." She made a sorry click with her tongue. "Bunné poisoned him, and cut him."

"Because he stole an egg-split?"

"I believe he recycled himself to hurt her."

For several moments, I just stood there. I didn't think I could have mourned my father any more than I had, but the notion that Bunné had mutilated him and that he recycled himself for spite raised my horror and fury from the dead.

"Your father was an extremely complicated man. Remon was just one of a dozen roles he played... or was."

I thought of the Warrior Remon jackets I had worn for Kira and how close I had been to the essence of his tragedy. "One last thing, that yarn I ripped from Bunné... what would have happened if you had gotten it?"

Vada just shrugged and shook her head. "I can't stay. The satins aren't far behind. I must go."

I gazed down at my now-scuffed Celine-Audis. "What I really want to say is that seeing you again, and traveling to get the Xi, has been a real journey. Of space and memory. But I'm glad you came to see me for this, it means a lot." When I looked up, the mannequin was stripped. Vada was gone. I hadn't heard anything: not footsteps, not the rustle of fabric, nothing.

"Vada?"

The room was empty and still. She'd done it again! Rushing through the studio, I sprinted out the front door, and dashed down the spiral entrance, across the jatoba heartwood, past the fabric testing machines and the yarn from my dad. I came to the entrance and found it vacant except for the echoing clatter of my footsteps.

"Vada? Vada!" My voice echoed in the space and then faded to nothing. She was gone. Gone forever. "Goodbye," I said in a whisper. "I'm sorry."

In the far distance the whine of several sirens began to converge.

YARN

Finding the braided cord that operated the wing sleeves wasn't easy, as frigid air blasted me, spun me, and hurtled me down. The blur of light from Bunné's building was rushing by faster and faster. Finally, after tugging frantically at the inside pocket, and feeling all up and down the slick lining inside the jacket, I found the cord, and yanked it. An instant later the sleeves of my jacket unfolded and inflated and a flap stretched between my legs. Using all my strength to push against the wind, I twisted around and, even as I continued to spin, got my head oriented the right way. Then I tensed and held the wings open. I wasn't flying, but I wasn't falling.

After ten black vans had come to screeching stops in the garage, I stopped counting. The satins that piled out barely noticed me as they stormed past, the sound of their thick-soled boots spiraling toward the doors to my showroom, office, and design lab.

"Stop," I told them, without volume or expectation. "No one's here. You're too late. You're much too late…"

I had practiced using the wing sleeves twice by jumping from the Pacifica, but it hadn't been at night, as high up, or anywhere as cold. When I saw the circle of orange lights atop the Parfum Spaceship that was my target, it seemed a thousand feet lower than I expected. I feared I would sail right by and tumble into the black of slubs.

"I found a suspicious girl!" shouted one of the satins.

A second later I heard her begin to cry.

"Back away!" I said, marching back into the room. "That's my adopted daughter. Don't touch her!"

"What's the matter with her?" asked a satin, his mouth a scowl.

"Nothing. She's fine. Just back up." Picking up the girl, careful not to touch her hair, I calmed her as best I could while the satins pulled apart my storage units, tore open all the boxes of needles, and dumped the fabric bolts and samples, thread and yarn spools, the bobbins and the notions across the floor.

The top of the Parfum was just a hundred feet wide. Approaching it, I could feel that I was going too fast and was too high. As I neared the front edge, I relaxed my arms and began to plummet.

"She was here wasn't she? Where did she go?"

Staring into the featureless black visor, I said, "My last client left quite some time ago. I don't know where that client was heading."

He leaned in and barked in my face. "Tell me who it was and what's going on!"

"There's the matter of client privilege."

The skin around the barker's mouth turned white. "Look, Cedar, you've been accused of sympathizing with the enemy. You could be condemned." He came so close I could smell the shit of his breath. "I'll beat in your leathery skull myself."

"Then find the damn woman," I replied. "Prove it, officer."

The barker's grin twisted. "I will."

You won't, I thought to myself with both satisfaction and heartache.

My feet slammed down against the roof. I fell forward in a twist of fabric, rolled, and came to a stop. A white flare of pain shot through my right leg.

"You okay?" The voice was Gregg's.

"My ankle!"

"Come on, I'll help you." He pointed a light in my face. "We have to get out of the city. You have the yarn?"

"No."

He stood there. After a split second, he asked, "No?"

"I couldn't get it," I lied. "I ripped it, but I lost it." Shrugging, I said, "I think Bunné was hurt bad."

The light in his hand fell from my face to the glossy-black tiles of the rooftop. "Yeah," he muttered, "I just heard reports… she's still alive."

"She was in pain," I said. I pushed myself up and found I couldn't put any weight on my right leg.

"Cut me," said Gregg sullenly. "I really thought you'd get it."

"Sir, come here! I've found something."

Still holding the Xi girl, I followed the barker into the studio, where we found another satin standing beside the mannequin. On the end of his dark purple-gloved index finger rested a single red fiber.

"What's that, Cedar?"

The Xi girl grasped me and nuzzled her face into my neck as she wept. I turned her so that her hair didn't touch my face. "It looks like a fiber," I said. "The place is filled with fibers."

"If that's Xi, I have orders to exterminate you."

While I patted the girl's shoulder, the other satin took a clear plastic bag from one of the utilities hung from his belt. After he had opened the fish mouth of the bag, he held his finger over the opening and shook. The fiber was gone from his glove, but wasn't in the bag. "Shit!" he said, dropping to a crouch to search the floor.

"What's wrong?" asked the barker.

"I don't know where it went, sir."

I turned to the galley, satisfied. All errant yarns and fibers would dissolve once they were away from the low 'tricity layer we'd built into the jacket.

"Don't go anywhere, Cedar! We're not done here."

"I'm putting her to bed," I told the satin. "And keep your voice down."

Twenty or so hours later, once Gregg and I had gotten out of Seattlehama, we split up—him traveling west and I east—I sat alone in a second-class compartment in the Rim Train, shooting across the continent at 2.2.

I had hidden the rip beside the yarn from my dad in my foundation when I re-dressed in the darkness at the top of the Parfum Spaceship. Only after I checked the aisle outside the compartment window, and then pulled down the blind, did I undress and take out the yarn from Bunné.

In many ways it was like my father's yarn, only much more advanced. It had several circuitry-imprinted matrix-fibril yarns, a tiny conduct yarn that I guessed was a signal-carrying system, around that was a z-twist spun part and what looked like a dozen super-denier monofilaments.

When the train began to slow into Shikago, I headed up to the observation deck, which opened during arrivals and stops. A few others passengers stood huddled in the swirl of air, the screech of other nearby trains, and the flood of sunlight. Holding up the ripped yarn between my index and thumb, I watched it flutter in the wind. It seemed almost alive—a helpless worm, or maybe part of me: my hope, my longing, and my dreams. Or maybe what it really represented was the twisted story of my youth.

I let it go.

AUTHOR'S NOTE

I am grateful for the help of the following people:

My wife, Elba, who read *Yarn* to me out loud; my daughter, Caroline; my dad and mom who looked at many drafts; Lee, who also slogged through some of the early versions; my agent, Ginger; my editors, Juliet and Marty; and at Night Shade Books, Jason, Jeremy, and Ross.

I would also like to thank Wikipedia, my professors at FIT, and my fans.

Jon Armstrong is the author of the critically acclaimed "fashionpunk" novel *Grey*. The son of parents trained in the Arts, he was raised in the shadow of Modernism and misspelled his way through school. In college, he spent a formative year in Japan. That neon/noisy culture forms the roots of the world in his novels. After college, he traveled the world as a by-product of stints at travel agencies and an airline, studied fashion design, did stand-up comedy, worked as a temp doing graphic arts, and (still to this day) designs web sites.

Jon lives with his wife and daughter in New York City. He is currently working on the third book in the *Grey/Yarn* series as well as the golf swing of the future.